THE ALTERED FIGHTING ACADEMY

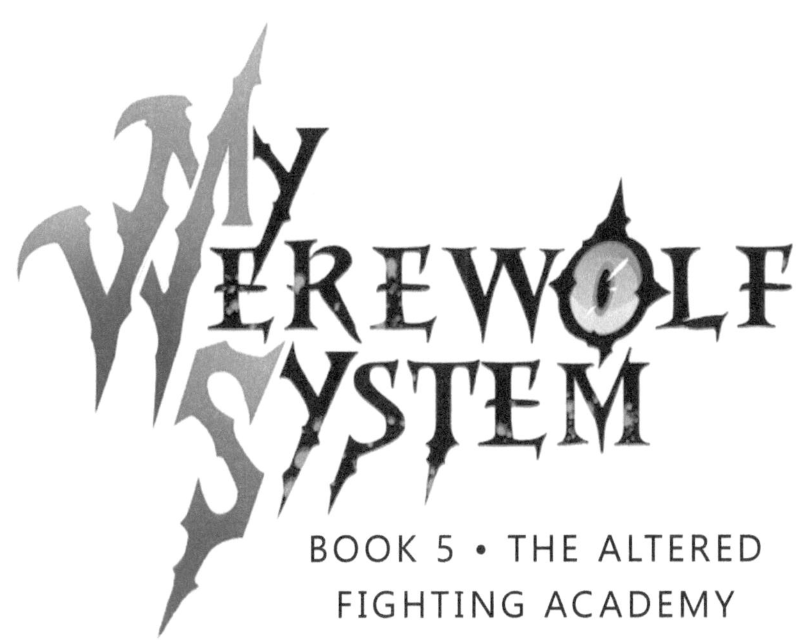

MY WEREWOLF SYSTEM

BOOK 5 • THE ALTERED FIGHTING ACADEMY

JKSMANGA

Podium

Published in 2025 by Podium Publishing
www.podiumentertainment.com

Podium

THE ALTERED
FIGHTING ACADEMY

CHAPTER 1

TEEN LOVE

There were multiple reasons why Gary had decided to join the AFA. It had been his dream since he was a kid, and he was now living out his fantasy, but one reason was because someone had advised him to.

When he entered the AFA, it was full of trials and hardships that were different compared to when he was in Slough.

With new friends he had managed to get through his troubles, and it was finally time for them to join the real AFA, but before that Eddy had one more surprise for them, and that was when Gary laid eyes on a certain individual in the Academy's training room.

"Xin!" Gary called out.

Everyone in the room had heard them call each other by their first names, and judging by their slow and awkward movement, it was pretty obvious that this wasn't the first time they had met. Slowly they inched forward toward each other, and when Gary was about a yard away, he stopped.

Now, the real question on everyone's minds, in both groups, was the connection between Gary and Xin.

"Hey." Ian gave Izzy a nudge. "From the way he behaves, Gary seems to be head over heels for her. I hope you didn't have the hots for him yourself, because their feelings might actually be mutual."

Izzy didn't say anything to that. Honestly, she wasn't sure herself about what her true feelings were with regard to the green-haired teenager. She still remembered how she had schemed against him to increase her chances to make it into the AFA. He might have forgiven her for that, but she still felt bad. On top of that, they had made it out of the facility together, but everything that had happened inside had made their relationship more than complicated.

The one thing Izzy did know was that seeing him act like a love-struck fool annoyed her.

"Hey, Xin." Ryan, the boy with blond spiky hair, nodded toward Gary. "Who exactly is Greeny over there to you? Is he your boyfriend or something?"

Xin and Gary looked at each other. Neither one was sure how to answer the question. Both of their faces lit up bright red, and Gary was struggling to control his heart as always. Any second now, he could end up transforming.

Ryan had merely asked it as a joke, yet seeing their reaction and neither one refuting it, he was more than just a bit shocked.

No way . . . are they really a thing? How is that possible? Is this really the same Xin who won't slow down for anyone? I mean, she rejected me . . . four times!

Gary and Xin had been unable to properly date, or get to know each other very well, because of the circumstances back in Slough. Nevertheless, Gary had made it clear how he felt toward her, and she hadn't completely denied him. On top of that, Xin was also thankful for him saving her.

Still, she hadn't really processed those feelings herself yet. She had thought they would be in the past. Her immediate goal was to go through the AFA and become a well-known AFC fighter, so she could live her life how she wanted.

"How did you manage to get in?" Xin asked eventually. "I mean, you weren't an Altered the last time we met, right?"

"Ah!" Gary scratched the back of his head, trying to come up with a good excuse. "I was sponsored by a . . . company. You know how I was always into fighting? They saw potential in me, and so they helped me apply for the AFA. Well, one thing led to another, and so I ended up here. It was just a stroke of luck, really."

There was a pause and an awkward moment between them. Gary had played this moment many times in his head. The reason for him coming to the AFA wasn't completely because of Xin, but it wasn't like she had nothing to do with that, either.

The last time he had met Xin's brother, Jayden had advised him to join the AFA and to go chasing after her. Now that she was before him, he was questioning if that was really the best thing.

"I'm happy to see you're doing well," Gary blurted out. "It can't have been easy to make it through, but you got to this place all with your own power. It's . . . good to see you again."

Eddy clapped loudly, as he didn't want to continue watching this teen drama catch-up. There would be time for that later. Besides, he had noticed Ryan mumbling profanities under his breath as he was trying to murder his fellow student with his eyes. However, that wasn't the main reason why he had called the students to this place.

"These students are the current top of the top that the AFA has to offer. The other teachers and I have given them our blessing to have their debut match in the AFC in the near future. Before that, though, they'll be showing you guys what it means to be the top dog in the real AFA."

Seeing the smirk on Eddy's face, Izzy quickly figured out the meaning behind his words. "Are you telling us to fight them? On our very first day?"

The others looked toward Eddy, semi frightened. Even Sty, who had acted cocky and confident, looked uneasy.

"I see that your files weren't lying when they described you as smart cookies," Eddy commented with a light chuckle at their overexaggerated reaction. "Even though you have made it into the AFA, you can't just take it easy, and this sparring match will be good for you, to remind you that there's always someone stronger than you."

The students looked across at their opponents. It was hard to tell how strong the others were, but they had had the advantage of attending the academy for some time already.

"Ryan, would you mind?" Eddy asked.

With a new wave of energy inside him, Ryan nodded and walked past the others. He stared at Gary, who was unaware of why Ryan was pointing his anger toward him.

Then, stopping in front of the black bag that they had all been standing in front of earlier, he readied his fist and threw it out, connecting with the bag with a loud thud as it swung widely back and up into the air.

The others who had tried to hit the bag earlier gulped. The difference between the performance of their groups was evident.

"Don't worry," Eddy said. "You will not be fighting today. Just like with any match, you're given a certain amount of preparation time. You have today and tomorrow to prepare as you see fit. Feel free to use the training facilities or rest during that free time.

"The day after tomorrow, though, you'll have to challenge one of these five."

Gary's mind went blank for a second.

"Sir . . . did you just say we have two days until our match?"

Eddy nodded, and the other students with Xin started to smile. They thought that Gary feared that it would be impossible to catch up in such a short period of time. Xin thought it was unfair, but she herself had been forced to challenge the future AFC fighters, and that experience had been both humiliating and encouraging.

However, the werewolf was worried for an entirely different reason. After all, he would have to fight during the day of the full moon . . .

CHAPTER 2

STARVING WOLF

In two days' time, the five students would officially enter the AFA by battling the current top five of their student body. For the time being, though, Gary and the others were taken to a temporary room. They were free to rest there as the temporary bedrooms were being prepared.

As the only girl among the group, Izzy was very happy about that last fact. The temporary room was located in the sparring building. On every floor, there was a large octagon filled with equipment for Altered to train with.

After placing their belongings down, everyone was allowed to order some food. Once more, the former top rankers were free to order whatever they liked. Eddy had even recommended that they use this opportunity to have their last "cheat meal." Once inside, their dietitian would decide what they were and weren't allowed to eat.

The teenagers didn't waste this chance, as they wished to gain every bit of energy before their matches. An Altered's body required a lot more calories on a daily basis than that of a regular human. Their bodies digested food in a short amount of time, which allowed their body to absorb it and produce the energy they needed to fuel themselves, especially if they wanted to transform.

Everyone was different in how fast that process was, but some could eat an entire three-course meal and fight right off the bat without it affecting them at all. Gary's friends had long since accepted that he was that type of Altered, so it came as a big shock when he only asked for one measly steak with potatoes on the side.

"Is everything all right with you? Does that measly meal even count as your appetizer? Usually you order steaks by the dozen. Are you feeling sick, or something?" Ian asked worriedly.

"No, it's not that. I'm just . . . not that hungry right now," the werewolf replied in a dejected manner.

His friends looked at each other but didn't say anything. They thought that he must simply be nervous about fighting in front of his old girlfriend. They couldn't blame him, as they themselves felt nervous about the tough fight in front of them.

What the fuck do I do? Gary screamed internally; his mind had been like this for a while now. *How can I get out of this situation? I can't tell them that I'm not feeling well when they have state-of-the-art machines to check me out. They won't take me seriously, especially not if there's nothing visible wrong with me! They'll just think I'm scared of fighting. Oh God, I don't want Xin to think of me as a loser when we finally meet."*

The werewolf still had no idea about what to do to avoid having to fight on that day. He knew only one thing; he had to make sure his Energy stayed under 30 that day. Thanks to the experiment during the last full moon, he had discovered that the key to surviving it was to starve himself so that he would lack the Energy to transform.

However, while he had already proven the success of that method, it came with a number of big problems. First of all, the overwhelming desire to eat made him act far more snappy than usual. He was also more likely to give in to his natural urges. Ideally, he would have preferred to avoid interacting with anyone at all, just to make sure he wouldn't accidentally devour anybody.

Shit, why couldn't it have been the day before or after? Am I really just meant to fight on an empty stomach? Should I just surrender and live with the shame? Gary wondered. He didn't like that course of action, but if he didn't come up with anything better, that might just be his fate.

When everyone's food arrived, the green-haired teenager enjoyed his meal . . . for roughly thirty seconds. After that, he had to force himself to stop glancing at the meals of the others. The scent alone made him hungry, and his stomach started to grumble. Nevertheless, he pretended that everything was fine.

In his head, he imagined his mother and sister in a room with him. No matter what, he would suffer through whatever it took to avoid eating them. This scenario helped him come to terms with his fasting.

Sty was the first one to leave the room. The Fly Altered knew that he was on thin ice, so he ignored everyone else in the room. After all, he knew perfectly well that they all hated him. He headed toward one of the empty rooms to train for the fight.

"What do you guys want?" Gary asked as he noticed that Izzy, Ian, and Numba were all looking at him expectantly. Izzy was a bit startled by the werewolf's tone of voice. He sounded annoyed, nearly angry.

"We just thought that you could teach us . . . You helped us improve before, so we hoped you could help us again. With only two days' time, we should do our best." Ian explained their reasoning, also having noticed Gary's erratic behavior.

"No! . . . Now is not the best time." The werewolf shook his head. He could see the looks of disappointment on their faces. It sucked, but he couldn't explain that he wanted them to keep their distance from him because he was afraid of hurting them. The hungrier he got, the more likely he might snap at them, and he had yet to find out how strong he currently was.

"I'm sorry, I need some time to myself. With how long I've been asleep, I want to focus on some basic conditioning training. Just repeat what we've been doing in the past, and you guys should be golden."

Before they could reply, Gary ran out of the room at his top speed. This way, he was continuously using up his Energy and it allowed him to focus on something besides his protesting stomach.

"I guess we were being a little selfish." Numba sighed. "We have relied on Gary for a while; it's not right for us to keep relying on him. We're in the AFA now, so we need to start acting like it."

Izzy and Ian let out a sigh each as well, but they agreed with Numba. Taking Gary's advice to heard, they headed over to a training room. After warming up together, they each trained in their own way, before they started to lightly spar with each other.

Late that night, Eddy called in the AFA students for a meeting.

"I hope all of you took the time to check out our batch of students. As is tradition, your rank 1 will fight their rank 1 and so on. I'm sure you all remember how it goes."

On the TV screen, the faces of the AFA students appeared with a number below each one. Numba at rank 1, Gary rank 2, Sty rank 3, Ian rank 4, and Izzy rank 5.

"This is great!" Ryan smiled to himself. "Let's see Xin continue to ignore me after I kick her boyfriend's butt!"

CHAPTER 3

HUNGER IS PAIN

"Is it just me, or do these guys look kinda weak?" Shingi, one of the top students soon to debut in the AFC, asked while twirling thick strands of his black curly hair.

"I guess you could say that," another student chimed in. Stark had the appearance of the typical Altered celebrity, with his neat blond hair and a perfect V-shaped body. "The last batch gave us quite a surprise, so it should be expected that nearly anyone after them would seem weak in comparison. Hey, Xin, you seem to know that green-haired guy. Is there anything you can tell us about him? It would be great if we could finish things early."

The reason he asked was that other than name and rank, no other information was given to them, to keep things fair between the two teams. The only thing they had to go off of was what they had seen earlier in the day.

Xin didn't really know what to say. She had only fought against Gary once, and at the time he had proven to be a hot-headed fighter who charged forward recklessly. Nevertheless, the one thing she still remembered was his tenacity. Despite her attack, which had even received Jayden's praise, he had stood up after it. And that was before he even became an Altered . . . at least she thought that was the case.

"My only advice would be to not go easy on him. I think he'll be a tough opponent for any of us," Xin replied eventually.

"Ha-ha, really?" Ryan chuckled. "A tough opponent? The guy didn't even make rank 1. Just look at the group of people he ended up passing with. You know the students get worse as the year goes on, since the top of the top have already left. Anyway, I'll take your advice, and I won't go easy on him."

"Just don't forget to do your due diligence," Shingi reminded him. "You know, if there is a conflict of interest and that crap. We should check out their backgrounds, and if it messes with any of ours, report it to Eddy, so we can change who we fight."

The others agreed and began doing their research for the rest of the night, while Xin was left wondering what had happened to Gary after she left.

The next day, Gary was down to 100 Energy. While the others were enjoying their breakfast, he had ordered a small meal once more, making his friends even more concerned for him. They could see the visible struggle on his face, not to mention the sounds of protest coming from his stomach.

"Hey, bro, I know you're meeting your girl and stuff tomorrow, but you don't need to diet for her. You look fine," Ian joked in an attempt to lighten the mood.

Alas, Gary didn't say anything and instead left the room to go train. Usually he would have at least let out a courtesy laugh, but right now every little thing was annoying him. Just during breakfast, he had felt his teeth starting to grow out, urging him to feed on something. The only thing keeping him sane was letting out stress by training.

During the last full moon the pack had come together and, following Kai's suggestion, they had performed a little experiment to discover the optimal way to deal with their common condition. After drawing straws, Olivia got to power herself out completely and barely ate anything during the previous seventy-two hours. Gary's task was to continuously power himself out for that same duration, whereas Kai was to power himself out completely on the last day.

From what they had been able to tell, Olivia's method had led to her being the most irritable of them all because of her prolonged hungry state. On the other hand, Kai had been the most aggressive, since his body had the least amount of time to cope with his starved state. Gary's path had been the middle ground, yet it was hard for the other two to copy because the alpha werewolf was the only one who could actively check how much Energy he had left, thanks to the system.

Unfortunately, this time, not only was he on his own, he also didn't have the luxury to tie himself up to make doubly sure he couldn't attack anyone. Tomorrow it would be a mental game; he would have to constrain himself in front of all those people, so he wanted to get used to the feeling of hunger and build up some resistance.

The hunger is one thing, but this stupid full moon is also making me feel like everything is pissing me off! Gary thought as he practically drained the entire water bottle in a few gulps. He was huffing and panting in the training facility.

Seeing how agitated Gary was, the others decided to stay out of his way for lunch and dinner. In the end, they also had to worry about their own training for tomorrow's match. Although they had been told that this match was mostly for show, none of them wanted to let themselves get beat up.

Around eleven p.m. all of them had gone to sleep. Only Gary remained in the training room, not feeling sleepy in the slightest.

My Energy is still high, and this damn pain is pissing me off! The werewolf cursed silently as he punched the bag in front of him. He continued to hit it with all his power, again and again.

"ARGHHH! Just a little more!" Gary shouted, and threw out an almighty punch.

Shingi was planning to go for a late-night training session himself. He was whistling as he walked down the hallway when he overheard the sound of someone hitting something.

No way, someone other than me is training this late? Man, what's up with these new guys? It seems like that Wu guy isn't the only gym rat. Oh well, the more the merrier, Shingi thought, amused.

Heading to the door, he decided to open it and take a look at whoever was powering themselves out before their big match. To his surprise, the green-haired teenager was only a few feet away from him, covered in sweat.

Shingi wanted to say something, but Gary's eyes seemed lost as he walked past him and down the hallway.

So it's Greeny training this late, huh? I mean, a light session is okay, but going that hard, he's not going to be able to fight tomorrow, Shingi thought as he got ready to train himself.

However, he stopped in his tracks when he noticed the state of the training bags. At the very end, the black bag, the heaviest of them all, had several large holes through it. It looked like cannonballs had been shot through the bag.

I . . . I've never seen anyone do something like this before. I need to warn Ryan before his fight tomorrow. If he doesn't take it seriously, he might end up with a hole in his body.

CHAPTER 4

DON'T FIGHT

It was finally the day of the big match. Izzy, Ian, Numba, and even Sty were dealing with their nervousness in their own ways to give it their all. As for Gary, he was currently sitting on top of his bed, his eyes closed. The werewolf had barely gotten any sleep. Unlike the rest, he cared little about the outcome of his fight, far more worried about the state his opponent might end up in.

During the last full moon, the werewolf pack had found out some interesting things, among them that it wasn't just the night that they had to worry about. Even before the moon came out, one was at risk of snapping. In Kai's case, the gray werewolf shapeshifter had gotten feral during his transformation, forcing Gary to subdue him, with help from Olivia, before he could cause any damage.

"Gary," Izzy called out in a soft voice as she knocked at his door. "It's time for us to head to the octagon."

The green-haired teenager slowly opened his eyes, wincing, like he was in pain. He took some controlled breaths before he changed into the outfit the AFA had prepared for them.

At the same time, in another room, the five that the group would be fighting today were also getting ready. Only the students from the AFA weren't in the least bit worried about today's matches. In fact, most of them saw these matches as nothing more than an annoying task that came with their position.

I . . . I just can't get that bag out of my head, Shingi thought in the boys' changing room. *It had not just one but multiple holes ripped right through it. The power had even reached the wall behind it. How the hell do I tell Ryan about this? It would be a total embarrassment for him to throw in the towel in front of a newbie.*

As the boys exited their changing room, Shingi tapped Ryan on the shoulder. The other two boys continued to walk toward the octagon, barely noticing that half of them had stopped.

"Hey, Ryan, I need to talk with you. Look, I know we haven't exactly been best friends in here. If anything, we're more like rivals, but I hope you know that I at least respect you in that capacity," Shingi began.

"Oh, come on, if you say it like that, it makes it sound like I'm the bad guy. We might not have hit it off at first, but as far as I'm concerned, you've proven in those tag-team trainings that I can trust you with my back," Ryan replied with a grin, not sure where his fellow Altered was going with this.

"Good, 'cause I want you to take what I'm about to say seriously, man. You see, yesterday, I went to train like I usually do at night . . . and I saw the black bag ripped to shreds."

Ryan had no particular reaction to that piece of information. Sure, the black bags were famous for being durable and sturdy, but they were a far cry from being indestructible. "So? Eddy or one of the other teachers must have been using the room. What's that got to do with me?"

Shingi shook his head. "Eddy is the only teacher who would come down here, and he's been busy with other stuff. No, it wasn't any of the teachers, man. Now I haven't seen him do it, but right before I entered, that green-haired kid left the training room."

Ryan laughed. "I didn't take you to be the funny type, Shingi, but that was just what I needed right now. There's no way it could have been him. I've done my research. The guy's a nobody. Someone who simply lucked out during the assessment and made use of the vacancy the last lot left."

"I told you I wouldn't joke about such matters," Shingi insisted with a serious look on his face. "I'm not talking about some teensy-weensy hole in the black bag. It looked like Swiss cheese, as if he had some grudge against that damn thing. If you get in that ring . . . you better take things seriously!"

Ryan placed his hand on Shingi's shoulder. "Are you even listening to yourself? If their rank 2 is already scarier than most of our teachers, doesn't that mean their rank 1 would wipe the floor with Xin? Did any of them look capable enough of such a feat?

"I'm telling you, it must have been one of the teachers. I got one of my contacts to look into Greeny's background. He's from the same town as Xin. The only difference is that he's a nobody who got picked up by a no-name gang."

"What did you just say?" a female voice asked from behind the two teenage boys.

Turning their heads, they both saw that Xin had come out of the girls' changing room and was ready to fight. She wore the same yellow-and-white AFA top that they did, only hers was like a sports bra, revealing her midriff and abs.

"About what?" Ryan questioned. "The backing of your old friend, you mean? His sponsor is this gang who call themselves the Howlers. My contacts told me they're not a big deal, but you should probably know better."

When she heard the name, certain conversations flashed through Xin's head. She hadn't been in contact with her family since joining the AFA, but she did remember her father angrily commenting about a new gang that was on the rise. She also recalled a news report about more and more businesses coming under the Howlers.

So that's why you avoided my eyes when telling me a company sponsored you. You actually became an Altered by joining a gang. Xin had hoped that Gary would have done better, especially after she herself had been captured by a gang. The fact that he had actually joined one didn't sit too well with her.

"The name doesn't really ring a bell. Come on, let's go and show these guys what we got," Xin said.

CHAPTER 5

LOCK ME UP (PART 1)

Eddy had arrived in the dormitory of the newly joined students. He had a big smile on his face as he looked over everyone, though he noticed that nearly all of them weren't looking too good, especially one of his favorites.

Hey, hey . . . don't tell me the pressure is getting to him as well, Eddy thought, looking at the sweaty and tired Gary. *I guess these guys are kids after all. They don't have much experience yet, but I thought he was different. Maybe I was wrong in the end.*

"Everyone, remember, the outcome of this match doesn't matter whatsoever," Eddy reminded those from the facility. "Even if you lose in one punch, you will still be granted entry to the real academy. You have already made it. That being said, I advise you to try and avoid that fate unless you want to get teased by your peers about it."

The joke made some of them chuckle, at least. "These fights are tradition and their purpose is to show you how far you still have to go, and of course what you can achieve by giving it your all during your stay in the AFA! If you give it your best, one day you'll be the ones teaching others a lesson!"

Eddy's little pep talk had lightened the mood a bit, especially for Izzy, Ian, and Numba. All they needed to do was show their best, and that was exactly what they intended to do.

The group followed the teacher through the large double doors, and just outside the fighting octagon, the students were seated on a bench, waiting. All the nerves that had disappeared from their bodies came back in a second when they saw their opponents again.

"Man, I'm worried I might let out a log during the fight. I should have gone to the toilet or something," Ian commented.

"You're so disgusting, you're going to make me sick," Izzy replied.

"Please don't be sick; when someone's sick, that just makes me sick," Numba replied.

The others could all hear this conversation and couldn't help but smirk, but at the same time, it just made the other group more confident that this whole thing was going to be a walk in the park.

Xin moved her head, trying to get a look at a particular student, and that was when she saw Gary, walking sloppily behind the rest of the group.

He looks quite pale . . . and he's already sweating, I think I just saw some drip from his nose. Is he really sick or something? Xin wondered. She couldn't help but worry, but the conversation from before had entered her head, making her clench her fist.

I'm sorry, I don't know what your situation is, Gary . . . but if what Ryan found out is true, I don't really know how to act.

Numba, along with the others, sat on the bench on the other side of the cage. Both groups could see each other but only through the cage, so they were unable to clearly see one another.

"The order of the matches isn't fixed, and I'll use a random generator app to put you in random order!" Eddy held out his phone, showing everyone. "A number between one and five will be assigned to you, and you will have to enter the ring and face your opponent.

"Just to let you know, your own rank will determine who you face on the other side, if you know what I mean."

Izzy certainly understood; both rank 1s would go against each other. Which meant that there were going to be no easy matches for any of them.

When Eddy pressed the button on the app, the numbers rumbled through and eventually stopped at 3. All heads turned to the first person, which had surprised them all.

"Ha, you guys are already shaking in your boots," Sty said, standing up confidently. "If you're worried about something like this, then you'll never make it far in the AFC."

For a second, Sty paused his tough talk as he looked at Gary, who still had his head held down and a towel over his head. The whole time he had consistently been drinking water, rehydrating himself.

No one had talked to him today. He had made it clear to his friends that something was up with him, so they had collectively decided to not bother him, at least not until his match was over and done with. "As for you, I'm the most disappointed in you out of all of them. I can't believe I lost to someone like you."

Sty walked over and entered the octagon, while his opponent did the same. Standing opposite Sty was a tall specimen of a person. If one thought Blake was the ideal candidate to become an Altered, then they had yet to see the student known as Stark, who was built like the superheroes in the movies they all used to watch.

"Rank 3, huh. Let's see if your group is as interesting as the last lot," Stark said, crouching down slightly with his fists away from his face, preparing to fight.

"Oh trust me, I'm the best of this bunch of losers, so tough luck!" Sty shouted as his whole body transformed. His wings came out, his mouth elongated into a fly's proboscis, and immediately he flew straight toward Stark.

Just like in the battle against Numba, Sty shot out a strange liquid from his mouth. Using just his toes, Stark pivoted, avoiding the strange liquid, and spun his body backward, throwing out a fist at the Fly Altered.

At the last second Sty flew upward, avoiding the attack. "Oh, you have fast reflexes. I guess this won't be a boring fight after all. Let's see if you can entertain me as much as that Wu guy," Stark taunted as Sty flew toward him, kicking out his leg.

CHAPTER 6

LOCK ME UP (PART 2)

Once again, Stark pivoted on his foot, changing position and making Sty miss. As Sty flew up into the air, he fired out more of the strange green liquid, hoping to hit his opponent, but Stark avoided it with swift minimal movements.

"Sty has gotten faster than before, but he still can't do anything against that other guy," Numba commented from the sidelines.

"It's because he's also just reacting," Izzy replied. "That Stark guy has managed to completely minimize his movements, just using his toes to pivot and swivel. Against someone like Sty who starts his attacks from a distance, it's easier for him to see everything coming."

"Easy?" Numba replied. "Trust me, Sty can change direction in a split second, which is why I could never hit him."

"I said it was 'easier.' Nothing easy about this, to move your body, to not blink or get scared, and to focus without losing sight of a flying opponent. The most impressive thing is that he's doing all of this without having transformed into his Altered form," Izzy explained.

For a while now Sty had been on the attack and hadn't managed to land a single hit. He was getting frustrated and tired, so instead of hoping for a lucky hit, he decided to take a risk. He flew up directly above Stark and immediately dove down.

While doing so, Sty spun his body with his fists held out, ready to hit Stark at the right time. The attack was faster than anything Sty had done before. Seeing this, Stark spread his legs wide in a sumo wrestler's stance.

As the Fly Altered approached, he leaned back to avoid the punch, grabbed Sty by his shoulders, and threw him into the ground. The others heard his body breaking when his head slammed into the canvas.

It bounced a bit as the material was flexible, but it was designed for Altered fights. Blood spilled out from Sty's nose and mouth. When he landed on the canvas again, he didn't get up.

"Fuck! Is he dead?" Ian shouted. "Damn, I hate the guy, but it seems like he is always getting beaten badly these days."

Stark knew the fight was over, so he picked up his opponent's body and carried him out of the cage. A few teachers seemingly appeared out of nowhere to collect Sty and take him away.

"Don't worry, guys, it takes a lot to actually kill an Altered. All of you should know that." Eddy laughed.

However, it didn't seem like a laughing matter to the others. For Izzy, Ian, and Numba, Sty was next to impossible to beat. So how would they fare against the rest? Before Stark headed back to the other group, he looked at those on the bench.

"You guys aren't as good as the last ones; it looks like it's going to be a boring day," he said before walking off.

He must mean Apollo and his friends . . . I wonder how they did, Izzy thought. It was hard to tell, because they had just seen Sty, who was originally part of Apollo's top five gang, get beaten without putting up much of a fight at all.

On the other hand, Ryan couldn't stop laughing.

"Come on, Shingi! Is this supposed to be the fighting group that I need to be so scared off? You have to be pulling my leg. If their number three guy couldn't even get Stark to transform, how strong could Greeny be?"

Shingi didn't reply. Ryan's mockery was annoying, especially since he had shared that information because he was worried about him. Now he was starting to think that it would be for the best if Xin's boyfriend could teach him a lesson. The only problem was, if what he had seen was true, then Ryan wouldn't just get taught a lesson, he would never be able to walk again.

His legs shaking nervously, Shingi didn't know what to do.

"So, what do you think about Xin? It looks like your friend has come with quite a weak group. Although maybe their rank 1 will give you a run for your money. That Apollo guy sure as hell had you sweating last time."

Xin looked at Numba. She didn't like judging a book by its cover, but he also lacked a certain aura that rank 1s usually had. Unless he was an actor worthy of an award, he seemed to be really nervous about their fight.

"If Gary has continued to improve from the last time I met him, I would not underestimate him. Least of all now that he has become an Altered who has managed to get to his position in record time. Which means I shouldn't underestimate their current rank 1, either. You should never judge a book by its cover," Xin said, serious about everything as always.

She seemed to be the only one in a fighting mood, and she had been the only one who warmed up beforehand.

"Gary, what did you think?" Numba asked. He already knew what he and the others thought, but Gary was beyond all of them, just like the people in front of them.

Honestly, having Sty lose like that was embarrassing, and Numba felt there would be more embarrassment on the way, but there was one person who could perhaps change that: the one right next to him.

"I . . ." Gary finally said. "It . . . hurts so much . . . I just want to make it stop . . . can't this day end quicker . . . please . . ."

Only Numba heard Gary's mumbling, but he was unable to make sense of it. He leaned in closer, because it looked like Gary had more to say.

"Numba . . . favor. Please . . . after the fight . . . lock me up . . . hold me back. Make sure I'm far away . . . from anyone," Gary mumbled again.

Numba wanted to ask what he meant, but Gary was clearly struggling just to get the words out.

"Sure, I'll help you with whatever you need after this, Gary," Numba replied, no longer caring about the outcome of the fight but instead worried about the person at his side.

"What is happening to you? I don't think you're just sick anymore, Gary. You've been acting strangely these last few days . . . I wonder if there is anyone who would know how to help?"

The Goat Altered looked at Xin, thinking she might know the answers.

"All right, everyone, stop thinking about the last match and get ready for the next one. Remember, just show us the best you can do." Eddy smiled and pressed the button on his phone. Finally, it stopped at the number 4.

"Ah, shit! I was hoping to go last!" Ian said, standing up. His legs were shaking as he walked toward the octagon, but strangely he saw that his opponent seemed to be a bit absent-minded.

Shingi wasn't looking at Ian but at Gary, who was sitting down on the other side.

"How do you think he will do?" Numba asked.

"Well, these guys are strong, no one can deny that, but Ian was able to get through the facility without using his Altered form, and now that he can, I think they might be in for a surprise," Izzy answered with a smile.

CHAPTER 7

A STRONG WILL
(PART 1)

"Teacher!" Numba called out. "Do we have to fight today? I don't exactly feel well."

The fight had yet to start. As the two opponents were getting ready in the ring, Ian was jumping up and down, trying to get the nervous energy out of his body. At the same time, Shingi couldn't stop looking past him.

"Hmm, I would say it's best if you just fight today and get it over and done with, even if you are sick," Eddy replied. "It's very rare for an Altered to get sick in the first place. However, if it's severe enough for you to be distressed, we can take you to the medical office and get you checked out."

Just then, Gary grabbed Numba by the forearm tightly. The Goat Altered was about to scream out in pain from the strength of the werewolf's grip, and he was barely able to stop himself.

"No, it's okay . . . it must just be my nerves," he said, excusing his earlier behavior. Fortunately, the teacher had been too focused on the two in the ring, so he hadn't noticed Gary's movements.

"These students are on a busy schedule, as they are currently the most promising ones in the AFA. It might be hard to find another window of time for a match, so I recommend you don't miss this opportunity."

As the fight started, Eddy's attention was now fully focused on it, and Numba could finally breathe without a claw of death holding his arm. The werewolf, as preoccupied as he was with his condition, registered that his friend had just been looking out for him, trying to give him a way out. Unfortunately, getting checked out today could only end badly. Either they would find nothing . . . or they might find something that would land the werewolf in much more trouble.

"Begin!" Eddy gave them the signal to start.

Still bouncing on his feet, Ian darted off toward Shingi the moment his feet touched the ground. He threw a punch, but just as in the previous match, the soon-to-be AFC fighter pivoted and moved away from it with ease.

At the same time, Ian had overthrown his punch and tumbled forward. Just before he hit the ground, though, Ian used his arms to lift his body and legs, then performed a side kick, hitting his opponent.

"That was a nice hit," Shingi said, holding his arm up to block the kick. "Still, you'll need to hit harder than that to take me out."

Pushing Ian's leg away with his forearm, Shingi threw a kick of his own. Just as he did so, he noticed Ian's smile and wondered, *Does he have something planned?*

The image of what Gary had done in the training room flashed through his head, and instead of kicking Ian when he had the chance, Shingi decided to retreat, making sure he could react in time to whatever was coming.

"Boo! What are you doing? We're here to show them who's boss!" Ryan complained from the sideline. "Come on, this isn't a serious match. Why are you being so careful?"

The fighter glanced at his taunting teammate. It was frustrating; no matter how annoying Ryan was, Shingi knew that his rival was right. If this were any other fight, he wouldn't have hesitated to use that opening. It was only because of what he had seen before that he was second-guessing Ian's capabilities.

"Hey!" Shingi changed tactic. "Why haven't you transformed? Do you really think you can beat me without transforming?"

"Right back atcha. Do you think you can beat *me* without transforming?" Ian taunted him, easily seeing through Shingi's trick to rile him up. "Besides, I got through the facility without needing to use my Altered form, so I don't see why I should use it now."

The others were quite surprised. They wondered if they had ever heard of anyone achieving such a feat and if it was something they could have done. However, it certainly did make those on the AFA side pay closer attention to the match. Of course, it had been a secret that Ian had actually only advanced this week because of special circumstances.

"If you're not going to come to me, I will keep coming for you!" Ian shouted as he ran forward; it looked like he was going for a punch, but once again, he leaned down and bent backward. He seemed to be falling, but with his powerful arms he pushed off the floor and flung out his legs, kicking Shingi in the chest.

Landing on the ground, Ian quickly got up and spun once again, trying to do a spinning back kick. This time, however, Shingi blocked the attack, yet more came his way, one after another.

"Is something wrong with Shingi?" Stark asked, noting that he seemed to be unfocused.

"Pfft, he's got it in his head that those guys have some hidden ace up their sleeves, that's all. I guess he's just being more cautious about the fight," Ryan answered, not sharing the whole truth, as the story about the black bag just seemed beyond ridiculous.

In the end, Shingi knew that he couldn't stay on the defensive. Ian's prowess was merely a conjecture on his part and when he saw the leg coming toward him, rather than avoiding it, he readied his fist and threw it out, sending it straight into Ian's shin. The strong punch caused the boy's leg to swing backward and his whole body to spin.

"Oh," Ian remarked, rubbing his shin. "Now, that was more of what I was expecting. I thought you might have forgotten how to punch."

Honestly, Shingi was surprised that his opponent's bones remained intact. It might have been a single hit, but the attack had been at close to full force.

"Unfortunately for you, someone on our team hits a lot harder than that," Ian said while standing up and heading toward Shingi again. If there was one word to describe the Altered, it would be *persistent*.

Ian spun his body, trying the same spinning kick as before, and Shingi decided to punch him in the shin again, only this time he would use more strength, aiming to break the other leg.

I can't let this guy's words or what I saw get into my head. I'm about to head into the AFC. My mentality can't be this fragile! Shingi threw his punch at the perfect time and faster than before, hitting Ian in the shin once again . . . yet this time there was blood.

CHAPTER 8

A STRONG WILL (PART 2)

Because of the angle of the hit, it was hard for the spectators to see who the blood belonged to, and since they were close to each other, even as they stood up and tilted their heads it was hard to tell.

Blood trickled down, dripping onto the mat. There wasn't a lot, but it was clear someone had been hurt; in the end, it belonged to Shingi. The blood was coming from his knuckles, and judging by the look on his face, it was more than just a flesh wound.

Shingi's fist had indeed struck Ian's leg, yet the leg had suddenly sprouted a load of dark brown, golden bristles, sharp little spikes that came out of his skin, and now they were stuck in Shingi's hand.

I was so caught up in trying to throw a punch that I was overthinking and missed the obvious. What is wrong with me? the Altered thought, chiding himself for his rookie mistake.

Observing how Shingi was stuck—with his leg in the air—Ian was able to hop forward on his other leg and throw out a fist. It wasn't an ordinary fist, though. Shingi raised his arm to block, and the moment it hit more bristles popped out from Ian's knuckles and dug deep into Shingi's shoulder, causing it to bleed.

Ian actually doesn't seem to be doing too bad out there, Numba thought. *Maybe we can do something against them after all.*

After seeing Sty lose in such a drastic manner, they had all lost some of their confidence. However, seeing how Ian fared so well against one of the best the AFA had to offer, as someone who hadn't been scouted, it made them believe that there was a place for them in this academy after all.

"*Screw this!*" Shingi shouted. "Why am I trying to be as impressive as *Stark*?" He took a step back, feeling each bristle as it dislodged from his skin. They were painful, but nothing he couldn't tolerate.

Immediately, he jumped back a few more steps until his back was up against the cage wall. Ian was quite a distance away, too far to land a punch or a kick, yet Shingi suddenly threw out his arm. The next second, Ian felt a hand on his head followed by his forehead being slammed against the canvas floor. He couldn't see what had happened, but the others had seen it clearly.

Shingi's arm had stretched in the middle of him throwing a punch, and it had done so faster than the punch itself. Before Ian had a chance to regain his footing, Shingi slammed the fist at the end of his long-limbed arm into the back of Ian's head, and his opponent was no longer moving.

"The fight is over!" Eddy declared with a concerned look on his face. He rushed in to check Ian's vitals. The latter's eyes twitched, and seeing his breathing, the teacher let out a big sigh.

"Did you really have to transform?" Eddy turned around and asked the other student.

Usually, Shingi wouldn't have had to, especially against an opponent like this, and perhaps if he'd let the fight go on longer, he could have tired Ian out and still have won. However, Shingi just wasn't in his normal fighting mood. He knew this from the beginning, and after getting played around, he had decided to take the extreme step to transform himself.

Before Eddy could give him an earful, Shingi decided to turn around and leave the area.

Damn it, it's embarrassing that I had to transform in front of a newbie like that. I guess I still have a lot to learn, Shingi thought.

"Hey, hey, before you try warning me, you should take a look in the mirror and improve yourself," Ryan said, mocking his rival.

"Whatever, man. Screw you and your stupid face," Shingi replied before turning away. "I won my match at least. Feel free to ignore what I said, but don't come crying to me if you get your ass kicked."

Shingi leaned against the wall rather than sit with the others; the wounds on his body had already begun to heal.

"That was some strange transformation," Izzy commented. "I guess as we get closer to the academy's top, we are more likely to see the unique Altereds and less of your typical kind."

Just as Izzy finished giving her judgment of the others and the fight so far, Ian came back to join the others while rubbing the back of his neck.

"It looks like I got knocked out in the end, but at least I didn't break any bones . . . this time." Ian chuckled, looking at Gary. Alas, he got no response; their friend just continued sitting there, his head held down.

"Gary said you did well while you were out. The training paid off, and he's proud of you," Numba chirped, answering for him. "You really managed to show them."

The blood on the floor was being cleared, and while the cleaners were busy, Eddy announced the next pair. There were only three more fights, yet none of those from Izzy's group wanted to go next.

The next number shown on Eddy's phone was 1.

"Whoa! Well, it looks like you're up, Xin!" Ryan cheered. "Go on, go show them what a real Altered match should look like."

On the other side, Numba stood up. He glanced at Gary for a moment, hoping he would say some encouraging words. Then again, he would be going up against his buddy's girlfriend, so would it be fair to expect him to cheer for him over her? Well, it didn't matter; the werewolf wasn't in the mood to support anyone right now.

"Numba, whatever happens, you have already achieved so much just getting in the ring, and don't underestimate the girl. She's ranked above them all for a reason," Izzy warned him.

"Numba . . . don't go easy on her . . . show her everything you have." A weak voice suddenly came from the stands as the two of them entered the ring.

Turning around, Numba saw that Gary no longer had the towel on his head and was keeping an eye on this fight. Although his opponent was Xin, Gary was going to support the person who was currently at his side.

Xin . . . let's see how much you've improved.

CHAPTER 9

ANOTHER HOUR (UPDATE)

At first, the talented top students from the AFA hadn't expected much from Gary's group. After all, it was common knowledge that as time went on, those who passed from the facility would get worse and worse.

On top of that, the last lot had proven to be beyond what any of them had expected. Although nobody on the AFA's side had lost their matches, they had been forced to take those fights far more seriously than they had anticipated. Apollo and his gang had been better than some of the students who had already been studying in the AFA for a year.

In fact, with their skills, they would be able to do relatively well if they were placed in the AFC right now. After all, the AFC accepted students from all Altered academies, not just the AFA. It was just that those directly from the AFA had an advantage because of their connections.

Still, after witnessing Ian's performance in his fight against Shingi, the others accepted that this lot was extraordinary, even though they might not be on the same level as Apollo's group. Nevertheless, they showed a lot of potential, and sometimes that was more important. With rank 4 being more impressive than rank 3, they were expecting a lot from the current rank 1.

I was informed that there were special circumstances with this group, but from what I've seen Gary is the one who should be fighting right now. Numba, let's see what makes you more special than him, Eddy thought.

The professors had kept their promise and hadn't told anyone about what exactly had occurred. So it was natural for everyone to think that the Goat Altered had a secret up his sleeve.

I'm in the ring. I'm finally here! I have to show that I deserve being here. I have to at least do something, so I can continue to help our family grow . . . and I want to show you, Gary, that I'm strong enough to repay you for your kindness, Numba thought after his friend's encouraging words.

"Fight!"

Unlike Ian, Numba transformed straight away. Aside from the horns on his head, the bottoms of his feet changed into goat's hooves. The change was apparent because the fighters didn't wear anything on their feet here. His already explosive power was further increased by his mastery of transformation, and the Goat Altered shot off like a rocket.

Come on, do what the others did, I expect you to pivot. It seems like you have all been taught the same thing. So I'll use the last few fights to my advantage, Numba thought, getting his fist by his side ready, his head pointed at Xin.

However, the female Altered didn't move out of the way; rather, she remained standing, as if to make a point. Xin took a fighting stance and just as Numba's horns entered her range, she threw the palm of her hand to the side. It hit the Goat Altered's large horn, and he could feel the energy from the palm strike rattle throughout his body. At the same time, his entire head was chucked off to the side.

The momentum in his legs made him crash into the cage. His horn went right through one of the mesh gaps, bent the metal . . . and got stuck.

I need to get out before she hits me! Numba began to panic, pushing off with all his strength. As soon as his horns were free, he felt his legs shaking, and he fell to the ground on one knee.

What . . . was that attack? What just happened to me? Why won't my legs work? He was unable to comprehend the strange situation. Confusing him even more was the fact that Xin had yet to move. She had the perfect opportunity to finish him off, yet for some reason she didn't.

"I won't strike you when your back is to me," Xin said, as if she could read his mind.

He heard laughter from down below, mainly from Ryan. "Are they serious? Has the AFA really gone downhill? The number one student that passed through the facility is a freaking Goat Altered. What's he going to do, spit and chew at his opponents?"

Hearing the taunts, Xin turned around and stared at Ryan, telling him to shut up with her eyes. She had used the palm strike, with the strange inner power she had, on others before, and they had been knocked out, but it was clear that this opponent had a strong will.

The question was, would he be able to stand up again?

People are laughing at me again . . . I can't take it. What is wrong with these guys who just sit there and laugh at others' hard work? Numba thought as he placed both hands on his knee. He pulled on it as hard as he could, hoping to be able to stand on it again.

His whole leg was shaking, and he was clenching his teeth. "AR-GHHH!" Numba shouted as he successfully stood up on two feet. He stumbled a bit but got in a fighting stance again. "I did it!"

"Yes, you did," Eddy agreed. "That's an impressive feat . . . but the fight is over. You're in no condition to fight any more."

The teacher was already entering the cage. Numba tried to argue his case, but when trying to move toward Eddy, he started to lean forward as if he were about to fall over. Fortunately, the adult caught him just before he made a fool of himself.

Xin returned to her seat. She sat down, folding her arms. She was ready to watch the next match, but there was one person who wanted to say something.

"You know how you always say that you only go out with those who are stronger than you?" Ryan reminded her. "You just beat their strongest guy with ease. So your old boyfriend over there can't be stronger than him. Why don't you go out with me, or was that just some type of excuse?"

"It's not an excuse," Xin replied. "Beating me is a minimum to my requirements, and as for my history with Gary, that is none of your business. Now stop bothering me, before I beat you myself."

Ryan *tutted* as he walked away, not really thinking it was fair, but then again what could he do? He only hoped he would be fighting next, so he could let out his frustration on Gary.

"All right, the next fight, rank 5!" Eddy declared.

It was time for Izzy to go, and when she stood up, she appeared the least nervous out of them all. She entered the ring while the others gave her words of encouragement; even Numba, who had just fought, cheered for her.

As for her opponent, he was a silent student with a bowl haircut. He had yet to say a single word since they had entered the room, and the expression on his face had stayed the same.

This is perfect, this is exactly what I need, Izzy thought.

"Begin!" Eddy called out.

Just like her teammates, Izzy ran out first. There were many disappointed faces in the audience, because it was clear that the tactic of attacking first wasn't working out. When she threw a punch, the other student moved his head and countered, hitting her in the face and sending her to the floor.

Izzy had a bit of blood in her mouth, and she stayed down for a full ten seconds.

"Well . . . I guess that's the end of that fight as well," Eddy said, shaking his head. After Ian's performance, he had expected more of them, making him nearly forget that this entire matchup could be seen as a form of hazing for the new students.

Meanwhile, Izzy thought, *There's no chance of me winning a fight against these monsters. I tried to figure out a way, and no one else could, so what difference would I make? This was the most efficient way to lose a match, and also without revealing my Altered form. This way, I'll have an element of surprise down the line. I don't plan to make it far in the AFC like everyone else. I'm just here to make connections.*

She wiped the blood from her mouth as she returned to the others with a smile on her face. She wanted to show them all that she was not upset about the outcome, and they all understood that she had lost this way on purpose.

"There is no reason to use the random number generator. There are only two of you left. Both of you, please get into the ring," Eddy told them.

Ryan was smiling and punching his fist into the palm of his hand, while Gary had taken the towel off his head and stood up.

"Let's get this over with," Gary grumbled in a pained voice.

CHAPTER 10

DON'T EAT HIM!

Eddy and those on the AFA's side had not noticed how nervous those on the facility's side were. They were all very concerned for Gary. It was clear that something was wrong with him, and having overheard those strange sentences, Numba was certain it wasn't his nerves.

The good thing was, whatever had been affecting Numba's body in the last fight, he was back to normal, so he could at least cheer for his friend.

On the other side, Shingi, while still pissed off at Ryan, had a gut feeling that his rival wouldn't make it out unscathed. As for how it would go, well, the black bag was still fresh on his mind . . .

As for Xin, her feelings were mixed. Her past high school life was now mixing with her current life. Part of her wanted to cheer for Gary because of their past connection, while another part knew it would be wrong to do so.

Gary, if you lose this fight, you should not be ashamed; even I lost to Ryan a couple of times when I first got here. As long as you show the academy what you've got, they'll guide you in the right direction, Xin thought.

As he entered the fighting area, Gary continued to hold his head down. At the same time, Ryan confidently went into the cage with a large grin on his face.

"Come on, Greeny, what's wrong? Don't tell me you're ill?" Ryan asked, since his opponent's movements were incredibly dull and slow.

"If only you knew," the werewolf mumbled under his breath. He repeated one sentence over and over: "You're not hungry, don't eat him! You're not hungry, don't eat him!"

His fists were tensed up, and his nails were digging into the palms of his hands. This was already his third full moon, and he was wondering if things would get worse and worse each time. He still remembered how things had escalated last time . . . which was why he knew if he ate now, he would go on a rampage in this very room.

"How long is this stupid day going to last?" Gary complained, but before he could look at a clock, Eddy made the familiar announcement.

"Fight, begin!"

For the first time today, the contestant on the AFA's side chose to act as the aggressor. However, rather than run across the floor like the others, Ryan used the edge of the cage.

"I don't care what your situation is, but I'm going to take you out in one hit, without even needing to transform!" Ryan jumped up the side of the cage and started to run across it without falling down.

It was as if he was defying the laws of gravity. It didn't take long for him to reach Gary's position, and he jumped off and threw a kick right toward the troubled teenager's head.

Surprisingly, although Gary had not moved an inch from where he had entered, he immediately lifted his arms to block the attack. Ryan's foot connected with a loud bang, as if someone had fired a gun. Gary felt his whole body shift, and he was sent crashing into the cage.

From outside the cage, the attack looked like a strong one. The sound itself indicated how much power and force had been used. Everyone got the feeling that Ryan deserved his spot as the second strongest Altered on the academy's side. His attack seemed more powerful than the others, even Xin's if it hadn't had a weird effect on Numba.

–3 HP
247/250 HP

The werewolf wasn't suffering from any pain or broken bones. With his current Endurance and HP, his defense was on another level. He was sturdy enough to act like a tank to protect those close to him.

"You're still standing after an attack like that, huh? I guess you're the rank 2 for a reason, but I won't give you a chance to hit me!" Ryan announced as he ran forward and started to jump from side to side.

He was energetic and showcased his agility. One of Ryan's traits was the fact that his opponents never knew what his next move was going to be. Jumping off his left foot, the Altered swung his arm in a hooklike fashion, aiming right for Gary's ribs.

His target was wide open. Once again, though, Gary slightly dropped his arm at the last moment, blocking the attack with his elbow.

–2 HP

It was a strong hit and the werewolf's body was chucked to the side again. However, that was it. There wasn't much energy in him in the first place. Seeing that Gary had blocked his attacks twice in a row, which Ryan had rarely experienced before, he leapt to the other side and threw the same punch, only for the same outcome to occur. It didn't take a genius to understand that this wasn't simply coincidence.

"ARGHH!" Ryan screamed, as he threw punches everywhere. He looked like a boxer trying to break through his opponent's guard but only throwing knockout punches. Unfortunately, each punch was met by Gary's defense, neutralizing most if not all of the power behind it.

–1 HP
–2 HP
–1 HP
–0 HP

If Gary had been able to think properly, he would have been beyond impressed with his Endurance, since one of the hits had taken 0 damage, which was the first time he had seen a message like that, but his head wasn't clear at the moment.

"Don't eat him . . . don't eat him . . . but I want to hit him so badly . . . *so I can freaking eat him*!" Those thoughts slipped in every once in a while. That was why the werewolf had been focusing so hard to remind himself to *not* do it. For the entirety of his fight, he had been acting on autopilot.

Eddy watched from the side with a grin on his face. *If I didn't know any better, I'd think he's a Turtle Altered. Still, his blocking skills are excellent, without even transforming. If his offense is just half as good, we might have a soon-to-be champion on our hands.*

Shingi was tapping his foot nervously. All of them had noticed what Gary was doing. At first, they thought that Ryan had the upper hand, but now they could see that their teammate wasn't pulling any of his punches.

Why hasn't that guy thrown a punch yet? Is he trying to tire Ryan out? Shingi was confused. Were it not for the green-haired teenager staying on the defensive, this would be an even more entertaining fight, especially since he was certain that Gary's power should be enough to end it all with one hit.

Even Xin started chewing on her nails. Sure, he was blocking all the attacks, but all that damage should be cumulative. He looked weaker compared to Ryan, as his body was being chucked all over, and from Xin's experience, Gary had a strong will. Given his unyielding character, going up against a strong opponent might not be the best thing.

It was then that the doors opened from the outside; those in the cage didn't notice it because they were too focused on their fight, but Sty had returned, somewhat healed and with bandages all over him.

He joined the others, watching everything. Gary was still taking hits from Ryan, and nothing else was going on, until finally the Altered had trapped him against the back of the cage, using his position to rain a flurry of hits.

"Is this guy trying to make me look like an idiot?" Sty shouted in disgust. "Why isn't he fighting against him properly? Just transform and get this over with."

Although Eddy didn't know the details about the werewolf's fight with the supervisors, he had been informed about the fight between him and Sty. It had not only been one-sided but also caused a huge mess.

Why hasn't he transformed yet? Eddy was starting to wonder. *Is he waiting for Ryan to do it first?*

"Gary!" Ian shouted. "Just turn into your full form and bite his head off!"

"Shut up!" Gary shouted with strength in his voice. Words like *bite* were triggering him into a rage, and for a second he had a surge of energy. Ryan even backed off unconsciously.

He looked at Gary, who was slightly bruised in some places but appeared to hardly be hurt.

218/250 HP

Ryan was breathing heavily; he couldn't remember the last time he had hit someone so much without them falling. A tingling sensation at the back of his head was telling him to back off, yet his pride couldn't take it.

Looking over, he saw that Eddy was about to raise a hand, stopping the fight.

Well, well, looks like I have just been given the go-ahead to transform, Ryan thought. *I don't care how I win, because winning is the most important thing.*

CHAPTER 11

WALKING ZOMBIE (PART 1)

There was a reason why Eddy was upset with Shingi when he had transformed during their fight. It was because before the matches had started, an agreement had been made that they were not to use their Altered forms.

The little spar wasn't just to help out those from the facility but the others as well. If they were truly ready to enter the AFC with a bang, then they should have been able to beat these guys without having to transform.

However, the last time Xin and the others had fought, the top three fighters had had to use their transformed states; otherwise, they would have lost. That was when Eddy had agreed with the others that this time he would give them a signal for when they could transform.

And the signal had been given. Not because he thought that Ryan would lose, but because he wanted to see what Gary could do. After hearing the students by his side, it was clear that Gary had yet to transform and was holding back.

Smiling, Ryan was happy with the decision, because it meant now he could use his power to the max.

You're going to wish you had never let me transform, Ryan thought.

In an instant, both of his arms started to grow larger—mainly his shoulders, which became three times as big. Then the rest of his arms grew, and soon Ryan had giant forearms that were bigger than his entire body.

His arms continued to get larger and elongate to the point where Ryan's legs were no longer touching the floor, and he had his knuckles pressed down on the canvas. Finally, the hair grew out from his forearms. Then there was one more change, but it was hard to notice except by those who were behind him.

Running up his back to the top of his neck was white-colored hair, almost like fur, while the fur on his two giant arms was black.

"Is his Altered form some type of gorilla?" Izzy said out loud, standing up from her seat.

Although the Altered beasts weren't based on real animals, they did share similar traits, such as the giant arms that now made Ryan's body look small. Without a doubt, they packed some power and punch.

Using his arms, Ryan leapt down and boosted himself off his knuckles, using his arms to jump into the air above Gary. He lifted both arms, preparing to slam them down on top of Gary's head.

"Block *this*!" Ryan shouted.

"Move!" Xin stood up, and she wasn't the only one shouting. Izzy was also screaming for Gary to move.

Just like before, though, Gary didn't move; he only lifted his clasped hands above his head. Both of the hands were held together as Ryan hammered his fists down. Bending his knees, Gary tried to take the impact. The canvas floor bent slightly, and the framework below seemed to be damaged.

−18 HP
200/250 HP

This attack is stronger than the supervisors, Gary thought.

The head supervisor was strong, and Kirk was strong, but it seemed like, as the professors said, there were many talented people in the world. The world of the Altered was new, so stronger and better beasts were rising all the time, and Kirk was only the rookie champion; plenty of people were above him.

−2 HP
198/250 HP

Ryan hadn't pressed another attack, but it seemed that as Gary resisted, he was still getting hurt, and he could feel his muscles tearing in his legs.

Energy 24/300

So far Gary had kept his energy at 29, not wanting to make it tick above 30. Because the full moon was today, if it did, he would transform, but also he didn't want to completely starve himself or have the energy to do nothing. If it got too low, he was worried he wouldn't be able to think at all.

In the end, Gary slipped out and rolled to the side, allowing Ryan's fist to bash into the floor.

My thighs feel like they're on fire, Gary thought.

As he stood up, though, a large fist the size of Gary's entire body was coming toward him, and this time he was unable to block it.

It hit him right in the chest with a loud crack, as his body was thrown backward against the cage.

−22 HP
176/250 HP

Blood was running from Gary's mouth, as a result of internal injuries, and he spat it onto the arena floor.

Your sternum is broken
Your energy is low
Unable to use emergency healing

Wiping his mouth, Gary stood there looking Ryan dead straight in his eyes.

I should just have fallen over and pretended I lost this fight, right? Gary thought. *It certainly would make my life easier . . . but for some reason, I don't want to lose to this annoying guy.*

Gary looked past Ryan, straight at Xin; this didn't go unnoticed by Ryan.

So that's why you're still standing, huh? You really think you can beat me without transforming? Ryan charged forward again, using his arms this time to push him from side to side as his legs dangled in the air.

He threw a punch at Gary's midsection; Gary blocked it with his arm, which knocked into his own body, breaking one of his ribs slightly.

–15 HP

More blood came out of Gary's mouth and he was flung to the side again; at that moment, Ryan hit him again from the other side.

–13 HP

This time he let his body crash into the cage, thinking it would be the end of it, but Gary stood strong, and not even his legs were wobbly.

148/250 HP

"You think you've beaten me?" Gary shouted, wiping more of the blood from the side of his mouth. "Your punches are weak."

CHAPTER 12

WALKING ZOMBIE (PART 2)

Gary the werewolf was standing strong and upright, like a tree.

Eddy and the others were amazed; an Altered who had yet to transform was under attack by one of the strongest raw-powered Altered, and yet he was still standing. It was hard for them to believe that Gary wasn't hurt; after all, there was blood coming out of his mouth, but Eddy didn't stop the fight, because Gary had yet to transform.

He had his reasons. He felt that Gary wouldn't risk his own life in this fight; if he truly felt like he was in danger he would transform.

"I want to see what this kid can do!" Eddy said, his whole body shaking with excitement.

Seeing this, Ryan charged forward and rather than throwing a punch this time, he grabbed Gary's entire body with one arm. His hand was large enough to do so.

He began to squeeze Gary tight but he could feel resistance, and it seemed like this would do next to nothing. So instead, he lifted Gary and slammed his whole body onto the ground, then began to punch Gary, stopping after four more hits.

"You cocky bastard, that's what you get for not transforming," Ryan said, breathing heavily. His Altered form was strong, but it was also tiring for him to keep up and use. By now in a fight, he would have lost or won.

But Gary stood up, staring directly at Ryan.

97/250 HP

"Screw you!" Ryan shouted, and swung his large arm toward Gary, only his nails had transformed into claws. They ripped across Gary's chest, and he was bleeding all over the canvas floor.

–12 HP
You are bleeding; blood loss will continue to take 1 HP every minute unless something is done about it.

It was a bad wound, an incredibly bad wound, and with the amount of blood they had seen so far, it wasn't natural for a fighter to still be standing after something like that. A normal person would be screaming in pain, but for Gary, there was no reaction at all. The hunger he felt was far more painful than anything he had felt so far.

Slowly, he started to walk toward Ryan.

Is Gary a zombie? Ian gulped. *How is he still standing after all that, and the blood loss? I don't understand why he hasn't transformed.*

Something strange happened in the arena at that moment. For the first time in the fight, Ryan started to step back.

What is my body doing? Why am I walking away from him? Ryan thought. *Am I scared? How can I be scared?*

Ryan knew he was scared; none of his attacks were working, and for some reason, his opponent just wouldn't fall no matter what he did. He had even used his secret transformation of his claws, and that hadn't worked either.

Ryan felt like he was facing an opponent that was far more powerful than him.

Gary. Xin seemed to be in pain at seeing the amount of blood. *You've shown enough strength; you can stop fighting. I know you're strong, but you're still an idiot just like before.*

Xin was remembering the fight the two of them had. She had hit him with her strongest attack and he had still gotten up. However, this time she was worried, worried for his life.

Biting her lip, she debated whether to go in and stop the fight herself, but Eddy was an experienced teacher; if he didn't go in, then neither would she, at least not yet.

"No! No!" Ryan shouted, as he felt his back touch the gate. "You don't scare me. You're just from the facility. You have not transformed because you can't transform. I guess you're just some type of turtle with good defense or something."

"Yeah, that's it, I just have to beat you before I tire out!" Ryan said, trying to regain his confidence through his own words.

Eddy thought this was a good learning experience for Ryan; he had never seen him act this way. The student's mind seemed to be more fragile than he had thought. It was important for a fighter to stay calm in a situation like this if they had any chance of winning the fight at all.

Feeling trapped, Ryan charged forward again and jumped into the air, like he had done the first time, clasping his hands together. He brought them down desperately on Gary with all his strength, and felt the impact again.

However, this time, Gary's hand blocked the attack.

"You . . ." Ryan was speechless; Gary was holding both of his arms, and Gary's arms had transformed into his werewolf form.

"I still have some energy left to do this," Gary mumbled. His energy was too low to do a complete transformation, but with the little Energy he had left, he could do a Controlled Transformation; focusing on his arms gave him the strength to stop the attack.

Ryan tried to pull his arms away.

"I can't move . . ."

"Finally, this is what I wanted to see!" Eddy rubbed his hands together, but others thought otherwise. Shingi felt like this was getting into the dangerous territory that he feared.

CHAPTER 13

THE NEXT MEAL (PART 1)

A long time ago, Ryan had been told that his Altered form was special. That it came from a rare beast that was related to the silverback gorilla. Those great apes were one of the strongest beasts in the world. Although many might argue that lions deserved the title "king of the jungle," without a doubt gorillas could claim that crown if they wanted.

The reason they didn't was that most gorillas were peaceful by nature. Nevertheless, in terms of strength, a regular gorilla could match nearly two dozen humans combined. Now, take their ancestors, who had been far bigger and more ferocious, and use their DNA to create an Altered, and the result would be an apex predator, especially in the right hands. This was what Ryan had been taught.

However, he was second-guessing all of that right now, since the "ordinary" human in front of him had survived so many of his attacks. The Gorilla Altered had fought against Altered whose defense had been their strongest trait, yet even they had been unable to take that many punches without it affecting them. Meanwhile, Gary looked like they had all been love taps. To top it all off, he was currently losing in a battle of strength.

How . . . how is he able to hold my hands like that? I know I haven't fully unlocked my power yet, but this is crazy. What type of Altered is this guy? Ryan wondered. His transformed hands were starting to hurt, and it was difficult to uphold the current standstill.

Am I going to lose to this guy? How can I call myself the second stron-gest if I get defeated by some grunt who just came out of the facility? The Altered was fuming at that thought. *No, I can't lose. I'm at the top for a reason, and I'm going to continue being at the top!*

With these thoughts in his head, Ryan decided to change his tac-tic, and stopped using just his brute strength. As he'd said to himself earlier, winning was the only thing that mattered.

He couldn't just think of Gary as someone at the facility, but as someone he needed to beat. At that moment, both of Ryan's arms started to shrink. They were getting smaller in size as he decided to revert to his Altered form.

The others thought this was a little strange; if he couldn't compete with Gary while he was transformed, how was he going to beat him without it? However, what the change did do, as both his arms were shrinking, was close the distance between the two.

"Are you going to do something or just hold me all day?" Ryan shouted directly into Gary's face now that the two of them were locked arm to arm. Gary was holding on to Ryan's forearm, and he was doing the same thing back, but it was strange to everyone that Gary had yet to do anything.

That was when Ryan opened up his large mouth and it started to change; his canines grew outward until they were almost as big as a walrus's tusks. But they were curved more sharply and had the power of Ryan's jaw behind them. He bit down into Gary's shoulder, and his teeth went through his whole body with ease. The pain this time was greater than any wound Gary had received before.

–30 HP
55/300 HP

This wound hurt, as shown by the scrunched-up look on Gary's face. He shoved Ryan off him, taking his teeth out of his body and sending Ryan close to the back of the cage.

Your blood loss has increased
–3 HP for every minute that passes unless something is done to ad-dress the wound

Unable to use emergency healing because of low Energy

From behind, the others saw two large holes just underneath where his traps were. They could only imagine how much it must hurt, but even more worrying the amount of blood that had already spilled onto the floor.

"Stop the fight," a shaky voice said. When Ian looked at who had said those words, he saw that it was Izzy, and she was on the verge of tears.

"What are you doing? Stop the fight!" Izzy said. "Can't you see his life is in danger? This is just a student match, not a real AFC match with a title on the line. Stop the fight!"

She was pleading with Eddy, but all she saw was a huge smile on his face.

"Stop it? Have you seen Gary? Does that look like the face of a person who wants me to stop this match?" Eddy retorted.

When they turned to look back in the ring, Gary had his head down, his arm over his wound, applying pressure. He was huffing and panting quite heavily, his chest rising up and down. When he lifted his head, his eyes were glowing red. What's more, the pupils had narrowed like those of a wolf, and his teeth had sharpened.

Gary had taken a low stance with his arms spread out; the fur on his arms had grown past his forearms and up his shoulders as his biceps got slightly larger. He finally went on the offensive by running straight toward Ryan.

The sick feeling in Shingi's stomach returned, and he could no longer stay quiet.

"Eddy, you need to stop the fight! Ryan, get the hell out of there!"

Alas, the warning came too late; the werewolf's clawed hand was headed straight for Ryan's chest, more specifically to the place his heart would be.

"*Gary, stop!*" Xin screamed at the top of her lungs.

At the last moment, a shred of sanity allowed Gary to realize what he was about to do. Before his hunger took over again, he did what he could to change the trajectory of his attack. Were it not for Ryan subconsciously listening to his rival's warning, and being in the midst of rolling out of the way, that would have been it.

As it was, the werewolf's attack merely scratched the Altered's chest before the claw ripped right through the specially built cage. The material used in its construction was sturdier than the black bag, making it suited for Altered fights, or at least it should have been enough for the students . . .

Gary's claw cut through the entire gate, causing a large slash, as he turned and looked at Ryan again. His eyes were back to glowing red. Even Xin's shouting from the side did nothing to calm him down.

"Screw this!" Numba shouted as he ran forward. The Goat Altered entered the damaged cage and transformed before placing himself between the werewolf and Ryan.

"Stop, Gary! The fight is over! There's no need to continue!" Numba tried to reason with his friend. "You asked me to stop you, remember? Let's just go, okay?"

Too bad that the only thing the red-eyed creature registered was that a tasty morsel had just volunteered as its hors d'oeuvres.

CHAPTER 14

THE NEXT MEAL (PART 2)

The others had still been hesitating about whether they should step in and help. In their minds, as an experienced teacher, Eddy would be able to step in at any time in case things turned hairy. No pun intended. However, seeing him stay gave them doubt. Unlike Eddy, who only cared about the outcome, they were friends of the fighters inside the cage and didn't want either one to be hurt.

However, none of them stepped in, apart from Numba. There were too many times when Gary had stepped up for him; it was now his turn.

Gary . . . I'm doing as you asked, and if I have to, I will hold you back with force just like you asked.

Numba had already transformed; he had his head tilted forward, ready to ram into Gary. If he got him at the right time, then his horns could dig into Gary's shoulders and pin him against the cage.

The only thing was, this was Gary. During training none of them had been able to get the upper hand on him; sure, he was more hurt now, but also far more dangerous as well. It was then that Gary charged forward; the red glow in his eyes was still there, and his mouth opened wide as if he was going to bite Numba.

His actions are wild, and he's not thinking straight. I just might be able to pull this off, Numba realized.

When Gary's feet touched the ground, though, he suddenly pushed off at an incredible speed, faster than Numba or the others had ever seen him move before.

Unsurprisingly, the Goat Altered was unable to react to this, but he didn't have to. Right in front of him, a long, large-scaled creature covered in golden armor had appeared. The next moment, everyone heard the screeching sound of the werewolf's claws scratching that surface.

Numba's attack didn't work, and turning his head toward his savior, he was surprised to see that it was the teacher, Eddy.

"You guys were right; perhaps I let things get the better of me, but you have nothing to worry about now," Eddy claimed.

His arms, legs, and strange tail were covered in large scales that were the size of a sheet of paper. They were a golden brown color, and it was difficult to say what beast he was based on just a simple look.

Whatever the case was, seeing how Gary's attack was able to break through the cage, it meant that these scales were solid.

"Gary, the match is over. You have shown enough power," Eddy reasoned. "If you don't get a hold of yourself, we'll have to send you off for testing."

It was clear that Gary's head wasn't there at the moment. He wasn't listening to anybody, and Eddy feared that perhaps the green-haired teenager had turned into a crazed Altered. After subduing him, they could easily test the color of his blood.

Truth be told, the teacher was hoping that it wouldn't come to that. Ideally, Gary had just worked himself into a frenzy, one he could break out of . . . if needed by force.

Whatever the case, Gary wasn't listening to reason and simply charged in again, this time leaping into the air. Turning around, Eddy whacked him with his large tail, right in the chest.

The teachers at the AFA weren't nobodies; although many of them weren't in the AFC or a large corporation, they were highly paid as if they were in one. The AFA itself was a high-level organization.

It wasn't that they weren't capable of competing, they just chose not to. In some cases, the teachers and the coaches in the AFA could be considered better than top-tier athletes.

Still, when Eddy's tail hit the werewolf, Gary grabbed it and opened his mouth wide, ready to bite through the hard scales. But a large hand reached behind Gary, grabbing him and pulling him off the teacher, throwing him against the back of the cage. It was Ryan, covered in sweat—not from being overworked but from fear.

"I'm sorry, teach, I feel like a lot of this is my fault . . . I should have just forfeited the match," Ryan said in apology. He was helping out because he didn't want his teacher to get hurt. Eddy was well liked among the students, and Ryan would have felt guilty if anything happened to him.

"Well, I see you two have this sorted, so I'm just going to step out of here now," Numba said, as he tried to tiptoe out of the place, but he soon heard Gary give out an incredibly loud yowl.

"*Awhooo!*" Gary howled to the sky.

"Gary, what is happening to you? You've been acting strange this whole time. You knew this was going to happen, right? Is that why you didn't fight today? We have to do something; *I* have to do something before you get killed in this place."

Numba had turned around, ready to help his friend, when one more person joined the party to help out. Climbing over the top of the cage, Xin dropped down right behind Gary and placed both hands on his shoulders.

"This might hurt a bit, but hopefully it will help you calm down a little."

A small yellow spark jolted from her hand, and Gary's whole body lit up. The convulsion made it look like he had been electrocuted, and him looking like a human lightbulb only strengthened that idea.

Xin was using an incredible amount of power, and Gary was shaking uncontrollably; his eyes were still red with anger as he gritted his teeth, bearing the pain, until his arms dropped to his sides. The natural color of his irises returned for a moment, before they rolled into the back of his head.

Once Xin stopped, the werewolf dropped to the floor unconscious. Everyone stood there looking at Gary, expecting him to get up again, like he had done during the fight many times, but he didn't, making everyone breathe a sigh of relief that it was over.

"Now what do we do?" Ryan asked.

CHAPTER 15

STRANGE BLOOD? (PART 1)

It was as if time stood still. Everyone looked at Gary, making sure that he had really been knocked out. The last thing they wanted was for someone to go and check, only for the green-haired teenager to take a bite out of their arm.

During this pause, Izzy was left in amazement about what she had just witnessed. *That girl Xin really deserves her number one rank. I've heard that there were beasts with elemental skills and powers, but I thought those were just baseless rumors . . .*

Unbeknownst to the rest of the audience, the AFC was well aware that some Altered were more special than others, which was why each fighter was informed beforehand that they were allowed to use only the advantages the Altered forms gave them and nothing else.

This led to the belief that some Altered were actually stronger during their official matches outside the AFC. The reports of Altered having special powers had come from those who belonged to gangs and organizations.

This Xin girl is the same age as us, but she has already reached such an advanced level. Just how long will it take me to catch up? Izzy wondered, but rather than get depressed that her own Altered wasn't that special, she intended to use it as motivation to get better, hoping to close the gap through training and using her brain.

After it became obvious that Gary wasn't faking being unconscious, the teacher assistants quickly entered and carried him away in the same manner as when Sty had been hurt in the first match.

"Wait, where are you taking him?" Numba asked, getting ready to follow him.

"Don't worry," Eddy said, stepping in between Numba and the assistants as they left. "He's going to be okay. The AFA has an incredible medical team and will make sure he'll be up in no time. Sty should know all about it."

Taking this as a dig, Sty crossed his arms and looked away. "I still don't understand why that guy just wouldn't fully transform," the Fly Altered mumbled, though not loud enough for the others to hear.

As for Numba, he had no choice but to watch his friend leave through the double doors, unable to stop him. *Gary . . . are you really going to be okay?* he thought.

"All right, everyone, head back to your rooms. You're free for the rest of the day. Make sure to go to bed early, since tomorrow will officially be your first day. The teachers will know this, so they will take it easy on you. Do your best to catch up to your peers," Eddy said.

Before the students left, Xin came up to Eddy. She looked a bit nervous as she rubbed her arm, but it was clear she wanted to say something. "Eddy, can you . . . can you let me know once he wakes up? I . . . I want to apologize for what I did."

"Sure." Eddy smiled back. "I'll let him know you were worried about him."

Xin's face went red as she quickly hurried off to exit the room with the others. Seeing this, Eddy was quite happy. He had been worried about her, since the only thing on that girl's mind had been fighting.

Throughout her stay, Xin had never seemed to care about anything else, which was why she had been able to improve so fast. As her teacher, Eddy was happy to see that the teenage girl still had normal interests. Unfortunately, he wasn't quite sure about the compatibility between the two, the "ice queen" and the "wild boy" . . .

If these two get together, the pair of them could cause trouble for whoever they meet, Eddy thought as he shook his head with an amused look.

There was another person who wasn't the same after his match. Ryan's cocky attitude was nowhere to be found, and he was not speaking to anyone. At the moment, he was looking at the cage itself . . . and its damaged state.

It made him wonder: if he hadn't moved in time, what would have happened to him? What would the outcome have been? Seeing the others leave, Ryan decided to catch up with one of his teammates.

"Hey . . . I just wanted to say I'm sorry."

Shingi looked at him, barely believing his ears.

"It's okay, man. I'm happy you didn't die. If anyone beats the shit out of you, it should be me as your rival."

The two laughed it off as they left the room, believing that they would never forget an event like today.

Gary was being wheeled through the facility in a hospital bed, and because of the severity of his wounds, they had decided to take him to the main facility. There, a group of experts could work on him, patch him up until he was good as new. He had already been attached to an IV drip on the way. When the werewolf arrived to see the specialized doctors, they were surprised that the wounds on his body were not life-threatening.

His heart was beating strongly, and just patching up his wounds had made a large improvement. With the IV drip, Gary felt a small spark of Energy return, yet his eyes were still blurry. He tried to open them but lacked the ability to do so.

"I've seen many Altered with great natural healing abilities, but it looks like he's on another level," a male voice said. "There's not much else we need to do, so we put him in his own private room for now. Also, lock the doors; the file explicitly mentioned that part. The supervising teacher suspects that he might be a crazed Altered."

"Would you like me to collect a blood sample and proceed with the tests, Doctor?" a female voice asked.

Blood sample? No, I can't let them take one . . . if they do . . . they'll find out I'm not an Altered. I don't know what would happen then, but I don't want to find out.

Gary tried to open his mouth to object and tell them that he was all right.

Alas, as someone who lacked the power to even open his eyes, he was unable to even move his lips. Everything was becoming burdensome, and before he could do anything, he lost consciousness once more.

CHAPTER 16

STRANGE BLOOD?
(PART 2)

When he awoke, Gary mustered enough strength to open his heavy eye-lids and was greeted by a bright white light above him. It was a familiar feeling, a familiar scene, as if he had been here before. The softness of the bedsheets in his hands acted as the last piece of the missing puzzle.

Shit! I'm back in a hospital bed again, aren't I? What happened this time? The green-haired teenager tried to recollect his thoughts as he clenched the sheets tightly. He could only remember bits and pieces, with most of it just being a reminder of how painful that hunger had been.

Eventually, the memories of what had happened slowly came to him, and thankfully in not one of them did he eat, kill, or injure anyone else. Still, he also had no clue how he had ended up in this room. He remembered the teacher Eddy getting involved with the fight toward the end, but that was it.

Well . . . I can always ask someone later. I guess it at least all worked out in the end. Gary let out a sigh of relief. He took in his surroundings. He was seemingly in a private room, though slightly different from the last one, with a potted plant here and there, but then he realized something.

Slowly the pain in his stomach was coming back to him, the pain of hunger.

10/300 Energy

Seeing the low value, he felt relieved. He was a bit surprised that he still had Energy left over, but then he noticed the IV drip connected to his body, ensuring that he would have enough nutrients to survive.

30 days until the next full moon

Wait, did I read that correctly . . . the full moon . . . it already passed! I don't have to worry anymore! Gary thought excitedly. He would have cheered if he had the Energy, but for now, he just enjoyed the comfort of the pillow. "Great, I can finally eat without holding back."

Unfortunately, his joyous moment didn't last long. The realization hit him how close a call it had been, the third turning. The pain he had gone through and the amount he needed to hold back was worse than the previous two times.

On the first night, surviving just the night alone had been enough, though he had been occupied with his fight against Blake at the time . . . Then there was the second turning, and suffice to say, three hungry werewolves being cooped up in one room had turned out to be a recipe for disaster . . . yet Gary had learned a lot from it. Enough to survive this third turning, at least that was what he assumed.

In a way, the starvation method coupled with his draining of Energy had worked. Perhaps without that match, he might have made it the entire day, but if things got harder and harder, then he might have no choice but to give in to his urges.

To just eat, and then transform on that night to go out hunting?

I guess I could always just make someone I don't like a hunting target. Gary tried to joke with himself, but he knew it was a serious matter.

In all honesty, he wished that either Tom or Kai would walk in through the door. Speaking of the beta werewolf, he was curious how his pack members had fared with their own turnings. Was it also getting worse for them each month, or was it just an alpha thing?

Whatever the case, he could at least put off his own suffering for another thirty days, and Gary was great regarding postponing problems he could do nothing about.

What is going to happen to me now, though? I didn't reveal myself, did I? Gary wondered. *Xin should have only seen my arms and my eyes transform; she can't think I'm a werewolf.*

If there was one person he wanted never to see him fully transform, then Xin was it. She and the rest of the gang had been attacked by Billy that time; although he had joined, he was in his werewolf state.

If she found out, it might take her some time, but eventually she would put two and two together. If she had to know the truth, then he wanted her to find out from his own mouth.

Just then there was a knock on the door. At least he didn't feel the need to escape from the room this time, but he was concerned about who might walk through that door and what they would say.

Surprisingly, Numba was the one to enter the room. "Hey, you're awake, I didn't expect that." The Goat Altered greeted him as he pulled out a chair and sat down next to him. "How are you feeling?"

"Hungry," Gary replied without an ounce of hesitation.

Hearing the green-haired teenager speak in his usual manner brought the largest smile to Numba's face.

"You're back to normal . . . I thought something had happened to you. I was worried you might stay like that forever . . . You knew something like that was going to happen, didn't you? That's why you told me to hold you back, right? It's why I came alone and didn't bring any of the others with me either."

"Hold me back?" Then Gary remembered mumbling something like that . . . At the time, he had been close to being delirious. If he hadn't been knocked out, then he'd wanted Numba to lock him in a secure room, making sure he couldn't escape.

"Thank you," Gary said, looking his friend straight in the eyes. "Thank you for getting into the ring. I . . . I don't know what would have happened if you hadn't . . . You've really proven to be a wonderful friend. I don't know what I can do to ever repay you."

Numba stood up from his seat and headed toward the door. "Stop that. Isn't that what friends do for each other? Let me grab one of the nurses to bring you some food. They might want to take your blood before that, though," Numba said, opening the door.

"Blood?" Gary shouted. "Hang on, Numba, does that mean they haven't taken my blood yet?"

The werewolf instantly remembered the voices he heard moments before he had passed out.

"Umm, no, I don't think so. I'm pretty sure they were waiting for you to wake up. To be honest, I shouldn't even be here. I snuck in here to make sure you were all right. Because of the way you acted, Eddy suspected you might have been turning into a crazed Altered, but since you're okay, there should be nothing for you to worry about."

Alas, there *was* something to worry about. Gary already knew about the blood test thanks to White Rose. And he also knew that his blood wasn't that of an Altered. While White Rose might not care, how could he explain to the AFA, an academy *exclusively* for Altered, how he had made it in and how he was able to transform without being an Altered himself?

"Numba, I don't have time to explain, but I need a huge favor from you. I need your blood to pass that test!"

CHAPTER 17

FAKE BLOOD (PART 1)

Hearing Gary's plea, Numba peeked out the door to see if anyone was coming their way. He slowly closed the door and kept his back against it, so he could buy them a few seconds if anyone did try to come in.

"Gary, what are you talking about? You're not seriously trying to pass my blood off as your own, are you?" Numba asked. "You seem normal enough, so what's the point?"

Numba was confused. Gary was behaving like his normal self. Even if he was easily angered, that wasn't the same as being a crazed Altered, so there had to be another reason. Perhaps he was just not feeling well, but in that case, why not just tell the nurses that so they could test him another day?

Gary sat there in silence. He had been in this type of situation before, and he remembered how Tom had taken him to the medical room at school. Back then, he had still been debating whether to tell the truth. Still, this was different. Tom had been his best friend who had arrived at the right conclusion on his own, whereas Numba, no matter how great a friend he had proven to be, was someone he had known for less than a month. Furthermore, as far as he and everyone else was concerned, Gary was just a wolf-type Altered . . .

"Look, Numba, I can't tell you everything right now, and I know that might make you feel like shit, but I promise I'm doing it for your own good. I don't want to get you into trouble," Gary explained. "I wouldn't ask for your help unless I really needed it, but if they take my blood . . ."

While the werewolf was still searching for the right words, Numba had a big smile on his face. "It's okay, Gary. We haven't known each other for long, but in that short period of time, how often have we stuck our necks out for each other? You came to me in the assessment. I helped you with that blackball test."

"To me, you are a person who can . . . accomplish anything, so if you need my help but can't explain things, then I'm trusting you that you're doing it for a good reason."

Gary was surprised by this reaction, though Numba's trust in him made him feel even guiltier for not reciprocating it. Still, there was just too much he didn't know about the Werewolf System, and the fewer people who knew about it, the better.

"Thank you . . . so you'll take the blood test for me?" Gary asked.

Numba pulled a strange face. "I mean, I'd be happy to, but how exactly are we supposed to do that? It's not like I can hide in your bedsheets and stretch out my arm when they come. I also can't just go out and tell a nurse that I'll bring them your blood, nor can I go out and pretend to be you."

Now that Numba had brought up the issue, the werewolf didn't exactly have a solution, either. Before they could rack their brains together, a slight pressure came down on the door handle. Numba immediately sprinted toward the bed, hoping to hide underneath it, but it was too late; the nurse had already opened the door.

"Hey, who are you? You're not meant to be in here!" she shouted. "Someone call the guards, we have an intruder!"

"I'm sorry, I just came to visit my friend because I was worried about him." Numba tried to explain. He made sure to put up his arms as a sign of surrender while showing off his AFA uniform so that she knew he was a student. The nurse simply looked him up and down before she pointed to the door.

"All right, I'll leave. I'm sorry for intruding."

As he exited the room, Numba gave Gary a disjointed look. However, the green-haired teenager didn't notice it. He was too busy staring at the tray full of equipment the nurse had brought with her, specifically at the needle and a strap.

I can't just leave Gary, he's not going to be able to figure this out himself, but I don't have any ideas either, Numba thought, but fortunately, he knew just the right person to help them out.

Running out of the hospital wing, the Goat Altered headed across one of the hallways that connected several of the buildings. He was headed for their new rooms and went straight to a room that turned out to be unlocked.

"Izzy, I need your help!"

"Ahhh! What the fuck do you think you're doing, close the door!" Izzy shouted.

Numba stood there motionless as he stared at Izzy, who had just come out of the bath. Thinking she would be alone, she didn't even have a towel covering herself, only one to cover her hair, allowing the teenage boy to get a great look at all her assets.

"Get out!" Izzy screamed, and Numba instantly escaped the room.

"Uh . . . I'm so sorry, but we don't really have much time. It's about Gary, he's in trouble," Numba said from behind the door. He was glad that there was nobody else around to see his beet-red face.

In less than a minute, Izzy came out of the room, now dressed in her AFA uniform. The only sign that she had been naked moments ago was her still-wet hair.

"He better be close to death for you to barge in like that." Her finger pressed into his chest, as she was barely resisting the urge to beat him up for what he had done. She took a step back, her arms crossed, as she waited for more information, yet Numba could only stare at the floor to avoid looking at her.

"Whoa, what's got you so mad?" Ian suddenly appeared from the hallway, coming back from the kitchen after his meal. He had heard the commotion on the way, but he had been too far away to make out details. "What did I miss? Did you confess to Izzy or something?"

"Shut up!" Both Izzy and Numba answered in unison.

Ian was shocked that they reacted to his teasing this way, but he let it go. Since he was already there, Numba didn't want to send him away, especially since they were all friends of Gary.

"Look, I came here because we need your brain," Numba said. "I've just come from Gary's room. He's awake and from what I can tell, he's back to his regular self. However, the moment I mentioned that they needed to test his blood to make sure his outburst yesterday had nothing to do with him being a crazed Altered, he started freaking out. He even begged me to cover him by taking the blood test for him."

"What? Why? That doesn't make any sense," Ian said.

Numba could only shrug. "I asked him the same thing, but from what he could tell me, it was best for me not to know. We didn't exactly have a lot of time to discuss what he meant by that because a nurse came in and tried to call the supervisors on me.

"Maybe his blood is a little crazed, and he's worried about what the school might do if they find out. Whatever the case, we need to help him. We owe him at least that much. If it weren't for him, we all would still be in the facility."

Hearing all of this, Izzy let out a big sigh. "All right, sounds like this is really serious. We might be able to do something, but it's going to be hard. The good news is, because of the rules around Altered, they are only allowed to test the blood for black particles, which means they aren't allowed to store or keep the blood sample in any way.

"After all, the corporations and other groups don't want to risk an independent company having their Altered's blood on file. That means giving our blood or swapping the sample before they test won't be a problem, it's just how we do it.

"If a nurse is already in the room with him, that means we don't really have the time to come up with something. We're just going to have to come up with a plan on the way there. Let's hope that Gary manages to buy us some time."

All three of them stood up. They knew that getting caught trying to temper with a medical test could land them in huge trouble, but for their friend, they were ready to take that risk.

CHAPTER 18

FAKE BLOOD (PART 2)

The three walked down the hallway at a fast pace; they didn't want to run to attract any attention, because they were now officially in the academy. Supervisors, teachers, and students could appear at any time.

Their reactions to this little mission were different: Numba nervous, Izzy focused, Ian excited. Never did he think his life in the AFA would amount to so many things happening at once.

He didn't even get a second to relax.

"All right, so there are two things that need to be done. First is to get one of the test tubes they use for blood, and also a syringe to draw out the blood. I'm guessing neither of you knows how to give yourself a blood test?" Izzy asked.

"I feel a little sick just thinking about it; they need to find a vein in your arm, and they wrap that thing around your biceps," Ian replied.

"All right, well, we don't know why Gary needs Numba's blood, but if I were to guess it doesn't matter who it comes from. So, Ian, that's going to be your job. The second task is to get Gary's blood sample and swap it. That's going to be harder," Izzy explained.

When they arrived at the medical bay, there were quite a few students with different injuries; what surprised them was that some supervisors were here as well. They guessed this was just a normal thing when Altered with all different types of abilities were training.

The medical ward wasn't too big; there was an oval desk in the center with staff members working at it. Nurses were walking back and forth, looking a bit too busy to deal with anything.

Then there were patients sitting outside a particular door on a cold metal bench.

"I was going to tell you, Izzy, I don't think the sneaking part will be so difficult," Numba explained. "When I came here earlier, everyone was so busy, and they seemed to trust the students not to do anything crazy here.

"The problem is finding out where they keep the blood samples. I mean, sneaking in and getting a few things, fair enough, but snooping around we're bound to get caught."

Before Numba could finish his explanation, Ian was already off; he had seen where the nurses were going in and out with their equipment. He went through the double doors, and everyone waited nervously for a while.

Five minutes passed, then ten. After fifteen minutes, Izzy was going to go in herself, but then she saw Ian walking back toward them. The group regathered and stepped a bit away from the reception desk.

"What took you so long?" Izzy asked.

"I was getting this," Ian replied. "I wanted to be careful, make sure it was a clean needle, where to dispose of it, and do you know how scary it is to stab yourself with a needle?"

"Aren't you a beast who makes needles?" Numba asked.

"That's different; anyway, it was terrifying, and I missed a few times, but I eventually got what you wanted. You know, on the internet I could probably sell my blood for a fortune, and here I am giving it away for free," Ian joked, but Izzy had already snapped the tube out of Ian's hand.

"So what are we going to do about the other part, swapping the blood? I couldn't find the lab," Ian replied.

"I'm going to need you two to make some type of distraction for me, just something to get all the nurses out here. Something big, and I'll go in and have a look," Izzy said.

"What if the door is locked; don't we need a key or to force someone to let us in?" Numba asked.

Izzy smiled.

"You know, I only accepted because I thought there was a chance of this working; you can let me deal with that."

The two boys thought about how they could create a large distraction, and then Ian came up with an idea and whispered it to Numba.

"No way, why would I let you do that?" Numba asked.

At that moment, Ian pushed Numba strongly across the room.

"Why are you trying to steal my girl, man, can't you get your own?" Ian shouted.

Like an actor, his facial expression and tone of voice had changed in an instant.

"Come on, why don't you fight me right here, right now!" Ian shouted.

Everyone had stopped, including the nurses, as they looked at the commotion happening in front of them, and one had even picked up the phone.

"Oh, so you're not going to say anything? Well, good defense!" Ian shouted, throwing out a kick and transforming his leg. Spikes grew out of it that dug right into Numba's own leg.

"ARGHHH, you bastard!" Numba shouted. Even if it was all an act, Numba was now annoyed.

"Stop fighting, please stop fighting!" the nurses were shouting.

It was perfect for Izzy, and she had already disappeared. It didn't take long for her to find the room that they were looking for.

There was a lab with a thick glass window, where she could see all the samples. It looked like the facility had on-site testing, so there was no need to send it off.

As Izzy placed her hand on the handle, her finger started to change, and the handle clicked open.

Closing the door and locking it again, she stayed low; Izzy was looking through the tubes and whatever she could find.

If someone came in, she was also looking for appropriate hiding spaces until they left. Eventually, she found the tube, in a tray with a couple of other blood tests.

There was a sticker on it with Gary's name. She removed the sticker and put it on the one Ian had given her.

Then she placed Gary's tube back in the tray, but the question was now what to do with the blood.

There was a bright yellow container for rubbish that was to be destroyed, and there was also a sink not too far away that she could pour it down.

Gary wanted us to get this for him, but why? Is he really a crazed Altered, or something else?"

In the end, rather than throwing the tube away, Izzy decided to keep it. Her curiosity about Gary had gotten the better of her.

CHAPTER 19

THE PLAN (PART 1)

After Numba had left Gary alone with the nurse, the woman had asked Gary a few routine questions before attempting to get his blood sample. Biding his time, the green-haired teenager asked for some food, but the nurse told him that the doctor had ordered her to get the test done first.

With no better idea, the werewolf told the woman that he really needed to go to the toilet, and since he had just woken up, she understood why he might need to go. Unfortunately for him, she had accompanied him right to the door, and when he stayed inside for over five minutes, the nurse was about to call the doctor. So Gary had to leave his impromptu hideout.

During that whole time, Gary was trying to think of a plan, any plan, to get him out of the situation, even climbing out the bathroom window, turning into a werewolf, and never coming back to the academy again.

In the end, he could think of nothing.

After he returned to the room, the nurse eventually took his blood, though not before Gary had destroyed one needle by "accidentally" flexing his muscles during the procedure. He was devastated. Now more than ever, he would have loved for someone to tell him what to do.

In the end, he just lay there, contemplating his troubles. The only good news was that he could finally eat, having taken the blood test. After a short while, the food arrived and he drowned his sorrows by eating.

Goodbye, academy; this could be the last meal I eat here, he thought as he stuffed his face.

Suddenly he heard a commotion outside, and since the voices sounded familiar, he decided to take a look outside. Walking down the hallway, he saw that everyone had gathered around the reception desk. He had to blink several times and rub his eyes, as he couldn't believe what he was seeing.

In the reception area, a Goat Altered was currently fighting a Hedgehog Altered.

"Numba . . . Ian? What the hell are the two of you doing?" Gary asked loudly, since they both had bloody wounds. He was confused about what could have happened in the short period of time since he had last seen his friends that might have led to the two of them to fall out this brutally.

While everyone's attention shifted to the new arrival, Izzy took the opportunity to exit the hallway, briefly giving the Goat Altered a thumbs-up to signal that she had completed her part of this mission, before disappearing.

Instead of answering him, Numba ran toward Gary and hugged him in front of everyone.

"We've got it resolved. You should be all good now," the Goat Altered whispered to him, before he let go.

Ian raised an eyebrow, unsure whether he should continue with the script about this merely being a spat over a girl. Ultimately, he decided to pretend to take this as his win.

"Yeah, you better run to your boyfriend. If I see you next to her again, nobody will be able to help you!" He loudly harrumphed and ran out before anyone could stop him.

This is what friends do, we look out for each other, Numba mouthed as he walked away. Gary received the message loud and clear: the fight had been part of a bigger plan to help him with his problem.

Later that night, Gary started to wonder if he had gotten the message from Numba all wrong. When the nurse entered, she told Gary that they had found no abnormalities in his blood, and that the blood had already been disposed of.

After that, he was told to go to his new room. It was a bit hard to find with the AFA being so large, but once he saw the red, yellow, and blue building he was sure that was in the right place.

The apartment building could hold around five hundred students, and although there wasn't a giant ranking system that dictated every student's quality of life, the colors did serve a similar function.

The AFA had such a great reputation for raising talented students because they wouldn't allow just anybody to progress to the AFC. For the time being, Gary had been told to head to the red section of the building and enter room 114, which was on the bottom. Once he proved his worth, he would eventually climb up to the other buildings.

Well, it looks like I won't be bumping into Xin any time soon, but it does make me wonder. All those students we fought should be in the blue dormitory, but if we had beaten them, would we automatically have been assigned to the blue dormitory? Or was that never possible and it was really just some type of assessment?

Gary felt a little left out since Numba and the others had probably been told earlier today what would happen. While they had all enjoyed their first day in the AFA, he had spent it in a hospital bed, praying that whatever Numba had done to his blood test had worked.

Since that had been taken care of, if he couldn't figure out a good way to protect himself by the next full moon, by locking himself up somewhere or escaping far away into the woods, then he would leave the academy before then. While here, though, he would learn as much as he could and make plenty of connections . . . at least if they weren't stuck-up assholes like Sty, that is.

CHAPTER 20

THE PLAN (PART 2)

Finding his room, Gary pressed the key card the nurse had handed him against the door, and it unlocked. He opened it and the smell of freshness wafted into his nose. It felt similar to the sensation one experienced when checking out a hotel room.

To the left was a nice kitchen area with a fridge and stove. To the right was a bathroom with a large bathtub that doubled as a shower.

Farther along was a large, empty space with a high ceiling as well as a few basic items, such as dumbbells, and finally a double bed. For an apartment for a single person, it was beyond what Gary had expected, especially since he still remembered where he had slept in the facility during the first few days . . .

Of course, it was nowhere near as plush as the luxury rooms he had enjoyed at the end, but as the professors had already stated, that was special for the facility's circumstances. Living the life he had lived, he was not one to complain that he had suddenly been robbed of his luxury.

Crap, why does my heart hurt a little? Gary thought. In the midst of the joy of this place and everything, he started to think about his mother. Before he had left, he had visited her at the hospital, but her state had not changed. He wished that she had woken up, so he could have told her not to worry about him anymore.

Alas, he knew that wishful thinking wouldn't change anything about her condition.

Gary saw that a sheet of paper had been left on the bed for him, and it looked like it was his schedule for the week: what time all his lessons would be and when he should arrive.

It reminded him of being back in school again. Just as he started to read it, he heard a knock on the door. He looked through the peephole and smiled as he opened the door.

"Hey, look at you, it seems like everything was okay in the end," Ian said as he walked in.

He wasn't alone; Izzy and Numba were with him as well. They instantly made themselves welcome, just like they had done in the facility. Ian casually took a seat, while Numba sat next to him on the bed.

"How did you guys know that I was here?" Gary asked.

"The supervisors told us." Numba chuckled. "After that little fight we had to distract everyone, it was impossible for us to get out unscathed. Fortunately, they bought our story about us fighting over a girl, and since we've just arrived they chose to be lenient.

"However, they did warn us that the next time we'll get a severe punishment, but we'll just have to avoid there being a next time. Anyway, when we asked about you, they told us that you'd already been discharged and sent to your room. By the way, we're your next-door neighbors."

It wasn't too big a surprise; it would make sense for them all to be in the red part of the building and next to each other.

"Thank you . . . thank you all for helping me, and I'm sorry for acting weird the last couple of days as well. I know what you saw might have been a bit scary," Gary said.

"Hey, I already knew you could break bones." Ian pointed at his leg. "And did you see the look on Ryan's face? I swear, he must have shat his pants when you nearly clawed him!"

"How . . . how did they stop me in the end?" Gary asked.

"It was Xin," Izzy replied. "She got up behind you and knocked you out on the spot."

Of all the people who had been present, Gary had expected that Eddy would be the one to stop him. He didn't remember the teacher doing such a thing, so he had assumed that one of the supervisors must have snuck up on him to knock him out. Xin hadn't even been on his list of suspects.

Is she really that skillful? I might have been out of my mind, but I still had a lot of Health left . . . I wonder how I would have fared if she had been my opponent from the start. Oh well, maybe we'll have a chance in the future. Now, should I thank her for knocking me out the next time I see her? There's Xin, the rest of the AFA, Altered Hunters, White Rose, and a number of gangs that still could topple me when it comes to power.

It was then that Numba picked up Gary's schedule off the bed.

"Ah, that's good, you have the same schedule as me," Numba said.

"Don't we all have the same schedule?" Gary asked.

"We do, but I'm guessing he's talking about something else," Izzy replied. "Numba's sheet was the only one with another lesson called 'Special Lesson.' It's a class that's taught once a week, but neither one of us has it."

Looking at the sheet, Gary saw the class on his schedule, and he wondered what it was.

"All right, I guess we should let you rest up." Ian stretched. "Today was pretty chill for us, but I imagine tomorrow they will start pushing us. Especially since we got in trouble. We should let you get an early night in a proper bed."

The others agreed and headed to the door, but before closing it, Izzy had one more thing to say.

"Take a look in the wardrobe; there is a nice surprise waiting for you." With that she closed the door.

The wardrobe? Gary thought. He opened it up and saw a small box. He pulled it out and opened the lid. Inside were a few of his valuable items that he needed to hand over before joining the facility.

The most important one of all was his phone. Picking it up, Gary immediately turned it on, and luckily it still had a bit of juice left.

I can finally contact the others, and see how they are doing, he thought with a smile on his face.

CHAPTER 21

UPDATE FROM THE OUTSIDE

Gary knew that he should focus on getting a good night's rest, but such a simple task felt impossible to him. Now that he finally had gotten his phone back, he was dying to find out what had happened during his stay in the facility.

For all he knew, something serious could have occurred without his knowledge. The Howlers might be in serious trouble and require his help . . . or they could be just fine on their own. Fortunately, his phone didn't let him wait for long. The sounds of several dings let him know that he hadn't been forgotten.

Noticing that his phone was about to die, with merely 3 percent battery, the green-haired teenager hurried to plug it in. The AFA had planned everything perfectly, allowing him to lie on his bed while scrolling through his contacts and their chat log.

Marie: Gary, I hope you're kicking some serious butt at the academy. It feels really weird without you here. I can't wait to see you on TV!

It was a short message, but sent during the beginning of his time at the academy. Of course, all of those in the Howlers knew what he was really doing.

Austin: Stay strong.

Short but precise. I might have had to worry if it had been anything but coming from him.

Innu: Happy that you're on your way to become a famous superstar. Sorry to have to ask you like this, but I'd like to borrow some cash from the Howlers Bank. Without you around, Kai is even more of a stingy asshole than before. I even explained that I don't need it for me, but to look after Kevin.

Gary pulled a face at that last one. Because he was a leader, it was only natural that from time to time he would actually need to make a decision, yet in terms of money he felt like Kai would know best. If he'd denied that request, then surely he had a good reason for it. So he merely told Innu that he would talk about it with Kai, stressing that he could not make any promises.

Tom: I got an apprenticeship at NIRV, so it looks like we are both on to big things. Don't worry, I won't hold it against you if you don't reply anytime soon. I know you're busy, and they must have rules about limited phone access. If you can, tell me that you're fine, otherwise, I guess we'll have a long discussion next time we meet.

Reading the message from his best friend reminded him of the bittersweet days in the past. During peaceful moments like this one, part of him wished he could just go back to playing video games, and not having to worry about so many adult things. Still, he knew that it was just wishful thinking. He had people to look after, especially his family.

I should give Tom a call at some point. Maybe during the holidays I could go see him. We should have enough money to visit a Tier 2 city, surely? Gary thought.

Amy: Gary, I never thought I would say this . . . but I actually miss waking up and finding your clothes lying around because you were too busy hurrying to school. I don't want to sound ungrateful. The apartment you got me is great, and your friends look after

me. I also managed to make some new friends, but . . . every time I come home it just feels so empty. I've been visiting Mom nearly every day, and while her condition is stable, there are no signs of her waking up. The doctor told me it could be tomorrow, next week, or next year, there's no way to tell. Anyway, I don't want to be your whiny little sister. I understand you have important things to do, but it would be nice if you visited once in a while.

This message pulled at Gary's heartstrings. It was painful to read, and it was the one that actually made him question his decision to come to the AFA in the first place. He cared about his family, everything he was doing was for his family, but was it really worth it, if he left behind the people he cared about?

Am I being selfish by joining the AFA? If I just spent time with the Howlers, then we could have lived off the income from that, right?

The more he thought about it, the more his heart tried to persuade him to leave, but taking a long breath he shook his head. His brain told him that he hadn't been gone that long, and leaving now would make his journey to this point meaningless. Besides, the life they had now could easily change at the drop of a hat.

Being in a gang wasn't safe, nor could a person in a gang . . . take it easy.

Finally, Gary scrolled back up to the message he had skipped earlier.

Kai: I bet you were expecting me to give you an update on the Howlers' progress and how we're doing, Gary, but you won't find that here. I don't want you to worry about any of that stuff. You've earned the right to be selfish, and even then your success will also help the Howlers, so just concentrate on your honeymoon with Xin. ;)

Kai: By the way, knowing you, you probably didn't bother reading their policy, so here is the short version. Once you're a student, you should be able to come and go as you please. They know that because of the students' connections, sometimes they have to leave. You'll probably have to ask a teacher or something for some time off. Don't overuse that privilege, though, and don't do it to meet up with us. We'll be fine on our own.

Then there was another message that was very recent.

Kai: You must have been worried sick last night, about how we dealt with the full moon. The short version is that Olivia and I are doing fine, so please don't worry about us. In fact, I'm more worried about what might have happened to you. I hope you didn't eat anyone. I guess we'll find out in a couple of days on the news. :P

For some reason, reading Kai's messages had caused Gary to grip his phone a little tighter. Perhaps it was the fact that Kai was nearly spot on with his prediction. Even if his smiley told him that he was jesting, they both knew that the possibility had been there . . .

Kai: I know I said I wouldn't update you with gang business, but the gang has gone through some big changes lately. Look forward to seeing it. Apart from that, things are going well and there have been no problems. Still, keep your phone on you if possible, perhaps I'll contact you.

After Gary read the message, his first instinct was to reply to his friend. He couldn't imagine what he would be needed for when Kai had the whole gang. The only scenario would be if they needed him for additional firepower, but who would dare to go against them in Slough?

Yet the context of the message said they were fine. In the end, Gary decided not to reply to any of the messages yet. Knowing Kai, Gary had been given all the details he deemed necessary.

Kai was right about one thing, though; I need to focus on me, Gary told himself. *Tomorrow is my first day in the academy. I need to work hard so I can catch up to Xin and even Jayden. If the group needs me, he'll let me know.*

Gary placed his head on the pillow, and it didn't take him long to fall asleep.

CHAPTER 22

THE FIRST DAY

Gary woke up in a great mood. After all, the first thing on his schedule was breakfast. The canteen was linked to the red section of the dorms, so unfortunately, just like before, he had no chance to meet up with Xin. At this rate, if Gary wanted to meet her, then he would just have to go over to the blue section, or outright go search for her during a free period, hoping that she would be free as well.

At breakfast, a kind of buffet awaited the students. The food there wasn't as extravagant as in the facility, but there was plenty of meat such as sausages, bacon, and chicken breasts. Since he had missed the first day, and thus the opportunity to meet his dietitian, he just picked everything he liked, which resulted in him carrying several plates of pure meat to his seat.

The eyes all around the room naturally landed on him as he carried his towers of meat.

"You know what, I'm happy for you, Gary," Ian said as the green-haired teenager sat down. All four of them were back together, enjoying their meals. "We were worried when you were fasting, but now that you're eating like that again, it's all good. It's also good to know that whenever you go on a hunger strike, we'll have to be careful that you might go all cray-cray on us."

Izzy kicked Ian in the shin, telling him to shut up. She was sure that their friend didn't need to be reminded of that event, but he was happily stuffing his face as usual, seemingly not caring about it at all.

Once breakfast was over, the four headed to their first lesson together. Gary was lucky that he had them to lead the way. Numba revealed that they had actually arrived ten minutes late for the first lesson yesterday, because of how big the AFA was and how many buildings they had.

The schedule had the name of the building and the class number, but that didn't help much when they had no idea where they were going. The initial tour with Eddy had helped, but it had been too much to take in at once.

The first lesson of the day was a theory lesson. It had nothing to do with fighting or martial arts, but the history of Altered themselves. It wasn't the most interesting subject in Gary's opinion, since he was only interested in the fighting part, but it was good that he didn't have to show off anything today.

I wonder when we will have a more combat-focused lesson? Gary thought. *Since I had to conserve my Energy in the fight against Ryan, I couldn't really go all out . . . at least not while I was conscious. I still don't know how much I've really improved compared to before . . . but it makes me think.*

Other than Xin and the teachers, is there even anyone for me to fight in here? Or learn from? If not, maybe there is a way I can skip all this and join the AFC as quickly as possible.

While Gary daydreamed about his debut match, he and his friends arrived in class. It was held in a large room, almost as big as a theater, and the seats were set up that way as well. There was a large bench with rows going upward looking down at the center of the class where the whiteboard was.

A staircase in the middle divided the rows of seats as well. It seemed like a bit of a free-for-all when it came to seats, but coming early allowed the students to sit wherever they wanted.

While they waited for the teacher, some of the new students looked Gary's way. They whispered about his green hair and his eating habits. Rumors were also spreading as to why he arrived today rather than yesterday.

The new students were always interesting to those who had passed, and just like in the facility, everyone had been here for different amounts of time. The classroom looked small, though, with about five other students entering.

I guess I shouldn't be surprised since this class is called Beginner Altered Theory. That means that there should be an Intermediate or Advanced Altered Theory class, though. I wonder how you go up . . . Is there a test for each subject or something? And you have to get a certain score before you go up another level?

While Gary pondered this, three more students arrived: Wu, Snow, and Apollo. Noticing the new arrival, Apollo nodded toward the werewolf with a big grin.

Well, I made it big, but sorry to disappoint you, I didn't make it through as number one, Gary thought.

The group went to sit on the other side of the room. Strangely, when Sty entered, rather than sitting with the three of them, he sat on Gary's side, but several rows above.

Eventually, the teacher entered and one of his helpers handed Gary a textbook and a bag with writing utensils to take notes during the lesson.

The first lesson was about beasts, and how they were related to Altered.

The teacher explained, "We have found that in the past, beasts had been ranked into different tiers based on the crystal inside them, which played a major role in how powerful they were. This could be one of the reasons why there's such a difference in Altered powers.

"However, we are unable to determine how strong the beast was that would be used for Alterification at this point in time. Or at least we haven't found an easier way."

The lesson continued, and Gary discovered that he found the subject far more interesting than he had initially anticipated, perhaps it was because it was his first day and everything to do with the Altered he had always found utterly fascinating.

After that, Gary had a personal session with the dietitian, while the others had a free period. He had to answer a few questions, such as what he would normally eat. He was a bit embarrassed, yet he answered honestly, because the one thing he wanted to avoid was to have his access to food restricted in any way.

"I think your diet is quite suitable for you," the female dietitian said jauntily. "Your Altered form matches quite well, so your stomach must have changed. Although if I hadn't seen you myself, I would worry that you might be overeating, but your body doesn't show any signs of that. In my professional opinion, I can only advise you to continue with your diet.

"I have made some adjustments, taking out some fatty foods for you, but tomorrow morning, at lunch and dinner, everything should be prepared for you. If you feel like you need any further adjustments, please make a booking at the reception desk and come and see me."

A free pass to continue eating like he had been doing put him in a great mood, and it was a good thing, because the next lesson was the mysteriously titled Special Lesson. It was in a completely different part of the building, and there seemed to be a lack of students.

Gary stood in front of a giant steel door, tapping his foot, waiting for his friend to arrive.

"Thanks for waiting for me. I'm glad I'm not doing this alone," Numba said.

"Me too. So what is this lesson?" Gary asked.

"I don't know. Eddy just told me that it will be something special, but it's the first time for me as well."

After waiting a while, they saw another familiar student arriving: Sty. This came as a bit of a surprise, though part of Gary had also expected it. Since neither Izzy nor Ian had it on their schedule, he had theorized that it might be something exclusive to the top three students.

A moment later, Apollo, Wu, and Snow arrived, further proving Gary's theory.

Whatever this special lesson was, apparently the AFA only wanted the top students to participate in it.

CHAPTER 23

SPECIAL LESSON (PART 1)

Despite everything Gary had been through, Apollo still had a strange aura surrounding him that told the werewolf on an instinctual level that he was quite dangerous. It wasn't that the Altered used it in any conscious way to threaten him, it was just there and made Gary aware that he should treat him with respect as he had done the head supervisor.

The visits between the two of them had been short, their interactions practically nothing, and yet his words the last two times they had spoken weighed on Gary's mind. Before he could even think about getting better than Xin, or anyone in the AFA and AFC, he needed to beat the person in front of him; he just had no idea what level Apollo was at, or the levels of his two teammates.

"I'm happy that you took my advice and made it through your group at the top," Apollo said.

It was good that Apollo had broken the ice, because the conversation between the two groups was lackluster for a while.

The three from each group stood opposite each other, looking into each other's eyes. Sty had his arms folded as he looked away from the group. Clearly something had happened, because Sty was a part of them earlier. First the classroom and now this; it wasn't hard to put the two things together.

Numba was feeling nervous. Out of the entire group, he felt out of place. After all, he knew that he hadn't done enough to deserve his position, and he felt like the weakest of the lot.

His draw against Sty could be considered a fluke, and he felt like if they were to fight again, Sty would surely win.

"Unfortunately, I didn't quite manage to stay at the top," Gary replied, pulling Numba into a friendly type of headlock, while he was still dazed and in the middle of his thoughts. "This guy took that from me."

Hearing this, Apollo looked at Numba.

"What are you saying, Gary? I only made it here because of you in the first place." The Goat Altered quickly refuted the praise, not wanting to set up the wrong expectations like he had done before with the last group of people they had met.

When Apollo heard this, the look on his face changed.

Huh, I didn't take him to be a softie.

For a brief moment, he even questioned his evaluation of Gary. He had taken the green-haired teenager to be the same as him, but if Apollo had been in the same shoes, he would have never given up the number one spot, even to a close friend. Yet there was still a feeling that the two of them were similar.

"Since you guys arrived here before us, care to tell us what this special lesson is all about?" Gary asked.

Snow and Wu looked at each other before giving an answer. "This is our first time here as well. Although it was on our schedule, we were told to wait until we were called, so here we are."

It was strange that only the six of them were involved in something, and it made Gary even more curious what they would be taught. Was it just a coincidence that the AFA didn't start those lessons before there were six of them? Did it have anything to do with the number? Was it hard to prepare, so they preferred to do it with a larger group all at once? There were too many reasons to guess. The only fact they did know was that each group were the top three students that had passed the facility.

"I've heard from the students before about this," Apollo said. "Those who pass the facility as one of the top three students in under a month get rewarded by the AFA by being allowed to take part in a special course."

Although the others started to get excited after hearing this, Gary was getting nervous. What if this special course was some type of training that only Altered could do? Lately, his werewolf self was getting into more trouble, and he had already come close to getting caught a few times.

Although he wasn't a cat, he felt like he had already used up many of his nine lives.

While Gary was worrying about the unknown, the double doors opened up. They appeared to be made of thick steel, an arm's length thick, and walking out was an extravagantly dressed adult whom they could only assume to be the teacher.

Black was the predominant color of his outfit, mixed with a few tinges of red. He was dressed in a black coat, black boots, and black gloves, and he carried a large staff with a large ring at the end. That ring was further adorned by many black feathers, seemingly coming from the same bird as the one depicted on his golden necklace. His onyx hair was pointed upward like a feather, and his neatly shaved and groomed beard covered up his round face.

"My name is Crowley Corvus!" The teacher introduced himself, lifting both his hands. "I will be the one to act as your teacher, if you choose to participate in my lecture. If you think you have what it takes, then please come and follow me." A bang of the staff on the floor ended his sentence.

The teacher said nothing else as he turned around and went back through the doors while also somewhat flapping his arms, making his cape look like wings. It was as if a human were trying to fly, but clearly Crowley was moving nowhere.

Numba looked at Gary.

"What was that all about?" the Goat Altered asked.

"I don't know, maybe he's just role-playing or something," Gary replied with a shrug. Unsurprisingly, all of them followed him into the room. As if on cue, the moment Sty entered, the steel doors behind them closed, and a locking mechanism clicked shut.

Gary was worried; why would they need such a thick steel door, and why did it need to be locked?

CHAPTER 24

SPECIAL LESSON (PART 2)

From the size of the large steel doors, everyone thought that they would be entering a fairly large room, but instead they were now in an even smaller room, with another locked door in front of them.

The room was hardly large enough to fit twenty people. There were a few seats, and a TV, where Mr. Corvus was standing at the back.

"You have been specifically chosen by the academy for this task. It is a job that not everyone can do. If you have a problem, please ask. Which is why, before we proceed, I must hand you all the documents you need." Mr. Corvus waved his weird staff, and from below each seat where the students were sitting a piece of paper emerged, landing in their laps or hands.

It was like magic, but clearly that wasn't the case. Gary assumed it had something to do with the Teacher's Altered power.

"Please read all the terms and conditions carefully before proceeding, and remember you have the option to accept or decline."

Honestly, Gary didn't like all this mystery mumbo jumbo. He would much prefer just getting a straight class, but remembering what Apollo had said, he at least wanted to see what this class was like. After all, this was most likely what had allowed Xin to improve at the rate she had.

Perhaps all of those who had become well known in the AFC had gone through this; it was hard to ignore such a special class.

By signing this document, I hereby agree to all the stipulated rules. I understand that this is a contract that binds me for life, and I hereby give permission for NIRV to exact the consequences should I break any terms of the contract.

The company name, NIRV, stuck out like a sore thumb. Although they had all heard that NIRV had connections to the AFA, they had all just thought that it was one of many corporations. This document made it look like the whole Special Lesson was somehow connected with it.

Rule #1: Whatever happens during the Special Lesson is to be kept completely secret. The only exemption from this rule is for those who also took the Special Lesson, as well as your handler, Mr. Crowley Corvus.

Rule #2: No electronic devices or recording equipment of any kind are to be taken into the Special Lesson. All personal items will be left in a basket before entering and will be returned at the end of the Special Lesson.

Rule #3: NIRV will do its best to ensure the safety of every student who agrees to take part in the Special Lesson. In the unfortunate case of a student's death, their respective corporations, sponsors, or family members will be compensated greatly. Please read the terms and conditions on the next page for more clarification.

"Gary, did you read rule number three?" Numba exclaimed. "Just what type of lesson is this? What do they want us to do that we might end up dead?"

Gary had just read the same rule and was wondering the same thing. At least now he knew why they only allowed the strongest students to participate.

"Stop being such a baby!" Sty sneered from the side. "As Altered there's always a risk of dying. Don't tell me you didn't know that when you chose to become an Altered. People don't enter the AFA just to become a better fighter to protect themselves out there in the real world. You can't just keep hiding behind your friends."

Numba closed his mouth, unable to respond to that point. He gave the Fly Altered a dirty look but otherwise continued to read the rest of the rules. Gary wanted to say something, but he had promised the professor to let bygones be bygones. As long as Sty was merely running his mouth without threatening him or anyone close to him, he would overlook those antics.

Rule #4: Anything found or obtained during the Special Lesson will be regarded as property of NIRV. Students will be rewarded with appropriate compensation.

Rule #5: By agreeing to every rule, the student will automatically become an Apprentice Recoverer. This means that NIRV will be able to call upon you at any point and time to do Recoverer-related tasks. Please read the terms and conditions on the next page for more clar-ification.

What is all of this Recoverer stuff? Signing this basically means I work for NIRV? They make it sound like there is no way to back out of this, and they don't really make the consequences for breaking these rules clear, either.

Looking around the room, Gary saw that Apollo, Snow, and Wu had already signed their pieces of paper and handed them over to Mr. Corvus. Numba was still wondering what to do, while Sty was also signing it, after noticing that the other three had done so already, and quite aggressively as well.

"What will the two of you do?" the teacher asked them. "There is no second chance. You can either sign it today or leave forever."

Looking at Apollo, thinking about Xin's rampant growth, and then considering the future of the Howlers, Gary realized there was a chance that if NIRV called on him, he might be unavailable. This would mean he would have to face the consequences . . . whatever those might be.

NIRV being involved just made everything more dangerous, but something inside Gary told him that he shouldn't miss out on this op-portunity. There was no way of telling whether there would ever be a time conflict in the future, but even if there was, he would just have to deal with it then.

Having made up his mind, he signed the piece of paper. Seeing this, Numba plucked up the courage and did the same.

"I'm looking forward to the special lesson, Mr. Corvus."

"Excellent. With all six of you, your survival chances should be great!"

CHAPTER 25

SPECIAL LESSON 1 (PART 1)

"I knew you would sign that piece of paper in the end. Still, I'm surprised it took you so long to make up your mind." Apollo addressed Gary in a teasing tone.

"I value my freedom, that's all. Getting told what to do by a giant corporation I don't really know much about doesn't sit too well with me," the Werewolf responded. He wasn't lying. If the AFA had been the one to organize everything, he would have signed a lot sooner. Especially if there had been no commitment clause to indefinitely serve them for as long as he was alive. However, suddenly finding out that NIRV was apparently the one behind this entire Special Lesson had been really off-putting, especially with all the secrecy they had to uphold.

Gary had already learned a few things about them from Tom.

Only time would tell whether he would regret signing that piece of paper. He could only hope that restricting his freedom was actually worth it. Of course, if Xin's powers actually originated from her having participated in this Special Lesson, then selling his services might be a small price to pay.

"I'm happy to hear that was your only reason for hesitating," Apollo added. "There aren't just downsides to this deal, though. NIRV is far more than meets the eye. They seem to have their hands in a bit of everything, not to mention they have enough influence to indirectly control the happenings of even Tier 1 cities.

"No matter your background, it won't hurt having a connection with them. This way, both parties benefit from it. This is just how things are in our world, and you have to get with the program if you don't want to lose out."

Gary chuckled. "I didn't realize you were the type who would rely on others just because they were above you," he replied, tensing his fist. "Because I never want to be in that situation again, where I'm helpless against those who are above me."

Before the two could continue their conversation, Mr. Corvus whacked the bottom of his staff against the floor.

"Please, children, if you wish to bicker, do it in your own free time. For now, let's rejoice in the fact that we have a full house. Although that is usually the case, let's just hope it stays this way. Everyone, please follow me, and make sure to not stray."

The second set of doors opened up, and just like the first pair they had gone through, it was made of thick steel, though not as reinforced as the first pair. From the looks of it, they were being led through a tunnel.

The flooring was white and so was the surrounding metal, and there was no end in sight. It made them wonder if their destination was going to be inside the academy or someplace entirely different.

Suddenly, Mr. Corvus stopped and turned around holding a basket in his hand. It had appeared out of nowhere, like magic.

"Now, before we proceed, I'll have to insist that you leave behind all mobile and recording devices. Don't worry, you'll retrieve them all once the special lesson ends."

Nobody protested, and one by one, they emptied their pockets, filling up the basket. When everyone was done, Mr. Corvus turned around, his hands free, with their items nowhere to be found.

He continued walking, and the students had no choice but to follow him. What Gary and the others did notice was that there were cameras every so often in the hallway. A red blinking light on each one indicated that someone was clearly watching them.

Eventually, the long tunnel split up. Without stopping for even a moment, Mr. Corvus took a right turn. Once it happened again, they ended up in front of three possible entrances, where he took the middle one. As time passed, the tunnel started to resemble a maze, and Gary wasn't sure he would be able to find his way back on his own with how many turns they had taken.

In the end, they arrived in front of a sturdy-looking door. This one had a palm scanner next to it. The teacher placed his hand on it, and a beep resounded. The next moment, the doors opened up.

The group entered a large square room, and for the first time they saw a change from the bleak white color. Half of the room was covered from the bottom to the top in red. There was a bench with different outfits. Seemingly par for the course, there was also a large metallic steel door. On the other half of the room, everything was the same, only in blue.

"First, if you could all please get changed into the uniform that has been provided with your name tag, and once you are done, remain standing in place," Mr. Corvus ordered.

The werewolf scanned through the outfits before he found his own name tag in the blue section of the room. As he walked over, the teenager looked at the other two outfits and stopped before turning around. At the same time, Apollo, who had been heading to the red side, met Gary's gaze. Both of them looked unhappy.

"Shit," Numba cursed. "Looks like we're not in the same group."

"You're correct. The teams have been created based on your performance reviews. This way, both groups should have roughly the same strength. Since we have an even number of you, I won't have to fill out the group," Mr. Corvus informed them.

Numba looked worried. The Goat Altered had been hesitant about signing up in the first place. A major part in his decision was him trusting his new friend, but now it looked like they would be split up.

As if that weren't bad enough, the red team consisted of Numba, Apollo, and Sty. At least the two of them knew each other, but his relationship with the former was nonexistent, and antagonistic with the latter. That was less than ideal in this special lesson that actually mentioned the death of a student as a possibility.

CHAPTER 26

SPECIAL LESSON 1 (PART 2)

Numba wasn't the only one unhappy with the teams. Gary had never really interacted with either Wu or Snow. Apollo had been the only one among the three who had given him the time of day, while his friends had treated the green-haired teenager like he was invisible during the meals.

Meanwhile, Apollo had paid special attention to Mr. Corvus's words. According to the teacher, the teams were the way they were because they wanted to distribute the strength of the participants as evenly as possible. He knew the strength of his friends, as well as of Sty, so the current team rosters told him a lot about the power of the other two . . .

Apollo was the first to change out of his outfit. Since they were all boys, there was no reason to waste time asking for a changing room. Besides, given his muscular body, he had nothing to hide. In fact, he was quite proud of his scars. Wu and Snow did the same, without uttering a word. Seeing this, Gary joined them as well.

It only took a few minutes for both sides to finish changing. The outfit that had been prepared for them was quite a bit thicker than their AFA uniform. It was flexible enough to bend, but hard like leather.

It was mostly black, with some accents of their team's color, and only covered the main parts of their body. Thinner pieces covered their arms, shoulders, and legs. It was clear it was designed in a defensive manner like a suit of armor, while not restricting their free movement.

The two groups stood opposite each other. Numba looked nervous because he'd thought of something. If there were two teams, then it probably meant they were going to be competing against each other in some manner. Still, there were also two separate doors on each side of the room, which indicated they might not be facing each other directly.

"It's time for me to explain what this special lesson is all about," Mr. Corvus said. "As you may have already guessed, I haven't led you here to teach you theory. In fact, I won't be the one teaching you at all today. How much you take away from this lesson will solely depend on your own actions and comprehension.

"However, we understand that this may be difficult for some students. Therefore, before the next special lesson, I'll prepare feedback on your performance, focusing on your weak areas. Nevertheless, I can only recommend that you do your own due diligence without solely relying on me.

"Now on to the lesson itself. Although there are two groups, you will both be given the same task. The goal of this special lesson is to provide you with the extra push you'll need to rise above your peers. Holding your hand too much will only slow your progress down.

"Let me stress to you that this is *not* a competition. I want you to work together, as that will be key to passing this lesson. Once you're inside, you'll know what you have to do. I understand that a lot of what I have said may not make a lot of sense. It's because I have been told to be as vague as possible.

"Which is why I will now leave you with a few words. To pass this lesson, you must survive. To fail . . . means death."

Numba gulped; he wondered how an academy could condone this. However, then he remembered the cruel way the world worked at the moment, and the contract he had just signed. It wasn't a saintly world.

They did say that they would do anything to ensure our survival . . . he must have said that last bit to keep us on our toes . . . right? Surely if we are in trouble, they will step in to help, Numba told himself.

The two steel doors opened at the same time, and both groups were told to walk in; on one side Apollo took the lead, and on the blue team, Snow was the one who walked in front.

"I know you can be a bit crazy at times, Greeny, but let's pass this together, all right? Wu and I have experience fighting together. Support us where you can and listen to my commands, and we should have no problems," Snow said.

Not wanting to get into an argument before he even knew what the task was, Gary nodded. Before entering the room at the end, he gave Numba a thumbs-up. The two doors then closed behind them.

Gary and his teammates entered yet another large white room. There was nothing inside but a steel door behind them, a steel door in front of them around fifty yards away, and some cameras that had been placed in every single corner and along one entire side.

"This is a pretty big room," Wu said. "I'm guessing it's going to be like those assessments we did, with the sticky black balls, or the last one to be hit. Whatever it is, I'm in!"

The two seemed excited, and as they were talking to each other, Gary went up to the wall, deciding to check out the room. That was when he felt a deep scratch in the wall. It was hard to see from far away because it seemed like they had painted over it, but up close the scratches on the wall were visible, and there were a lot more than one.

The next second, the closed door started opening up.

GSHH TCH!

Strange noises could be heard from behind the door. The moment it was fully opened, both Wu and Snow froze in place from shock.

GSHTY HHH!!!

The moment Gary saw it, he received a new notification.

New Quest received
A beast has been discovered
Kill the beast in order to gain Exp
Optional Quest: Consume the beast in order to gain stats

CHAPTER 27

THE RED TEAM (PART 1)

There was a relatively large room with several screens inside in an unknown location. Some monitors showed what was currently going on in the special lesson.

The cameras could rotate 360 degrees and zoom in and out, and there were so many that they could view whatever was going to happen inside from any angle.

The outside of the monitor, which took up half of the room, was painted blue, while the other half was painted red to indicate which room they were watching. On top of that, several people were inside.

A few people wore white lab coats with the letters *NIRV* written across the chest. They had tablets in their hands and were looking at other screens, monitoring a number of different things.

Finally, there were also the three professors who made up the head of the entire AFA academy: Humfree, Wood, and Hai. They were busy people, but they always insisted on being present at the beginning of everything:

the arrival of new students, the assessment, and now the first special lesson.

By their side was a female teacher. Her hair was a light red, shoulder length, straight and parted in the middle. Her clothes were quite sporty and were a dark red color, as if she was ready for a fight at any moment.

According to the deal between NIRV and the AFA, a teacher from the academy would always be present while these lessons were taking place, just in case something occurred that was outside their expectations. Currently, the four of them sat in the back of the room so they could see every single one of the monitors.

At the same time, a man wearing round glasses stood in the center of the room, as if he were about to give a presentation. In contrast, the others continued to adjust levels, type away, and input data, checking everything.

"It always is fun for me at the start of these, sharing my passion with others," the man said in an energetic and upbeat voice as he pushed his glasses up. The screen behind him had suddenly changed; it no longer showed the room, but instead displayed a 3D image of what looked like a beast.

"Before the lesson begins, I wanted to give you some information about the beast that we have been able to procure for today," the man explained. "Of course, since it is the first lesson, we have tried to not give the students anything too overwhelming, while at the same time we didn't want to give them something easy, as it could make them too confident in their next lesson. As requested by the AFA, of course.

"However, I do have to remind you that although we have attempted to gather as much information about the beast as possible in order to determine what difficulty the students might face, it is impossible as this is a new type of beast even for us."

The man looked down when he said this, avoiding eye contact with them all.

"A new beast . . . so you are experimenting on the students with a new beast? Why couldn't you have used one for which you know all of the details, like you have done before?" Humfree asked.

"As you know, we have to get something out of this as well. A basic beast that can turn a person into an Altered isn't going to do much. We need to keep expanding our research, and our technology has always improved and has gotten better in terms of figuring out what the beast will be like before we . . . bring it back, let's say."

Humfree folded his arms and gave out a big huff, showing that he was displeased. Although the three professors ran the AFA, they were not the owners of it. This lesson, the whole deal, was set up between people who were much higher than them, and they could do nothing about it but ensure that the students were safe.

Now that that was over, the NIRV employee turned to his screen to have a look at the beast. The 3D render showed its body in full. According to a scale chart, it was larger than a lion, yet smaller than an elephant, about the same size as an SUV.

The beast had six eyes total, but three eyes on each head, because this beast had two heads. They were split apart and had two large fangs sticking out of each mouth. It also had a single large tail that looked somewhat like a hammer at the back.

The beast itself looked to be bulging with muscle, having next to no fat at all.

"This beast is meant to be difficult to deal with because of the two heads, but the group should be able to figure out some way to defeat it. Still, they will need to watch out for its powerful tail as well. It's the perfect beast that will promote teamwork between the three of them.

"We have yet to receive a crystal from this type of beast as stated, so we have no clue how a human Altered would be able to benefit from this. However, from our tests, we have determined that it is unlikely to have any powers, skills, or abilities. This is why we have considered this safe for both groups of students.

"As always, we have our special gas ready and staff available to help if we believe there's a chance of one of the students dying. Without further ado, it looks like the students are now ready."

He stepped to the side; the screen showed both teams entering and the doors opening up for both of them.

With Apollo and Gary on either team . . . I doubt we will have to worry, Humfree thought.

CHAPTER 28

THE RED TEAM (PART 2)

The dreaded two-headed beast had entered the room. Saliva was dribbling from its mouth and onto the floor. It made constant noises that were unheard of and out of this world.

The second that Numba saw it, his legs started to shake, and he almost collapsed.

I knew something had to be up . . . all the red flags were there, talking about death and getting involved with NIRV. They're making us fight real beasts! How are we meant to win against that? Numba thought. *How are beasts even a thing . . . how is one standing in front of us?*

Even Sty seemed hesitant to attack such a creature. It wasn't what he had expected either. To be honest, he hadn't actually read the document and just signed the thing when he saw that the others had as well.

"Ha-ha, now this is more like it. I knew coming to the AFA was the right thing to do!" Apollo said as he punched his fist into his other hand.

They didn't have time to think because the beast was already heading straight toward them. It ran across the floor on all fours like a crocodile, but each footstep was hard, loud, and clear.

The first one to change into their Altered form was Sty, who flew upward in an attempt to avoid confrontation with the beast. Numba was still too nervous about moving but knew he had to do something, or he would end up being eaten by the two heads. He could already imagine his body being split in half.

Just as Numba was in the middle of his transformation, he saw Apollo running straight toward the beast, smiling. When he was partway there, his arms started to change, becoming larger and turning white, with soft fur sprouting on them.

Then, just like the beast in front of him, Apollo was running on all fours. The beast opened its mouths wide, baring its fangs. Apollo leapt into the air; his two large, white fists had turned into deadly claws, which he used to bash both of the heads into the ground. Its mouths closed shut in an instant.

The floor shook when Apollo's feet landed, as if he weighed several tons. The beast had been stopped in its tracks. All that momentum it had built up had come to nothing.

Wow, this is the first time I have ever seen Apollo fight, Numba realized. I wonder what type of beast he is, to have white fur?

Soon though, the heads of the beast started to struggle. It was moving about, shaking left and right. Apollo kept his large paws on the beast, holding it down, not allowing it to move.

"Well, are you guys going to do something to help or what?" Apollo shouted. As he finished saying those words, the tail behind the beast, which looked to be too short to reach him, had extended itself and swung around.

The tail hit Apollo right in the chest, sending him crashing into the wall before falling onto the floor. Blood spilled from his mouth.

"It looks like that thing has some power after all," Apollo said, getting up. "If only it didn't have two heads, this would be no problem, or if you two were a little useful. But don't worry. Even if you don't help, I'll kill this thing on my own because that's what I always do."

Apollo's eyes started to change, becoming completely black. It looked like he was ready for round two. However, the beast didn't turn to look at him. Instead, it was now looking at Numba, who was closest.

It then ran toward him with its two large mouths gaping open.

Numba thought, *Crap, do I charge forward just like Apollo did? I have a feeling if I did that, I'd be the one who was knocked forward, but I have to do something!*

In the middle of his thoughts, liquid rained down from above and hit the three eyes on one of the heads. Numba recognized this liquid and knew the acidic pain that it would produce.

One of the heads was screaming. The creature had veered off course and didn't know where it was going.

"Sty, make sure one of the mouths is shut!" Apollo shouted.

Hearing this, Sty flew into the head that he had spit his acid on and kicked it hard. He continued to fly around, hitting the beast in the head. Its tail was swinging recklessly, trying to swat Sty out of the air, but Sty's fast reflexes were working for him as usual.

Damn it, even that damned bug is being more useful than me. I have to . . . I have to help in some way, Numba thought.

He used his explosive power to charge up to the beast, and since its tail was in the air, he was able to run right up to the base of the tail and hit it with his horns, digging in.

They were stuck quite deep into the beast, and Numba started throwing fist after fist.

"Well, it looks like this team isn't too bad after all. It's time we finish this!" Apollo said as he grabbed the head that Sty wasn't attacking and began to lift. It was unbelievable, but the next second, the beast was in the air.

Sty had stopped his attacks, and using his legs, Numba pulled his horns out of the tail, falling to the ground. Then Apollo fell on his back, slamming the beast to the ground. It was now on its back, wriggling with pain, and before it could roll over, Apollo was above it, looking down at its belly.

He landed right on top of the beast with his two feet, and they all heard loud cracking noises as its bones broke and its halves bent upward as if a large weight had been thrown on top of it. It let out its last few squeals, and then the beast was no longer alive.

"Well, the red team has done well," the NIRV employee said. "I didn't expect there to be such a strong fight. Now it's time to see how the blue team will fare."

CHAPTER 29

THE BLUE TEAM (PART 1)

Both Wu and Snow were stunned as they saw the beast. Their brains needed a moment to handle the surprise of seeing one in the flesh rather than in a textbook or documentary. The feeling of having to face something that should be extinct and was now threatening your life was hard to describe.

It was a natural reaction for them to think that everything they were experiencing now was just a dream, but their senses and their inner Altered beasts knew it wasn't true. They could feel something react inside their bodies when looking at this thing. Meanwhile, the last member of their team had a different take on the situation.

Huh, somehow I pictured them scarier . . . Am I going crazy? Or is it because I fought against Billy, who turned into a bloodthirsty werewolf? No, that's not it. Even Damion was more of a monster than this thing before us. A simple beast did cruel things in nature, whereas humans did stuff to each other for what reason? Gary didn't understand; but a human had put his mother in the hospital. To him, those who could hurt someone like his mother were the true nightmares that people needed to be scared of.

For a while now, the werewolf had believed that his only way to grow stronger would be by leveling up through the system. One of his quests wanted him to reach Level 25, which would reward him with a class promotion. Given how much stronger he got from reaching a higher class, it was a no-brainer that Level 25 would make him even more powerful. Unfortunately, the system had been really stingy these days in terms of giving him Exp. The days of just fighting against his local high school mates and challenging strangers for Exp were over, but fighting against beasts would surely fix that.

On top of that, it allowed him to raise his stats.

After all, how many chances would he get to consume an Altered and actually get away with it? Each one was a precious resource to whatever background they belonged to, so unless he was willing to face the backlash, he could only forget about it . . .

"Hey, Greeny, forget about the whole supporting-us bit. I'm sure you want to pass this in one piece, same as us, so whatever chance we get, we need to attack this thing. Don't hold back and let's take this thing out together!" Wu said as he regained his composure.

"I'll distract it, so the two of you better make use of that time!" Snow shouted as he ran forward. His two front teeth started to elongate until they went past his chin. At the same time, the teenager's ears grew larger, while white fur grew on the back of them.

The special armor they had been told to wear was not only strong, it was also flexible, able to accommodate their transformation without a problem.

Ha, so he really is a rabbit. No wonder that guy would only eat carrots. Still, I shouldn't forget that he was ranked number two in the facility, so I shouldn't underestimate him just based on his Altered form.

Gary had to admit that he was impressed by both Wu and Snow. They might have been stunned at first, but they only needed a moment to understand that they couldn't let their fears get the best of them, not if they wanted to survive this.

The beast had only stared at the trio, seemingly deciding whom to target first. It ran toward Snow, and it was picking up speed. The Rabbit Altered seemed to be trying to escape, and naturally the beast wouldn't let him.

"I bet you think I'm a tasty rabbit! Well, let me show you that you're nothing but an ugly oversized dog!" Snow shouted as he zigzagged around the beast. Pissed off at failing to catch him, the beast followed him as he neared the wall.

Just then, when the beast looked like it was about to bite down on the agile Snow, he leapt up and his feet transformed. They grew long and flat like a rabbit's, and their bottom surface was now larger. Immediately, Snow jumped off the wall and landed behind the beast.

Given its momentum, it was unable to change direction, and it crashed into the wall, letting out a howl of pain. Its tail was thrashing left and right, trying to hit Snow, but he would hop and jump out of the way with his strong legs.

"I guess I was being generous comparing you to a dog; you're far stupider. Did even one of you get a functioning brain?" Snow taunted it.

Turning around, the beast opened its two mouths. It had suffered some damage, but far too little to slow it down. But Snow had never believed that this little would do the trick. Instead of letting the beast build up momentum and run toward him again, Snow jumped from the ground, and his large feet hit the top of one of the beast's mouths. He pushed off, jumping backward, slamming the beast's mouth shut, while also avoiding the other mouth of the beast.

"Do the two of you need some sort of invitation? Am I supposed to do all the work here? I mean, I'm sure I could beat the thing myself, but I thought Mr. Corvus said the idea was to work together! I don't fancy getting hit by that damned tail or by its mouth, so get off your asses and do something!"

"I thought your buddy was the silent type . . . looks like that is only true when he has a carrot in his mouth," Gary sneered, and Wu could only add a quiet "Tell me about it" under his breath.

"I have no idea what this mutt can do, but to be honest, I'd rather not find out. Let's just both use all our strength to take it down in one hit!" the former rank 3 suggested as he ran forward and began to transform mid sprint.

CHAPTER 30

THE BLUE TEAM (PART 2)

Before Wu could transform, it looked like there was a type of routine that he would need to perform. He let out a few punches as they neared the beast, and he got into a stance. Sweat started to cover his body, and in less than a second there seemed to be a pool of water below his feet. It was amazing how he was able to sweat so fast. Gary had been focused on the pool of water, but then he noticed the two antennae on Wu's head.

What type of Altered is he? Gary thought.

Looking at Wu again, he saw that his forearms were slightly larger than before, but the rest of his body was not much different. He could only assume it was a partial transformation, but even then, what difference would a pair of antennae make?

"I know that I don't look as impressive as those two, but I promise you, as long as we're talking pure strength, I'm no weaker than Apollo."

At the same time, Gary had transformed himself, though he didn't fully transform into his werewolf form yet. Apart from his shoulders, his legs turned into those of a werewolf, providing him with extra speed, enough to reach Wu's side.

"I'm sorry, but I have no clue how strong Apollo is, so I don't know how strong you are," Gary said with a smile. Wu saw this smile and, coupled with the green-haired teenager's earlier remarks, he realized that Gary didn't seem tense at all. Rather than a life-and-death battle, he appeared to be treating it like a sparring match.

Meanwhile, Snow continued to distract the beast, mainly concentrating on one head. He would jump off the ground and throw a punch straight at the left head, hoping to take it out. He was damaging the beast but not causing major damage.

Snow would have been able to launch a stronger attack, but he was being careful, worried that the beast might hide some nasty surprises. There was no need to overexert himself if the others were there to help, especially Wu.

If Green Hair helps, then it's a bonus, but me and Wu will be able to take on this beast. I guess that's why they made the teams like this in the first place, Snow thought.

Charging forward, Wu and Gary readied their fists, and at the first opportunity they threw them right into the side of the beast's body. Turning his head slightly, Wu was surprised.

His punch is as fast as mine . . . and he hasn't even transformed fully. I hate to admit it, but Apollo was dead on about him being more than meets the eye.

The second their fists hit the wall of muscle under the beast's hide, it rippled, and the beast's entire body was lifted on its side before it crashed into the wall. Snow was left there stunned because one moment the beast was in front of him, and the next it wasn't.

"Whoa!" Snow exclaimed. "Well, you guys finally woke up. Wu, your nightly training is paying off. I've been hoping for you to damage it, not send it flying away. I know they said there aren't any points for this lesson and stuff, but man, you earned some big ones there if there are."

Wu didn't say anything; he just glanced at Gary by his side. It was hard to tell which hit had been stronger, but he wasn't arrogant enough to believe that he could have managed this feat on his own.

Either way, the beast wasn't dead yet; a bit of black blood had come out of its mouth as it got back up, and it started to growl deeply. Drool dropped from its mouth, which was covered in blood, and it looked like it still had plenty of fight in it.

It sprang off the ground and leapt into the air. Its mouths opened wide; it saw both Wu and Snow as tasty snacks. Snow jumped back, while Wu was getting ready to hit the beast from below.

However, at the same time, the large tail had grown in length and had swung to its side, looking to hit them. Seeing this, Gary moved over to take care of the tail. Judging by the speed of its jump, he was sure that his current power would be insufficient.

Skill activated: Full Transformation
–20 Energy
Transformation has begun

Gary's size started to change, and the next second he grabbed the beast's tail. His foot dug in and with all his strength he stopped the tail from hitting the others. Lifting his hand, he slashed it toward the base of the tail, making a deep cut, and then pulling with all his might, he ripped the tail off.

Blood spilled all over the floor, and turning around, Gary stopped his transformation as he could see that both Wu and Snow had finished the beast off.

"Hey, man, you could have helped as we—" Snow stopped his complaint the second he saw the werewolf holding the beast's tail in his hand.

The two of them hadn't noticed that he was doing his part as well.

You have defeated your first Beast
Quest reward: Instant level up
Additional rewards: 5,000 Exp
5 Pawn points have been awarded
Congratulations, you have now reached: Level 22
A stat point has been granted
Optional Quest (Waste not want not) is still in progress
Consume the body of the beast for additional stat points

Now . . . how exactly am I supposed to do this without making them think I'm crazy . . .

CHAPTER 31

SECRET MEAL (PART 1)

Usually, Gary was fascinated by the rewards the system presented to him. They were like an incentive for him to keep working harder and getting closer to reaching the Level 25 he was aiming for. It was an addictive feeling and quite thrilling to see himself progress.

However, this time, he was far too obsessed with something else: the beast's dead body on the ground.

The beast's body is right there. It's right in front of me. If I just took a quick few bites of it, it wouldn't be a problem, right? Otherwise, it's just going to waste. Maybe I can just say I'm really really hungry or something. Would that work? Gary considered the option, but he soon remembered that everything in the special lesson belonged to the group called NIRV.

It made him think twice about whether he should do such a thing, but instead, he realized there was another solution: the beast's tail that was still in his hand. Quickly turning away, Gary didn't know if just the tail was enough for him to gain stats, but he was going to try anyway. Bringing the tail closer to his jaws, he went to take a bite.

He paused for a second, seeing the blinking camera in front of him.

Will I get in trouble for this . . . ah, screw it! Gary thought as he elongated his teeth to make it easier to dig through the beast's skin. It was still much harder than expected, and he imagined it would be relatively impossible to bite through it with his regular set of teeth.

However, just when the tip of his upper canine had pressed against the beast's skin, a buzzer suddenly rang throughout the area, forcing him to stop immediately and drop the tail. It was as if he had been caught red-handed doing something he shouldn't have.

The special lesson has come to an end.
All students should refrain from touching the beast for the time being until the invigilators come to collect you.

Gary had an awkward look on his face. He was unsure if that message was directed at him; maybe someone had seen him, or maybe it was just simply a coincidence. However, after hearing the announcement, Gary walked over to stand by the others. Although he was quite upset, he was still trying to devise a way to consume the beast, and he wouldn't miss an opportunity if he got one.

Not for just this lesson, if he somehow found a way, in every special lesson he would be able to eat a beast and get even stronger than before. Even the title of champion of the AFC would be within sight, and he could possibly do what Kai wished as well: get to the very top, where the Tier 1 cities were.

The door in front of them opened, and for a second, all of the students, including Gary, flinched. It was the same door the beast had come through, and with the trauma of what they had just been experienced, they feared they might have to do it again.

It wasn't a beast, though; instead, five men in hazmat suits came out. With them was a man with round glasses and a lab coat with *NIRV* embroidered on his chest, and also the professor that Gary had seen a few times before, Professor Humfree.

As for the other lab coats, professors, and teachers, they had gone to the other colored room.

The staff in hazmat suits swiftly began working with all sorts of equipment, including a special carving tool that looked like a chainsaw. However, the end was a lot thinner, and when they turned it on, it didn't make as much noise.

The students noticed that they were carefully carving part of the beast out, as if they were looking for something.

"Congratulations." Humfree walked up to the students with a NIRV employee standing next to him. "All of you did incredibly well in this lesson, and you didn't get injured either; I am truly impressed.

I have to say that you are one of the best batches to have taken part in the special lesson."

The students were pleased with the compliments, but they were unsure if this was just something that he said to all of the students for further encouragement or if it was actually the truth. But it didn't matter much.

"Yes, you have helped out NIRV greatly, and I am sure you all will make great Retrievers in the future." The NIRV employee also broke his silence and introduced himself, "My name is James Kent, and I will oversee the special lessons you will be taking from now on, so you will get to see me more often."

Going by the first impression, Gary wasn't really getting a good feeling from this NIRV scientist guy. The vibes just seemed all wrong, as if he always received a greater benefit than those he made a deal with.

"We found it!" A shout from the right suddenly attracted everyone's attention.

One of the men in the hazmat suit held a tennis-ball-sized crystal in his hand. He lifted it in the air for all of them to see, and almost immediately James left the students and walked over to him in excitement to take a closer look.

"I guess I should continue from where he left off." Humfree shook his head and cleared his throat. "NIRV wants to have a good relationship with those who are the future of this world, and they believe you guys are that future. So, in addition to this, for becoming a Retriever, those who take part in killing the beast to get crystals that create the Altered, NIRV will give ample rewards for your efforts.

"The more dangerous the task is, the better the reward they will give you. And since this is your first special lesson, as a kind gesture, they will be happy to have open ears to your demands, and they, along with the academy, will do their best to accommodate your request.

"Whether that be Altered DNA for a family member, or first pick at rare Altered DNA to be used for yourself, or maybe even a meeting with NIRV, and more. Whatever request you can think of, please ask for it now, and we will try our best to match it as closely as possible. It's the least the academy and NIRV can do for you for risking your lives."

Gary's eyes lit up because he had finally found his way to get the beast's dead body. He just needed to find a way to word it so it didn't sound so weird.

CHAPTER 32

SECRET MEAL (PART 2)

The NIRV employees looked to be having a field day with the crystal they had extracted from the beast. First, they handled it carefully and delicately, using large metal prongs to hold the crystal, and then they gently placed it into a container as if it were an explosive that could go off at any second.

It was a slow and steady process, and James was occupied with overseeing the crystal restoration and would be busy for a little while longer. This gave the students enough time to think about the rewards they wanted, and eventually Wu was the first to make a request.

"I would like to request a new type of Altered DNA. One that has yet to be used on others, and at the same time, for that Altered DNA not to be made again. I and my cooperation should gain exclusivity over the Altered DNA." He carefully worded his request to avoid sounding like he was asking for too much, although it was hard to tell if he succeeded.

Hearing what Wu had asked for piqued Gary's interest. It sounded like a big request. Although they likely would give Wu a special type of Altered DNA, the request to make it exclusively for him was not quite easy. In the end, it all depended on how valuable they considered these Retrievers, and it was also a chance for Gary to observe this fact.

As for the reward itself, it could be sold or passed on to someone in Wu's group, increasing their power and status in the outside world. It made Gary wonder if he should change the request he had in mind. If he got his hands on some Altered DNA, he could use it to change one of the Howlers' lives, maybe get it for his sister so she would be safer and be able to protect herself.

However, in the end, Gary decided that getting the beast's body was a better reward. Being an Altered had its own risks, such as having to avoid the Altered Hunters. He just wanted Amy to live a safe and sound life, which she already had at the moment, and Gary would deal with whoever attempted to harm her.

While Gary was musing, Snow put forward the next request.

"I didn't get my Altered DNA from NIRV, but if possible, I would like them to make a replica or get hold of the same type of Altered DNA I have and pass on that information to my group. Also, a year's supply of carrots for me, if you can add that as a complementary reward."

With the information from the Altered DNA, Gary could guess what Snow wanted to do. He wanted more Altereds like himself in his group. If his group received the information he had requested, maybe they could create more versions of the Altered DNA.

"The year's supply of carrots can be done." Humphrey smiled. "Even though you made two requests, I will give you that. As for the requests regarding Altered DNA, I will have to pass them on to James and see what he can do."

Then glancing at the young man standing at the left end, he asked, "What about you, Gary? What would you like?"

Gary had had some time to think about how to phrase his request, and in the end, he couldn't really think of a way to not make it sound weird, but he just had to go for it since this was a great opportunity.

"My request . . . is the bodies of the beasts we kill in these special lessons," Gary asked. "I can see that NIRV cares a lot about the crystal. I don't need that, but just the body and a private place for me to do research."

Gary saw the others looking at him, and he decided he needed to explain himself.

"If I can investigate the beast's body, then maybe I can figure something out regarding how Altered DNA is created."

Humfree stared at Gary for a while, observing his body language. With his over explanation and the slight nervousness in his tone, it was clear the student was lying. Which made Humfree think, why did Gary want the corpse?

Another thing was that he hadn't asked for the corpses to be sent to his group. Instead, he had asked for them for his personal use.

Does this have something to do with before? Humfree wondered as he recalled the image of a bloody Gary in his head. *It never made sense why he ate his teachers, but from what I saw on camera and now this, it's most likely that Gary wishes to eat these beasts as well, but why?*

Has he figured out a special trait of his Altered? A way to get stronger based on what he eats? If that's the case, then that is incredibly rare, and it makes me wonder what his limit is. Either way, seeing this student grow is making the bones in my body shake again.

By now, James and the other staff had safely extracted and stored away the crystal, and he had joined Humfree's side once again.

"One of our students had a particular request," Humphrey asked. "Since it can be granted right now, I guess I should talk to you here. The request is for the beast's dead body. Will it be all right if he takes it with him, and also the beasts that die in future lessons?"

James's jaw dropped, showing how stunned he was to hear the request.

"I mean, it's not really a problem for us, but are you sure that you want that to be your request?" James looked at all the students, not knowing which student he was really speaking to since he wasn't there when they had made the requests.

"You see, the corpses have no use to us, so that's not really a problem, but there is a reason why they have no use to us. Once the crystal is removed from its body, they tend to disintegrate quickly. So in half an hour or so, nothing will be left."

Immediately upon hearing James's words, Gary walked past the other staff toward the beast. He used his strength to lift it up and put it on his shoulder.

"That's great, don't worry about that. Just show me to my room where I can have a look at this thing in peace," Gary said.

Seeing the strange excitement in the boy, James decided to take note of who had asked for each request.

Come on, let's eat this meat and gain some stats! Gary was more interested in what was about to come.

CHAPTER 33

EATING A BEAST

It did not take long for them to heed Gary's request and give him a room. The area they were in was large, wherever it was, and there were plenty of rooms in the place. The only problem was that all of the rooms had a camera system set up in them.

The beast's body was laid out on a large table. Using his sharp claws, Gary had split it up to make it easier to consume, but he couldn't help but look around the room at the cameras.

Humfree said they turned them off, and that red blinky thing is no longer blinking, Gary thought. On top of that, for extra safety they had placed a cap on each camera, so even if they were on, they would see nothing but darkness.

In the end, Gary had to check the entire room, just in case they had hidden a camera somewhere, but he could find nothing. He also noticed that just like the NIRV employee had said, the beast's body was already disintegrating.

The skin on its leg was turning slightly ashy. Small particles were breaking off and disappearing into the air.

That guy said it was because they moved the crystal out of the body. Does that mean the crystal is what is needed to create Altered DNA? I guess that's why they don't care about the body so much.

It makes me wonder, if I eat this now, will I still gain stat points even without it having the crystal inside?"

In the end, there was only one way to find out. Although Gary was now used to eating such things, animals and more, most of the time he had done so out of desperation. Either his instinct or the situation would force him to do such things, but none of that applied now. He needed to willingly eat the "food" in front of him.

Gary started with the leg because it seemed like the easiest part. He had begun his challenge.

The whole thing had taken a while since there was a lot of flesh, but Gary was more impressed by his own stomach. Even after consuming enough meat to bring his energy back to 300, he could still keep going.

On top of that, after he had eaten around two-thirds of the beast, Gary received a message from his system.

The beast that you have defeated has been consumed
You have received the following stats
+1 Strength

Gary waited for more messages to come, but they never did, which left him seriously disappointed.

Just one stat point, but I got so many for the other Altered. Is it because the beast is considered a weak one . . . or maybe it has something to do with the crystal that left its body.

After overcoming the disappointment, Gary thought about it for a while and decided it was still a good outcome overall. For one, he had gained a single stat point as a bonus, something he only usually gained from leveling up.

On top of that, he gained Exp and a bonus Exp reward for killing a beast for the first time. From the way the professors had explained things, he was sure that in the future the beasts would get stronger and stronger.

I guess I should wait here for a while; there are still parts of the beast's body left inside, but it's disintegrating even now. If I wait for it to completely disappear, then I can explain that's just what happened.

While he waited, Gary saw it as a chance to check out his current stats.

Gary
Class: Warrior
Grade: Bishop
Level 23
Exp 1788/11564

Health 250
Energy 300
Strength 36
Dexterity 26
Endurance 32

The recent point was added in strength, and because of the Exp he'd gained from killing the beast, Gary had leveled up twice, bringing him closer to his Level 25 goal. This also meant that he had two stat points to use.

At the same time, he still had two Pawn points but was saving them to use later on, if they were needed.

Originally I was thinking about increasing my Energy, but I'm starting to see that as a problem after experiencing the full moon. The more Energy I have, the longer I can go without food and starve myself, but it just seems to add up to this aggressive side in me that I can't control.

A large Energy pool requires a lot to eat to fill it up, and that means it will be harder to get used to on the day of the full moon. I also imagine that if the Werewolf side of me goes crazy, it will keep eating at least until its Energy is full, maybe beyond.

Thinking of other ways to use his points, he thought back to the fight with Ryan and how well it had worked out. Sticking to his original plan, he decided it was best for him to add his points to Endurance.

Endurance 34

His endurance was linked to his health, and with tougher opponents and now beasts to go up against, it would be better for hits against him to take less damage.

Man, in some ways, I wish I could fight Ryan again, and fight him properly. Then I could show off in front of Xin, and everything would work out. I mean I would still have to figure out the whole werewolf thing, but we could be a powerhouse fighting couple or something.

Now that he had waited a bit longer, the entire body of the beast had disappeared. Gary left the room, planning to find Crowley in order to get out of here and get a good night's rest. As soon as he opened the door, though, a person was standing right in front of him.

"Hello," James, the NIRV employee said with a smile.

CHAPTER 34

THE BEST FOR THEMSELVES

It was a surprise to Gary to see this person of all people; he'd thought Crowley would be waiting, or Humfree, but there was no one apart from the NIRV employee. Honestly, James was already making him nervous, and the fact that he must have been standing outside for a while, waiting for something, was putting him ill at ease even more.

"Did you get to play with the body and find what you wanted?"

It was a probing question, and Gary didn't know how to really answer. It wasn't like he was a scientist; Tom would be best for this.

"I did, but I still would like to do more research. So as long as you don't want the bodies, then please send them my way after the lessons," Gary said, and the easiest way for him to get out of the awkward situation was to walk away and head back the way he came.

"I have a question if you don't mind me asking. What type of Altered are you?"

When he heard this question, Gary's heart started to throb, and he didn't know how to answer. He had yet to turn around but had stopped walking. It was clear he had heard James, and his hesitation wasn't helping.

"You see, I looked into our files, and NIRV has never given any type of Altered DNA to the group known as the Howlers, which would suggest you got your DNA from somewhere else. Maybe an auction, another corporation, or even abroad.

"Your Altered form, the way you ripped off that tail, was quite impressive, so we would like to know what our competition is, that's all."

Thinking hard, Gary wanted to answer the question in a way so he would no longer be involved in NIRV, or at least get James off his back. However, the answers just weren't coming to him. He'd never expected James to be there when the door opened.

"What are you doing?" a voice said down the hall, and Crowley, the teacher dressed in all black, came around the corner of the hallway.

"The students are only supposed to complete tasks for you as a Retriever. They are still apprentices. They do not have to do your bidding outside of the special lesson, and it is now over. Come over here, Gary," Crowley said.

Out of all the people to come and help him, Gary never thought he would be thankful to see the strange bird/magician teacher, but he was, and he rushed over. They turned down the hallway and began to head back.

They walked for a good five minutes, and it seemed they were heading down the long hallway back to where they first started, taking several turns just like before. When they were finally in the tube-shaped hallway that Gary recognized, Crowley stopped.

"I have a warning for you as one of our students," Crowley said. "NIRV are a group of people that only care about themselves. They will do anything for the sake of science. You know that some people are against Altered; well, these guys are *pro* Altered.

"If they could, they would turn every single person into an Altered, but they aren't foolish. They would do it, so in a way they are at the top. NIRV is a corporation that supplies Altered DNA, even to Tier 1 cities, creating the strongest Altered the world has seen.

"Now imagine, if that's the Altered DNA they are willing to sell, then what about the DNA they are keeping for themselves?"

Gary had read about similar conspiracy theories online, but hearing one directly from a teacher who was connected with and worked with NIRV gave him a different feeling.

Maybe the world hadn't seen everything Altered could do, and with expanding technology there would be breakthroughs at every corner, creating better Altered.

The double steel doors opened up, and Gary was back in the room where they had started, with the seats and the signed sheets of paper. To his surprise, the others were there waiting as well.

When Gary's eyes met Numba's, they smiled at each other, happy to see that the other was okay. With Apollo in the group, he wasn't so worried about what might occur during their lessons, though.

He was sure, after seeing Wu and Snow fight, that they would be able to deal with the beasts as well.

"Everyone is to leave and enter the special lesson at the same time," Crowley said. "These are the rules, even if someone is being held back to be healed or something else. But don't worry; while your teammates were waiting for you, I gave them all their feedback as well.

"As for you, Gary, they actually didn't have much to say about your performance, apart from the fact that they would like to see you be more active, but I would say that is for you to decide.

"For me, I think when you enter the special lesson, you should just focus on surviving, no matter what."

The special lesson was only once a week, so they would have to wait to see what their task was or who they would go up against next week. In the meantime, they were to continue their lessons like normal, while not speaking a word about the special lesson to those outside.

Now that the lesson was done, Crowley made the basket appear in his hand, and all of their mobile devices were returned. The doors were open to the outside, and it was around eight p.m.

"Ah, man, I really want to talk to you about what happened there, but rules are rules," Numba said. "No doubt the others are going to ask. I wonder what we should say to them?"

Gary was thinking the same thing, but he was distracted because as soon as he turned on his phone, he noticed there was a missed call from Kai, and he had received a message.

Call me as soon as you can, we need to talk.

CHAPTER 35

A MESSAGE FROM HOME

Seeing the text message caused Gary's heart rate to rise a little. He knew that because his system's messages were telling him so. It was odd; Kai was always calm and collected, and hardly anything fazed him.

On top of that, he and Olivia were now like him. Their strength and more had increased, and there shouldn't have been many people in Slough who could cause them problems.

Now that Gary was being contacted, he felt like it was a serious matter.

Is it the people that the Underdogs worked for? Or maybe something has happened to their werewolf forms, Gary thought.

"Hey, Gary, are you just going to stand there all day? Come on," Numba shouted.

Putting his phone away, Gary followed Numba back to their rooms, but he couldn't stop thinking about what had happened. When they had arrived at their rooms, Numba headed to Ian's room rather than his own.

"Oh, hey, aren't you going to come chill with us for a bit?" Numba asked. "I know we can't talk about what happened, but Ian wouldn't stop texting me to come over after the special lesson ended."

Gary had automatically gone to his own room; he'd noticed that he had received a text from Izzy as well about a little get-together, claiming it would be nice for their first day.

"I just need to sort something out first. It might be a while; I'll send you a message when I'm done." Gary smiled and went into his room.

"Hmm, Gary was looking at his phone the whole way back; maybe he had a message from someone at home. Come to think of it, I got a message as well," Numba mumbled to himself as he let himself into Ian's room.

Ian and Izzy were already playing some music and had a load of snacks out on the table: popcorn, chips, and more.

"I mean, I know you said that we were having a party, but is it really smart to be eating all of this junk on the first day?" Numba asked.

"Will you relax, it's okay to have a cheat day once in a while even if it is on the first day," Ian replied, getting up from the sofa. "Besides, the food they recommend is just a recommendation. They can't stop us from eating this stuff."

Although Ian had a point, Numba wanted to take this whole thing seriously, especially after what had happened in the special lesson. He kept imagining if Apollo weren't there and it was just him and Sty; could they have taken out the beast? Soon they would be facing bigger and stronger things than today.

Izzy had come out of the bathroom and was doing her hair, and she saw Numba standing by the door.

"Where's Gary?" she asked.

"Oh great, so I guess you're not happy to see me?" Numba replied. "Gary needed to sort something out first; he said he would text us when he's free."

In an instant, Numba saw the look of disappointment on Izzy's face. And it was at that moment that he realized the feelings she had for him, even if she didn't know about them herself.

"So come on, what made this special lesson so special?" Ian asked, and the excitement shone in his eyes. "I can't even imagine what lesson would only have you and Gary in it. Did you get personal sparring training one-on-one with the teachers, or maybe meet some AFC athletes?"

Before the lesson, Numba had wondered the same things, but the truth was far more terrifying, and he didn't want to show his fear in front of the others. Knowing that he had something that Ian wanted, Numba folded his arms and put a smug smile on his face.

"Unfortunately I can't tell you any details; those are the rules of the special lesson," he said, loud and proud. The others weren't sure if they were imagining it, but it looked like his nose had gotten larger as well.

"Look, stop playing around, just tell us what it is!" Ian said.

"I'm serious," Numba replied. "Gary will confirm when he comes over here; we can't tell anyone about what is happening. But I will say one thing: Apollo, Wu, and Snow were there as well."

Hearing those names lit a fire in Ian's belly.

"Ahhh, it would have been better if you'd said nothing. Now I'm really jealous. Maybe I should have just waited and passed through as the top three with the next lot. This seriously sucks."

In his room, Gary sat down on his bed and nervously called Kai.

Come on, Kai, pick up, pick up . . . please don't make me worry.

But the phone continued to ring. Gary was squinting at this point, because his worst fear was coming true; something drastic must have happened while Gary was away and he wasn't there to save them.

"Hello." He finally heard a voice on the other end. "Hey, Gary, are you there? Sorry, I was having a nighttime shower. Sorry about that."

"You were taking a shower," Gary replied. "I thought something had happened to you. Are you okay? Is everyone okay?"

Gary was speaking so loud that Kai was forced to pull the phone away from his ear. He eventually set it down and put it on speaker while he dried himself with a towel.

"They're all okay, everyone is fine, your sister is fine as well. I just wanted to talk to you, that's all," Kai replied. "I didn't realize you would panic this much. I mean, if I was well enough to send you a message, then that means everything is all right, right?

"Anyway, I won't keep you for long. An up-and-coming electronics company that sells parts for phones wanted to expand into our city. They are looking to produce more than just small parts for phones and need to broaden their contacts.

"There are quite a few skilled but unemployed people in Slough, so it's a good place for them to set up base, hire people, et cetera. At the same time, of course, they're looking to be protected by others, and since we're the current top gang in Slough, they have come to us."

So far the news sounded good rather than bad, and everything was kind of going over Gary's head, so he was waiting to hear why he needed to be involved in this.

"The company is known as Cardenez Electronics, and we had a meeting with them. They were quite honest with us, and they are also thinking of joining a Tier 2 city. Of course, they needed protection there as well.

"The Tier 2 city might be able to offer them more but at the same time will take a bigger cut. I think since we are an up-and-coming group, they have a feeling that we will rise, and rising together is much more attractive to them than being under another gang. The problem was that their leader could tell, Gary."

"Tell what," Gary replied. "That you're a werewolf?"

Although that didn't make sense, it was the only thing he could think of.

"No," Kai replied. "He could tell that I wasn't the leader of the gang. He said he will only do business with us after meeting the real leader. If he is putting his future on the line with us, then he wants to meet you.

"I know you're busy with the academy, but I can set up the meeting to be held in the evening, and Olivia and I will be there as well. You'll just have to come down after one of your classes, maybe one day you finish early."

Gary thought about it for a while; he didn't have a problem with what Kai was suggesting, but he was nervous. What would he say, what would he do, and how should he act? This was something that he had never done before.

"It's okay, maybe I should take a couple of days to come to see you again anyway. A few days won't hurt, and it would be good to catch up."

"That's great. We can sort out the details about the whole thing at a later time."

With that, the call ended, and it looked like Gary was going to go back to Slough and meet the others again. He couldn't wait to see what they had been up to, and seeing his mother and sister was something he had to do out of respect, but something was bothering him.

Cardenez Electronics. I'm sure I've heard of them before. But why would I know that name? Gary thought.

CHAPTER 36

I AM A WEREWOLF

Curious, Gary searched for Cardenez Electronics on the internet, but all he found was the company's products, which did little to help jog his memory. He let out a sigh and decided to head over to join his friends and enjoy the rest of the evening. Tomorrow there would still be more than enough time for him to worry about how to help the Howlers.

As he walked down the hallway, he thought back to the last time he had seen all of them together. It had been at the Wolf's Pool Club, and Gary had gone there straight after school because Kai had informed him that there would be an important meeting with everyone.

He still remembered the lack of reaction when he had told the Howlers about his decision to give up school, followed by them telling him that they had decided that it would be for the best for him to leave the gang, albeit temporarily.

Fortunately, the misunderstanding hadn't lasted long, and after agreeing to try out for the AFA, he had made sure to leave the gang at its strongest by granting Kai a Unique Class. Of course, the most memorable moment had been when Gary came clean about what he was . . .

"Guys!" Gary exclaimed, and everyone in the room turned to look at him. "There's something important I need to tell you all. I'm aware that all of you already know my secret . . . and I'm thankful that none of you have asked me about it. Before I go, I want to set the record straight. I'm not an Altered . . . I'm actually a werewolf . . ."

The room that had been filled with the laughter and jokes of the Howlers went silent at this sudden declaration. The green-haired teenager had been so focused on his words, and how to phrase them, that he had forgotten that White was also in the room, although the pool club was currently closed, as the barmaid who practically lived there.

On top of that, there was Tyler, the Howlers' driver, who had been coming here more often lately, and Miss Degrace, Marie's mother. In the end, both of these people were important to the future of the Howlers. So to keep the truth from them was rude as well.

In the midst of the silence, Tyler's legs were shaking. He took Gary's words seriously and although no one knew it, he had watched the fight between the werewolf and Kirk many times.

Innu soon broke the silence with his laughter.

"A werewolf? Do you mean like those creatures from the movies? I don't understand, Gary, we already figured out that you're an Altered, so what's the point of lying to us about something so crazy?" Innu asked, but judging by their gang leader's reaction, this wasn't a joke of any sort.

"I know that it's hard to believe, but I swear I'm not an Altered," Gary insisted. "I wanted to tell you all earlier, but I was afraid . . . afraid that if I did, you might all be scared to be around me."

"Why would we be afraid of you?" Marie asked, still not fully comfortable with the unexpected revelation.

"Because of what happens when I lose control. It already happened once . . . at the park . . ."

The first one to understand what Gary meant was surprisingly Innu. With all the puzzle pieces in place, how could he not realize it? It wasn't like he could forget what had transpired in the park, when they all had nearly died because of two Wolf-type Altered . . .

Talking to Kai, Innu had somewhat figured this out, but confirming their thoughts was another thing altogether.

They could all see that Gary was worried, and that was when Austin decided to stand up.

"Altered, Werewolf, what's the difference?" The large teenager shrugged it off. Innu gave him a meaningful stare, yet he refrained from arguing that he hadn't been there.

"You're you, and you have helped out this gang so much. I only have one question. When we first met on the rooftop, were you already a werewolf? The way you say it, I assume you weren't a werewolf since birth, so how and when exactly did it happen?"

"Yeah, and if you're a werewolf, are you one from birth? Does that mean your sister is one as well?" Innu asked.

Gary wasn't expecting this type of reaction; he had been prepared for all his friends to scream and run, perhaps call him a monster and leave, but if anything, they were simply curious about his condition.

"You're right, I haven't been a werewolf for long, and to answer your questions, you've only met me after I became one. And no, my sister isn't a werewolf, and truth be told she knows nothing about this and I would like to keep it that way. I hope you understand." Austin showed him a wide grin after hearing the answer. Gary wasn't a mind reader, but he knew his friend well enough to understand why he did that.

"You all seem to have a lot of questions, and since I've already told you this much, let me start at the beginning."

Gary went on to explain to the group what had occurred that night as a transporter. After that, he went into the details of the park that day, where most of them were present. They now also knew about the full moon and the problems that plagued him during that day.

The only thing he didn't tell them about was the Werewolf System. Its existence was a pure enigma, and he didn't feel like it would help anyone knowing about it. Neither Olivia nor Kai had one, even though they were werewolves as well.

When he was finally done with his story, Gary sat down at the bar and finally rested. He let out a big sigh, feeling like a big weight had been lifted off his shoulders.

"Gary . . . thank you." Marie finally spoke, having waited for the right time. "You know, I feel like I never got to thank you for that day. When I was trapped in that container because of the twins. I know you went through some bad things, and all of this is scary . . . it is for me as well. But if you didn't have this power, I wouldn't be alive today."

"She's right," Innu agreed, despite being the most shocked out of everyone. To tell the truth, he was scared, and hearing what had occurred to Billy, how he had been turned by accident, frightened him even more, but Marie had made him consider the positives.

"Not just Marie, but you pretty much saved Slough. It's on video! If it weren't for you, a lot more people would have died, and it's because of you that we Howlers are the top gang now. We can really make a change in this town!"

From behind the bar, Miss Degrace pulled out a drink and set it on the table.

"I'm a mother, and believe me there are not many people I would trust with my daughter, but you are one of them."

"And I still want to be your driver!" Tyler shouted with passion. Which made all the others laugh.

Honestly, all the positive support brought a tear to the werewolf's eye. After losing connection with his mother, there weren't many people he could share this burden with; in fact, he couldn't even share it with her, and hiding it from these guys every day was hurting him each time.

He had always been scared of how the Howlers would react, but seeing them now, he actually felt a bit stupid for hiding the truth for this long.

"Speaking of which," Kai said, clapping his hands. "I hate to interrupt this moment, but there are a few things I should tell you. Not only will Gary attend the trial to get into the AFA—I know I brought it up to all of you earlier—but it has been confirmed. So we should have a big leaving party.

"It also means there are quite a few things we need to set up. A place for his sister, people to keep an eye on his mother, and of course, all the Howlers' duties. While Gary is away, we will do our best to keep this gang growing, and when he returns, we will be the ones to shock him with some news."

All the gang members smiled at this, and that included White. The truth was, that day when Gary had fought against Olivia, she had seen a lot of it, but she too had decided to keep it to herself, as she was enjoying her life right now.

"Oh, and since we're on the topic of sharing secrets, Olivia and I are werewolves as well, and we need to start preparing for the next full moon, and for that, we're going to need your help."

CHAPTER 37

THE SECOND MOON (PART 1)

A few days had passed since Gary had told everyone the truth, and during that time things seemed to be going well. Using Olivia and the rest of the Howlers, they were working on a strategy to control Slough better.

There were still the midsize gangs to worry about, as well as the mayor, who had yet to make a move, but now that the Underdogs had been dealt with, it looked like everyone was laying low for now.

On top of that, Gary had been spending more time with his sister, although he had yet to tell her he was going to be leaving the city, or had anything to do with the gang. He still couldn't quite bring himself to do any of that yet, but he knew he was delaying the inevitable.

Finally, though, there was a big day ahead of them. It was the night before the full moon. The main members of the Howlers had been preparing for this for a while, and with only them knowing the truth, they were also the only ones that could help.

Currently, the whole gang was spending the night at the abandoned police station. It was one of the properties that originally belonged to the Underdogs but was now under the control of the newly created Howlers.

It was also the place where Gary and Kai were kept for a while. Only this time they weren't in the cellars but in one of the meeting rooms where the police usually conducted their cases.

Everyone sat down and were quite nervous. Although they had all accepted the fact that they had three werewolves in their gang, words and actions were two different things. They hadn't seen Kai or Olivia transform, and they'd seen Gary only partially transformed when he was asked to help move things.

Inside the room were Marie, Austin, Innu, Olivia, Gary, and Kai, of course. Although there were more who knew about them being werewolves, Kai felt it was too dangerous for them to be here, although he didn't tell those who had come to the meeting that.

"All right," Kai said, clapping his hands, standing up in front of everyone to get their attention. There was also a large TV behind him with a PowerPoint titled "Operation Full Moon 2."

"This is everything that we know about the full moon, thanks to Gary. First if we do nothing, it all starts at midnight. All three of us will turn into these huge monsters called werewolves."

The screen changed, showing a cartoonlike image of a werewolf that didn't look scary at all. Kai had done this so the others would be more inclined to take part.

"On this night, apparently we will lose our minds. We won't really know what we are doing and also won't be able to control ourselves. Instead, we will eat and kill people to satisfy our hunger. Does anyone have any questions on this part?"

During his talk Kai had gone through a few more slides, this time showing cartoon characters being killed, and some pictures of food. When he looked at the others, the cute pictures no longer seemed to be working so well.

Innu gulped and slowly raised his hand.

"Doesn't this mean that those of us who are working closest to you are most likely to be . . . eaten by you?" Images of werewolves chasing after him were flashing in his head.

"I mean, you are correct, but hopefully it won't get to that point," Kai replied. "You see, once the sun rises at six a.m. and the moon goes away, then the dangerous night is over.

"According to Gary, his transformation ended earlier on that night. After fighting the Altered Hunters and the White Rose agents, he tired himself out. According to Gary, this is because he ran out of energy, and what werewolves need for energy is food.

"Both my and Olivia's appetites have become far larger now that we are werewolves. So it seems to be true. Gary has suggested that we tire ourselves out while also not eating the night before, which is today."

Although this was true, and Gary was confident of his theory, there was one problem. Gary had the system to know when he didn't have enough energy to transform, while the others didn't.

If they were like him, then they could just transform before the full moon and try to use up all their energy, but he wasn't too sure they wouldn't give in to their natural urges.

"And what if that doesn't work?" Austin asked with his arms folded, looking toward the corner of the room, which contained a few strange weapons that weren't there before.

"This is where you guys come in. The Underdogs did a good job of keeping Gary here last time. In fact, they still have some chains and more to tie us down. Each of us will be put in our own cell and chained to the floor. You are to keep watch over us in the camera room.

"When we have successfully survived the full moon, you can free us and treat us to a nice meal. Now, the camera room and the cells are quite far apart, but just in case, there are Anti-Altered weapons for you to use.

"They are for your protection and seem to work quite well against us. Even if we do turn, I imagine we will be quite weak. So after a few hits with those, you should be golden."

"Yeah, 'should,'" Innu said, shaking his head, not believing what he was getting himself into.

"All right! Let's head down to the cells and start this long night, shall we." Kai smiled as if he was going to enjoy this.

CHAPTER 38

THE SECOND MOON (PART 2)

Olivia, Kai, and Gary weren't given another morsel of food to eat, and they were already feeling the effects of their hunger. The closer it was to the full moon, the higher their alert level would be.

"Ahhh, this sucks!" Olivia screamed from her cell.

The three of them had been chained up next to each other, and they could see one another through the metal bars, but because of the chain length they were unable to reach each other or the bars that were in front of them.

The order of their cells was Kai, then Gary, and finally Olivia.

"You never said this was what was going to happen when you turned me!" Olivia complained.

"Will you relax?" Kai replied. "Remember that all of us are in the same pain, and besides I'd have thought you would be used to your emotions getting high-strung once a month."

"Ah, I swear if I turn into a werewolf, the first one I'm going to kill is you, pretty boy," Olivia said, licking her lips.

Gary immediately turned his head to look at her and stared her down. It was a fierce look and his eyes had slightly transformed, appearing a little redder than usual.

It was a reminder to Olivia. In the first place, turning her into a werewolf was meant to be a punishment. Gary didn't really care what happened to her, and he had decided that if he was unable to control her during the full moon, or at least restrain her like they were attempting to do now, then he would get rid of her.

He didn't want another Billy situation, never again. However, Olivia had helped them out a lot with her Pincer gang, protecting his sister and even helping out in the fight with Kirk.

But Gary still didn't forgive her for all the bad things she had done in the Pincers and for attempting to kill him, but she was more useful alive than dead.

Olivia remembered challenging Gary when she had first been turned, and although she had grown stronger after seeing him go up against the Underdogs, she didn't want to challenge him again. Besides, her life was good at the moment; she was in the top gang of Slough. Everything was going well apart from this.

There was quiet among the three of them as they focused on their breathing. They were trying everything to forget about the pain in their stomachs. Kai even resorted to exercise; he attempted to hit the air, do push-ups, and more.

After a while, though, Kai was beginning to feel incredibly weak. For a werewolf, just keeping one's body awake for the day took up more energy than the average human. It was why they needed to eat so much.

Gary could also see via the system that his Energy was now below the required amount to transform. Since the others had been doing the same as him, they should be below the Energy amount, but it was the moment of truth.

"Just one more minute, right?" Innu said, holding the spear-type Anti-Altered weapon. All of them were holding onto their weapons, but it didn't feel right, what was about to happen.

"Yeah, it's the moment of truth, whether their plan will work or not," Marie replied, looking behind her. The door had been bolted shut, and multiple heavy objects had been placed in front of it just in case.

However, this strategy was a catch-22, because if the werewolves needed to escape it would be impossible, but there was only one way in and out of the room. With their weapons, the Howlers were confident they could at least control them.

"You know, there're three of them and three of us; we need to start thinking about what to do if they all turn," Austin said, and it looked like Innu agreed as well.

However, Marie wasn't too sure, because Gary seemed pretty confident about not turning; he had told her that she didn't have to worry about him but to keep an eye on the others.

BEEP BEEP

The alarm they had set on their phones had gone off at midnight. They had also left one phone in each cell so the others would know what time it was as well. After waiting around thirty seconds, Gary let out a big sigh.

It is the night of the full moon
The power of the moon is at its fullest
Your bloodlust is at its max
There is not enough Energy for you to transform

They all felt something in their bodies as soon as the clock struck midnight, a strange twinge, but it soon calmed down as their bodies realized they weren't able to do what they wanted to do.

"It worked, your plan really worked, didn't it?" Kai said with a smile.

"It looks like it has . . . but it's just begun; here comes the real hard part," Gary replied.

What Gary said was true, because they would have to survive six more hours, through a pain that was unimaginable. It was similar to being starved, but instantly rather than over a period of time.

The pain was rushing through their heads and their stomachs all at once, so much that they were unable to properly focus. It was hard to even tell what was around them because of the pain.

Several times, the shackles were pulled and slammed onto the ground.

"We have to keep fighting!" Kai shouted.

Olivia seemed to be suffering the worst, as she was constantly screaming.

"Let me out! *Let me out!*" Her wrists were bleeding from the repeated pulling of the chains.

It was hard for them to tell how much time had passed, but it felt like minutes were becoming hours, until . . .

BEEP BEEP *BEEP BEEP*

"Is that—?" Gary said, looking up. "It's six a.m., we did it!"

A few seconds later the others came into the room, with a meal in their hands and their weapons by their side. They waited a couple of minutes just in case, but it was hard for them to watch.

There had been a few times during the night when the Howlers wanted to go to the cells and help the werewolves, but they knew it was for the best. Now that they were down here, they had brought some raw steaks that had been bought just for this occasion.

Austin opened Olivia's cell first, and when he got close, she snatched the food right out of his hands.

"Whoa . . . I thought you were going to take my head off there!" Austin was so shocked that he took a step back and pointed his spear toward her. *I guess she was just hungry, after all*, he thought.

The others were getting ready to open the other cells as well, until they heard the sound of growling.

"Guys, it's happening!" Austin shouted, and immediately he stepped out of the cell and slammed the door shut, locking it as quickly as possible.

It's happening? What's happening? How can this be . . . it's past six, so why . . . why is she changing? Gary thought.

Whatever the reason, Olivia had turned into her large black-furred self, and immediately, everyone pointed their weapons at her cell.

"What are you guys doing? Run!" Kai shouted.

"Run?" Marie replied. "And leave you two with this in the room? That's not an option."

CHAPTER 39

THE SECOND MOON (PART 3)

Before the day of the full moon, Gary had already informed Kai and Olivia that he was nearly 100 percent sure that as long as they starved themselves, and therefore kept their Energy low enough, they shouldn't be able to transform during the full moon.

Taking their leader's words with a grain of salt, Kai had come up with some theories of his own on how to achieve that starvation, so he had suggested they test themselves to find out more about their condition.

After drawing straws, Olivia had ended up being the one who was forbidden from eating for seventy-two hours before the full moon, making her by far the hungriest. Although she had been complaining a lot, the Lady Boss had acted fine when the clock hit midnight, and only toward the end had she displayed signs of aggression.

Gary was selected to stop eating meat starting one day before the full moon, and he had even used Claw Drain a few times before midnight to get his Energy down.

Then there was Kai, who stopped eating meat the same day, and who was still expending his energy in his cell. He was exhausting himself by doing push-ups and other physical exercises. Although he didn't tell the others, he had clenched his fist hard so many times that he'd drawn blood in the palm of his hand, and that was without transforming.

At the same time, the more exhausted he became, the more each and every little thing irritated him—the sound of dripping water, Gary's and Olivia's breathing—but rather than lashing out, the beta werewolf had continued to work out to keep his feelings bottled up. Never had he experienced pain like this before.

Looking to his right, Gary saw Olivia in the midst of her transformation. The black fur on her skin was starting to spread, while her mouth was changing. Without a doubt, this change resulted from her eating.

However, the thing Gary didn't understand was why?

Is it because of the methods we used . . . no, that can't be right, the alpha werewolf thought, his mind hazy from the lack of food. *That little bit of food shouldn't have been enough to make her transform, so what's happening? Is this because of her class, or is there something I didn't know?*

"Quick, give me some food, so I can whack that werewolf bitch!" Kai demanded uncharacteristically. It was the first time they had seen him act like this. But he couldn't hold it in anymore, as his patience for this whole thing was wearing him thin.

"You think we're going to give you some food with what is happening? Dream on!" Innu shouted back. The three Howlers were hesitant, unsure what to do, yet Olivia looked like she had already finished her transformation. Drool was dripping from her maw as she looked at the trio.

All of them wanted to run, but running right now was not an option. They were no fools who believed that the chains and bars would keep the transformed woman inside. Werewolf Olivia probably didn't even recognize Gary and Kai as anything but tasty little treats wrapped up for her.

"If you guys are going to stay, then attack her now!" Gary ordered. "Right now is your best chance to overwhelm her. Quick, before she manages to get out of those chains!"

The group seemed hesitant, but the more the black-furred werewolf struggled, the clearer it became that the chains wouldn't hold her forever. In the end, Austin was the first to heed the alpha werewolf's words. He opened the cell door and thrust his spear forward, hitting her right in the torso.

Olivia started to light up as sparks hit, but it seemed like the only thing it was doing was pissing her off. Fortunately, two more spears quickly helped out the first. Thanks to that, her entire body lit up, and a loud growl escaped her before it slowly started to fade. In front of their eyes, the Lady Boss began to revert to her human form, though her clothes had been partially ruined.

Gary thought, *I'm sorry, Olivia. I know firsthand how much those Anti-Altered weapons hurt, but you can't argue results. When the Underdogs used them on me, they managed to knock me out, even when I still had a bit of Energy in me. With how little food Olivia got, she shouldn't be a problem until this is all over.*

"Hey! Hey! Is everything okay? Will you guys answer me? For fuck's sake, stop ignoring me!" Kai shouted from the third cell down.

"You did a great job, but I think it's best if you leave now," Gary told the Howlers. "It seems like I was wrong earlier. The food you guys are holding isn't helping us. In fact, it's only making it harder for us to hold on."

"We can just take the food back and keep an eye on you here," Marie suggested.

"It's not just the food." Gary shook his head.

They understood what he meant and didn't need to be asked twice. Leaving the room, they headed for the monitor room to keep an eye on the werewolves again. On the way, they thought about what a close call they'd had.

Inside the cell, around half an hour passed before Olivia eventually came to. The chains were still around her wrists and legs. They were made to contract and expand in size just for this occasion, and thankfully it didn't look like she would be turning into a werewolf anytime soon.

"I turned, didn't I?" Olivia asked. "I wasn't really myself when it happened, but now I'm starting to remember. Good thing they stopped me."

"Fortunately, you didn't hurt anyone, so I'll let you off this time," Gary answered in a weak voice. "At least we'll know not to do that next time. How are you feeling right now?"

"Hungry. *Very* hungry. I remember that I ate something, but it feels as if I hadn't. Honestly, the hunger doesn't really seem any worse than yesterday's, but the moment I smelled the food . . . I didn't even think about it, I just went for it."

"Will you two shut the fuck up?!" Kai yelled from his cell. "You're yapping so much that I can't focus!"

Until now, Gary had believed that Kai and his way of dealing with the full moon were better. After all, both of them seemed to be dealing with the hunger better than Olivia, most likely because they had starved for a shorter period of time, but after the beta werewolf's outburst he was no longer so sure. In his case, one might argue that he could endure it because this wasn't his first turning, or perhaps because he was more concerned about keeping his pack in check.

Then again, perhaps Kai had endured it for this long because he was in a good mental state, or it had to do with what they had done before today. Whatever the case, the more Gary thought about it, the more his mind pointed in one direction . . .

"Guys, you can hear me, right? I think . . . I might have been wrong about another thing. Because of how it went last time for me, I was sure that we could outlast it, but now I'm starting to worry that it's not just the night that we have to worry about . . . We might actually have to endure this for the whole day . . ."

CHAPTER 40

THE SECOND MOON (PART 4)

The night of the full moon, or rather the day of the full moon, was putting an immense amount of pressure on the mental strength of every werewolf in the room. It had been hard enough already, and as the following midnight approached, everyone was starting to feel a bit relieved, knowing that it would all be over soon.

Alas, the moment Gary brought up the possibility that they might have to continue with the current situation for the rest of the day, everything changed. It might have been a different story if it had been for a few more hours, but this . . . this was simply soul-crushing.

"All right, Gary, I can see where you're going with this, but maybe you're wrong," Kai said after a minute of silence. He focused all his energy on breaking out of his cuffs. Fortunately, he was far too exhausted at this point, so his efforts stayed at the level of attempts. He was only becoming more exhausted and annoyed, sweat dripping down his forehead onto the floor.

"Wrong about what?" Gary asked. He was trying to focus on the pain himself. The only reason why he was doing well was that he was afraid. As the alpha werewolf, and the only one among them who had gone through this once before, he couldn't show that it was affecting him in the same way as it was them.

"About your theory. Why don't we just eat some food during the next six hours? That's six more than you originally thought, and then that would be okay, right?" Kai said.

Gary stayed silent. Although it might work, he didn't want to test it, because any test they did meant putting the others at risk.

"Stop fucking ignoring me!" Kai shouted.

For the others watching this from the monitoring room, seeing the usually calm-headed teenager act this way was rather entertaining. Innu even suggested that they should keep the security footage and use it against Kai in the future, because it was almost as if they were looking at a completely different person.

"I'm not ignoring you, I was considering your idea," Gary replied, before he lifted his head and looked into the camera. "All right, you guys, listen carefully, because I want you to follow my instructions based on what I say now. Ignore whatever I say in the future because it could be a different me talking to you."

Based on Kai's behavior, Gary was worried that he was only a few hours away from acting the same way Kai was.

"Every two hours from now, come in and give us each a bit of food. *However*, make sure that it is *less* than what you gave Olivia. Our Energy is already low, but if we don't eat anything throughout the day, we could actually die. Also, make sure to *not* come into the cage like you did last time. Just chuck the food over so it's close enough for us to eat it.

"It might feel wrong, since you'll be treating us like animals, but right now we're worse than wild animals."

Although this was true, Gary imagined that if they got a little bit of food, it could make the hunger harder for them to deal with. He wasn't sure if they should exclude Olivia or not. Right now she seemed fine, but who knew what could happen.

"Then, two minutes before midnight, I want you to feed Kai, feed him until he's full. If there are any signs that he's starting to turn, you have my full permission to zap him. If what I think is correct, then even if he starts to turn, you will only need to survive a minute."

The instructions had been given and they were clear. There was a lot of extremely loud moaning coming from Kai and Gary this time. Olivia, who had been complaining before, was still in pain, so she wasn't making too much noise.

Once the two hours were up, Austin and the others came and did as Gary asked, giving each one of them a bit of food. The timing seemed quite perfect, as they practically collapsed on the floor, nearly unable to move.

The color of their skin and some of their Energy was coming back, but none of them had transformed, and just like Gary had warned them, all three werewolves were doing all they could to convince the trio to let them out or feed them some more.

Kai was the worst of them all, going from promising them everything they might ever want to threatening them all with kicking them out of the Howlers and even hurting their loved ones. It was tough to listen to, but they reminded themselves that this was the hunger speaking through him.

Another thing that Gary had gotten correct was that after eating, the pain seemed to worsen. The small taste of food made them even hungrier than before, and it was true for every one of them.

Once again, though, it affected Olivia not as much. Gary thought it couldn't be a coincidence; it had to have something to do with her fasting before. She was the only one who had done something drastically different from them all.

It had been a long and tough day; even Austin and the others were tired from watching, giving out insults, and more. They had stayed up the whole day, only giving each other two hours of sleep as they worked in shifts.

When they went to the cages, they all went together; they agreed this was the safest thing to do.

"All right, it's time, we have five minutes until midnight, let's do this," Innu said.

They approached with the raw food just like they had done before. Then both Innu and Austin had their spears ready to attack Kai at any moment, while Marie was the one who would feed him.

She threw the food toward Kai, who began eating it immediately, ignoring everything around him. At the same time, Marie picked up her spear from the floor and pointed it toward Kai, waiting for any signs of him turning.

"Come on . . . please don't turn, please don't turn," Innu begged in a low voice.

Eating the food at an incredibly fast rate, Kai suddenly stopped, and everyone's hearts started to thump louder.

"Screw this!" Innu screamed as he thrust the spear forward, unwilling to take any chances. Alas, having expected this, the beta werewolf grabbed the spear head just below the tip and looked up at the dark-skinned teenager.

Saliva was dripping from his mouth as his now blue eyes stared at Innu.

CHAPTER 41

GRAY VS. BROWN

When Kai grabbed his spear, Innu immediately tried to pull it back. The Anti-Altered weapon only worked by touching the tip of the spear. As long as the end didn't directly touch the target, then it would electrocute nothing but air.

Damn, what is this strength? This scrawny blond kid would not have been able to overpower me this easily in the past! Innu thought, but the next moment he gulped, as he noticed that Kai's attention was fully on him. Those blue eyes glaring at him made him aware that he was in great danger.

"Why the fuck does it always have to be me? Help me, guys!" Innu yelled as he tried to push down the weapon as best as he could. He understood that letting go of the weapon at that moment would be a death sentence.

Fortunately, he wasn't alone, and when his friends noticed Kai's eyes, they ran up to help Innu by shoving their spears into the werewolf's body. Sparks appeared at the end of the weapon, and just like with Olivia, his whole body lit up like a Christmas tree. The sparks continued for a while, but unlike the female werewolf, instead of reverting to his human form, Kai continued growing bigger by the second.

"ARGHHH!" Growls escaped the transforming teenager's mouth, as his back grew in size, his forearms changed, and gray fur covered his body. It started on his arms and spread to his face. The transformation looked slightly different to Olivia and Gary, as his snout didn't protrude as much compared to theirs, yet his sharp canine teeth didn't look any less terrifying than those of his pack members.

Pulling the spear toward himself, Innu was almost dragged forward, so he let go at the last second, leaving him with no weapon to defend himself. Although both Austin and Marie had been using their weapons at the highest setting, Kai was now standing up, with the chains barely holding him in place.

"Get out of there!" Gary shouted from his cell. "Release me quickly! It's the only chance we have!"

Immediately, all three of them listened to Gary's order and ran out of the cage. Suddenly they all heard a clunking sound, followed by a loud bang. Innu didn't want to, but he turned his head and saw what he had been afraid of.

"Holy shit, he didn't just break the cuffs, he took out the whole freaking floor!" Innu shouted in disbelief, which didn't really help the tense situation. Austin opened the cage, and Marie quickly flipped through her keys.

"Come on, Marie, hurry up!" Innu insisted.

"I'm trying!" Marie shouted back as she went through the ring of keys. Her hands were shaking, hindering her from finding the right one.

A loud bang sounded from the rightmost cell. Rather than following them out, the gray werewolf was trying to make a path to get them directly. He had charged forward into the bars, bending them outward.

"Hey, Gary, even if we let you out, how are you planning to deal with him? If we give you food, won't you just become the same as him?" Innu asked, suddenly questioned the validity of their plan.

"I don't have to beat him," Gary answered. "I just have to keep him busy for a minute until it's midnight!"

They all could see that Kai was charging up to have a second go at the bars again, and they weren't so sure they would be able to hold out this time. Then Kai lifted his hand and his claws grew longer, looking incredibly sharp.

"Shit, why does he have to use his brain *now*?" Austin cursed.

"Success! You're free!" Marie said.

Having gotten free, Gary turned to face Kai. It was already a frightening thing to face a fully transformed werewolf, not to mention that

Gary only had 15 Energy points. Nevertheless, he didn't have much of a choice, so he ran past his friends, using Controlled Transformation on his arms.

I can only hope that my Endurance is good enough to keep him occupied. All of this is my fault, so if anyone has to get hurt, it should be me. I knew that I might have to face you when I created you, Kai, but I wish it hadn't come to this! Gary thought as he transformed his arms.

Kai leapt up and swiped at the cage, his claws slicing through the bars like hot butter. His body did the rest, making them bend further. Luckily, this caused him to lose a lot of his momentum.

With his transformed arms, Gary held on to him, keeping him down. The green-haired teenager didn't have to say anything; Marie and Austin saw their chance and helped their leader by poking Kai in the ribs with their spears. Even Innu grabbed his weapon to help out.

Kai let out a pained howl and closed his eyes. Grasping this opportunity, Gary pushed him down and started slashing Kai's belly with his claws.

BEEP BEEP *BEEP BEEP*

"That's the sound, it's midnight, it's midnight!" Innu cheered for joy.

You have survived a full day of the full moon.
The moon no longer empowers you.

Seeing this, Gary let out a sigh of relief, but he knew that it was not over. Not until Kai reverted to his human self. At the moment, he still had a wild look of defiance in his eyes.

"Kai!" Gary shouted, hoping that it would get through to his friend. Unfortunately, all it did was make him squirm.

"Damn it, he doesn't listen. Give me some food so I can make him submit!" Gary shouted, and Austin threw some food to the alpha werewolf, who caught it with one hand. But Kai took advantage of that distraction to push him off using his feet, and he got free.

Skill activated: Full Transformation
−20 Energy
Transformation has begun

Immediately, Gary's body began to turn, with brown fur covering his whole body. He charged in, running at the other werewolf on all fours. Seeing this, the gray werewolf did the same, and their bodies clashed together.

However, there was a clear winner in terms of strength. Kai fell to his knees in pain, and Gary lifted him by the chest and threw him over his shoulder, then slammed him onto the ground. He followed up by slamming his foot onto the beta werewolf's chest.

Stomping on him a few times did the trick; Kai's body began to shrink as his transformation became undone.

CHAPTER 42

LEAVING SLOUGH

"No wonder you're the leader. However, if this is what you all have to deal with every month, I guess I'm all right staying human," Innu said. Marie and Austin nodded along, sharing his opinion.

The horrible day had finally come to an end, and the three of them spread out on the floor. All the built-up tension from watching the werewolves, the lack of proper sleep, and the adrenaline that had left their bodies left them with no energy.

After filling up his own Energy, Gary carefully gave Olivia some of the meat to eat. Once he was sure that she wouldn't become feral once more, he ordered her to keep watch over Kai, while he carried each of his friends upstairs to a more comfy place.

Grabbing a phone, he called Tyler, telling him to bring over some burgers, pizza, and other junk food, so the trio could have a feast. Gary was positively surprised when Tyler told him that there was no need for it. Apparently, Marie had informed her mother earlier that their "thing" would take the whole day.

So Miss Degrace, with White's help, had cooked an entire feast for the Howlers and was just waiting for them to be done. A few minutes later, the three of them brought out all the food and Marie, Austin, and Innu began eating as if their lives depended on it.

Never in their lives did they want to feel the same way ever again as they had during the last twenty-four hours. At some point, Gary left them and went downstairs, where Kai and Olivia were waiting for him.

The gray werewolf was still injured, but it was clear that those injuries would heal on their own in due time.

"I guess Olivia was affected the last time because she had fasted for a couple of days before, getting her body used to the pain," Kai said, dressed in a new set of clothes he had brought along just in case. "Although we survived the night with nothing horrible happening, we need to learn from this experience for next time.

"After all, Gary, you most likely won't be here for the next full moon. If you hadn't been here today . . . well, let's just say Olivia and I already have enough to apologize for . . ."

After the "success" of this turning, Gary was actually reluctant to leave. There was no guarantee that the AFA would let him be there for them next month. He knew that at some point he might have to leave them on their own, but was now really the best time?

"We will be okay without you, brat," Olivia said, having noticed Gary's sudden change in attitude. "Don't we just need a bigger and stronger area to hold us during those twenty-four hours? Also, now that I've actually experienced it, I know what to do and not to do. I even have a plan where I can go the next time."

"Great, I also have a plan on what to do for the next time. How about we discuss it together later?" Kai offered. "She's right. For now, the Howlers are doing great on their own. Because of your methods, the businesses in Slough are willingly seeking us out.

"Because we are the only gang with a confirmed Altered, the other gangs don't dare to do anything but curse us. It's actually funny, usually the large gangs use their power to bully others into getting more money, but we're doing the exact opposite. In a way, I have to admit that I'm surprised how well all of this seems to be working out for us.

"Although we're not flush with cash, we still have enough for a few projects. And that's even after I've made the arrangements you asked for. Your family will be safe during your absence, I promise. All you gotta do now is tell her whatever you feel is right."

With business out of the way, the trio of Werewolves went upstairs and joined the others. The Howlers continued their feast, with all three of their "wardens" reminding Kai how obnoxious he had been during his hangry phase. Unable to defend himself, Kai just took it and kept apologizing for his behavior.

The merry mood continued for a while, but after Olivia excused herself, Gary quickly followed suit, since there was one thing he had put off for a long time.

After walking through the broken door of their apartment building and up the stairs, Gary reached the Dems' door, where the numbers were hanging crooked. He had lived there seemingly forever, ever since his father had disappeared, but it was finally time for them to leave this place.

Opening the door, he found Amy in the living room, having fallen asleep in front of the TV. Unfortunately, the creaking of the door woke her up.

"Hey, you're back." Amy groggily greeted her big brother. Although she wouldn't admit it, she had been quietly lonely these past few days. With her mother in the hospital, Stacy dead, and her brother hardly being at home, the previously cramped flat had felt too large for her.

When she saw her brother's serious face, Amy quickly became more awake.

"What's wrong, is it something to do with Mom?" she asked, starting to sweat.

"What? No, no, Mom is fine. She's better than fine. In fact, they're moving her to a better hospital. She'll get the best treatment possible," Gary quickly answered as he moved to sit next to her.

"Huh, but how? No, why would they do that? Gary, we don't have the money to afford that!" Amy said. Healthcare wasn't free, and although her brother had allegedly been able to pay the bills with his part-time job, a better hospital would naturally cost a lot more money.

"This is why I wanted to talk to you," Gary admitted.

Amy felt nervous; she already knew that he had been hiding a few things from her. Still, she had known Gary long enough to know that whatever he was doing was for their sake. Not wanting to get in his way, or worry him even more, she had promised him that she would stay out of his business and had merely offered to listen whenever he felt ready.

Is he finally going to come clean? Amy thought as she gulped.

"There are going to be a lot of changes around here, and I know I'm not Mom . . . or Dad, but I am your older brother. So I want you to listen to me, and I promise you that everything is in your best interests.

"You'll have a new apartment in Cipen. You will be staying there, but don't worry, you won't be alone. You'll be living with White. You've already met her a couple of times at the Wolf's Pool Club. She knows how important you are to me and since you're both nice people, I'm sure you will get along.

"You won't have to worry about anything. All the bills will be taken care of, and you'll even get a weekly allowance to do whatever you want. I know that Stacy's death has been weighing on you, and I'm sorry I wasn't there for you to talk about it, so if you want, I'm sure we can transfer you to a different school entirely. If there's anything else that you need, just tell me, all right, Amy?"

It was quite a shock to her. As someone who had lived her whole life in Slough, she knew that Cipen was the most expensive district in their town. To suddenly move there, and to live with a stranger after staying here all this time . . .

Still, Amy had picked up on one thing when Gary was speaking.

"Gary . . . the way you've been talking. You're making it sound like you'll be leaving . . . Are you no longer going to be . . . living with me?" Amy asked.

This was the hard part he still wasn't ready to admit. The lump in his throat made it hard to swallow, but eventually, he blurted out the words. "I'm sorry, Amy, but I'll be going to the AFA."

CHAPTER 43

A LAST MEAL

It took a second for Amy to realize what Gary was talking about. Unlike him, she wasn't really into fighting sports, but she had heard the name before, and it finally clicked in her head.

"The Altered Fighting Academy, but that makes no sense. You're not an Al—" Suddenly, images flashed through Amy's head of everything she had found. The bloody clothes, how Gary had gotten them out of a tricky situation, and even more things, including the money to pay for everything.

"I'm working with a corporation, and they sponsored me, so I'm an Altered now, but part of the deal is that I have to join the AFA and become a mascot for them," Gary explained.

Gary had thought long and hard, but it was impossible to come up with a reason to tell Amy about why he had to leave her and where he got the money from, and eventually, she might even see him on TV if things went well. That was why it was easier to mix lies with the truth, just enough for her not to ask any more questions, but tears started falling from Amy's eyes.

"I . . . I can't believe it." Amy sniffled. "You're doing something so dangerous . . . and it's to look after us, and now . . . now we won't even be together anymore."

The tears didn't stop there, and all Gary could do in this moment was to pull her toward his chest in a hug. Amy continued to cry for fifteen minutes before she eventually stopped.

"Come on, let's go for a meal on Burnham Street. It's my treat." Gary smiled. He never wanted to see tears in his sister's eyes and would do anything to keep her safe and happy.

The two of them enjoyed a nice meal at one of the steakhouses, which was Gary's choice, of course. Amy didn't mind because the steak was expensive and a luxury. She thought that if Gary was leaving her, she needed to treat him nicely and not let him worry too much about her.

The two of them started to talk about the good times in the past and more, and eventually, they got to the tough subject of what she would be doing next. Gary would be leaving soon, so she was to move in with White.

If she needed anything and couldn't get in contact with him, she could go to Olivia or Kai, whose numbers were now saved in her phone.

During the meal, Amy kept asking if it was okay for her to order as she wished. The prices on the menu put her off, and never before had they done such a thing. After she had called the waiter over a few times, only to send him back, Gary decided to order for her, and she filled herself up until she felt like her belly was going to explode.

After letting it settle down, they decided to head back home.

"Hey, don't you need to pay?" Amy asked.

"I settled the bill already while I was returning from the washroom." Gary smiled.

While they were leaving the restaurant, two waiters were standing by the door. It looked like one was about to stop Gary, until the other looked at him and mouthed *He's fine.*

They exited without a problem, and Gary thanked both of them.

"Who was that guy? They ate around three hundred dollars' worth of food, and you just let them leave like that? And they're just kids! Don't tell me they're the owners' kids or something?" one of them asked.

The other waiter smiled back.

"Not quite, and to be honest, I don't know either. I know that Olivia Pearl said if we ever see a green-haired teenager, we should not charge him. In fact, I think when I was talking to the others, I found out every restaurant on Burnham Street was told to do the same."

The other waiter's face went a little pale.

"Olivia Pearl? Well, I guess it makes sense, then, but I wonder who that kid is. Even her own men don't get free meals, and she's not old enough to have a kid that age."

Unaware of the discussion between the two waiters, the siblings continued onward toward home.

In the past, Gary and Amy would have never visited such areas, nor would they have walked so late at night. Slough was just too dangerous a place.

"Is it just me, or have things settled down in Slough these days? There seem to be fewer fights, scuffles, and even fewer color gangs on the streets," Amy noted. "I kinda like our hometown now."

Of course, Slough still wasn't safe enough to allow his sister to walk home on her own, but right now, she had one of the best bodyguards out there, even if she didn't know it.

"I agree," Gary replied. "Things seem to be changing in Slough, and I'm glad they are. After what happened to Mom, I hope no one else ever has to experience something like that again."

One of Gary's orders was to eliminate the color gangs completely. If anyone in the Pincers or the Howlers saw them, they were to give them a warning they wouldn't forget and, simultaneously, make them spill information about the day of the attack.

"Gary, I never want you to forget about your hometown, Slough. Even if you become some famous AFC champion, use the money to make this a better place or something. I think this could really become a good town."

Gary patted the top of her head and smiled.

"Of course; this is my town."

Heading home, Gary helped his sister pack the heavy things she needed. The moving company would come in the morning, and he would be off after that. He had left it till practically the last moment to tell his sister because she was so afraid.

While in the middle of packing up, Amy was going through some letters, which caused a question to pop up in her head.

"Gary, since we won't live here anymore, what should we do if Dad tries to contact us?" Amy asked.

CHAPTER 44

THE BIG AUCTION

Once everything was set in motion, Gary left to go to his trials at the AFA. His friends and acquaintances sent him off with their farewells and goodbyes, trying to make him worry as little as possible. At the same time, Amy had now moved in with White.

The two seemed to get on well. Although White didn't talk much, that was all right with Amy since she wouldn't be living alone. And at the same time, there would also be two guards who would follow them when they went out or while they were heading to school, even if they didn't know about it.

This left the Howlers to make their next move, and Gary had called a meeting between the original gang and Tyler, since the latter would be somewhat involved. The Wolf's Pool Club had been closed for the morning as they all sat around a table.

"All of us will be going on a trip," Kai began with a smile.

"A trip? You mean out of Slough? But I still haven't sorted things here. Kevin is about to go to secondary school," Innu complained.

"Wow, having a kid at your age, it's almost like you are the father and Suzan is the mother," Marie commented.

Innu's face instantly went red, but he didn't deny anything as he imagined himself and Suzan holding hands. Although there was a bit of an age gap between the two, that wasn't a problem for him.

"You can put that on hold because this is important," Kai replied. "Remember, a while ago, I talked about the Dark Guild Auction House? Well, the auction is in two days, so we need to start preparing."

"Dark Guild Auction House?" Tyler commented, not really following, especially since he wasn't there the last time.

"It's the auction house that sells nearly anything but is more known for their Anti-Altered weapons and Altered DNA," Austin explained with a grin on his face, because he had been waiting for this for a while.

"This time, the auction will be quite big because they are holding it in Morfran, a Tier 1 city that the Dark Guild controls. Usually, they just hold auctions in other cities, using a few of their men as guards, but because it's in their own city, they must have some pretty interesting items this time," Kai explained.

"Does it mean we're going to a Tier 1 city?!" Marie asked, her eyes lighting up as she imagined what the shopping malls would have to offer. Of course, it was unlikely she could afford anything, but just window shopping would satisfy her in a Tier 1 city.

"Isn't everyone else going to think the same thing?" Austin replied. "Which means there's going to be a lot of gangs there from everywhere."

Upon hearing this, the others froze. The Underdogs were a Tier 3 gang and not even one of the top ones in that category. Yet they were so difficult to deal with. At this auction, there would surely be gangs and organizations from all over the country far more powerful than them.

"Don't worry too much. No one tends to cause trouble at these auctions. It's usually afterward. One group gets an item another wanted, and then maybe a fight occurs, but they won't do anything risky for fear of angering the Dark Guild.

"What I'm hoping is that because the others are holding out for something impressive at this auction, we will be able to get what we want for cheap. Altered DNA," Kai stated.

The fear of everyone in the room had gone away, as their hearts started to tremble with excitement and smiles appeared on their faces. Both Innu and Austin wore smiles so large that one couldn't see their eyes, and when they looked at each other, they stopped for a second.

"I know why I'm smiling, but why are you smiling, you big ape?" Innu asked.

"Because of the Altered DNA, of course," Austin replied. "Now we can finally match up to Kai, Olivia, and Gary."

"I mean, you can get all excited if you want, but you know that I will be getting it first, right? I mean, I was in the Howlers way before you," Innu replied.

"What, by a few days? And what does that matter? It should go to the strongest person in our group, and that's clearly me," Austin replied, grinning from ear to ear.

"Ha, you!" Innu laughed.

"Will you two calm down?" Marie shouted. "Kai didn't say we would only be buying one Altered DNA tube; the gang's finances are doing well from what I've heard, and besides, technically, I was the first, so I should get dibs."

The three continued to argue for a while, and Kai was waiting for a good time to interject to tell them a few more things, but it seemed like it never was going to come.

"Listen!" Kai couldn't hold back in the end and banged his hand on the table, putting a large crack in the wood, and the memory of Kai nearly attacking them all returned, making them listen immediately.

"Unfortunately, we only have the funds to buy one tube, and that's if we're lucky. Honestly, at a push, maybe we could buy two, but we don't want our funds to hit rock bottom just when we have taken over everything.

"In the future, we can always get more, as for who gets the Altered DNA . . . it would depend on what we find and for whom it will be the most suitable. I think that's fair and best for the gang," Kai explained.

With that, everyone spent the next two days beaming with excitement over visiting a Tier 1 city and going to an auction with the top of the top. Then the day had finally come, and Tyler pulled up in a limo to take them all to Morfran, under the control of the Dark Guild.

CHAPTER 45

TIER 1 CITY

The limo ride was intense for the gang and they talked about multiple things on the way there, mostly about Gary and how he was faring. Since he hadn't sent them a message yet, they took it as a good sign that he was doing well.

Then the conversation steered to where they were going today.

"Why are you all nervous? You should all be excited for today!" Kai said.

"How are you *not* nervous? We're going into a battlefield where all the top gangs will be around us! You know how they act," Innu replied. "Some of them will be worse than the Underdogs; one wrong look and they might decide to destroy us and take over our town!"

"You better not do anything stupid, then. Oh, wait, I think that's impossible for you," Austin teased.

Grinding his teeth, Innu wanted to retort, but that was when he saw the sign saying *Welcome to Morfran*. Shortly after that, they entered a tunnel, and the atmosphere of the tunnel was something they had never seen before.

There were long digital screens across the entire tunnel, and the image was seamless. The video seemed to be advertising some type of beverage, with a male and a female model in it.

"Hey, isn't that Lulu and Matthew? They're both in the top ten Altered!" Innu pointed out.

"Well, these cities can afford to pay them. Plus, each Tier 1 city will have a few of the AFA stars under their belt," Kai explained.

Soon the car came to a standstill; at the end of the tunnel was a barrier that scanned the license plate of each car as it passed through.

When they reached the barrier, every person in the car was also required to have their photo taken. After all was done, they were allowed to continue traveling onward.

"That's quite the security system," Marie commented.

"A lot of the Tier 1 cities have them. It's so whoever causes trouble isn't allowed to leave," Kai replied. "It makes attacking a Tier 1 city extremely difficult, as the tunnels are the only way to normally enter them. Unless you drop out of a helicopter or something."

Eventually they finally entered the Tier 1 city. To be honest, although Kai didn't mention it to the others, it would also be his first time seeing such a place.

"This . . . is not what I expected," Tyler said as he stared through the windshield, unfocused on the road in front of him.

The word *city* made them expect giant skyscrapers with apartments on top of apartments; however, Morfran wasn't like that at all. Instead, they saw plenty of large, green parks and giant mansions.

There were indeed skyscrapers, but they looked like office buildings and were covered with advertisements.

"I guess that makes sense," Kai commented. "The Tier 1 cities are a place where truly only the top of the top can live, the top one percent of the population. So they aren't overcrowded like other areas."

Of course there were still apartment buildings here and there, for those who wished to live in a Tier 1 city, rather than live a larger lifestyle in a Tier 2, and there were many reasons for that. Just seeing the beauty of how the city was laid out, everyone could understand.

"There's . . . there's just such a huge difference between their lives and ours," Marie said, clenching her fist. Even in Slough there was inequality, but not quite like here.

"Who knows, Marie, maybe we can change all of this one day, who knows," Kai said with a smile, because seeing all of this was inspiring him even more to complete his goals.

"Damion, I wish you were still alive to see what exactly I'm going to do to this whole world."

Following the car's satellite navigation, they had finally reached the auction house. It was an incredibly large building that had a unique architecture compared to the rest of the city. Most of the city was made out of glass and fancy designs, giving the whole place a modern look. The flooring and pathways throughout the city were made of marble, rather than the standard concrete or stone flooring. But the auction house looked like something out of the Victorian era.

There were carved details everywhere, and it even had large pillars at the front with a huge entryway. In front was a gigantic garden with a fountain, along with hedges and flowers that had been perfectly trimmed and arranged.

There was also plenty of green space behind the auction house. The place was quite busy, busier than they had thought it was going to be, with several cars pulling up to the entrance.

Directly in front were valet drivers parking cars off-site. While waiting in the queue, they saw that the auction house itself had yet to open its doors, and groups of people were enjoying drinks outside, where there was a pop-up bar for guests.

Some were dressed in expensive outfits that cost more than a whole house in a Tier 3 city. Others appeared to be wearing their gang's clothing and more.

"I'm shaking, man, I'm seriously shaking," Innu said, holding out his hand to demonstrate. "Look at them all, look at all these people. I have no clue who they are, which makes it worse."

It was true; many of these people were known by name, but no one knew what group they belonged to. Many of the gangs behind the scenes didn't publicly display their faces, and as for the Kings who ran the gangs, only a few were quite flashy in proclaiming who they were.

"All right, everyone, my best advice would be to not talk to anyone for the time being. If someone does approach us asking us questions, send them to me," Kai said as he pulled out the black-and-gold fox mask and placed it on his face.

"Do the rest of you have your masks as well?"

Pulling them out, they all did the same, covering the top half of their face. Unlike Kai's, though, theirs didn't have a particular design, only a solid near-black color that just went below their hairline.

Since they were a new small gang, and the current people in the car, minus Olivia, were the pillars of the Howlers, Kai didn't want their identities to be revealed to everyone. Even Tyler wore a mask as he stepped out of the vehicle.

They were all dressed in their black-and-gold gang uniforms as well, and the strange masks certainly attracted some attention.

"Who are they? I have never seen them before," a person commented.

"Probably some up-and-coming group from the new cities. They do this stuff all the time in hopes of getting noticed," another person replied, and turned their head away.

There was certainly some interest, but it quickly faded with the higher groups. It was only the lower ones that gave them another look.

The whole group stayed together, with Kai leading the way, and he went up to the bar and ordered a drink. He did so confidently, even though he was underage, and the bartender didn't give it a second thought.

Never in their wildest dreams did they think that a bunch of high school students would be attending such an event.

"Hey, I feel like I've seen that uniform somewhere before, and those strange masks. Aren't they that gang that was on TV?"

At the time of the broadcast, many of the Tier 3 and below cities had taken great interest in it, and their little show along with their uniforms seemed to do the trick.

However, what Kai didn't expect was to catch the attention of one of the Kings, who was standing toward the back of the crowd of people with a drink in his hand.

"So those are the Howlers, who recently took over Slough. It might be worth talking to them," said Sin, one of the Kings, as his drink had evaporated into the air.

CHAPTER 46

A WORLD OF GANGS (PART 1)

Looking around, the Howlers could only guess who belonged to a gang, because everyone was dressed similarly. Of course, without special knowledge, that didn't tell them where those gangs came from. It was of the utmost importance to avoid conflict with those who had established themselves in high-tier cities, especially as a new gang.

To prevent anything from occurring, the Howlers were staying together, and they were enjoying their drinks and some casual chat. Still, Marie noticed that a certain person was continually looking their way.

At first, she decided to ignore it, wondering if she was just imagining things, but as time went on, she could see his eyes following them.

"Have you noticed that flamboyant man over there? Ever since we came here, he's been staring at us," Marie whispered to Kai. She felt tingles running up her entire back when she looked over. The creepy thing was that the man didn't even try to hide the fact that he was looking at them, and he even smiled and waved at one point.

"I have noticed him, but I have no clue what he wants," Kai replied, feeling uneasy. At the stage the Howlers were as a gang, there should be nothing warranting Tier 1 gangs looking at them, especially not someone as flashy as that man.

As the son of a gang leader, he knew far more about the underworld than the other members, so how could he not recognize the man with dyed red tips in his hair dressed in the large red overcoat in his white fur hood?

Practically everything about Sin screamed *Look at me!"* and everyone in the bar appeared to be actively trying to come close to him. At the same time, others chose to stay far away. After all, unlike the other Kings, Sin had made it a point to show off. His actions had shown the entire country why the Kings deserved their moniker.

In the past, a Tier 2 gang had stolen something that was supposed to go to him. When Sin had learned that fact, he had offered the gang one chance to return it, no questions asked. Of course, the gang had refused to do anything of the sort, and so Sin had paid them a personal visit.

Usually gang wars lasted weeks, if not months. After all, the larger the gang size, the more territories they controlled to fight over. Funds and more were tied into assets as well as businesses. A gang war would break out when one wanted to take over the other's businesses or to expand their own. So it was important that they did it right.

What's more, other powers at work would not just sit on the sidelines and watch the show. Perhaps not White Rose, but the local police force, the mayor, and other gangs would all try to intervene in some way, making the situation difficult to navigate.

And yet one person had managed to eradicate an entire gang in the span of one day, and in the process he had nearly burned the whole city to the ground . . .

Rather than hide his involvement, Sin had made his actions quite public, even hiring a team of professional videographers to film it all. Their job had been to show off his vast power, and that was what they had done. The video was spread and talked about in other cities for months, and the craziest thing about it all was the fact that he had suffered zero repercussions for his heinous act.

Sin had returned to his own city as if nothing had happened. After that, life for the Tier 1 cities got easier, because everyone understood the possible consequences if they didn't follow orders. Now, whatever any of the Kings asked, not just Sin, the task was completed. The lower-tier cities were to do their bidding, whether there was large involvement with other gangs or not.

The Underdogs and the Gray Elephants were both working for higher groups. Could it be . . . don't tell me that Sin is related to one of them? Or maybe he did business with one of them. I hope not, because even all three of us might not stand a chance against him. Even if Gary were here, it wouldn't make a difference, Kai realized as he continued to pretend not to have noticed the king staring at him.

Unless Sin came up to them, he would continue that charade . . .

As they waited for the doors of the auction house to open, more and more people started to gather. It looked like there were around five hundred in the garden to the side, all here for one thing, from all over the country.

The Dark Guild also had auctions in other countries as well, but this was their homeland so they tended to keep the best items for themselves. Although wars had come to somewhat a halt.

The level of Altered and how strong they were was a sign of a country's strength. Some thought it was why the government was so lenient on the gangs roaming around. It was also why there was next to no regulation on Altered solutions and DNA either.

They realized their mistake too late, as the situation had become what it had become.

Eventually, a certain group came up to the Howlers and decided to try to make conversation. White Rose was their answer, but it was too small and weak to stop the powerhouses at the top.

CHAPTER 47

A WORLD OF GANGS (PART 2)

"I haven't seen you people here before. First time?" an older gentleman asked politely. He was dressed quite nicely, with a shirt and blazer that barely covered his large tummy. Behind him were two men who appeared to have weapons strapped to their sides, checking out the gang.

The others turned toward Kai, just like they had been instructed, and let him speak for the group. The fox-masked teenager had expected that their new appearance and new faces would attract some attention, yet so far nobody else had come over.

Of course, all he hoped for was to meet people from lower-tier towns, as those above them would already have all the connections they needed.

"I doubt we're the only ones who've arrived here just for today. We're the Howlers from Slough. Perhaps you've heard of us. It's nice to meet you, Mr.—?" Kai placed his hand out for a handshake, which the old man accepted. Feeling the werewolf's grip and seeing him up close, he was in for quite a surprise.

"My name is Harry Cardenez, and I represent Cardenez Electronics," the old man admitted, after staring at the rest of them and noticing that they were all young. "I thought I recognized you all, though you're younger than I expected. To be honest, I'm a bit surprised that you are here."

"Why wouldn't we be?" Kai asked, trying not to sound the least bit surprised. "There are some things that we need to get, and it's always good to make connections. As someone whose company is located in a Tier 3 town, I'm sure you understand. With the boom in electronics, your company has been able to expand quite well, and perhaps demand has even gotten a bit too much for you to handle in Brighthum Town alone. You know, Sl—"

The old man raised his hand to stop Kai right there. "I have to admit, I've underestimated you and your group. You've really done your research. However, you should understand that there is no use in us talking . . . not until you hold the key to your town."

Hearing this, Kai smiled and sent the man off with a polite bow.

"Hey, what was that? Why did that guy come over if he wasn't interested in doing business?" Innu asked.

"He was, and he is," Kai said. "We aren't the only ones who have done their research, though. As much as we might want to expand, it's too early for us, because there is still one problem that we have to take care of."

The others started to think about what Kai could possibly be talking about. The Underdogs had been able to do as they wished, and only the Gray Elephants had been able to match up to them, yet both of their gangs had been eliminated.

So then who were the Howlers supposed to take care of?

"You guys may not have noticed, but they have been causing problems for us from behind the scenes," Kai explained. "However, the real problem is our mayor."

The mayor of Slough, Xin's father, Ben Clove, had quite a few medium-sized gangs under his fist. Individually they were all weak, but as a unit, they were just as troublesome as the Gray Elephants or the Underdogs.

Originally, they had planned to swoop in and take over the city just after the new war between the Underdogs and the Gray Elephants, but in the end, the Howlers had joined the fight and had done that instead.

However, the mayor was quite a powerful figure if not controlled by a gang, because he was fighting in ways that only he could—for example, by rejecting proposals to rebuild new areas and not offering tax breaks to new businesses that were coming in.

Any progress to do with the city that had the Howlers name on it had been halted in some way. When the Howlers made a deal to protect a new business, legally these terms as well as a percentage were written into the contract.

All of this information was passed on to the mayor, so it was easy for him to reject anything involving the Howlers. There were ongoing legal battles, but the lawyer that Olivia had introduced them to had told Kai that there was nothing that they could really do about it.

Fighting back would take a considerable amount of time, especially since the mayor had the power to make the judges delay these things until the last day. Until a decision really got overturned, they would have to fight on a case-by-case basis.

Kai gave the other gang members a summary of those problems, making them realize why he had been holed up in his office for most of the day. He wasn't just sitting and planning mastermind things; there was a lot that needed to be done to run an efficient gang.

"Then what are we supposed to do?" Marie asked.

"It's actually simple. Cardenez said it right there. He is interested in working with us, not with the mayor. The people on the outside are rooting for us. We just need to control him, giving us full control over all of Slough."

Not many others approached the gang after. There were a few people from Tier 4 towns and such who said hello out of respect for the Howlers, but none of them mentioned any business.

This was fine for them, though, as everything else was secondary; they were here for the actual auction itself.

The large double doors creaked as they were pushed open by two large men dressed in dark purple outfits. A giant man who was a wall of muscle came out.

"The auction house is now open. The event will be starting in fifteen minutes. Please come inside, where you will be escorted to the right area!" the man shouted.

Finally, it was time.

CHAPTER 48

DARK GUILD (PART 1)

Following instructions, the people formed two lines, five yards apart from each other, at either side of the hall. Behind the large door were several staff members dressed in the same dark purple clothing as those outside. They stood straight and proud like guards.

This wasn't the type of group that Kai was expecting. The Dark Guild was a well-known gang. Although gangs operated differently and ran different businesses, all the guards were gang members, but this was almost like a well-tuned army.

Guiding the guests in the front was a woman who was dressed in a black skirt, a white shirt, and a purple waistcoat. Next to her was a man wearing a purple waistcoat and a top hat. They didn't say much, other than for the guests to follow them for the time being.

The hall they were being led through was littered with giant paintings that depicted scenes of old armored knights, kings wearing ornate crowns, and fantastic beasts such as dragons. At times, the hosts talked about some of the paintings as they explained the history of the Dark Guild.

However, the farther they went, the more modern the décor became. Rather than paintings, photos started to fill the walls, depicting items that had been sold in prior auctions. Apart from weapons like swords, axes, bows, and shields that looked to have been created with unnatural materials, there were also fantastical creatures next to syringes.

When a guest asked whom these items were exactly sold to, the hosts just smiled as they carried on.

The Dark Guild seems to have quite a history, Kai thought as they silently followed the group. *All I could find out was that their gang has been around for quite a long time, but for some reason they have stayed out of the way of others, mainly focusing on their auction house.*

Strangely, I haven't found even a single report about anyone daring to attack them. I'm still not sure whether this means that somebody might have tried and that information got buried by them, or something is actively stopping others from even trying it.

I doubt that an unspoken rule not to attack them would keep everyone in check. They must have made a deal to have the others guarantee their safety . . . or else they have the means to protect themselves.

Although it was rare for Tier 1 gangs to face each other, because of the potential fallout of such a confrontation in terms of damage and the problems it would cause, small disputes were normal. After all, the larger a gang was, the harder it was to control each and every member.

On top of that, there were plenty of people with big egos who had a lot of pride: those who had to prove themselves or thought that their gang was better than others. They just couldn't help but get into a fight. So at some point, every group had some type of report come out about them causing a bit of trouble; the sole exception to this appeared to be the Dark Guild.

There was not even an attempt to see if they were truly as strong as people thought they were. Or at least not one that had been reported.

It makes me wonder, how strong are these guards in this hallway? If we want to rise to the top, we have a lot of work to do, Kai thought.

Suddenly, the two guides leading them stopped and turned around.

"All those from a Tier 1 city, please follow me upstairs to the gallery seating. There is a bar and we've prepared refreshments for your convenience." The woman's soprano voice filled the hall as she lifted her hand toward the staircases on either side.

"As for the rest of our guests, please follow me to your seats," the man added in a deep baritone as he started opening the doors on their level. Inside was another bar area, allowing the guests to order as they wished provided they were willing to pay for it.

"I guess there's always someone higher up than you," Innu noted with a big sigh, but it wasn't because of the division of people. "Goodbye, pretty ladies."

"Oh . . . I thought you only had eyes for one," Austin said. "Maybe I should come with you next time you pay Kevin and—what was her name again?—a visit."

"Will you get out of the way?" A man's loud voice disrupted the previously somber atmosphere. The commotion was coming from upstairs. A group of three men, all with shaved heads that looked like they had been slightly waxed, were stopped at the top of the staircase, blocked by the purple-clad guards from taking another step forward.

"Why are you stopping us?" asked the man at the front, gritting his teeth.

"Because you have disrespected the rules," the guard in the middle answered. "You've been informed that the upstairs is only for guests from Tier 1 cities. You're not one of those. Please head back down and make place for those who deserve to be here."

"And how would you even know that?" One of the gang members pointed at the guard.

Watching the situation, it wasn't hard to figure out what was going on. Unless the Dark Guild's staff had decided to single them out, the trio must be pretending to belong to a Tier 1 city. With the large number of gangs and organizations each section could hold, there was no way to tell who was and who wasn't from a Tier 1 city, unless they asked for some kind of proof.

Judging by their behavior, Kai assumed that the trio was trying to sneak in. He himself had entertained the idea, yet the risk would far outweigh the potential benefit, so the werewolf had refrained from acting upon it.

"Sir, we'll ask you once more to leave on your own," the Dark Guild member repeated, raising his hand and placing it on his chest. "Please, enter the appropriate way, or we will have to escort you out."

Maybe we will see just how strong this Dark Guild is, Kai thought.

CHAPTER 49

DARK GUILD (PART 2)

The bald man was filled with rage, but when he glanced at the people staring at him from below, he also felt embarrassed. They had garnered too much attention to simply step down now.

As a Tier 3 gang that had recently risen to the top, they felt like they were now in a place of respect. Getting to be seated with the king would allow the man to progress further, and he would feel respected. Having risen to the top of their town, the group felt like they needed to ride this momentum and continue to push themselves further.

At that moment, Sin, who had been the first to go upstairs, went out to look at the commotion. When he saw the three men, he just sneered.

"You think you have finally made it, huh? That is because you are able to be in a place like this, where you can do what you want. Let's make this clear: people like you can be replaced at any moment. Look around; there are plenty of people at your level, but your place is down there."

He snapped his fingers, and a small flame appeared right above his hand, burning upright and strong.

"Would you mind not doing that in here?" The woman in the purple skirt stepped out behind the king. "Mr. Mutav, as much as we treasure you as a valuable guest, you should be aware that the Dark Guild does not differentiate between troublemakers. Should you choose to start anything here, I'm afraid we'll also have to remove you from our premises. "

It was an interesting development. After all, the guide had just threatened to remove a king. What's more, Sin was known for not taking orders from others, so everyone was wondering what would happen next. Could the Dark Guild really make good on their threat?

The bald men appeared nervous as they looked at Sin, but they weren't backing down. In a way, the fact that they saw him and still chose to act this way made him want to burn them even more.

"Fine." Sin shrugged and put out the flame before he turned around and walked back in. "Just make sure they know their place."

Hearing this, the bald man tried to push past the guards, but the moment he took the first step, a raised palm rushed out. Everyone heard a loud bang, it looked as if a shock wave had come out of the bald man's back.

All the guests turned around, worried that a gun had gone off, but that would have been impossible. The bald man fell back and started to roll down the stairs, banging his head repeatedly until he eventually stopped midway down.

"Slappy!" one of the other men shouted as they chased after him. "Are you okay?"

"You have a minute to take him away before we do the same to you," the woman noted before announcing, "Dear guests, please ignore this little incident and enjoy yourselves at the event!"

What was that? One hit without any transformation? Kai wondered. *Surely everyone who is here has to be an Altered, but the guard didn't even look as if he was serious. Just what kind of Altered is he? Are the rest the same?*

I guess it would only make sense for the Dark Guild to keep the best Altered solutions for themselves, and they need strong people in order to protect their assets.

After this little demonstration, Kai was sure no one else would try anything, so it seemed like it was pretty safe inside the place. He also overheard others commenting that, "Every year there's always one new group that causes trouble."

The main venue hall was similar to a large theater. There was the seating area above, reserved for the Kings, and then there were the rest of the seats down below.

As they entered, each group was handed a paddle with a number on it; the Howlers received number 23. If they wished to bid, they would raise paddle.

"Oh man, I'm so excited. We're really going to see cool weapons and stuff, right?" Innu exclaimed. "I mean, maybe we don't just have to get an Altered solution, maybe we can get some cool weapons as well.

"The ones we have are good, but it was still difficult using them on you guys last time, and didn't Olivia say she got her whip from here?"

"We'll see about that," Kai replied. "Our first priority will be the solution. Even among the Altered solutions, there are variants. The cheapest are the common ones, the type that most people can get anyway. Then there are those that are proven to be strong since they're either the same as or similar to that of an AFC fighter.

"Finally, there are the mystery types that are quite expensive but a gamble. Those are the never-before-seen types, meaning they can be either super strong or a total bust. I would prefer to go for one that we know is strong and suits one of you, but depending on how much competition there will be, we'll barely be able to even afford one, much less two," Kai explained.

"How much is our budget?" Marie asked.

"Five million, and that will leave us with pretty little for the next few months."

When they heard that number, the Howlers' eyes lit up.

CHAPTER 50

FIVE MILLION DOLLARS

Everyone had been comfortably sitting in their seats when they heard Kai mention their group's budget, but the moment he revealed the number, all of them nearly jumped up in shock. Five million dollars was an unimaginable amount for any of them.

Instantly, they were all thinking about what they could do with that kind of cash. Coming from a Tier 3 town, they could go practically anywhere, select any apartment and car they fancied, and still have enough left over to live a happy life . . . and yet for some reason, their blond leader had mentioned it as if he were talking about fifty bucks.

"I know what you're thinking, but it shows that you guys have no idea how much it actually costs to run an organization as big as ours. While we get paid protection money from various businesses, we have dozens of people on our payroll, not to mention that each property we own has costs associated with it.

"This money we're using will be gone. We won't be able to upgrade our businesses or reinvest it into Burnham Street or other areas that have been run down. To give you an example, think about the apartment building where Gary lived. That much money would be enough to renovate the entire building, but think about how many of those there are in all of Slough.

"What's more, to get this type of liquid fund, I had to sell off a couple of Underdog buildings. Because of the rush, and certainly because of the mayor's interference, we got less money than they would be worth, but I had to do it because we can't handle their costs at the moment.

"Besides, in a place like this, this kind of money is pocket change to those sitting up top. Don't forget, everybody who has come here to bid is the leader of a town, a city, or a large corporation. Worst case, we'll go home with nothing from this auction."

The others fell silent as they realized how naive their thoughts had been. Altered DNA was something everyone would be fighting for. Unlike other luxury items, they could all use it, as without it their fancy lifestyle would be short-lived.

"Doesn't that mean that if we end up not buying any of the tubes, we get to keep it all to ourselves?" Innu asked.

Immediately, Marie, who was sitting next to him, slapped him on the back of the head. The sound was loud enough to cause the others in the room to look over, making Marie a little embarrassed. "Did you not just hear a word he said? There are plenty of uses for that money in Slough, and we all know the mayor isn't going to do anything for the city."

"That's true." Innu rubbed the back of his head. "Say, why don't we get someone we know to run for mayor in the next election? Won't that solve a lot of our problems? Surely we could use our gang's influence to help them get votes. What about Olivia? She's the oldest among us and already known by others."

Kai stroked his chin, considering that idea. The Lady Boss might not be the most optimal choice given her gang connection, but the idea certainly held some merit.

While their group was discussing things, the werewolf had used his super hearing to listen in on the conversations around them. It had allowed him to learn that a large percentage of guests on the bottom floor consisted of new gangs, mostly coming from low-tier towns.

Crime was more rampant in those areas. Everyone was fighting for the few scraps that were there, which meant they were quite dangerous, but it also meant the leaders and those at the top changed constantly, unlike in the Tier 2 and Tier 1 cities.

The Howlers were also a relatively new group, and they were treated with a bit more respect only because they had appeared on the news rather recently. Additionally, their current appearance with the masks made them quite mysterious.

On the Howlers' left sat an all-female gang that called themselves the Amazons. They were an established gang that was well known and even quite popular in their hometown. On the other hand, the No Land Gang was the polar opposite of those ladies.

To the right of Kai sat gang members who shared neon-green dyed hair, all of them with several missing teeth and torn clothing. Were this any other place, they could have easily been mistaken for a group of hobos, but this was just the style of this Tier 4 gang.

"Hmmm, isn't your boss with you? I remember his mask was different from the rest of youse!" the man sitting next to the werewolf asked. Kai had purposely been sitting on the very edge, not just to stay with his friends but also to be as far away as possible from the other gang's stench.

"There's no need for him to come personally. This is just an auction, not a fight, so let's just enjoy the event for ourselves, shall we?" Kai answered as he tried to keep down his disgust.

The man smiled, showing off his silver teeth, and began to slap the armchair of his seat over and over. "You're right. Let's get this started!" he shouted, and the other members of his gang shouted along with him.

As if on cue, a spotlight appeared on stage, and underneath was none other than the man in the top hat, who had been leading the main group this entire time.

CHAPTER 51

EVERYONE IS HERE

"Thank you all for coming today. We're especially happy to see so many new faces, but of course, we're also elated to see the old ones return. Allow me to remind you all that it's in your own interest to stay respectful and follow the rules of our auction.

"For the first-timers among you, be aware that any bid you make will be binding. Should your group be unable to pay the full sum, we have our own ways to get our money," the man in the top hat said with a mischievous smile, without elaborating.

It was pretty brazen to start an auction with a threat directed to everyone in the room, especially in a place filled with leading figures who all had massive egos, yet not a single one said anything.

"With that out of the way, I won't bore you any longer. Let's give you all what you are here for and introduce our first items," the man said, and pointed to the side.

The spotlight shone on a staff member who rolled the first item in: a large crate. He opened the crate to reveal a load of illegal melee weapons inside. Immediately, multiple gangs raised their paddles, bidding one by one. Even the No Land Gang showed interest, though not a single Tier 2 or Tier 1 gang paid any attention.

Once the bidding was over, the crate of weapons was rolled away and another one was rolled in. This one contained ranged weapons with ammunition. The man onstage explained what they did and showed off their power a little bit. He fired a bolt at a target, electrifying it.

After Kai had seen a few ordinary Anti-Altered weapons, the next set of items surprised him. Only a screen projector was brought out; the screen showed images of land and the names of each city.

Oh . . . they're selling land and buildings from their cities. I didn't know this was a thing. Hmmm, it's quite a good strategy for expanding. It allows a gang to enter another city without causing trouble, and if a higher gang buys it, then it's also a sign of cooperation, Kai thought.

The buildings and land were being sold for a crazy high amount, though, with the Tier 1 and 2 cities fighting over it. Although selling land was a quick way to make money, for a gang that wanted to rise like the Howlers it wasn't a good idea to invite others in, at least not if they wanted to purchase it back.

They would have to either pay more for it or force the other gang to give it back somehow.

"You seem to be lacking funds, young one," the man next to Kai commented. "Your group has yet to bid on a single item. If you plan to keep your position and protect yourself, these items are valuable to have, you know.

"In a way, even this auction house is a battlefield. Some people are taking note of what others have bought, and it is a way to show off your power."

Kai already knew this, so he didn't engage the conversation with the No Land Gang leader. Because of the way Gary had asked the gang to make money, their source of revenue, despite being the top gang of their town, produced far less than what the Underdogs or even the Gray Elephants would have brought along.

They didn't extort the people down to the bread line so they could gain higher profits, nor did they delve into extremely illegal things like Olivia had been doing. They still made a lot of money. But they didn't have as much as the surrounding gangs.

If only the guy knew how many Anti-Altered weapons we still have left over from the Underdogs. Even better, we have three werewolves, who might be even stronger than your average Altered. Kai smiled to himself.

"You think what I said was entertaining?" the man asked, having misunderstood his expression. "Let me help a fellow newcomer out. If you take off that mask and show that pretty face of yours, I will be happy to lend you some money so you can have a bit of fun with the grown-ups."

Although Kai hadn't been laughing at the person originally, he was doing so now as he turned his head toward him.

"You seem very interested in what lies underneath my mask," Kai said as he leaned toward the gang leader. "However, are you sure you can afford to pay the price? Because it will cost you your entire city."

The moment he said those words, Kai's eyes started to glow blue, narrowing slightly, making him resemble a predator looking at his prey. The gang leader felt shivers run through his entire body and shifted his attention to the auction once more.

The next item that had been brought out was another weapon, this time a sword, although it looked different from the one in the first batch. It was one of the old-style weapons; it looked as if it had been carved out of an animal, quite similar to those that they had seen in paintings.

These weapons . . . are they similar to Damion's axes or Olivia's whip? I'm guessing these are what those more experienced Altered Hunters use as well, Kai thought.

The bidding started and people raised their paddles one after another. It was the most popular item that had been shown today, and it made Kai believe his hunch was right.

That was when he felt a nudge from Innu. "Hey, are you seeing what I'm seeing?"

The dark-skinned teenager was pointing downward to the lower seats. One of the guests holding their paddle up had a recognizable face.

"That's . . . Blake Hunt," Kai said in surprise, not having expected to see him here.

CHAPTER 52

STARTING BID!
(PART 1)

As an upperclassman, Kai had never really interacted with Blake Hunt. The former had only known the latter as a result of being Westbridge's rugby ace, making him famous in their school. Only later did he discover the younger teenager's double life as an Altered Hunter, and that was mostly from Gary.

During Slough's big gang war, involving the Underdogs, the Gray Elephants, and the Howlers, Blake Hunt had come out to help. One could argue that he had merely acted as an Altered Hunter who wanted to get rid of the infected Altered, but it was undeniable that his intervention had helped out their entire town.

Have the Altered Hunters sent him on his own? No, I doubt that. He would make too easy a target if that were the case. I should assume that either the ones next to him are Altered Hunters, or they're hidden elsewhere in the room. Have they come here to buy Anti-Altered weapons . . . or are they here for another reason? Kai wondered.

They were in a room with many Altered. The more Kai thought about it, the more perfect the location seemed for a large-scale attack. The only thing was, that wasn't how the Altered Hunters operated. They attacked isolated Altered in small groups to avoid the risk of anyone else interfering.

Besides, the unknown number of Altered would also pose a giant risk to them, as there was no guarantee the Altered Hunters could take out everyone involved, and if they failed, the retaliation was bound to be very bloody.

"Sold!" the auctioneer announced before he slammed his gavel down on the lectern. "For 1.2 million."

Shit, if a single weapon costs a fourth of what we have, do we even stand a chance to get an Altered solution at all? Innu was left flabbergasted at the kind of money being thrown around.

The others were also beginning to doubt the likelihood of winning anything. The longer this auction went on, the more expensive the items seemed to become. Before the various parcels of land and buildings had come out, things had been relatively tame. At least with the batches of weapons, it had seemed less shocking, since they could justify the high prices because of the quantity of sold goods, but now . . .

A couple more weapons followed, and one of the adults next to Blake Hunt had actually managed to win the bid for two weapons. Unfortunately, he was unable to purchase a third one, as the trident he was interested in had also attracted the attention from a patron above them, and perhaps because of their earlier acquisitions, they had ended up conceding the following bidding war.

Kai thought, *Considering that the Altered Hunters are regarded as a terrorist group, it's a bit surprising to see how much money they appear to have. I'm not even sure if they gave up because they lack the funds, or simply because they wish to avoid standing out.*

Either they have very rich members among them, or someone must be backing them. Perhaps a private company? Hmmm, it could actually also be one of the Tier 1 gangs or even a King. I suppose there could be a symbiotic relationship between them. They would make the perfect pawns to take out a rival gang's Altered, Kai realized, though he was also aware that most of this was wild speculation on his part.

It was hard to do research on such an elusive target. Just like Blake, their members were leading normal lives during the day, so it was near impossible to find out who was a member and who wasn't. Up until this point, Kai had also focused mainly on other gangs or organizations that they might have to fight at some point, but now that they were delving into Altered territory, they were bound to become enemies with the Altered Hunters. Assuming they weren't already. After all, only Blake knew that the Howlers' werewolves were not the same as Wolf Altered.

"And with that, we're out of weapons. Let's move on to the next category of items," the host declared as he wiped the sweat from his forehead. The bidding had been quite intense on the last item, and he knew there was more to come. "The first Altered solution of the night."

Rolled out from the back came a tray table with a solution. It was further protected in a glass container displayed on a red cloth.

"Thanks to recent developments from labs around the world, nearly everyone can become an Altered with but a simple injection. This item will let you become a cat-type Altered, granting you fast reflexes, better night vision, and power-climbing abilities among other perks. All who watch the AFC fights should be aware of the prowess of feline Altered. The bidding starts at five hundred thousand!"

The people at the front cheered a bit, and nearly everyone in the room put up their paddle, each one trying to be the first to shout out the starting bid.

"Seven hundred thousand!" a man shouted as he raised his paddle.

"Seven hundred fifty thousand!" another shouted.

"Eight hundred thousand," the gang leader next to Kai shouted. He had a large smirk on his face and looked at the masked teenager, seemingly challenging him to participate.

"Hey, should we go for this one?" Marie asked. "I think I might be suited to be a Cat Altered, and the bids are quite low at the moment."

While they talked, the bids were continually going up; if Kai were to make a prediction, then this solution would sell between 1.5 million and 2 million in total. So far nobody from upstairs had made a bid, else the others would have backed out.

However, there was a good reason why they refrained from doing so. As much as the auctioneer had hyped it up, it didn't change the fact that this was a rather simple Altered solution. Sure, it increased one's strength greatly, and depending on the person, one could utilize it better than others, but a cat just wasn't the same as a lion.

It just didn't have an impressive enough track record to warrant the current bids, and perhaps the crowd had merely fallen for the silver tongue of the Dark Guild's representative.

The auction house is truly clever, not telling us how many tubes there will be. This way, we're being pressured into spending more for fear it might be the last item, eventually.

"Sold!" the host announced, pointing toward the No Land Gang. "For 1.1 million."

STARTING BID! (PART 2)

"You're going to be an Altered, Boss Kit!" one of his members cheered. "We'll be able to make the others submit to us, and all of us together will be able to take over a Tier 3 town!"

Overhearing their group, Kai learned that the leader sitting next to him was called Kit, and their strategy was very typical for a low-level gang. Rather than improve their own town, they planned to use all the money they had gained to improve themselves before attempting to invade another nearby town. No wonder they were spending their money without worry. This was also the reason why it was almost impossible for lower-tier towns to rise a tier.

Hmm, but the item sold for a lot less than I expected, Kai thought. *Either the other guests are smarter than I gave them credit for, or the bidding was mostly done by newcomers like them. The others must be aware that better stuff is coming soon.*

Keeping it interesting, the next item to roll out was not one but three solutions at once, this time allowing the people who ingested it to become rat-type Altered. This, however, did not seem to stop people from bidding. After the bidding passed three million, some voices from above called out their bids, eventually ending at four million.

After a while, a single solution was rolled out, but the screen behind it showed what type of beast the solution came from.

"As you can see in the video, this Altered DNA has great power. This solution is already showing great results in the AFC. This fighter might be a rookie at the moment, but he has been rising through the ranks, so the solution's potential is guaranteed."

The video showed a man transforming into a bull-like creature. It had great strength, and horns grew out the top of its head. It also displayed a high amount of endurance when another Altered from the AFC hit it without causing any notable damage.

This . . . this is the one that we should bid on, Kai decided. It should suit Austin perfectly. He was already large and a natural powerhouse when it came to strength.

"The bidding starts at one million!"

Paddles were raised, and almost instantly the price had been boosted to 1.5 million.

For the first time, Kai raised his paddle. There was no need for him to say anything, as each bid would always be 10 percent of the starting bid, meaning that his bid was one hundred thousand dollars more than that of the previous top bidder.

"One point six million to those in the masks!"

"Two million!" Kit shouted, raising his paddle and glancing toward them. "So this is what you were waiting for, huh? Well, let's see who has the deeper pockets."

The masked teenager just raised his paddle, not reacting to the clear provocation.

"Two point five million!" Kit shouted with a smile, not even caring that he had just outbid someone from the top floor.

"Three million!" the same person bid. He wasn't one of the Kings but the leader of a Tier 2 gang; he wouldn't give up easily, not without a fight. This sign that someone important was really interested in the solution made those on the bottom back off, but not Kai.

"Three point five million!" the werewolf stated loudly.

Damn this guy. This is far higher than I wanted to go, and this is for just one solution. I was really hoping that we could buy another one, or other items . . . but who knows when we might get another chance, Kai thought.

"Four million." Kit outbid him without hesitation, and this raise even silenced the Tier 2 gang leader. Sure, this was a rare Altered DNA, but not a super rare one. He could continue, but at this point it was likely that his peers would make fun of him for overpaying. So he simply remained silent.

Is he really that keen on winning one over me? Kai wondered as the auctioneer was about to accept the bid. Swallowing down his reluctance, he raised his paddle, but Kit did the same, making the new bid 4.2 million. The masked teenager let out a regretful sigh and lowered the paddle.

"Sold for four point two million!"

"Ha-ha, is this the best you fools can do? What type of gang are you running? At first I thought you were buying nothing because you were holding back for something, but it turns out you're just a bunch of beggars."

Kai was dying to argue about the stupidity of overpaying for the solution, but he understood that it would just be a waste of time. It would merely make him look like a sore loser. Still, just like many others, he expected that despite all the mysteriousness, the Dark Guild would follow the typical auction scheme of saving the best item for the end of the auction.

With this solution being the first rare one, there were surely more and even better solutions to come. The only issue with that was that if they were too good, the gang wouldn't be able to afford them. In other words, if they wanted to go home with something, they would have to strike soon.

"Okay, folks, to keep things interesting, the next item will be a mystery solution. The Dark Guild can guarantee that this type of Altered DNA has never appeared before. However, everything else is up to chance. It may turn you into a slightly stronger human, or incredibly strong. This is the risk that you'll have to take with this item," the host claimed as he started the bidding.

"Two million!" Kai said straightaway, doubling the starting bid from the get-go. Given the description, he hoped that not too many people would be interested in it, and this move might make it seem even less interesting.

"You know, you really shouldn't have threatened me earlier," Kit sneered. "If you had apologized earlier, I might have even forgiven you, but now I'm going to buy every little thing that you guys want!

"Three million!"

Those who had been slightly interested in the mystery solution were now put off. The real show now became the bidding war between these two gangs who clearly had it out for each other.

"I'm warning you, you better back off." Kai looked straight at him, and his eyes were glowing blue, even fiercer than before. "If you're that keen on crossing us, I'll personally pay your shithole of a town a visit and make sure not a single member of your gang has any limbs left!"

When he opened his mouth to speak, Kai didn't realize that his anger had gotten the better of him, making sharp fangs grow from his mouth, while his nails had turned into claws.

"*Five million!*" Kai shouted at the top of his lungs, turning his voice into a powerful howl.

Seeing this from above, Sin smiled at the sideshow. *Those guys are idiots. Only desperate people would bet on a mystery solution, especially the first one, but I have to admit, that shout was quite intimidating.*

Kai looked toward Kit, his body language telling the gang leader that he would pounce on him the moment he opened his mouth, so he never did.

"Sold for five million to the fellow in the fox mask!"

CHAPTER 54

WHO GETS WHAT?

When the Howlers heard Kai bid their entire budget on the solution, their hearts stopped for a moment. Even after the gavel struck the lectern, they didn't really feel like celebrating. Since Kai was responsible for their finances, they could only hope that their de facto leader had had a good reason for his behavior.

Kai would be lying if he said that his emotions hadn't influenced his action in any way, but it hadn't been fully without logic. Admittedly, it had been a calculated risk, and if someone had bid higher, the Howlers would have been unable to do anything about it. At that point, they might as well have packed their bags, as it would have been the same as admitting that their entire budget was capped at five million.

The werewolf had bet on the fact that the others would be holding out because the Dark Guild was bringing out more and better items each time. With this being the first mystery solution, it was clear that there would be more to come. Had this been the final item, though, then those who wanted to buy something and use the money they had brought with them would just use it anyway, even at the risk of paying for the item itself.

Part of the risk was that he had to trust the Dark Guild that this was truly a never-before-used mystery solution. In that case, even they should be unable to find out what type of Altered one would become if they used it, and thus it would make no difference if they purchased the first or the last one, as it would remain a gamble.

"Kai, did we really have to blow our whole budget on that one Altered solution? We have no idea whether it's good or not. Worst case, we can always get turned," Marie whispered to him as the auction continued.

It was something all of them had considered. After all, Gary had turned Kai and Olivia, so why not them. Of course, after living through the night of the full moon their enthusiasm for becoming werewolves had greatly decreased, but it was nevertheless an option on the table.

"It's far more complicated than that. What happened to us on that day is just the tip of the iceberg." Kai shook his head, able to talk with her about it since she was already aware about the existence of werewolves, and thus was not breaking the last pack rule. "Trust me when I say none of you will want to experience what it feels like. If it hadn't been for the circumstances, Gary wouldn't have turned me, either.

"According to him, there is always a chance of something going wrong, and even if that chance is incredibly low, we don't need to take it if it means risking your lives, especially not when there are other ways to increase our strength!"

Of course, there were other reasons for their refusal of turning the rest of the Howlers. It was safe to assume that those in Tier 1 cities, at least the core members who belonged to the top gangs, were all Altered. Admittedly, the werewolves' bodies seemed strong and comparable to that of a good Altered, but every gang could use some variety.

Different Altered forms meant a diverse portfolio of strength. What one Altered could do, another couldn't. They backed each other up, creating a horrifying team, and the Howlers needed to do the same.

What's more, if all their members were werewolves, it could invite a different set of trouble.

The bids continued, and the Dark Guild kept everyone on their toes by mixing known Altered solutions with mystery ones, keeping everyone guessing how much of each they might have. Just as Kai had predicted, it didn't take long for the final bids to cross the five million mark. It wasn't the exact Altered Solution they wanted, but it was something, and it could even turn out better than what they originally wished to get.

"Fine people, with this item, today's auction has come to an end," the host stated. "We thank you for your patronage and we shall inform you about the next auction through our website. We further ask those who have successfully purchased at least one item today to remain in the auction house so we can finish the formalities."

The doors opened and everyone began to exit. Many groups left with disappointed looks on their faces, with some even muttering that it would be better for them to go to a smaller auction in the future, where there would be fewer people with high amounts of money.

In total, fifty-three sets of items had been sold today, and yet only about sixteen groups stayed behind, two of them containing Kings, though Sin wasn't one of them. In a place like this, certain groups were just more dominant with their financial situation. If Kai had tried to remain conservative with their money, the Howlers would have ended up with nothing.

"Please come to the stage, where we will give you the details to send the money into our accounts. Once we have verified that your payment has gone through, your items will be delivered to you in person," the host explained, now surrounded by the other staff members to prevent anyone from trying something stupid.

Kai stood up with the others, and so did the No Land Gang, and they walked down the staircase toward the stage. This was a chance for him to check out the Kings who had purchased a few items.

Walking down was a mountain of a man whose former muscles were now hidden under his large belly. He was dressed in a red robe, and the crown on his head was the only item that made one associate him with the term *King.*

This man called himself King Henry, though most assumed it was a fake name. Nevertheless, he was one of the few Kings who showed themselves in public. Some even theorized that Henry's dress code, coupled with his actions in his prime that had led to him taking over one of the Tier 1 cities, had coined the term *Kings* in the first place.

As for the other King, Kai had no idea who she was. The woman was wearing a small black leather jacket; she had long legs in tight-fighting trousers and dark boots. Strangely, she had a majestic aura as she strutted forward in her purple lipstick, her casual gait treating everyone as if they were beneath her.

There was no one else with her, which was the strangest thing. The only reason why Kai suspected her to be a King was the way even King

Henry seemed to treat her as an equal. Was she just that confident with everyone around her?

It was hard to say, although one might be confident in the Dark Guild's presence. It wasn't the same and if this person was a leader, or even if she wasn't, she could be dealt with easily without anyone even knowing.

When they all had reached the stage, the two largest groups were the Howlers and the No Land Gang, who had brought along more than just one or two bodyguards like the rest. That was also where they made eye contact with Blake Hunt, who had two others with him as well, although both of them seemed quite a bit older than Blake himself.

"Please use your phones to scan the QR code we've prepared for you. It will take you to a site with the total amount you owe us. Once confirmed, one of the staff will deliver your item."

Everyone did as asked, and honestly it was hard for Kai to sign away this amount of money, but in the end he had made the choice. Pressing his hand up against his ear, the host nodded with a smile on his face, and members of the Dark Guild appeared from behind the curtain with the items. Some of them had to get their items in crates since there were so many.

However, the Howlers didn't care about the others so much; instead they were focused on what was in front of them. The mystery solution was in a small, shiny metal container.

As soon as they had the solution, the group exited the auction house with no problems.

Kai had warned them not to stay too long, as he had a feeling that either the No Land Gang or the Altered Hunters might be looking for a fight.

"Tyler, go grab the car, and let's get out of here."

In the end, they left the auction house and later the city with no trouble, and all of them couldn't stop staring at the syringe with the strange liquid inside.

"At least we got one solution out of it . . . but who should be the one to use it?" Innu asked. "After all, we have no way of finding out what's inside, and it's not like we can try again if it turns out to be garbage."

CHAPTER 55

THE ONE-STAR HUNTER

It wasn't too long ago that Blake had become a one-star Hunter, thus officially joining the Altered Hunters. Of course, now that he was officially recognized as one of their members, there were certain responsibilities on his shoulders.

No longer was he able to just travel and piggyback with his father doing hunts in the local area. In the first place, Ozacas Hunt was away more often, being called by the organization for important tasks involving the mysterious black liquid.

This was one of the responsibilities of being an Altered Hunter, to always answer when they call you, and it was why Blake was where he was now.

Of course, Hunters could choose where they wished to live, and they could also act as they saw fit, as long as they followed certain guidelines, but the guidelines weren't the law.

However, now as a one-star Hunter, Blake could be called out for tasks that were planned by the leader and the other five-star Hunters, and that was why he was currently in the Dark Guild's auction house in Morfran.

Currently standing onstage waiting for the items they had bought were Blake, another one-star Hunter, and a three-star Hunter. This was the first time he was working with these people. They had only been told about the great task that they would have to accomplish today.

The other one-star Hunter was a university student who was a little older than Blake. He was taller than him, at a height of around six foot four, with black hair and a serious look on his face even now. The young adult had introduced himself as Kane, and unlike Blake, his promotion wasn't as recent, making him his senior, despite sharing the same number of stars.

Then there was Josh, the three-star Hunter in his mid-twenties. Unlike the serious Kane, he seemed to be far more amiable, always having a smile on his face, and coupled with his light brown hair parted down the middle he had the appearance of a charming gentleman.

These people had been selected for the auction because they were relatively new members of the Altered Hunter Association. Although all Altered Hunters were required to wear masks during their nightly outings, it was impossible to guarantee that they would stay on during fights.

The more senior members knew that their faces had been passed around to the higher-tier gangs. This made it impossible for them to attend the auction, though they didn't want to cause trouble during it in the first place. So who better than to send a few harmless-looking young members to buy a few new weapons.

So far they had achieved their task; the first part had gone smoothly, but while Blake was standing on the stage, his hands started to sweat a little.

This is my first time going on a group outing. I have to do well. No doubt my father will hear about this, Blake thought.

Having been focused on his task during the auction, he was only now really looking at the people around him. With the crowd clearing out, he saw the familiar black-and-gold uniform of some of the other people on the stage.

Those are the same colors that Gary and his gang would always wear.

Looking at the masks on their faces, Blake couldn't help but gulp. He and the fox-masked leader made eye contact with each other. It lasted for just a moment, but the young Altered Hunter was sure that they knew each other.

Why . . . why did you guys have to come here? Why now of all times? Is Gary with you? Blake wondered. *Without him, you guys might be in a lot of trouble, and I can't help you.*

Seeing them made Blake think back to the meeting before he entered Morfran.

Back in Slough, Blake had been called upon, and he was to wait at home at his father's dojo. He was pacing back and forth after he had prepared a table along with a few chairs.

He was nervous because he was meant to be meeting quite a few people from the Altered Hunter Association today, and they had chosen his place as the meeting area.

Blake had been given only a few details; they were meeting in Slough because it was on the way to their actual destination, Morfran. Eventually, the speaker in the dojo sounded, indicating that someone was at the door.

Walking through his relatively large front garden, Blake checked the camera on the door and saw five people present. Immediately he opened the door and bowed to them all.

"It is my pleasure to meet all of you, seniors. I will do my best to make your stay here as comfortable as possible," Blake greeted them.

"You can raise your head, for starters," Josh the three-star Hunter replied with a friendly smile. "There's no need for all that formality. We're all friends here, so you can relax a bit."

Blake was happy to see that there were Hunters close to his age. In fact, everyone on the team looked quite young. While he led the group out to the dojo, they all introduced themselves.

Aside from Kane and Josh, who was the leader of the group, there were three two-star Hunters. It was a little strange, as Josh looked younger than one of them.

But it reminded Blake that not everything was about age; it was also about skill and talent, and the stars just indicated that Josh had the talent to kill a number of different Altered. After the introductions were done, each of them sat down and Josh's smiley face had gone to quite a serious tone.

"Now, all of you have been briefed on the task. We are to head to Morfran and buy supplies for the Altered Hunter Association. They have given me a budget and a set of requirements, so you guys can let me deal with that.

"The only thing you need to keep in mind is to avoid trouble. The best way to do that is to stay at my side and to remain silent."

This was part of the task that Blake already knew, but he was no idiot. If that was the only thing they were attempting to do, then there would be no need for six Altered Hunters to be sent on this task.

"The association wants to test the waters a bit. Because of how big this event will be, they're sure that quite a few new gangs will turn up. We'll be ignoring the established gangs and keeping an eye on the up-and-comers. They'll be the ones to improve their strength the most by buying supplies, and of course Altered solutions.

"Our main goal is to do our best to get rid of these new gangs by eliminating at least their leaders and if possible the entire gang. However, there is a good chance that we will be unable to do so with our current strength.

"If it proves to be too much of a hassle to take them out, plan B will be to focus on stealing their Altered solutions, so we can at least cripple their growth. After we've achieved that goal, we'll flee and meet at the predetermined location later."

Blake looked toward Kane to see if the other one-star Hunter was nervous about the situation. Judging from what Josh had said, there was a chance they could be going up against more than one Altered Hunter together.

On top of that, they would be in Morfran.

"We will only target those who buy Altered solutions from the event. We also will only target the new groups, since for a lot of you this will be a first experience. If there are no groups that I think we are capable of taking out, then we will not proceed with the task, understand?"

Everyone nodded, and Josh pulled out a few thick sheaves of paper. It was information on the newly rising gangs, and he handed the paper out to each of them so they could be updated on the situation.

"Now, there is a chance that some of these gangs will not even appear at the auction. Or perhaps they'll be unable to buy the Altered solutions, but I want you to go over the proposed plan of what we are to do, and keep up with all the possibilities."

Everyone was silent as they worked through the sheets of paper, looking at all the information.

The No Land Gang is a Tier 4 gang; there is a star stating that this is most likely one of our targets . . . and it looks like there is another star on another gang, Blake noticed.

He looked at the names and the descriptions given. It stated at the top that one of their targets was a gang that called themselves the Howlers.

CHAPTER 56

THE HUNTERS CHOOSE

Given the information provided on the gangs, it appeared that the Howlers had been selected because they were deemed a relatively easy target. For one, there was only one confirmed Altered in their group, and that was Gary. They had his appearance and still frames from the filming that day, along with a few details here and there. When Blake saw their name, he could only hope that they wouldn't come to the auction.

Reality was often disappointing, and there was nothing the young Altered Hunter could do after the gang had stayed behind to pay for their purchased Altered solution. It might have been different had they bought nothing, or simply weapons, but their single purchase had, unfortunately, put them on today's radar.

After everyone received their items, the Altered Hunters proceeded to leave the venue on black motorbikes that they had used for today's trip. They were not only stylish, but more importantly, they had been tinkered with to allow them to reach a speed surpassing the average car while fitting two people on each one.

On top of that, their weapons were placed in cases that hung from the sides of the bikes for easy access. After exiting the auction house, the three of them met up with the other half of the team, stopping on a side street and entering an alleyway together.

"Okay," Josh said, blowing out a big breath. "Two groups on our list have purchased an Altered solution. Usually, those gangs plan to stay here for a couple of days. The city is currently full of influential groups, gangs, and corporations, making this a prime opportunity to make connections.

"Since we don't know how long they will stay here, we'll have to act fast, especially since we want to avoid attracting another group's attention. Should we go for the No Land Gang or the Howlers?" Josh asked.

Everyone seemed to be deep in thought, but given that he knew at least some of their members, Blake obviously didn't want to go after the Howlers. He and Gary had worked together in the past, so he felt like he at least owed it to him to try to make his group consider going for the other option.

Blake knew that he would someday have to fight Gary, since he was believed to be a Wolf Altered. It was impossible for him to correct that mistake in thinking, at least not without any proof or admitting that he had worked with the "enemy."

"I think it would be for the best to go for the No Land Gang," Blake suggested. Josh raised an eyebrow, his sign for the youngest member of their group to elaborate.

"The Howlers might all have been wearing masks, but according to our information their leader is known to be wearing a black-and-gold wolf mask. The one who bid on the items and accepted them, though, was someone in a fox mask. In other words, at the moment their group has no Altered with them.

"Our main goal as Altered Hunters is to fight Altered, ridding the world of them before they become crazed and cause more harm than good. Like our ancestors did in the past with beasts.

"Taking down a gang of normal people is not the Altered Hunter Association's goal, but police work."

Blake spoke strongly and passionately, and they felt that he had a point, but there was also an opposing opinion.

"Isn't that a good reason to go for them, though?" Kane asked. "I mean, if their leader isn't with them, then there is less risk involved for us. Without an Altered stopping us, it will be child's play getting their solution and destroying it, completing our task."

Blake hadn't considered that, and now he was worried because he had to agree that Kane had a good point. Judging by the other Hunters, it was more likely that Josh would take the easier approach. The three-star Hunter was considering both opinions.

"Kane is right . . . but so is Blake. Taking away their solution will not get us any closer to earning our stars. According to the information, there is one Altered here today in the No Land Gang. If they have already used the solution that they have just received, then it will be two Altered. There is a chance for all of us to get closer to a promotion.

"There won't be many opportunities like this," the older two-star Hunter said. "We have to have some backbone if we want to rise."

Blake was thankful this was relatively a young group, because the younger members of the Altered Hunter Association always wanted to improve themselves and climb the ladder in the organization. It was the same for Blake, but given the circumstances, he wanted to avoid fighting one side.

"All right, I have heard your opinions on the matter . . ." Josh continued. "And honestly it's not a simple decision. At the end of the day, it's not just my life but yours as well that we would be risking, so I want to take that into account. "Which is why we'll decide this by majority vote. I'll accept whatever decision the five of you come to."

Blake gulped. It all came down to this, and just in case, he needed to create a backup plan.

The Howlers didn't want to waste their first visit to a Tier 1 city, and Kai had promised a certain someone that they would visit a particular area before they returned to Slough, which was why they were currently in the main shopping district in Morfran. The group stood at one end, in complete awe, with their mouths open. They saw all the stylish people walking down the street, wearing clothes that shouted *Look at me.*

On top of that, the street itself was super impressive. The ground was paved with marble and there wasn't a speck of dust or grime on it. It reflected the sunlight, making it sparkle even more, and the shopping malls were no different, large and palatial. Marie found the place so beautiful that it brought a tear to her eye.

"I know it looks really cool and all, but do you really have to cry?" Innu asked.

"You don't understand. Just going to a shopping area where there are dozens of people around, it makes me feel so free," she said, smiling and hugging herself with excitement, but that excitement soon dwindled down. "And . . . we can't even afford to buy anything."

"There's no use looking at me. I've already told you, the gang's funds will be sparse the next few months. Besides, all of you get paid, so it's time to use that money," Kai complained.

This caused the rest of the group to stare at him deeply, because their pay for being core members wasn't exactly the best. It was similar to working a normal nine-to-five job in Slough; it certainly wasn't the high-life treatment that the main members of the Underdogs had enjoyed.

Kai had cut corners to save as much money as he could, and he knew that those closest to him would be able to take the hit better than the others. If he tried cutting the pay Olivia's gang members had grown used to, there would be an uproar and they could forget about loyalty. Coincidentally, it was for this reason that Olivia was actually one of the best-paid members of their group.

"If you really see something you like, I'm happy to pitch in and help you buy it," Austin said. "I don't really have any need for my money in the first place, and I think you would be happier with it."

Marie was so over the moon with these words, she felt like she could kiss Austin right now. She took his hand and thanked him, and looked over toward Innu.

"If you're expecting me to do the same, you must be crazy. Did you forget that I'm using my money to look after Kevin and Suzan? And despite all my complaints, Kai won't raise my pay!"

After a bit of back-and-forth, the group decided to let Marie drag them around through the shops. Kai stated that it was best if they stayed together, and so the gang ended up going to a lot of shops and got tired of looking at clothes and more clothes.

At first, they enjoyed seeing the shopping mall and the robots that would guide you to certain places, but it was extremely tiring and after trying on lots of clothes, Marie had simply bought a small red purse.

However, the guys understood because even with Austin's money, it was the only thing she could really afford without going broke.

After a full day of shopping, the sun was starting to set and it would soon be dark out, so they returned to the car. Tyler was ready to drive them home, as their visit to Morfran had come to an end, and they were ready to return to Slough.

The whole group was in the limo, traveling across a large bridge that went over the river. They saw the lights turn on in all the buildings as the sky turned dark, and it was extremely beautiful.

The bridge was mostly empty, as there didn't seem to be a lot of people going in or out of Morfran, as they headed toward the tunnel. The Tier 1 cities were certainly different compared to the rest of the cities.

As they drove along the long bridge, they heard the sound of a high-revved engine. In the rearview mirror, Tyler saw something coming up behind them very fast. He decided to slow down because he didn't want to get in an accident.

"Who is driving so fast, and at night? Do they want to get in an accident?" Tyler mumbled to himself.

Kai turned his head to see what was making that noise, but it quickly passed them. That was when they noticed it was a motorbike. After getting in front of Tyler, though, it skidded to the side and stopped right in front of the limo.

"What the hell?" Tyler shouted as he slammed on the brakes, forcing the car to come to a halt about five yards away from the person on the bike.

"I don't like this one bit," Kai stated. "Get ready to drive away at any second."

CHAPTER 57

AN ALLY OR A FOE

With the motorbike coming to a halt while it was dark outside, it was clear the person was here for them. Since he had waited for the group to be in a secluded area, and at a time like this, it was safe to say that this person was looking for trouble, or at least didn't want to be seen.

Kai looked around to see if there were others. *I have a bad feeling about this, but whoever this is, if there is only one of them, there will be no trouble at all. I doubt that they know about me or the fact that I am the ace in the hole for the Howlers. I just didn't think that I might have to step up so soon.*

However, since the person on the motorbike kept their helmet on, Kai had one dreaded thought: What if this was one of the Kings after them? What if right in front of them, right now, was Sin? If that was the case, then it would be better for them to retreat immediately and get away.

Thinking about that, Kai imagined that Sin could just explode their car with a single snap of his fingers.

"Keep your foot on the gas, Tyler. Worst case, just run this guy over," Kai ordered. No matter who the person was, if things turned hostile, they wouldn't go down without fighting back.

However, Kai's words made Tyler gulp because he wasn't sure he could go through with such a thing. Sure, he knew what his position was now, but to actually attempt to hurt someone wasn't the job he had originally signed up for. Still, if his life was in danger, then he might just have to.

Slowly, the man removed his helmet, revealing dark, wavy hair underneath. Innu sighed with relief when he saw the man's face.

"It's just Blake," he said.

"What do you mean, it's just Blake?" Marie frowned. "Isn't that a bad thing? Did you forget he's with the Altered Hunters at the moment? Doesn't that mean he might be after us?"

This was one of Kai's guesses as well: that the Altered Hunters would go after those who were here for the auction. The only thing was, with so many gangs crowding the place, Kai had believed their gang would most likely not catch anyone's eye.

Wait a second, why is Blake alone? Even though Gary isn't here, he couldn't possibly think of taking us on alone, right? Kai frowned.

On the other hand, Blake continued to stare at them while standing in the middle of the street, which was why Kai had decided to open the door.

"Hey, hey, what are you doing? Do you want to back up? Should we stay in the car or what?" Innu asked.

"Just stay in the car for now," Kai replied as he closed the door and walked up to Blake.

The others were interested in what was going to happen and why Blake was there, so they rolled down the car windows slightly so they could overhear the conversation.

"If you wanted to talk to us, then you could have arranged a meeting back in Slough." Kai began with a bit of a lighthearted comment because he needed to see where Blake was.

Blake shook his head before answering.

"This discussion couldn't be delayed. I had to meet you about this because I have been told you're a smart guy, Kai. Gary always spoke highly of you, and I'm sure that you probably don't trust me, but the matter at hand is serious and you must trust me. I just want to ask one thing: do you mind if I see the solution that you bought?" he asked as he held out his hand.

When he did so, he seemed to wince a little from the strain on his injured arm.

"You want the Altered solution?" Kai raised an eyebrow and stared at Blake to see if he was joking.

For a second, Kai even wondered if Blake was trying to take him for a ride. Did an Altered Hunter just ask for the solution out in the open? Was this some kind of prank?

Or is this his way of telling me that he doesn't want to fight? That he will let us go if we just give him the Altered solution? I guess then he can go to his teammates and tell them he did the job he was meant to do.

"I'm sorry, Blake. I know you helped us out before in the past," Kai said. "But we have a lot of targets on our backs. Gary has a lot of targets on his back, including from you guys. If you're his friend, you should understand that we can't just sit by and let him bear all the burden."

Blake hesitated for a moment but eventually put his hand down.

"You don't have to give it to me. Just show it to me," Blake replied. "I will stay here and have a look. I just want to let you know that I am looking out for you guys."

There was a lot in Kai's favor, and since he was sure Blake still didn't know about him, he took the solution out from under his blazer and lifted it up for Blake to see.

"Is this what you wanted? I'm afraid until you give me a good reason, I can't just give you a closer look," Kai said.

"Fine," Blake replied, partially annoyed and looking down the motorway as if he was expecting someone. "The Altered Hunters are after the solution sold by the Dark Guild for a reason. Also, if you haven't noticed, the number of crazed Altereds has increased in recent times.

"After the attack on Slough, the Altered Hunters are trying to find the source of the Altered solution that causes people to go crazy. It is the association's top priority. It is unlikely that something like this is coming from corporations such as NIRV, which is why we have been looking into the solutions from the Dark Guild.

"There is an easy way to tell at the moment if the solution is different compared to others. Inside there is a dark substance; it can be a small amount or large, but it will slightly tint the color. What stands out about it, though, is that it moves as if it's alive. I can't see that well from this far, but your solution seems to be okay.

"Now that I am done here, I will take my leave," Blake said as he walked back to his bike and started to put his helmet back on.

"Wait!" Kai hesitated for a moment and said, "Thank you for the advice. Your arm hurts, right?"

Blake didn't say anything, but he could feel the pain, and some blood had already dripped down his sleeve onto his helmet.

"I don't know what you have been through, but I know that you are already helping us more than you should. Warning us, and I guess stopping the others in your group from coming after us. Blake, this might sound like a shot in the dark, but I do have a question to ask you," Kai said.

"Why don't you join us?"

Everyone in the limo let out a loud gasp. They had been listening to the conversation the entire time, but they never expected Kai to ask an Altered Hunter to join their group.

I guess Kai is always one step ahead of everyone. It wouldn't surprise me if he had already been thinking something along these lines for a while, Marie thought.

"Ha!" Blake chuckled. "First of all, it's naive of you to think I want to leave. My family have been involved in the Hunter business for much longer than you think. This isn't something that I can just give up.

"And besides, even if I do join you, then what? The Altered Hunter Association would not just come after me but after your gang as well. There is no one who can protect me."

With those words said, Blake put his helmet on prepared to drive off.

On the other hand, despite getting a straightforward rejection, Kai wore a large smile.

"So are you saying once we get big enough to protect you, so that even the Altered Hunters won't touch us, then you would join? Well, it's a deal."

It was unclear if Blake had heard these words or not as he started his bike and headed straight past Kai, after leaving them with a few final words.

"You better get out of here now. I can't stop them," Blake muttered as he drove off.

CHAPTER 58

SKILLED HUNTER

Blake rode his motorcycle back down the highway and across the bridge, heading to the meeting place they had agreed on. On the way, he was trying to come up with a believable excuse without implicating himself. Clenching the handlebars tightly, he was also trying to forget about the injury to his arm.

According to the media, we Altered Hunters are supposed to be the bad guys, but I know that's a lie that people simply believe because they've been told so, Blake thought. *But am I really any better if I believe that every Altered and every person who wants to become one is automatically bad, simply because I've been told that since I was young? Even though I know for sure that Gary and his friends are not like the rest?*

"All right, it's decided then," Josh said with a big smile as he looked at the show of hands. "Since the majority wants to go after the Tier 4 No Land Gang, we'll ignore the Tier 3 Howlers for now. As Blake said, it's not our job to clean up after normal gangs, and we'll focus on the gang who have a confirmed Altered with them."

Blake felt like letting out a sigh of relief, but he controlled himself, not wanting to make it obvious that his opinion was based on more than logic. He was just happy that the older members seemed far more interested in taking down an Altered to advance their own promotion than in simply getting the solution.

The Altered Hunters had their ways of tracking down the gangs, and Josh didn't really explain how they knew their current location. At the moment, the No Land Gang seemed to be heading to the underpass of a bridge.

It went over the river in the city, but underneath it was a walking path, and it was also a popular hangout for some of the younger people. At the same time, according to Josh, the No Land Gang were there to do some type of deal.

It was detailed information, down to even knowing what gang they were going to meet. It seemed impossible to gather this type of information unless they had someone on the inside.

If they know this much about the No Land Gang, then does it mean they also know a lot more about the Howlers than what was on the intel? Blake thought.

There wasn't really a plan; Josh just waited for a while, and then when he said it was the right time, they got on their motorbikes in pairs and rode off toward the location.

At the underpass, a group of eight men, all with dyed green hair and ragged clothing, were walking confidently on the pebble-like surface. They stomped their feet as they walked, and eventually stopped.

The men in back were carrying quite a few things, including some of the Altered weapons, that they had gotten from the auction. They were holding them as if they were ready to use them at any point.

"Come on out!" Kit shouted. "You were the ones who called us out here, remember? At least show up on time, damn it!"

A group of men wearing brown leather clothing appeared from around the corner. There were ten of them, all armed, although just with ordinary weapons.

"Hey, what's the big deal?" Kit asked, not dropping his smile in the least.

The man in the front straightened out his leather jacket a bit before speaking.

"We had a deal," the man began. "We were supposed to pool our money together and split the goods, but how exactly do you plan for us to split a single Altered solution, huh?"

Kit's shoulders shook as he laughed.

"Well, it's simple; you guys should have used your heads a bit more. You should never make a deal with a group that's stronger than you."

Immediately Kit grabbed what looked like a crossbow from one of his own gang members and pulled the trigger. A bolt came shooting out, but the man in front had moved out of the way. Unfortunately, one of his fellow gang members was too slow, and the bolt pierced right through his head, leaving behind a hole and a corpse.

"Kill them all!" the man in the brown jacket shouted, and their fight turned bloody instantly. Knowing full well that the No Land Gang had an Altered among them, the Brown Jackets had brought more people to suppress them.

However, because of the movement restrictions in Morfran, it was impossible for them to bring more in. The fight was scrappy, with faces being punched, bodies being kicked, and rocks being thrown.

Regardless of how dirty the Brown Jackets fought, they soon realized that the Altered weapons, bought with the money that they had supplied as a Tier 4 gang to the No Land Gang, had become their downfall.

With his face covered in blood, Kit had just finished pounding in the face of the leader of the Brown Jackets. His knuckles were as bloody as his smile, and he lifted his head.

"Haha, that makes another territory for the No Land Gang," Kit announced loudly, earning cheers from his men. Suddenly, the gang leader's ears twitched at the sound of something revving in the distance.

It was clearly the sound of several motorbikes racing toward them from above. A few seconds later, the motorbikes landed on the pebbled path and stopped.

Keeping their helmets on, the riders began to pull weapons out of the holders on the sides of their bikes. One had a double-edged sword, another a strange toothlike weapon, a third two red blades, and the fourth had a sword that looked to be made of bones from the handle down. It was the weapon that they had seen at the auction.

"Well, I can't say I didn't expect others to come after us," Kit said. "It's clear that you want our items for yourselves, but you will end up just like them."

One of his gang members fired a crossbow toward the guys in the masks. Josh started to move out of the way of the bolt, but before he could, Blake dove in and struck the bolt down with his red sword, eager to prove himself and show off his skills.

Is Blake really just a newly advanced one-star Hunter? What he did was skillful, with perfect timing and a strong powerful strike. He is one to watch out for, Josh thought.

Meanwhile, Blake's move had shocked Kit and the No Land Gang. Their faces dropped as they realized that these guys weren't going to be as easy as the Brown Jackets.

Instantly the young Altered Hunter charged in and avoided a spear attack, knocking it away with one sword and attacking with the other, making a strike at his opponent's chest.

"I can see them again, these white lines that show me my opponent's strike path and the best place to attack."

Blake was back in the zone, just like when he had fought against Billy. He had tried reaching it during his training, but he had never been able to achieve it . . . until now.

Another member came toward him with a ball and chain. It had an electrified end, but the white line showed Blake where to strike. His blade hit the middle of the chain, causing the ball to wrap around and cut short. Then he pulled his sword back, forcing the gang member to let go of his weapon. Blake prepared to strike again, but the other one-star Hunter thrust his spear forward, stabbing the man in the stomach.

It was a quick strike, and more importantly, the Altered Hunter's footsteps were so silent that Blake didn't even hear him approach.

"Hey, you're doing good, kid," Josh said. "Let us take care of the extras. Why don't you take care of the leader there, and be careful, okay, because remember he's an Altered."

CHAPTER 59

GROWING QUICKLY

The Altered Hunters were used to fighting Altered. It was their main task and what they trained for, and on top of that, most of the group were two-star Hunters. Although the gang was using Anti-Altered equipment, it just wasn't the same quality.

For one, their weapons were enhanced with electrical power that anyone could use, but with real Anti-Altered weapons, one could draw power from them. This was a technique that anyone could learn; however, those weapons were expensive, and the Altereds were trying to collect them.

Because of this, fighting everyday gang members, especially from a Tier 4 city, was relatively easy for the Altered Hunters. There was only one person that they needed to worry about. With his teammates fighting with the rest of the gang members, Blake was now face-to-face with Kit, the leader of the No Land Gang.

"You think I'm as easy as the rest of the guys? Well, that's where you're dead wrong!" Kit shouted as he threw a punch. It was fast, but Blake was faster; he dodged the punch and in return he dashed in and struck Kit's body with his sword.

It ripped through his clothes, but Kit was wearing some type of leather armor underneath. He seemed surprised because the armor had been scratched as well.

"I should have known you guys aren't some wannabe gang that wants to take us down. You're Altered Hunters!" Kit shouted. "Well, you have come to the right place, boys!"

Most of the men had been beaten and were on the floor. The Altered Hunters had actually tried to avoid killing them. Usually when their opponents were willing to kill them they didn't hold back, but the difference in strength and skill meant they could defeat the gang without killing them.

But the gang members were still conscious, and they threw their weapons over to Kit. He stretched himself and suddenly two more arms had sprouted on each side, giving him a total of six.

He grabbed two swords and two spears, keeping his other two hands free so he could deal out physical pain with them.

The report was right! This Altered can create extra limbs, and He's quite skillful at using weapons. This is going to be a bit more difficult.

On top of that, ever since Blake had started to fight against Kit, the white lines had disappeared. He still didn't know why.

Two powerful spear thrusts had gone straight toward Blake, and he had no choice but to use his two red swords to deflect the attack. As he did so, two more swords came down toward him from above.

I have to avoid this.

His quickest option was to roll forward. The spears were still blocking his path, and the sword strikes would probably damage him, even with the Altered armor he was wearing.

But the gang leader chucked two fists toward his head from below, smashing them into his helmet and breaking it, causing him to fall back onto the ground.

"Hey, we're done over here, shouldn't we help him?" Kane, the one-star Hunter, asked. Fighting an Altered would put them a step closer to getting the next star.

"Don't worry, if he needs our help, then we will join in," Josh answered with his foot on top of one of the gang members. "One has to be put in situations like these to grow. It's the kid's time to shine."

Blake was unaware that the rest of his teammates had already dealt with the gang members; he was focused on the opponent in front of him, and at the same time he was frustrated.

What was I doing before, that I'm not doing now? Blake thought.

However, Kit wasn't going to give him time to think by just standing there. He came forward again, thrusting his spears toward Blake, and this time Blake spun his body, using his momentum to knock the spears out of the way. Then he charged in again, shoulder first, and barged into Kit, knocking him back.

With his arms free, Kit tried to grab Blake, but Blake pulled his swords up from below and sliced Kit's hands.

"This is getting annoying!" Kit shouted, dropping the spear in his hand and throwing a hook, hitting Blake in the side of the head, knocking him to the ground and his helmet off.

Seeing this, Kane charged forward; Kit picked up the spear and threw it at Kane. He was a lot faster than Kane had expected, and on top of that, Kane had thought that Kit hadn't been paying attention to the rest of them.

The Hunter had thought he would be able to sneak in and take Kit out, Kane knew instantly that the spear would pierce his body. He just wasn't fast enough.

This person isn't just an Altered, but a skilled one at that. I took him as too little of a threat after taking out the rest of the gang. This one rose up and took over a Tier 4 city, which means his strength could be higher.

Kane was braced himself, but at the last second, a sword hit the spear, sending it to the ground.

"That's one way to test this sword out. It's pretty good if I do say so myself," Josh said, swinging the huge sword with a single hand. "Still, I can tell that your opponent is tougher than we gave him credit for. Do you want a little help?"

Blake was standing at this point, and with his helmet off his face was now in full view.

"What the hell?" Kit said. "You're just a kid!"

"What does that even matter, if I'm going to beat you?" Blake said, charging in again.

This time, when he thrust his spears forward, Blake avoided them by stepping out of reach.

Watching the fight carefully, Josh felt like he already knew who the winner of the fight was going to be. It was clear that Blake was improving at an incredibly fast speed during this fight, and it would only be a matter of time.

"This is going well. It looks like none of us have any injuries, either. At this rate, we might be able to go after the Howlers gang as well," Josh said. "If the information was right, they should be crossing this bridge soon, so it shouldn't be far either."

Blake's heart thumped louder, and for some reason, he could see where to strike on the gang leader once again. Not wanting to lose this moment, he charged in, as he could see the path of Kit's spear.

Although he could avoid it, he imagined that the white line across Kit's neck would be impossible to hit, unless he did one thing. Moving just an inch to the side, he allowed the spear to pierce his arm.

With his other sword he whacked the other weapon away. Finally, leaping forward and slashing vertically with his sword, Blake cut right across Kit's neck before he could do anything with his other weapons, all in one smooth motion.

That was incredibly impressive. This kid is going to go up the stairs in no time, I just know it, Josh thought.

Kit fell to the floor holding his neck, trying to stop the bleeding, but his eyes were starting to fade and it looked like it was the end for him. As the others stepped forward to congratulate him, though, Blake hopped onto one of the bikes and rode away, leaving the rest of the Altered Hunters confused.

"Let's clean up here, and go after Blake. Something is up," Josh ordered.

CHAPTER 60

ONE DAY

Kai and the rest of the Howlers were nervous as they drove back. They had managed to safely exit Morfran without any problems. Even after half an hour, their group continued checking out the back window, expecting to hear motorbikes coming after them. Everyone had heard Blake's warning and it had sent chills down their spine.

"All right, guys. It doesn't look like we'll have to worry about them today," Kai said eventually. "If they wanted to take us on, they should have caught up to us by now. Looks like we owe our little Altered Hunter friend a favor now."

With those words, the others did indeed calm down a little, yet every few minutes one of them still turned around. They only calmed down fully when they were close to home.

I'm happy that you helped us today . . . I just hope you didn't have to pay too steep a price, Kai thought.

Blake's arm was throbbing with pain. Even a layman could tell that he needed a professional to patch him up. The cut on his arm was quite deep, and once his body had stopped producing adrenaline, there wasn't much but willpower that kept him going. In fact, having been on the move, Blake hadn't even noticed just how much blood he had lost.

While he was on the bike, his vision started to turn hazy, his body was beginning to weaken, and he no longer revved the throttle to accelerate. Soon he heard the others approaching, and he could see them in the distance in his mirrors.

I still don't . . . what should I tell them? Blake wondered as he drifted off and the bike started to lean. Fortunately, he had put on the spare helmet, as the bike began to skid across the ground. Just as Blake fell off, another bike went past with no rider on it.

Instead, the person was sliding on the gravel with their specialized boots and grabbed Blake before he hit the ground.

"You stupid kid," Josh berated Blake as he held him in his arms. "If you're injured to this degree, why didn't you just tell me?"

A few moments later, the rest of the Altered Hunters caught up and stopped on the bridge to check the damage.

"What should we do?" one of them asked. "Should we continue on and chase the Howlers? That was the original plan, right?"

Josh looked in the direction that Blake had just come from. It was where the Howlers would have been. Taking off Blake's leather vest and looking at the armor underneath, the leader saw the large cut on his arm but was unable to find any other wounds.

Just why did you run off like that, and why were you heading back toward us? It doesn't look like you had a scuffle with them, and you had a bit of a head start compared to us, the three-star Hunter thought.

After defeating Kit, they also needed to retrieve the Altered solution from him. Their task had been completed, and their rising newcomer was now one step closer to his next promotion.

"As much as I hate leaving things unresolved, we can't just leave Blake like this. Splitting up and going from one fight to another also isn't the best idea. We'll take him to a hospital and focus on recuperating. We can always take the Howlers on another time," Josh declared.

The older Altered Hunters weren't too happy about that decision, but nobody complained. One of them produced a first-aid kit, and with their basic knowledge they bandaged Blake's arm. After that, the group exited Morfran and headed for the closest Tier 2 city to get more professional treatment for Blake.

They needed to head to a place that wouldn't raise too many questions. They were sure that it would take some time until news reached the Dark Guild about what had happened. The guild would certainly be in a tight spot. They had always boasted about the safety of their auction, yet several members from two gangs had died right underneath their noses . . .

The Altered Hunters changed out of their armor into more normal clothes. At the hospital, nobody suspected them to be anything but normal citizens. Some of them looked bored, but Josh was keeping his eye on the TV screen.

"We interrupt this program to bring you breaking news. The Altered Hunters have struck today. Their calling card has been left at the scene of the crime, where members of Morfran's police force are investigating with the help of White Rose.

"The gangs that were targeted were known as the Brown Jackets and the No Land Gang, a newly rising gang that had recently taken over a Tier 4 city to . . ."

The news report went on, and of course, no one from the Dark Guild had made a public comment, since the actions themselves were a secret known only to its members.

I hope this has the effect that you're looking for, Blake. It's the first time something like this has been done, Josh thought as he tried to understand his task.

"Visitors for Billy Hunter may now enter his room," a nurse with a clipboard called out. Josh immediately headed into the room to see Blake still alive and kicking.

"Thank you so much for saving my life, leader," Blake said with a still-weak voice. "I am sorry for causing you trouble and inconvenience."

Josh looked at him and let out a deep sigh, relieved that his injured team member would survive without any permanent injuries. "Remember, there was a chance that we would not have to attack anyone on this trip. The whole thing was a huge success. We took out an Altered and managed to get the solution as well.

"However, what I do want to know is what exactly happened? Why did you go off like that?"

Blake had been awake for a little while, but the doctors and nurses were still doing a few checks on him. Altered Hunters were stronger than the average human, but as non-Altered, they unfortunately lacked the supernatural healing factor.

Blake's arm had needed about twenty stitches. Regardless, he'd had a lot of time to think about how to answer Josh's question.

"I wanted to take out the Howlers as well, for myself," Blake answered. "I don't know what happened, but while I was fighting, there was something different about me this time. I could feel myself getting stronger."

Blake paused for a second as he turned to Josh.

"When you're fighting, have you ever seen those . . . lines?" Blake asked. Josh raised an eyebrow.

"When I'm fighting, it feels like someone, or my own mind, is telling me where to strike. It shows me the path where a weapon will go, and it shows me the best place to strike as well.

"I only see these lines sometimes, but today I saw them again, and because of that, I thought I could get a head start on finding the Howlers. But when I got to them, my body was starting to feel weak.

"I'm guessing it must have been a loss of energy or something, but I could feel that I wasn't up to the task and that the white lines would no longer be there."

This was Blake's answer, mixing in some truth with a few lies, and it sounded plausible because it would be a reason for him to jump the gun.

"I see," Josh said. "I think I have heard about this before. Maybe when I head back, I will speak to management about this and see if anyone else has any information. Don't worry about the Howlers. Sooner or later you're bound to get your chance . . . just promise me you won't go at it on your own."

This was what Blake was partially worried about. The Altered Hunters were now clearly targeting the Howlers. It couldn't be helped, as they now had an Altered solution, making them even more troublesome in the Altered Hunters' eyes.

"They're from your hometown, Slough, right? When the time comes, you'll most likely be the one we'll call to deal with them," Josh said to cheer him up.

Blake didn't know what to say to that. Although he had gotten away with not taking out the Howlers today, it felt like his actions had merely delayed their execution date. The worst part was that he was now the one who was supposed to wield the axe.

Only time could tell whether he would be able to follow through on that order . . .

CHAPTER 61

A NEW ALTERED IN THE HOWLERS

After a tense ride back, the group's destination in Slough was unsurprisingly the Wolf's Pool Club. Although it was rather late, there were still more than a dozen people around the pool tables, though none of them were teens. While the business continued to be a popular hangout spot for teenage delinquents, during the evening it had turned into a bit of a meeting spot for university students and young adults.

Austin's three friends who earned extra cash as waiters during the day had already clocked in, though they were now playing a round of pool free of charge. Meanwhile, the ever-popular hostess White continued doing her job, helped by Miss Degrace, who often chipped in during the evenings and acted as a bartender.

Although she had started selling alcohol, there had yet to be a fight breaking out. Then again, the locals knew that the pool club was connected to the Howlers. Of course, nobody knew that the gang used this place as their de facto headquarters.

"Make sure no one follows us downstairs," Kai said to Miss Degrace. "Tyler, you've done a great job. Here's some extra cash. Feel free to have a drink and go home. I'll call you when we'll need your services again."

When they reached the refurbished office in the basement of the club, everyone sat on the sofas except for Kai, who sat at the table and placed the Altered solution in front of everyone.

"Now that we don't have any Altered Hunters on our heels, we should resume our earlier discussion about who gets the solution," Kai began. "Do consider that becoming an Altered will definitely place a giant target on your back, so you should do your best to grow in strength as much as possible.

"Of course, that also applies for those of you who don't get the solution this time. Aside from the Altered Hunters, other groups will also be out to get us. They might be from the lower-tier towns, or the higher-tier cities, and heck, there are still the other gangs and the mayor here in Slough."

Kai glanced at a few letters that lay on the table, most likely left there by the lawyer who used to work for the Pincers gang but was now part of the Howlers.

Kai had given him a lot of tasks, and he was keen to look through the letters. However, this was more important.

"Originally, the plan was to give the Altered solution to the person it suits best, but seeing that we had to purchase a mystery solution, that's not really a choice. Since we don't know what type of Altered solution will be inside, we have to come up with something else. I feel silly asking this since we have no idea when we'll be able to get another one, but would one of you voluntarily pass this time around?"

The room was dead silent, with everyone's eyes darting around the room.

Come on, guys, just give up! Didn't we talk about this before? I was the first to join the gang, so I should get to be the first one to pick! Innu thought.

I could really do with the Altered DNA. However, we don't know if it's strong or weak, but whatever it is, I could improve my strength. But then what about the gang?

"It should go to the strongest," Austin said, with his arms folded. "This group needs to get stronger. It's not about putting everyone at an equal level. So I think it should go to the strongest, which is clearly me."

It was the most words they had heard come out of Austin in a while, so it was clear that he wanted the solution quite badly. Just as it looked like everyone was getting ready to fight over it, Marie raised her hand.

"I'll pass," she said. "Like Austin said, it's in the gang's interest to make sure we're the strongest we can be. Giving me a mystery solution won't accomplish that. I have been practicing every day using the Anti-Altered daggers that we received from the Underdogs, so I don't mind waiting a bit longer.

"I have even practiced using ranged weapons like their crossbow. I can help out in my own way, but if possible I'd prefer supporting you from the back rather than from the front line, so I think you guys deserve it more," she said with a sweet smile.

"In that case, don't mind if I do!" Austin was ready to grab the solution.

"Hey, you oaf, did you forget about me?" Innu stood up and grabbed Austin's hand before he could reach the tube.

While the two of them bickered, Marie felt Kai's hand on her shoulder. "Thank you for being a lot more sensible than those two idiots. Don't worry, Marie, I'll do my best to make sure your kindness gets repaid someday soon. In the meantime, you can be sure that all three of us will do our best to protect you.

"As for you two overgrown children," Kai said, clapping his hands to get their attention. "It's obvious that neither one of you will budge, so let's do it the good old-fashioned way. One match, no rules, winner gets all."

Suddenly the two of them were outside. Since they had just come back from the Tier 1 city it was late at night and the sky was dark. But they weren't the only people outside.

All the customers, Austin's friends, and White and Miss Degrace had joined them. In total, about twenty-five people had formed a circle and were ready to watch the fight.

"All right, everyone!" Kai shouted. "These two have a little dispute that they would like to solve, and since neither one is a talker, this is the way it goes.

"On the left side, our dark-skinned friend is a Muay Thai street fighter who has won a number of underground fights. On the right side, this giant fellow used to be the leader of the few schools in the area, able to blow away most of his enemies in a single punch. This will be a close match, so please place your bets now."

Kai would never miss an opportunity to make some money, and he started to gather bets from the onlookers. As a nice bonus, the betting might help spread the word about the pool club and earn them a few more customers.

"What the hell? Why are my odds that much worse than Austin's? Are you saying I'm going to lose this?" Innu shouted in protest.

"Don't blame me. Most people here believe in Austin, making you the underdog of this fight. It's on you to prove them wrong, Innu. If you need any extra motivation . . . well, you know what's on the line."

CHAPTER 62

FIGHT FOR THE PRIZE (PART 1)

Austin and Innu readied themselves for the fight ahead. Innu had gotten into his usual fighting stance and surprisingly Austin had as well, putting both of his fists out like a boxer.

"I guess that means you're really serious about this thing, huh?" Innu said. "You just can't let me have anything. Well, I guess I'm just going to have to earn this myself."

Austin didn't say anything but just clenched his fists harder. Seeing this situation made Austin think back.

Every day, the two of them had a morning training session, as requested by Kai. When they decided to leave their respective schools, they continued to train. Instead of one training session a day they had upped it to two.

During their everyday training sessions, though, Austin realized that Innu was a monster, especially when it came to anything to do with his legs. Innu was able to lift more with his lower body; he was also able to mentally deal with more pressure. On top of that he was more hardworking than Austin as well.

It was clear when watching him that the strength Innu had achieved was from hard work. He was used to this type of training, honing his skill and technique in fighting, whereas Austin was a natural fighter. He had been naturally gifted with a large body, and he had a hard punch that could knock down most students his age and size with one hit. He had never had to train before to take out the delinquents around him.

However, watching Innu train had unlocked his competitive side. Because they were in the same gang, it wasn't as if they could have an all-out fight. So the only way they could compete was through hard work and training.

It was grueling at first; there were aches and pains that Austin had never felt before, but soon he was catching up to Innu. The thing was, Innu saw this as well. Innu had always believed that if they were to fight, it would be a close match.

Now that Austin was training, it worried Innu, but he only upped his training even more.

However, training wasn't the only thing the two of them competed in. Kai had often sent the two of them on tasks. Shortly after the Howlers had taken over Slough, a few troubles arose here and there down the streets that were owned by the gang.

Some of them involved gang members, and others just involved rowdy students, and it was the Howlers' job to prevent trouble in the first place.

"You know I can deal with it myself," Innu said as they walked down the street one night toward a trouble spot.

"I can too; I'm just doing what Kai ordered," Austin replied.

When they arrived at the bakery that was being harassed, there were ten adults holding mainly bats, but a few other weapons as well. Seeing this, Innu gulped for a second. He was good at fighting one on one, but not in a scene like this.

"Hey, it's those freaks in masks; I guess it's true what they say about the Howlers!" a man at the front said, laughing.

Austin was confident as he walked up to the group, and while the leader of these attackers was busy laughing, Austin threw a punch as hard as he could. The leader placed his bat in front of his face, trying to protect it, but it split apart and Austin's fist collided with the man's face, knocking his teeth out.

Another person attacked, swinging a bat toward Austin, but before it connected, Innu jumped up with his knee forward, hitting the attacker in the face and causing him to drop the bat onto the ground.

The other eight were stunned, as their two strongest fighters had been knocked out just like that. Regardless, Austin and Innu weren't going to let the attackers get away with it; they continued to fight them and soon defeated them.

This wasn't a onetime occurrence, either; the two of them fought and fought, continuing to train and getting stronger each day.

One day, though, outside of their regular Howlers work, Austin got a call from one of his school friends. He had stayed in touch with some of them because they came to the pool club sometimes, and Kai had also told him to keep up those relationships.

These delinquents could possibly be the future of the Howlers, after all.

"Austin . . . East Boys are giving us trouble without you here! We need your help, man!" his friend shouted.

Austin thought about it; it wasn't the first time he had gotten a call from his old school friends asking him to help them fight. Finally he made a decision.

"Gather everyone and tell them we're going to be taking care of the whole of Slough. They will learn that the Howlers own all of the delinquents in the area, and to not kick up a fuss," Austin replied.

He had been training long enough, fighting long enough, and now Austin set out to do what he had always dreamed of doing when he was in school. That day, every school had a visit, not from the masked individual, but from Austin himself.

In an alleyway, Austin had just finished dealing with the last of the schools in Slough. His hands were bloody, his knuckles were sore, and bruises covered his face and body.

This was the dream that I used to have . . . and now I am here, Austin thought. *King of the high schools of Slough. Well, this sucks balls. That was too easy. I guess I'm done with this child's stuff. I need something a lot more interesting.*

Now Austin was here, in front of Innu, in front of the Howlers . . . and ready to make a name for himself.

CHAPTER 63

FIGHT FOR THE PRIZE (PART 2)

"All bets are in, and the fight will now start!" Kai shouted.

Innu was the first person to charge in as he ran across the hard ground.

I know Austin is big and strong, and it's like going up against a solid wall. So I need to use all the momentum I can get.

When Innu was close enough, he decided to use a move that never failed him when taking on a big opponent. Jumping into the air, with his knee forward, Innu leapt up to an incredible height, aiming his knee for Austin's face.

Quickly, Austin raised his arms in defense. Innu's knee banged right into them, causing them to start throbbing, but it was nothing that Austin couldn't take.

Next, Austin threw a punch of his own. It looked heavy and strong. Innu spun around to avoid the hit and get closer to Austin at the same time. He swung his elbow out and hit Austin right in the face.

The crowd heard a loud crack, and they couldn't help but wince as they imagined how much the attack had to have hurt.

"I think people might have underestimated Innu too much just by looking at the size difference," Kai commented. "These are the core members of the Howlers, and no one is weak on our team!"

Austin shifted all of his weight to his other leg, to keep himself from falling down. From this awkward position, Austin started to throw a punch toward Innu.

"I knew you wouldn't go down just from that!" Innu shouted; after all, he had seen Austin get hit with a baseball bat to the head and remain standing. That was why Innu threw a kick toward Austin even though he was already falling down.

However, Austin grabbed Innu's leg with his left hand and threw a punch toward Innu's side. He let go of the leg and Innu's body was propelled into the air; everyone could see Innu's eyes bulging out, and spit shot out from his mouth.

Eventually Innu landed on the ground, his hands holding on to his side. Everyone was stunned.

"Is he okay? That punch, I could hear it! I think he might have broken some ribs!" one of the onlookers said.

To them, it seemed like the fight was over. Innu was still on the ground, trying to gather air into his lungs, as he was winded by the blow.

"Innu, I thought you were different from the rest," Austin said. "Is that why you want the prize so bad, because you realize how weak you are?"

The veins on Innu's neck started to bulge. All of the hard training, the faces of those who needed him appeared in his head. Without using his hands, Innu stood up.

"There's a big difference between me and you, Austin," Innu said as he caught his breath, but he could feel the pain in his side. He was certain that something had broken. "I have a real reason to fight, so I will always get up!"

Innu charged in again toward Austin, and just like before, it looked like Austin was ready to block whatever was coming his way, but instead of jumping up, when Innu got close, he used all the strength in his legs to deliver a powerful and devastating kick right into Austin's thigh.

Immediately Austin felt the impact, like a sledgehammer, but before he could react, Innu performed a second kick.

Austin's thigh had gone numb, and he wanted to move away, but his legs were already shaking.

These are incredibly strong kicks, and if I hadn't trained I would have fallen down by now!

Innu could tell that Austin was on his last legs, if he just kicked him a couple more times, Austin would fall and Innu could finish him off with a knee to his chin, rattling his head and ending the fight.

Innu threw another kick toward the same thigh; no one could see but it had already started to swell, and everyone could see Austin's legs shaking.

Regardless, Austin grabbed the leg and pulled Innu forward, then grabbed him by his shoulder with his other arm. Innu attempted to hit Austin in the face to break free, but Austin lifted Innu's body into the air, then slammed his body onto the concrete.

The second Austin finished his move, he fell to one knee; his leg could no longer support his body. At the same time, Innu couldn't get up off the ground.

"It looks like we have our winner! Let's take them both to the hospital as soon as possible, and after that . . . we can give you your prize. Congratulations, Austin." Kai smiled.

CHAPTER 64

THE LAST PROBLEM

Opening his eyes, Innu found himself staring at a dark ceiling. He could feel the spongy seating underneath his body and slowly lifted himself up. Looking around, he recognized the seats in the back of the Wolf's Pool Club.

The place was quiet and devoid of customers now, though he could see that Miss Degrace and White were busy cleaning the bar area. As for the others, Innu couldn't see them. Moving his body slightly, he winced as he felt the pain from his injuries.

My body and my sides are killing me. Just what the hell has that big oaf been eating to have such power?

Looking down, Innu saw some bandages, but overall nothing too serious. Still, his current condition made him aware of one important fact.

The fight . . . I lost. Damn it, I lost, which means that damned meathead got the Altered solution. With his head held down, Innu kept replaying the fight, pondering whether there was anything he could have done differently.

In hindsight, it was the first punch from Austin that had knocked him off his game. If he had been more patient after throwing a hard punch, and only then proceeded to attack his opponent's thigh, perhaps he could would have won.

Even when he was kicking the thigh of Austin, he shouldn't have rushed, though he had mostly done so because of the pain. Innu had been in enough fights to recognize that his broken ribs and hampered breathing would slow him down if the fight were to drag on.

I can't just make up excuses for myself. At the end of the day, he won and I lost. If it had been a real fight against a rival gang, I would be dead right now. If that happened, then who would look after Kevin and Suzan?

Being in a gang was a dangerous business. Alas, it came with corresponding high rewards, meaning he couldn't just quit.

"Looks like the doctor was right about you only needing a couple hours. You're not too bad off after all." Kai smiled, having come up from downstairs along with the others.

"Doctor?" Innu asked.

"Yeah, we had a doctor come out and check on you. Why, who did you think bandaged you? Fortunately, in his medical opinion, you should be in top condition in a couple days. Perk of being a big gang is having an on-call doctor for these types of situations. Hospitals are busy places and we don't want to endanger others because of our identity."

Innu understood, but he was a bit distracted because he could see that Austin had a syringe in his hand.

"I wanted to wait for you," Austin explained. "Knowing you, you would have made a fuss about missing out on such a moment."

The comment annoyed Innu, making him tense up his whole body, which unfortunately just caused him more pain. Closing his eyes, he was surprised by what he saw the moment he opened them.

"These are . . . but these are yours."

"And now they're yours," Kai said, as he held out the two red axes that had originally belonged to his father. "I had always planned for them to be a consolation prize for the loser.

"These axes were what gave Damion his power, and now they will do the same for you as well. Don't feel bad about taking them either. Every time I see those things, I'm tempted to throw them away because they remind me of him. The only reason I don't is because it would be a huge waste.

"If you learn how to use them properly, they will boost your powers immensely. Given your fighting style, they will be a good fit."

Innu didn't know what to say, but he could tell that the blond teenager was serious, so he accepted both of the axes. For a second, he had a strange feeling of being energized. The pain in his body even lessened a bit, and he felt more powerful.

All this from just holding some weapons? Just what are they made of? Innu wondered. The feeling quickly faded, though, but he'd had a glimpse of what they could do. Now he was starting to understand how Damion had been able to face Altereds as a normal human.

"The club is closed, so now that we're all conscious, let's see what this solution brings to the table for our group," Kai said.

Austin handed the solution to Marie. There were no instructions, but from what Kai had gathered online, it was pretty self-explanatory; one jab to the shoulder would do it.

"All right, three . . . two . . ."

"I don't need a countdown, just jab it in!" Austin said, closing his eyes as he looked away. Apparently, the big teenager was afraid of nothing . . . but needles?

Marie didn't take his outburst to heart, and she simply did as she was told. Once the needle was inserted, she started to push the solution in. She worked quickly, making sure all of the liquid was used up before pulling the needle out again.

The next second Austin fell to his knees, with a burning and itching sensation all over his body.

"No one told me this shit was going to hurt!" Austin wanted to claw at his skin, as it felt like ants were inside his body, crawling around and changing everything inside.

Kai didn't say anything, because he was sure Austin would be able to endure. He doubted the pain could be any worse than what he had gone through back in the cell, or before Gary had left.

Quite frankly there were other things on his mind. When he had gone back to the office, the vice leader had checked the letters that their lawyer had left behind. It had been one rejection after the other. No matter what approach the Howlers had taken, be it direct, indirect through a proxy, or even the offer of an investment, the answer had stayed the same.

With the way the mayor was acting, it was going to be hard for the Howlers to expand. Who would want to work with a gang that was unable to get their own yard in order?

How would the Underdogs have dealt with this situation? As far as I'm aware, Ben Clove avoided getting in the way of Damion and his plans, yet now that our influence has undoubtedly overtaken theirs, he somehow has the confidence to take us on? Is it because we haven't re-taliated?

Now, as he watched Austin recovering, Kai stood up with a smile on his face.

"Well, if he doesn't want the carrot, perhaps we'll have to pay him a visit and convince him that he won't like the stick . . ."

CHAPTER 65

ONE LESS PROBLEM

After Austin and Innu's match concerning the ownership of the Altered solution, Kai told everyone to prepare themselves for something big. His choice of words had been pretty vague, yet the fact that Olivia would accompany them made his fellow gang members suspect that there would be a fight soon.

As to who their enemy was going to be, nobody questioned it. They all trusted in the blond teenager's judgment, so each one spent the next few days training. Marie continued her daily training with a variety of weapons, while Innu started to incorporate his two new axes into his fighting style.

Austin was undoubtedly the one who had it the hardest, though. After all, becoming an Altered didn't really come with instructions. In a way, it was similar to what the two beta werewolves had gone through, yet in his case, the big teenager had yet to find out just what kind of Altered he was.

One night, Kai stood on the roof of a restaurant. It was three stories high, and the wind was blowing his hair as the backdrop of a crescent moon shone behind him.

A few more days and we should be ready to take the other gangs on. Austin is getting the hang of his powers, and he got relatively lucky with the mystery solution. Once we take care of our local problem, we can look into taking over the other Tier 3 towns in the vicinity.

I know I shouldn't rush it, but Austin's power has me shaking with excitement. Still, I need to keep in mind that gang wars are a different ball game than a straight-up fight. Gang wars require funds, and after our last purchase, we're lacking in that area.

We need to build up our finances and power to be able to protect our increased influence. Taking over an area doesn't mean a thing if we're unable to protect it.

While the others had been busy training, the werewolf had been preparing their next step by snooping around. He had also asked Olivia and her people to complete a certain task for him, and to pass on what they heard about other gangs. There was one opponent that was of significant importance, and that was the mayor.

Gary's blatant disrespect during the meeting of the midsized gangs had already made the Howlers into a public enemy. However, since the Howlers had established themselves as the most powerful faction by taking out the Underdogs, the others had kept to their territories. Of course, they all understood that this peace had an expiration date, so it hadn't taken Ben Clove a lot of convincing to get them all to agree to form into one large alliance to stay relevant.

On the surface, it looked like they were all equal, but in reality, the ones calling the shots were the Rising Dragons. They had been working for the mayor before the change in the status quo, so he naturally trusted them the most. There wasn't much the other gangs could do about it, except to curse their situation.

If possible, it would be best if I could get them to fight among themselves by having one or more gangs defect to our side. Since Gary left Olivia alive and her gang is thriving, it shouldn't be too hard to convince them. As for how much we can trust them . . . well, I'll cross that bridge once we get to it, but first I need to find out what has made the mayor so confident, Kai thought as he continued to track tonight's prey.

Outside the Chinese restaurant, there were gang members who were already lightly intoxicated and in the midst of discussing a seemingly important event.

It's a good thing that Gary made an adjustment to the pack rules. Because I'm going to need it.

As Kai jumped off from the third floor, his body shifted into a much smaller form. Rather than growing in size, his bones became more compact, and fur began covering his entire body.

When he landed, his body was no longer that of a human, but that of a gray wolf.

This was one of the advantages of Kai's werewolf type. His Unique Class wasn't called the Gray Werewolf Shapeshifter for nothing.

Like an obsessed man, he had spent every free moment to learn how to use his newly granted powers, to the point he felt that he had grasped complete control over his transformations.

This form was far more suited to reconnaissance, especially since he looked not too different from a normal dog. His senses were even sharper in his animalistic form, allowing him to listen in from a distance without making the gang members suspicious.

Even if someone were to see him, they would think he was a simple dog, and nine times out of ten, even if they saw his face, most people didn't know what a wolf looked like; they would just assume he was a husky or some type of dog they hadn't seen before. It was rare for humans to interact with wolves, at least in the town of Slough.

"Did you come here?" one of them asked. "Rizer asked us all to get ready to move, and to keep track of the Howlers."

"Oh?" the other replied with a hiccup. "I'm guessing this has something to do with that meeting that the boss said they had, right?"

"Yeah, from what I hear, the alliance has been asked to come back together again. Based on the actions and the word from the other gangs, it looks like the mayor is wanting to make his move."

"Move against the Howlers? But they took out the Underdogs, and they have an Altered as well. There's no way we can take them on."

The man flicked his cigarette into the middle of the road and let out a huge puff of smoke.

"Word is, the mayor managed to get his hands on a pretty strong Altered solution himself, and it's enough for the boss to believe we have a chance of getting rid of them. If we get rid of the Howlers, then we own a pretty big piece of Slough. Our alliance will have all the say, and with the mayor we can rise up. Nothing is stopping us now."

The men continued to chat for a while, but it was useless information; what Kai needed was a date and time. He continued following them until the perfect opportunity presented itself.

Going down the alleyway, one of the men seemed quite drunk; he was wobbly on his feet and decided to take a leak. As he was relieving himself in the fresh air, he noticed something to his right.

"Oh . . . Fuck, that's a huge wild dog, I need to hurry up and finish this," the man said, but as he stood there with his pants partly down, a hand grabbed the back of his head and slammed him into the wall.

Blood dripped from his nose and forehead as his vision blurred. His hair was pulled back, but he could see what looked like a blond teenager.

"You scream, you die. You call for the others, you die. You speak before I tell you to, you die," Kai whispered. The man was about to say something, but before he could, Kai grabbed his head and slammed it against the wall again.

"I didn't give you permission yet. Just nod if you understand."

The man was incredibly shaken, but out of fear he nodded.

"Good. I'm going to need some answers from you."

The man's lips turned out to be incredibly loose; it seemed like these men weren't too loyal to their gang, at least not for such simple information as where a meeting would take place.

"Please . . . will you let me go?" the man whimpered.

"I'm sorry, but no one can know that I know about this. I can't trust someone as loose as you," Kai said as his whole head transformed and he bit down on the man's neck.

Kai knew that while Gary was away, the gang would have to use violence, and possibly go as far as killing someone. Gary had changed the pack rules. Olivia was trustworthy enough by now, at least to the point where he trusted Kai looking over her. The one thing Gary didn't want was for them to suffer because of his rules.

The gang member died a few moments later. Back in his wolf form, Kai let out a few barks before he started to dig in. The others, hearing the commotion, followed the noise, where they found him with blood all over its mouth.

"That fucking street dog killed Umar!" one of the men shouted as he discovered the corpse. "Kill the damn dog!"

Now that they had seen the scene of the killing and believed it was done by an animal, Kai turned tail and ran away, too fast for the intoxicated gang members to even attempt to catch up.

A big meeting, huh? Now should we strike them all at once, or do so before they have a chance to gather?

CHAPTER 66

TIER 4

"Those fucking Howlers and their fucking Altered have ruined my fucking plans! Just why the fuck did they have to come here of all places?" Ben internally cursed the appearance of the gang for the umpteenth time as he stared at the pile of documents on his desk with hateful eyes. The paperwork was stacking up to his chin, because he had recently instructed his staff to bring everything that needed his approval directly to him.

It wasn't a coincidence that had led Ben Clove to Slough. The politician had done his fair share of research before he decided to campaign in this particular Tier 3 town, and unlike what he had claimed during the election period, his true reasons were far less utilitarian.

The thing that had made Slough stand out among the dozens of other Tier 3 towns he could have chosen was the delicate balance in its underworld. There were signs that the two big gangs that controlled most of the town would clash in the foreseeable future, and he had intended to be there to reap the benefits when it happened.

Of course, he would have been unable to do it on his own, but fortunately he wasn't the only one who was interested in biding his time. The five small-time gangs had long since held gatherings to decide on a common course of action to not offend the big gangs, keenly aware that their continued existence was tied to staying off the radar.

At one of those meetings, Ben Clove had introduced himself to the gang leaders, and using his charisma and glib tongue he had managed to win them over. In time, they had helped him win the mayorship, some directly, others indirectly, and all of them had waited for the inevitable falling-out between Damion and Brandon . . .

Unfortunately, the outcome had turned out drastically different from anything they could have foreseen, leading them to a situation far worse than before. Instead of enjoying full control over Slough, the mayor was currently doing all he could to hinder the Howlers' growth.

I can't allow them to expand their influence any further. According to D, the other gang leaders are starting to complain more and more openly about this alliance. If I don't do anything soon, some of them might consider deserting, Ben Clove thought as he picked up the telephone by his side and dialed a few numbers to set up a group call to inform the alliance about the location for their next meeting. It was a place he would never go to if circumstances hadn't demanded it.

Tier 4 towns had a nasty reputation of being cesspools of filth, housing factories that caused mass pollution. The people who lived there had fallen so low, leaving them with nothing else to lose. Nevertheless, those who were well-off considered them a necessary evil, producing many things the Tier 2 and Tier 1 cities required to run.

Admittedly, aside from the worker areas, the residential districts weren't bad to look at. The same couldn't be said about the people, though. The population could roughly be divided into those who tried to live by doing the only honest work they could get, and those who wanted to get rich or die trying, with the latter not being a rare occurrence.

After all, there was something dangerous about those who lived in a Tier 4 town, painfully aware that they were the dregs of society. Given how crazy and hectic the constant fighting and power struggles tended to be, the ones in charge rarely got to enjoy that privilege for long.

The top floor of this town's highest building was a fancy restaurant with a red and gold theme. In the center a large round table was set up, surrounded by a group of outsiders who had secretly traveled here.

"Gentlemen, let me thank you all for meeting me here. I understand that it must be out of your comfort zone, but I assure you this should be the only time," the mayor said as he raised a glass of champagne to the present gang leaders.

With him in the room was Tony from the Lock gang. The gang leader was sitting at the table while two of his gang members stood behind him. Opposite him were the three Red Blood Triangle brothers; the oldest brother was seated, while his two younger brothers acted as guards.

To the right of the mayor was D, leader of the Rising Dragons, while to the left of him was D's little brother, Little Dragon, who had recently taken over leadership of the Hook gang—now rebranded to . . . the Little Dragons.

"Let's cut the bull and get to the chase," Tony yelled, as he slammed his glass onto the table, causing it to smash. "I don't want to stay here a second longer than I have to! Heck, the fact that we have to hide from them is already saying everything that needs to be said about the current situation, don't you think so, Mr. Mayor?

"More and more of my men are either leaving me to work for the Howlers or at least thinking about doing that soon. I have no idea what their leader is thinking, but his jackass angelic morality is making all of us lose money. I'm only afraid that if things continue the way they are, we'll go out of business before they do."

All of those around the room agreed as they nodded in unison.

"Well, Mr. Lock, today's topic just happens to be strictly about the Howlers and our next course of action to get rid of them once and for all," Ben replied with a smile, not caring the least about the gang leader's tantrum.

Outside the restaurant, the strongest gang had been paid a handsome commission by the mayor to ensure that nobody would disturb the meeting. Their gang leader had happily agreed to lend out his men to show off his muscle.

"Hey, check the list. I'm pretty sure we've already let in all the VIPs today," a gang member who stood in front of the door as a sort of bouncer said to his buddy who had the list.

"Yup, everyone is accounted for. Well, you heard the boss, let's give those masked freaks a beating," the other gangster answered, happy that this evening was about to get fun.

"Looks like they sent over the welcoming committee. Let's crash this little event of theirs and move on," a teenager in a foxlike black-and-gold mask said to the ones next to him.

CHAPTER 67

NEW ALTERED
(PART 1)

The confidence in the mayor's voice as he revealed each and every way he had rejected the Howlers' many attempts to expand was invigorating for the gang leaders to hear. Nevertheless, when Ben told them that he needed their help in stopping the Howlers' revenue streams by doing things that he, as a public figure, was unable to do, the hesitation from their side was palpable.

"You do understand that doing that is the same as crippling Slough as a whole, don't you?" Tony from the Lock gang pointed out the issue they all had with the mayor's proposal.

"Mr. Block, weren't you the one who said that the Howlers would win without having to do anything if things continue as they are? I admit that forcing most businesses to pause their operations is a drastic step, but it's necessary, though I assure you that it's only for a limited period of time.

"I have it on good authority that the Howlers have liquidated a large amount of their buildings recently, which is a sure sign that they intend to purchase something big. In other words, their reserve is about to take a real hit soon.

"What do you think happens when their businesses, which appear to be their only reliable source of revenue, stop all of a sudden? Without money, they will be unable to pay their people . . . and what will happen then? There will be a large-scale revolt!"

There was a large smirk on Ben's face as he reached this point of his monologue. Seeing this, the leaders of each gang all came to one shared realization: the mayor might be an even bigger crook than any of them, because he truly cared only about one thing, and that was himself and his own well-being.

The fact that his plan would further decrease the quality of life of his constituents seemed to be merely an afterthought. A minor factor in a complicated calculation. The most sinister part of it was that he would be handing those businesses over to the gang members on a silver platter, and once things returned to normal, he intended to take credit for solving a problem he himself had instigated.

"That plan sounds great, but isn't there a huge problem?" the youngest brother from the Red Blood Triangles asked with a small frown. "Even if we don't account for the fact that they may not have spent that liquidated money, what do we do when the Howlers decide to take action?

"They might have ignored us before, but if we go after their source of revenue so brazenly, how is this any different from an open declaration of war? They're bound to come after us, and if we had the power to stand against them, we wouldn't be meeting here in the first place."

Ben started to laugh out loud. "Do you really think I would have suggested my plan if I didn't account for that fact? Besides, if they were completely sure about taking us out, they would have done so already. That's just another reason to go after them, before things chan—"

A few grunts interrupted his speech, and all of those present turned to look at the only door into the room. Outside were the Tier 4 gang leader's so-called best men, whom the mayor had been forced to hire when choosing this venue, as they came with the package.

Just as Ben was about to make an offhand remark about how difficult it was to find good personnel before continuing their meeting, they heard raised voices outside the door.

"Who the hell are you guys? You're not allowed to be up he—"

The sentence was cut short as the double doors swung wide open and an incoming human projectile crashed into the wall.

"Sorry for the disturbance, but one of you must have forgotten to put our name on the VIP list," a man with a black-and-gold fox mask explained with a wide grin as he stepped over a downed gang member and entered the room.

He was followed by four individuals who were also clad in black-and-gold clothing, with different masks on their faces to cover their identity. The black-and-gold uniform had become a symbol for their gang, and it was already common knowledge that those with these masks belonged to the inner circle of the Howlers.

"Who the hell told them about this meeting?" the leader of the Red Blood Triangle shouted as he looked around, suspecting that one of the other gangs must have betrayed them, yet the confusion on the faces of the other alliance members was genuine.

"Do you have a problem with us being here? Would you have rather continued cursing us behind our backs?" Kai asked calmly as his gaze slowly fell on each one of them, sending shivers down the backs of the grown men.

Ben looked over at the man who had been sent flying. Without a doubt, he was one of the supposed guards. When the mayor looked behind the Howlers he saw many others in similar or worse condition, yet none of the five newcomers had so much as a scratch on them.

Still, he also noticed that they were short one very prominent member.

"Tsk, just how little do you guys think of us that you sent the B team?" Ben asked after regaining his composure. "Your leader, the guy who defeated Kirk, isn't even with you. None of you match his body shape or are wearing the same mask as him!"

When he pointed that out, the others let out a sigh of relief. As impressive as the feat of sending someone flying was, the person they all feared the most was the wolflike Altered, as he had managed to take out the AFC's rookie champion.

"You really think I don't recognize you, Olivia?" Tony asked after regaining his confidence. Given their shared history, it was easy enough for him to recognize her proportions. "How low can you sink? They kicked your ass, yet you follow them like a loyal dog?"

He slammed his hand into a fist and punched the chair that he was sitting on, breaking it in a single blow. His knuckles were bleeding, but with a smile he licked away the blood.

"Had you run into my Pincers headquarters and defeated all my guys, I might have considered tolerating your presence long enough for a single date. Besides, where did you get the audacity to question me working for them, when all of you rats gathered together to stand a chance against us, huh?" Olivia retorted. The Lady Boss swung out her whip at a lightning-fast speed and wrapped it around Tony's shoulders, then lifted him into the air and slammed him down at full force, breaking part of the wooden flooring.

Ben ground his teeth as he saw that his side was losing momentum.

"You guys have annoyed me for long enough!" the mayor shouted as his body began to transform. His new status as an Altered was supposed to be their side's ace in the hole, and without Gary, now was the best chance for him to use his advantage to deal a critical strike to the other side.

No wonder he grew the balls to mess with us directly, Kai thought.

"All right, big guy, it's your time to shine," the vice leader ordered Austin, who happily walked forward to meet the Altered.

CHAPTER 68

NEW ALTERED (PART 2)

Olivia was facing Tony Lock and the two goons by his side. While it didn't look like they would give her any trouble, it would still take her a few moments before she could help out the others. With their way out blocked by the rest of the Howlers, the ambushed gang members decided to act.

The Rising Dragons who had worked under the mayor the longest took the charge. D leapt up onto the table and ran across it, making his way to the masked intruders. However, before he or his men could reach them, they were met with an incoming bolt.

The gang leader managed to avoid the first one, but one of his men wasn't so lucky. The projectile pierced a few inches deep into his body, not enough to kill him but more than enough to make him scream in pain, unable to move.

It looks like all that training wasn't for naught, Marie thought. A proud, satisfied grin formed on her face as she held the crossbow in her hand.

"You bitch!" the injured gang member yelled out. However, he was unaware that his pain was just the prelude to the actual effect. Were he able to look down, he would see that the bolt had started to light up, sparks forming as a high-voltage current was released inside his body.

The effect was far more potent than any ordinary stun gun,

as it was a weapon designed to be used against Altered. The man fell onto the table as Marie continued to place bolts inside her new weapon.

D had only stopped briefly to gauge the lethality of the weapon. Although it sounded painful, he was at least relieved that it appeared to be designed to restrain rather than kill the target. Nevertheless, he had no intention of allowing himself to be hit. He leapt through the air, aiming straight for Marie with his fist wound up.

We need to get rid of her first! the gang leader thought as he looked at the teenage girl's thin frame. *One punch should be enough to take her out and use her as a hostage!*

"Do I look like decoration to you?" A mocking voice resounded as Kai used a seemingly casual gait to move into the perfect position to intercept D. He moved his head to the side, thus avoiding the incoming punch, and countered with a right hook of his own. The punch was hard enough to flip the gang leader's body completely, shattering a few of his front teeth as he fell to the floor.

"Next time, think about how you'll dodge when you're in the air, dumbass."

The werewolf was slightly surprised that a single punch was all it took to knock D out. All of the leaders present had a reputation for being relentless when fighting, yet the Howlers were dealing with them with ease. They had all changed since beating the Underdogs, and they were growing stronger by the day.

"Just keep firing away at these idiots, and I'll make sure no one gets close to you," Kai ordered Marie, as he turned toward the remaining Rising Dragons members. He crossed his arms, taunting them to come and try to get past him.

At the same time, Innu locked eyes with the Red Blood Triangles, trying to differentiate the triplets. Each of them was bald, and each was using the same type of weapon: a long staff with a metal cap on the bottom. They had slowly surrounded Innu, locking him inside a triangular formation, but the teenager wasn't unarmed.

Innu charged forward, swinging his right axe toward the opponent in front of him. Unfortunately, he was unable to hit his target as the brother to his left hit the top of his axe, causing the weapon and his whole body to shift to the side. Presented with the opportunity, the other two brothers hit the teenager right on the thigh.

It was a hard whack, more like a slap, which made Innu grunt with pain. He wanted to scream but he wouldn't let himself. Innu then tried to kick another one of the wannabe monks, but they lifted their staffs, blocking the attack and hitting him on the back leg as well as the side.

Arghh! This shit hurts! Their stupid poles give them the range advantage, so my fists are useless in this situation. There's no way I can go against three experts like this after training with these axes for this short period of time!

In the middle of his thoughts and with his leg back on the ground, all three of them struck from above, this time aiming for Innu's head. He saw their movement and their feet this time, so he lifted both axes to block the incoming attack.

They had pushed him down slightly as they all hit the tops of the axes, but with his strong thigh and leg muscles Innu pushed up, making them all back away as they marveled at their opponent's surprising strength.

Innu charged forward and jumped in the air this time, swinging both of his axes down toward one of them. The youngest of the Red Blood Triangle brothers was startled by this, yet he managed to lift his pole in time. The axes slammed into the weapon, bending it and cracking the wood.

The bladed part didn't even hit the pole! How much power does this guy have?

Meanwhile, another large pole had whacked Innu in the ribs, sending him off to the side. He gritted his teeth and bore the pain again.

Come on, you useless things! Kai said you were supposed to have some sort of power, but right now it just feels like you're dragging me down! Innu screamed in his head. *If you're not going to do anything, then I might as well throw you away.*

Getting up again, the furious Innu didn't even realize that the surge in power didn't stem solely from his anger. With a fire lit in his belly, he went after the bald-headed men again, throwing a kick as hard as he could.

Just like before, the man held his staff sideways to block the attack, but Innu's shin hit it and broke it in half. It was the strongest kick that

Innu had ever produced. As soon as he landed on his feet, Innu leapt up from the floor, just missing the other two poles.

Holy shit! I've never felt like this before! Is it really because of the weapons? How is that possible?

As Innu reached the bald-headed man, he kicked the man's shin with the side of his foot and felt it fracture; the leg bone hadn't completely broken, but the man was in severe pain. When he knelt over, Innu shoved the axe up from underneath and hit his opponent's chin with the top of his axe, shattering the bottom of his jaw and causing him to fall to the floor.

"That's one brother down, two more to go," Innu announced with a challenging gaze.

Perhaps I didn't get the short end of the stick after losing that fight.

Turning his head slightly, though, he abandoned that thought as he saw that both Austin and the mayor had transformed.

CHAPTER 69

FULL TRANSFORMATION

One after the other, the gang members were starting to get more and more self-conscious about their chances against the Howlers. Olivia was using this opportunity to settle her score with Tony and his Lock gang. In the past, the Lady Boss had had no other choice but to endure his ceaseless attempts to woo her, but now she was giving him a taste of his own medicine, teaching him an entirely different meaning of "*No doesn't always mean* no."

Suffice to say, her whip wasn't idle, and while his two goons had long since passed out, the gang leader didn't get to enjoy the same privilege. Olivia made sure to hit him hard enough to hurt, but not enough for him to lose consciousness. Were it not for everyone being busy with their own fights, the loud screams would be very distracting.

As for Ben Clove, the person responsible for this entire meeting, he had removed his suit to reveal his large belly. One look was enough to convince anyone that the man was definitely no fighter. He didn't look like a gang member either, but he didn't need to. Seeing him transform made it clear why the chubby man had remained so stoic in the face of the ambush.

The sleeves covering the mayor's forearms ripped open as muscles bulged, revealing sharp, long fins on his arms. His face elongated and a tail emerged, ripping a hole through his trousers. The color of his skin was changing to a grayish blue, while his teeth sharpened and his eyes slanted a bit.

Depending on a person's Altered form, it was hard to tell what beast they came from since Altered were based on animals that didn't exist today. However, in Ben's case, it was safe to wager that he was based on a sea creature, more specifically one that was related to today's sharks, predators of the sea. According to research, most beasts were predatory anyway, at least back in the day.

Still, there was a clear distinction between beasts and animals. Scientists had discovered that their DNA, their blood, and a number of other things were different. Nevertheless, comparing both types of fossils, they did find some relation. Through evolution, the animals of the past used to take on some forms of the beasts around them.

In nature, predators tended to take on the forms of the most dangerous of beasts. Since the mayor knew his beast was related to sharks, he was certain that NIRV had given him a powerful Altered, even if it paled in comparison to Xin's.

It's shameful to envy my children for their Altered forms, but that NIRV employee promised me that this was one of the best out there, and in a Tier 3 town like ours no one will get in my way, Ben thought as he smiled, baring his razor-sharp teeth at Austin.

The mayor had grown larger and his form looked dangerous; however, Austin had a trick up his sleeve as well, his own transformed state. Ben might have been a pencil pusher for most of his life, yet he understood that it would be idiotic to allow his opponent to finish his transformation by doing nothing. He spun his body, leading with his tail. This particular Shark Altered had huge muscles in its tail that could knock over a ton of bricks.

"You guys are done for!" Ben shouted as he put all his strength into his tail. When he tested it against cars, it had been enough to fully destroy them, so no human would be able to survive that impact.

When the tail whacked into Austin, a loud bang echoed throughout the whole room. It sounded like a gun had gone off. Everyone stopped their own fights for a moment and turned their heads, just in time to see that Austin had caught the tail, though not without being shifted back a foot.

"Now I'm a confused!" Innu said as he stared at Austin's Altered form. This was the first time he had seen his fellow gang member in this form, since the big guy had been practicing using his Altered self alone or with Kai.

Innu was confused because Austin's whole body had grown larger and more muscular, the tight-fitting uniform stretching even more to accommodate his new form.

His legs had grown two hooves, and his newly enlarged head had two horns sticking out from the top. Finally, he had larger nostrils as well.

"I thought we didn't get the Bull Altered type serum! And how has Austin learned to partially transform so fast?" Innu asked out loud. Kai just smirked; as much as he would like to take credit for it, he had only helped out in that regard.

He too had been surprised when Austin had asked him for some help. For a while the two of them had been trying to figure out what he was. When he looked at reference videos and photos, Austin had been unable to find anything that matched his own form.

At the same time, what was confusing was the transformations. Usually, there was partial transformation, allowing a person to just change one part of their body. This was the easiest and at the same time the hardest to control. For many it was the first step in figuring out how to use their Altered forms; an expert could control minor details such as transforming just their fingernails.

Then there was the hybrid form; this was usually the preferred form for fighting, and it was what every new Altered focused on obtaining. How long it took to obtain a hybrid form was different for everyone. And then there was full transformation, turning completely into a beast.

Full transformation was advantageous depending on the situation, and some found it easier to go straight to this form rather than the hybrid form when practicing. What Kai and Austin had realized was that this was Austin's real form.

"You think you're strong? Just because you're an Altered?" Austin gripped tightly onto the tail. "You're nothing compared to me!"

Exerting both arms, he lifted Ben into the air, then swung his tail and his entire body over his shoulder, slamming his head into the ground, partially breaking the floorboards underneath. As Austin let out a big breath, it looked as if steam was coming out.

We might have lost out on the Bull Altered, but this mystery solution was worth every penny. I have no idea where they got it from, but a mythical beast is far stronger. With this Minotaur Altered, we seriously hit the jackpot! Kai inwardly laughed to himself.

CHAPTER 70

THE PERFECT FORM

Austin had not learned how to enter into a hybrid state, but his particular beast DNA had allowed him to enter his fully transformed state. Every once in a while, he would let out a big huff of hot air, and steam would come out of his nostrils. This was happening when he looked down at Ben Clove on the floor.

It's as if this Altered form was specially made for me, Austin thought once more. As a Minotaur Altered, his strength had gone up an entire level, and the best part about it was that there had been no need to change anything about his particular fighting style. *If Innu or Marie had used it, I'd have certainly regretted it for life, but now I can help the gang defeat anyone who stands in our way.*

As he slowly pushed himself off the floor, the Shark Altered tasted the blood in his mouth. He spit it out, and a few shark teeth also fell on the floor. The attack, which could have killed a normal human, merely dazed him. When he looked up at his opponent, he flashed his teeth, showing that he had a full set again.

"You think you can beat me in one hit?" Ben asked. "You think I could have reached my current position if I were the type of person to give up at the first hurdle? You were merely lucky, punk!"

Ben charged in, his movements relatively slow as he pumped his foot side to side. Austin couldn't help but think Ben would have been far better off if this fight were underwater. Right now, the mayor was faster than a regular human, but against Austin's Minotaur form . . .

When the mayor got close, once again he spun his body along with his tail. This time, Austin didn't try to grab it; instead, he moved backward just enough so the tail skimmed past him. Then, using his strong hooves, he burst and charged in.

Ben covered his face with both hands, bracing himself. However, the punch had come from below as it hit him in the stomach, and the sheer power lifted him into the air.

Trying to breathe, Ben dropped his hands, and an overhand fist smashed into his face, sending him crashing into the wall.

Despite being an Altered, Ben was in severe pain, as Austin's punches were heavy and hard. By the time he had recovered, the Minotaur Altered was standing in front of him. Desperate, the Shark Altered threw out a punch, but Austin simply slapped it away to the side and kicked him in the stomach again, causing him to land on the floor.

Then Ben felt a heavy hand on the back of his head. "Since we're both Altered, let me tell you that this form is truly wasted on you."

"*What?*" Ben raised his voice, only to cough the next moment. He was still finding it hard to breathe and his energy was spent. His fingers and toes were even starting to revert slowly, giving him the appearance of a half monster.

"Did NIRV lie to me? I gave them everything because they promised me that this Altered form was special," Ben mumbled to himself as he watched the change happen.

"I don't know about you being lied to. Anyone with half a brain would agree that this form is better than your average Altered," Austin replied. "See, the problem is not the Altered itself but the one behind it.

"The second we started to fight, I knew I had nothing to worry about. It's obvious that you're the type of person who has been doing things behind the scenes for his entire life. Always pulling the strings of others, never directly involved. I'm sure that you thought becoming an Altered was enough for you to beat us.

"However, since you've never been in a fight in your entire life, it's impossible for you to bring out this Altered form's potential. I bet even the lowest gang member with a somewhat decent Altered form could take you on. Thinking about how many people would kill to become an Altered, it's truly a waste that you're one."

Still holding on to the back of Ben's head, he shoved it into the floor, breaking the floorboards before bouncing back.

"Hey, why did you kill him?" Marie shouted. "We were supposed to keep him alive."

Austin's form started to revert back, and he crouched down next to the mayor.

"Relax, he's still breathing. He might be a waste as an Altered, but he still has the durability of one," the teenager replied before turning to Kai. "By the way, I'm going to need a new mask. The inside of this one gets all wet after I transform."

It was practically soaked because of the steam that involuntarily escaped his nostrils; the small holes only allowed for a little bit of air to come out.

"Sure, we can look into that, but first we have other things we need to do," Kai said.

Everyone in the room had dealt with the enemy at hand; all of them had been beaten to the point of either passing out or being unable to get up. They were rolling in pain or just drained of all the will to fight again.

That was when Kai knelt down next to the mayor. He lifted his head and unceremoniously gave him a big slap across his face. The shock made him regain consciousness.

"Look, your little plan failed," Kai began. "Everyone was dealt with before you could even make your first move. You must have thought that with the Underdogs gone, you could take over, but you were dead wrong. Although we may be nice to the common folk, we don't show the same courtesy to other gangs, especially not ones who plan to stand in our way."

Looking through his swollen eyes, Ben saw that the small body frame of the fox-masked leader of the Howlers indicated that he wasn't even fully an adult yet. With the others, it was clear that they were a bunch of teenagers, not counting Olivia, so he was wondering just where it had all gone wrong.

"Speaking of which, I've been trying to play nice with you, but what did you do? You used your position as the mayor to spit on all my proposals time and time again. Do you have any idea how annoying and time-consuming it was to fill out all of that stupid paperwork, only for you to reject it when you most likely didn't even take a look at it?

"Well, that ends today. After today, Slough will change, but it won't be in the way you wanted. The only thing we still have to decide is what your role in all of that will be." Kai lifted his mask slightly, allowing the mayor to see the giant maw and long tongue that was licking its lips.

CHAPTER 71

A NEW SLOUGH

"Holy crap, is that who I think it is?" Tyler exclaimed in disbelief. "Are you sure we should be doing this? I really don't think I can help you with this."

"Get a grip, Tyler!" Kai shouted at their panicked driver. "Nobody's asking you to get involved in this any more than you already are. All I need you to do is to drive us to that location. Unless, of course, you'd prefer me to drive and get home on your own."

The thought of having to stay in the Tier 4 town was enough to quiet the university student. His whole body was still shaking, but he kept his mouth shut and drove the car onto the highway, occasionally looking back at their unwilling passenger.

Were it not for the specks of blood on the Howlers' clothes, the casual tone between the passengers would make it appear as if they were nothing more than a group of teenagers enjoying a casual drive. Of course, if one were to listen in to what they were talking about, just as a certain driver had been doing, their only reaction would be bafflement.

Because right now, Tyler was sure that the large man with the bag over his head was none other than Slough's mayor. Never in Tyler's wildest dreams did he imagine he would meet the politician in this type of setting, yet his encounter with Gary and the subsequent job opportunity had changed his life completely.

"Come on, Tyler, this is the big life. You've always wanted to be more than just a small fry; this is your chance," he muttered to himself as he followed the GPS to the destination Kai had programmed in. The closer they came, the more obvious it became where he was driving them all, and the more his face continued to drop.

Is it too late to get down? Tyler thought a short while later. He was finding it hard to fully open his eyes, but not because they had gotten out and it was a particularly windy day, but because he was on the rooftop of a multistory apartment building.

On top of that, the mayor was still with them. Rubbing his eyes, Tyler didn't want to believe it, but it was clear what was happening. The mayor no longer had the bag over his head, yet he was still tied up and Kai currently held on to him, tilting him over the edge.

"In case your situation wasn't clear enough, let me spell it out for you. Right now, the only thing standing between you and certain doom is me holding on to this rope. If you try to attack me, if you try to play wise and turn into an Altered, or if you give me any attitude, I will let go. You might be an Altered, but this height is at least more than enough to cripple you for life."

Turning his head, Ben stared into the abyss before he turned around, facing the blond teenager who even without the fox mask looked like a devil. It was hard for the mayor to understand just how it was possible for him to fall so low that even a brat like this could threaten him, especially after he had become an Altered.

Alas, with his life hanging on a proverbial thread, all he could do was nod along and accept what was coming his way.

"Great. First of all, let me tell you, Mr. Mayor, that I'm greatly disappointed in you. You're just like all the other politicians, the kind who promised the world during the election period, but once you won and got the power in your hands, what did you do besides sitting on your ass?" Kai began. Judging by Ben's expression, he had some choice words on his mind, but given the situation he could only swallow them down.

"Tell me, are you happy with the current state of Slough? Don't you find it ironic that you chose a Tier 4 town to hide in, so you can hold a meeting because of safety concerns? In my eyes, your actions are no different from the common man who had to keep his head low when heading home from work, trying his best to not stick out and become prey for one of the gangs. Do you still think yourself above those people?"

"No matter my current situation, I was voted in by the people," Ben coldly replied.

Hearing these words, Kai let go of the rope slightly, so that Ben was more inclined to fall. A wet spot appeared on his trousers, and he was silently saying his prayers with closed eyes.

"You don't even believe that pile of bull yourself, do you? The people don't really get a vote, you just used scum tactics to get where you are," the teenager said. "Do you even remember what you promised the people on the day you took office? Not only did you promise them that you would do everything in your power to make it safe for them to go out, but you also said that you wanted to make Slough great again, to turn it into a Tier 2 city.

"Now you might have forgotten about this fact, but I haven't; I want it to change, and you should as well," Kai explained as he pulled the rope up, making sure the mayor could listen to him without having to be afraid.

"There are two scenarios how things can go from this point on. You can either leave with us or go first by taking the direct route. It should be in your best interest to partner up with us. It's not like I'm asking you for anything outrageous in the first place. The first thing you will do once you're home is to accept the proposals that the Howlers have made. You know exactly the ones I'm talking about.

"They will not only benefit the Howlers but also Slough as a whole. If you're honest, you should be able to admit that you're merely rejecting them out of spite. In the future, if you ever reject one of our suggestions without a valid reason, I'll send over Austin, though next time he will tear your whole house down, do you understand?"

The mayor had no choice; he didn't want to agree, but he had to, so that was what he did. Never in his life had he been treated in such a way, but what worth did his pride hold when weighed against his life?

"Good. Now for the second condition, you're not to go up for re-election. What's more, you'll have to recommend a successor, and we will be choosing who your successor will be."

"No!" Ben shouted immediately. "I can't do that! This was just my first term! If I don't even become a candidate, it will affect my whole career and my entire family! You need to—"

Kai, not impressed by the shouting, let go of the rope until the mayor's body was hanging over the edge.

"I know you're just threatening me! You're not a killer, you're just a teenager!" the mayor shouted. "You're asking too much from me. You have no idea what I had to do to get this far. I can't give it all up now. It's worth more than my life, it *is* my whole life."

For a second, the eyes of the two met, and Ben could see something different about Kai's blue eyes. There was something inhuman about them.

"Fine . . . don't say I didn't give you a choice," Kai said as he let go of the rope.

CHAPTER 72

CHANGING SLOUGH

Tyler was unable to close his mouth, but he didn't even care that saliva was dripping on his clothes. He had been prepared that things might get a little crazy, especially after what had happened on their way back from the auction, but this was on another level. If someone had told him hours ago he would be a front-row witness to the brutal murder of his own mayor, he would have called that person crazy.

That's . . . there's no stopping this now. We have long passed the point where the Howlers can be considered just a small group, and I'm simply a driver. I ignored everything that was happening because I trusted that Gary was a good guy, but this Kai . . . I can't deal with this.

Dragging his face with his fingers, he gathered his resolve to tell Kai that he wanted to quit. But looking around, he noticed that the other gang members looked confused as well. They were just as surprised by Kai's actions, not quite understanding why he would use such an approach with the mayor, but before they had a chance to question him in any way, the Howlers' vice leader jumped off the roof.

The blond teenager had purposely let a few seconds pass before following behind their still-tied-up hostage.

"Catch my shoes!" Kai shouted, flinging them off and transforming into his werewolf self, he used his powerful legs to kick off the building to give himself an extra boost, allowing him to catch up to the mayor, who was praying to all deities to save him from certain death.

Kai used his transformed hand to stab through the mayor's back, making sure to get a strong grip. Ben screamed in pain, unable to understand what was happening in his panic. Blood was dripping from his back, and he experienced a tingling feeling throughout his entire body.

Kai's head was still mostly normal. Not so much wolf, with his nose only elongated slightly, and his teeth a little sharper than sharper usually would be, allowing him to speak a little easier.

"Do you still think that your ideals are worth dying for? Or are you ready to talk to this 'dumb teenager'? I promise you that this is the last chance that you will get. I suggest that you open your eyes now," Kai said, slightly muffled, as he was struggling to speak clearly with his larger teeth.

The mayor opened his eyes, only to see that he was halfway down the building and there was still quite a fall to go. His trousers were completely soaked.

"Do you agree to the conditions that I set, or do you wish for us to change something? I'm ready to listen, but you better make it quick," Kai prompted once more.

"Whatever you want, you crazy kid, just save me first!" the mayor shouted. "You should be locked up! I can't believe you're running this gang."

Kai smiled as he grabbed the rope still attached to the mayor before reaching over with his claws to grab the stone. Slowly, he clawed his way back up, carrying the cursing mayor with him, and eventually tossed him over the edge of the roof as his body reverted.

Seeing that the mayor was still alive, Tyler let out a sigh of relief, reconsidering his plan to quit. Still, he planned to have a talk with Kai once they were back home.

"Thank you for complying with our conditions, but I just need to correct you on one thing. I'm not the leader; just remember that." Kai said as they all left the rooftop. He untied the mayor, but he had no plans of giving him a lift. Since Ben was an Altered, he didn't worry about him not making it back, and some cardio couldn't hurt.

"Olivia, get someone to repair the walls of this building. We need to start looking after this city; we can't just leave a mess behind," Kai ordered.

The next day, Kai sat down in the basement of the Wolf's Pool Club, searching for the copies of his previous proposals. He was eager to see if the mayor would be stupid enough to deny them again. It was easy enough to understand the applications they had previously sorted, but Kai also knew that they needed to do something bigger than this to get Slough up and running and to give it a new life.

I should probably contact that electronics company. They showed interest last time.

It didn't take long to get a reply back, and a meeting was set, but the company had set one more condition.

So they want to meet the actual leader of the Howlers. I guess it's time to contact Gary and see if he's up for it, Kai thought.

Ben was in his office; he had healed up from the fight, but he wasn't so sure if he would ever recover from that horrifying experience. His hands were constantly clenching, and his back hurt every time he thought about what had happened.

"Soon everyone will be talking about the Howlers, when it was meant to be my time to shine! I worked so hard for so long, and now this!" Ben shouted at the top of his voice, his face red.

Eventually he calmed down and looked at the envelopes in front of him: the proposals by the Howlers.

Fine, I will play along with your games for now, and do as you request, but don't think I will take it lying down. There is still something that I can do. You gang members think you are strong, the new rising group.

Well, let's see how strong you are when you have to face an experienced Altered! The mayor inwardly smiled as he began writing an email addressed to his son.

CHAPTER 73

BLACK AND GOLD RETURNS

"Now arriving at . . . Slough station."

As the doors slid open, a crowd of people got off the train, surrounded by other people who were eagerly waiting for the chance to get on. Among the arrivals was a teenage boy wearing a plain white T-shirt, jeans, and a pair of running shoes. Were it not for his green hair color, he would hardly stick out from the masses.

Looking to his left and right, he recognized the dirty gum-filled spots on the floor tiles, as well as the slight smell of the nearby wastewater plant and the people that argued and shouted at each other at the train station.

Spending time at the academy had almost made him forget about how filthy his hometown actually was, but this was clearly the same old Slough that he had left not too long ago.

I guess some things don't change, but at least there aren't any gang members I have to hide from. It feels nice being able to walk around these streets without a hoodie over my head.

Leaving the train station, Gary took a right turn and continued walking down the familiar streets until he was back in the neighborhood he had grown up in. Although Gary had said he was coming back, he actually hadn't told them when he would arrive, as he wanted it to be a nice surprise for the others. Only when he was about to head farther in did a sudden realization strike him.

Shoot, I completely forgot about getting Amy that apartment in Cipen. I went in the completely wrong direction. Slapping his head, Gary turned around, wondering whether to walk or call Tyler to give him a lift.

During his absence the other core members had other things to do, so the plan was to meet up at the Wolf's Pool Club in the evening to get him up to date before the big meeting tomorrow. Until then, Gary planned to spend time with Amy.

He still regretted how he had decided to move her in with White without asking for her opinion, even though one might argue that the new apartment was an upgrade in every sense of the word. Still, he knew that he had messed up, and as her big brother he wanted to spend some quality time with her, especially since he wasn't sure when he would be able to return again.

On his way to Cipen, Gary walked past a bakery. The smell of freshly baked goods wafted into the air. He wasn't really into sweets these days, but the smell reminded him of a few pleasant memories from his childhood. Coming back with some of those blueberry muffins should certainly earn him some brownie points with his sister.

However, this wasn't the same bakery that had been there back then. The previous bakery had long closed down because of pressure from the Underdogs, so it was nice to see another one in its place.

From outside, Gary saw three young adult men wearing black-and-gold clothing through the glass window.

That's definitely the Howlers uniform, but I don't recognize those guys. They don't look like any of Austin's friends, and I also can't remember seeing them among the Pincers? Must be new members, I guess.

It was nice to see that the Howlers gang had expanded in his absence. He hadn't really paid attention, but now that he thought about it, he was sure to have passed quite a few people their colors. They were all over the place, just like the Underdogs were in the past.

"How come you are asking for a larger cut *again*? You just raised it the week before!" a woman was shouting. "I have been speaking to my friends, and their percentage has stayed the same throughout. Why does only our district's rate keep increasing?"

Gary's enhanced hearing was able to pick up her voice even from the outside. He had wanted to go inside, but now he was curious to see what was happening. In the past he might have ignored such a thing, but this was his gang. If something was affecting his old neighborhood, he needed to know it.

One of the men started to tut and wave his finger toward the woman. She was in her mid-twenties, wearing a large chef's hat and white baker's clothes. It was strange because her appearance was quite similar to that of the baker that Gary used to go to, which would have been impossible because of the amount of time that has passed.

"What are you complaining about? If it weren't for us giving you the cash, would you have been able to renovate this place? You're talking as if we haven't done anything, but who is keeping the streets safe, huh?

"Thanks to us there are no longer any gang fights or any color gangs loitering around in the streets. You could say we're keeping public order, and your business is also profiting from this, right? So don't you think it's only fair that we deserve a bonus once in a while?"

One of the three men grabbed one of the loaves of bread that were wrapped up in plastic and stacked in a basket to the side and opened it up, taking a big bite out of it. Clenching her fist, the baker was holding back her anger, restraining herself from slapping the man.

"I understand you guys helped us by getting rid of the Underdogs, but if you keep hiking up the prices, how are you any different from them? If things are going to just be the same, then I won't pay; go ahead and do your worst."

The woman then folded her arms. She was going to take a stand. In the past she had witnessed how the other members of the public didn't take a stand against these gangs, and they were able to do what they wanted. Under the Underdogs she had been forced to use up her reserves. Thanks to the change in leadership, she had been able to save up a bit again, but she was unwilling to give that up again.

There was also a deeper reason: no matter what, she needed to make this bakery a success. Since it was new, she still had a lack of loyal customers and a lot of start-up costs. Every penny she had went into this bakery, so she wasn't able to pay either way.

The man in the Howlers uniform was beyond annoyed, and he reached out and slammed his hand on top of the chef's hat flattening it, and then through the hat he grabbed the blond girl's head and pulled her forward.

"You think you're a smart bitch!" the man shouted, right in her face, his spittle hitting her face. "Do you even know who the fuck we are?"

"Of course," she replied, with a pained look on her face. "Typical that you resort to violence. I guess this makes you feel big, huh? Do you think it somehow compensates for the fact that you have nothing down there?"

He started to pull her forward even more, but before he could he felt a hand on the back of his head.

"What the fuck are you doing in my town?"

The other two men looked at the green-haired teenager who had just entered the shop and was holding their friend by the back of his hair.

The man tried to turn around. "How dare you touch a member of the How—"

Gary slammed the man's head down into the counter, breaking his nose and cracking the wood. When he let go, the man slid onto the floor.

"Are you crazy, boy? Do you know what you just did?" the others said, shocked. "Do you have any idea who we are?"

"Yeah, you're an utter disgrace to that name, so I will make sure you're never allowed to say it ever again," Gary said.

CHAPTER 74

THE LEADER RETURNS (PART 1)

Naomi stood behind the counter with her hand covering her mouth. She was in disbelief at what had happened right in front of her. She hadn't been running the bakery for a long time, but to be honest, these people who asked for protection money every once in a while were getting to her.

She knew that having to pay protection money was simply a necessary evil if one wanted to work in any town, but the frequency with which these gang members were harassing her about it was getting out of hand. At times she'd wanted to slap them herself, but she knew that it wouldn't end with that. The Howlers weren't just any gang in Slough, but the biggest one, so doing any such thing would only make it worse in the end.

Naomi had merely resisted today because she was out of options, never expecting someone to intervene on her behalf, much less to see one of the gang members slumped over on her floor with blood dripping out from his mouth.

"You fucker!" another gang member shouted at the teenage boy whose back was toward her.

The boss told us something like this would happen since it's a new area, and since the gang hasn't quite made their name everywhere, some people would test us. Regardless, he was only able to take Joe down because he caught him by surprise! the man thought.

"Don't mess with the Howlers!" the man shouted as his fist flew toward the boy's head . . . only to hit nothing but air. Gary had calmly moved his head to the side, and now he grabbed the attacker's forearm, a deadly grip that caused the gang member to scream out in pain. He felt that his bones were on the verge of breaking.

"I just told you that you should keep that name out of your filthy mouth!" Gary threw a punch cleanly into the man's face and let go of his forearm at the same time, sending him flying back. He crashed into the door of the shop, causing the glass to crack but not break.

"Dillan! Are you okay? Wake up, man, wake up!" The last gang member crouched down next to him, but Dillan had been knocked out completely. Realizing this, the man stood up, his legs shaking slightly.

"You! You will pay for this!" the man threatened as he pulled out his phone and ran back out through the entrance of the shop.

"That damned coward! He left his friends lying on the ground," Gary mumbled to himself; it didn't look like they would be getting up anytime soon.

"Do you— Do you realize what you've just done?" the baker asked.

Glancing around the room, Gary saw that some of the shelves had been knocked over, the countertop was damaged, and the glass on the front door was broken. The place was a mess, that was for sure.

"I'm sorry about all of this," Gary said, scratching the back of his head. "I promise you won't have to worry; I'll have everything fixed up for you in no time."

Folding her arms, Naomi let out a big sigh. She knew that it wouldn't be right to be angry at him. After all, he had gotten involved to help her, seemingly unaware of the consequences of his actions.

Who is this kid? How can someone say those words so easily? He doesn't look like he has any idea how much these repairs will cost. Not like a teenager in Slough even has that type of money in the first place.

"I wasn't talking about the shop," she clarified. "You can forget about that. What I'm concerned about is you. Look, you might be some strong student who likes fighting, but you just messed with one of the Howlers gang members. You need to get out of here and hide. Those guys aren't the type who are quick to forgive, and I don't want you here when they come back."

Naomi moved from behind the counter and started to push Gary out of the shop. He resisted and pulled an awkward face.

This woman is really nice, I can tell she is concerned for me, but how do I convince her she has nothing to worry about? It's not like she will believe me if I tell her that I'm the head of the gang that was harassing her.

"Will you stop being so stubborn? Come on, just get out of the shop quickly before more of them—" Naomi's voice trailed off as she looked at the street in front of them.

About ten men in black-and-gold uniforms were coming toward them. They didn't exactly look friendly, and standing in the center of them all was a bald man with a scar on his face, carrying a wooden sword over his shoulder.

"That's him, Park, that's the one who's causing trouble!" the man who belonged to the trio from earlier said as he pointed at Gary.

Park shook his head as he tapped the wooden sword on his shoulder.

"I can't believe that there is someone dumb enough to try to cause trouble here, when everyone knows this is Howlers territory. Unfortunately for you, boy, the Great Park has been assigned to this area, and the boss said we need to do everything we can to protect this place."

Taking the sword off his shoulder, Park pointed it right toward Gary.

"Get him!"

CHAPTER 75

THE LEADER RETURNS (PART 2)

Gary couldn't help but shake his head at the sight in front of him. In the past, if he had been surrounded by ten gang members like this, he would have been shaking in his boots. However, after everything he had been through, fighting off a group of normal thugs seemed like child's play. His system seemed to agree with him, not even bothering to issue a quest.

I don't mind beating them all up, but that wouldn't exactly reflect well on the Howlers. Is there any way for me to get out of this without a fight? If I tell them that I'm their leader, they won't believe me. Should I call Kai or Olivia and get them to vouch for me?

"Watch out!" Naomi shouted as two men threw their fists at the same time to teach the teenager a lesson.

Gary calmly grabbed the men's incoming fists and quickly twisted their arms, then kicked one of them in the back. The blow was so strong that it knocked the man off his feet and into his friend, sending them both tumbling down to the ground.

Kai told me that it's important to hide my identity, for my sake as well as Amy's. The leader of the Howlers should be feared but remain a mystery, and it's kinda too late to put on my mask.

One of the larger Howlers rugby-tackled Gary with full force, yet the man was unable to push him even an inch. The teenager slammed his hands down on the man's back, causing the gang member to yell out in pain as he fell.

Damn it, I have to keep in mind that these guys are more fragile than the Altered from the academy. These guys won't be able to recover in a short amount of time. If I don't hold back my strength, I might accidentally end up killing or crippling them. That would be bad, especially since they're technically my gang members.

Naomi stood at the door, unable to believe her eyes. It had already been impressive enough to see this stranger come into her shop and defeat two adult men. Part of her had still thought that the green-haired teenager had been lucky to be facing only a few inexperienced gang members, but now it was clear that he was really extraordinary.

The cuts on these gang members' faces and their enlarged knuckles were proof that this batch of Howlers were more experienced, but somehow the teenager was dealing with them without much effort. Three men charged toward Gary with a kick and a punch, while the third one stayed a bit farther back.

Moving in quickly, Gary closed in on the man before his kick connected and pushed him, knocking him off balance. Now he was dealing with the other one by kicking him in the backs of his legs, making him fall to his knees.

Arghh, this whole situation is super annoying. You guys aren't even worth a single Exp point.

In the middle of his thoughts, Gary heard something cutting through the wind. Lifting his head, he quickly made out what it was. He opened his palm to stop the flying object.

–1 HP

Gary looked at the small knife that was now stuck in his palm. The wound hardly did anything to him, and if he took out the knife he knew his body would just heal it up. Regardless, he was shaking with anger.

The kneeling man who had been kicked from behind saw this as an opportunity and tried to grab Gary's leg, intending to restrain him so others could finish him off. However, Gary quickly stomped on the man's hand, which cracked loudly as he crushed it against the concrete.

"I was going easy on you guys because it was clear to me that this was mostly a misunderstanding," Gary said in a gruff tone that sounded slightly like a growl. "That ends now. I won't overlook what you bastards just did. It's one thing for you to attack me, but since when is it okay for the Howlers to drag innocent bystanders into their fights?"

The gang members were unsure what he was talking about, but Naomi figured it out. She was standing in the path of where the knife was thrown. Gary could have easily avoided the knife, yet he had deliberately blocked it, so she wouldn't get hit.

This . . . this is definitely not the actions of a kid, Naomi thought, feeling bad for how she had treated him earlier. *This man saved me, and he still is thinking of me, even at a time like this.*

Although she had no clue how old Gary was, she was starting to see him in a different light. She had never felt indebted to someone like this before. Pulling the knife out from the palm of his hand, Gary immediately threw it back, piercing the leg of the original thrower, who yelled out in pain.

I was in a good mood today . . . I was happy that I was going to see Amy again, but you just had to go and ruin it. I thought it was okay to leave everything to Kai, but it seems I'll need to help him sort out some of the rotten members.

The energy coming off Gary was giving Park the creeps. It was like every cell in his body was telling him to run away, but his brain argued that it was just one teenager when there were nearly a dozen gangsters on his side. If they caved, it would be a disgrace to the Howlers name. Unsure what to do, he pulled his phone out of his pocket.

In his office, Kai was doing his paperwork as normal when he received a phone call. The caller had been saved as *Team Leader #17 (Park)*. The blond teenager let out a sigh as he accepted the call and pressed speaker.

"Sir, I know you told me not to contact you unless there is an emergency, but there is big trouble on Bader Street!"

"How many?" Kai asked nonchalantly as he continued to sift through papers.

"It's just one person, sir, but if someone doesn't come soon, we're going to be in big trouble."

Bader Street? Kai thought. *We've invested quite a bit in that area since it's where Gary's old apartment was. It won't look good if something happens to it, especially when he should be coming today.*

"Just hold out for a little longer. Help will be on the way," Kai replied, and he hung up before calling another number.

CHAPTER 76

A SPECIAL BOY
(PART 1)

A powerful right hook sent yet another gang member flying through the air, leaving only two gang members in fighting condition. Park and the man who had called over Park's group looked quite nervous, because it was far too late to run away.

Just where did that guy come from, and just what gang is he working for? Park wondered, aware that he needed to buy enough time for reinforcements to arrive. *Could he be the leader of a color gang from another town who has come here to take over our territory?*

Park's appraisal would have been a compliment for most. After all, color gang leaders were strong fighters, but of course Gary was on a completely different level. The team leader didn't even consider the possibility that the green-haired teenager might have been holding back.

At that moment, the image of people in black and gold masks appeared in Park's head. Their leaders were naturally the strongest fighters of their gang, with one of them even rumored to be an Altered. As long as this teenager wasn't one himself, he would be finished if one of their leaders had been sent over.

"I have to admit you are skillful." Park chuckled as he looked forward to seeing Gary get beaten up. He held his wooden sword firmly in his hand. "But I bet you've never had to go up against someone who can use a weapon like this."

Park ran toward Gary carrying the wooden sword with both hands above his head. The street had cleared out. The pained screams of the injured gang members had been loud enough to make the people in the area aware that there was a fight going on, and nobody wished to get involved.

The only ones watching the fight were the shop owners and a few customers who had refused to leave, out of fear or sheer curiosity. All of them looked at the commotion that was happening outside.

As the wooden sword approached his head, Gary calmly stopped it with his previously injured hand. "You have courage, but the right thing to do if an opponent is far stronger than you is to run away!" the teenager lectured as he tensed his muscles and snapped the wooden sword into pieces.

Looking directly into Gary's eyes, Park fell on his backside and started to scoot away. At that moment, the two men who had been knocked out in the shop came outside as well, limping and bleeding.

"What . . . is all of this? Did that guy do all of this?" one of them asked. Seeing the frightened look on Park's face and the person standing above him, he had no doubt that this was all caused by one person.

"Park, look behind you!" one of the men from the shop shouted.

Turning his head, he saw five people in black-and-gold clothing running toward them; not only that, but one of them wore a black and gold mask.

Tears of joy fell from Park's eyes when he saw that his silent prayers had been answered.

One of the leaders of the Howlers has really come. Turning back toward Gary, he smiled confidently. "You are truly done now. We told you that messing with the Howlers was a bad idea, and now you'll understand!"

Park stood up quickly and ran to join those running toward them, but stopped as the one in the mask lifted his hand, telling the others to stop before him.

"Lieutenant! Thank you for answering our call," Park said, bowing down. "We are sorry we were unable to get rid of the one causing trouble in the area. He is skillful, but now that you are here, I'm sure that you will be able to deal with him. Please help us!"

Park lifted his head and saw the person in the mask walking toward him with his fist clenched. He was looking forward to watching the green-haired punk be punished for what he had done.

"Haha, your life is over!" Park said with a sadistic smile, but as he turned around, he saw a fist approaching his face. Ironically, it didn't belong to the green-haired teenager; instead it was coming from his very own leader.

The fist landed strongly, knocking Park's face to the side, and once again he fell to the ground.

"Leader!" Park exclaimed, his mouth throbbing. "What did I do?"

"You idiot!" the masked man shouted at him. "All of you are idiots! And the worst part is that none of you even have the slightest idea about who you just tried to hit right now! All of you, get on your knees and beg him for forgiveness."

Seeing this, the masked man looked at Gary, who stood there with a smile plastered on his face. He knew exactly who was behind the mask, and he was happy to watch how he treated the gang members.

I'm glad they sent you, Innu, Gary thought.

"Make sure that none of you so much as look at him without express permission in the future! Now you, explain everything that happened to me right now!" Innu ordered.

Naomi, who had been watching everything from behind the safety of her damaged door, was just as confused as the Howlers members. Nevertheless, they knew better than to argue with Innu, so without understanding the reason they crawled their way toward him, with aches and pains.

Those watching from their shops were curious about the sight they were seeing, to the point where they pulled out their phones and began filming the event. Never in their life had they seen a gang act this way, in front of what looked like a teenager.

"I appreciate the gesture, but I'm late for a meeting with my sister," Gary said as he patted his friend's shoulder. "Please make sure that this woman's bakery will be up and running as soon as possible. As for this one?" Gary pointed to the man who had thrown the knife. "Kick him out of the gang, and do the same with the other three who were in the shop. I'll be honest, I'm not sure if that sword-wielding guy really knows what is going on, but I'm sure you can run an investigation into what happened. I will leave these matters to you and we'll catch up later, okay?"

Innu nodded as Gary ran off toward Cipen.

He just ordered one of the leaders of the Howlers like that . . . and they all listened to him, even about fixing the shop? Namoi scratched her head. *Who was that guy?*

CHAPTER 77

A SPECIAL BOY
(PART 2)

There were now many bases of the Howlers gang spread around the town. They were used to pass on information, work as a base of operations, handle income, devise outcomes, and more.

In fact, many of the bases were just places that the old gangs used to use, and the Howlers had taken over. It was impossible for Kai to micromanage everything, which was why these bases were being used.

Each area had a captain of a squad, and they would pass down the information that was received from the core leader, who was in charge of certain districts.

In this case, Kai passed the information to Innu, who then passed the information to the captain of the squad and in this case, the captain of this squad in that particular area was Innu.

However, each squad captain also had Kai's number, which was only to be used in emergencies, and Park had deemed the situation enough of an emergency to contact him.

Kai had set up this system to control all of Slough as well as the Howlers gang as it got bigger and bigger. He knew they would need to make adjustments here and there, but this was his concept.

If it worked, then it would also work when they spread outside Slough and started to operate in other cities as well. For now, Kai was imagining each district as a separate city.

There was another reason for doing things this way, and that was to keep the identity of the core members, or the lieutenants of the gang as some of the members referred to them, secret.

When they met up with other members of the Howlers gang or were in the area, the core members wore the masks on their faces to hide their identity. Of course, some people knew the real appearance of these core members.

Olivia was a prime example, as nearly everyone recognized her with or without a mask, but the masks still made it harder to identify them. In the end, each core member could decide when to reveal their real face or to whom.

Currently, Park and all of the members involved in the bakery incident were in one of the bases. This base was inside one of the sporting goods shops that were part of their territory.

In the back of the shop was a stockroom with a cleared-out area for them to conduct their meeting in. All of the members, including the injured ones, had been made to go down on their knees.

This was all on the orders of Innu, who stood at the front with his arms folded.

"I can't believe you guys. I explained to you all about the importance of this area to the gang," Innu said, shaking his head.

"An investigation is currently ongoing to find out what happened. Now, I don't like to waste my time, so I'm going to tell you all now. If we find a reason why what happened today happened, your punishment will be a harsh one. Or you can tell me now whatever it is you are hiding, to make your punishment lighter."

Although Gary had told him to get rid of certain members from the gang, Innu felt that these people were his responsibility, and in order for something like this not to happen again, he needed to find out the truth of the matter.

The three men at the back glanced toward each other, and eventually the one in the center, who was unhurt, lifted his head.

"It all started with us," he admitted. "We were collecting our payments like we usually do and . . . we asked for a little more. We thought the gang could use the funds. The owner said that she was struggling. Because of that, she refused to pay and . . . that's when that kid got involved."

"You asked for more?" Park repeated as he turned his head to look at them. "Didn't you numbskulls listen to anything I said? We don't ever ask for more, and those who are struggling you report back to me!"

Park was furious, because he knew that the lieutenant had emphasized this point several times.

"What is so wrong?" one of the beaten-up members asked. "Why are you making a big deal about asking for a bit more money? We were the ones who got hurt. I mean, we're a gang, right? We're already extorting people, and we're bringing in money for the gang. What's wrong with that?"

Innu stomped his foot loudly on the concrete floor, causing everyone to shut up.

"There is nothing I can do. All three of you are to leave the gang immediately. You are never to use the Howlers name again or apply to join the gang in any way or form." Innu was blunt with his words, and since this was an order from Gary in the first place, he would have had to do it anyway.

Immediately, the three of them stood up.

"Wait, you're really going to listen to that green-haired punk and kick us out of the gang? I don't understand! What the fuck did we do wrong, other than getting our asses kicked trying to protect the gang's name?"

"Because those are the leader's rules!" Innu shouted back. "We made it clear when everyone joined the Howlers that we are different from other typical gangs. Our protection fee is more like a service to the shops, so the other gangs don't touch them and they feel safe.

"But your actions undermined that. We're trying to build rapport with the people in this community. In truth, if there were no other gangs and the police actually did their job properly, there would be no need for us to even do this.

"But our leader has said that we are the necessary evil that has to exist in this world. That's why we do what we do."

Innu then looked toward one more person, who had his entire foot bandaged up.

"You as well, you are no longer part of the Howlers gang. The leader has said clearly that there is another rule. The Howlers are to try not to involve the general public.

"Gangs may fight with other gangs, those who know what they are getting into, but we are not to involve the general public who don't wish to live the same life as ours. Only if you feel like your life is on the line are you allowed to be aggressive toward them, which is why throwing that blade without thinking means you are no longer allowed to be in the gang."

The member stood up, clenching a shaking fist, and paused a moment before protesting.

"That green-haired person, he *is* someone, isn't he?" the man asked. "No normal teenager is that skilled at fighting, or can throw a knife like that. On top of that, you followed his orders down to the letter by getting rid of us. You've just done it in a roundabout way so we don't get suspicious." The man smiled. "I guess we just messed with someone that we weren't meant to touch."

Then he bowed down. "Thank you for the opportunity that you have given me."

With that he started to walk away, but suddenly he whirled around.

"This is bullshit! What kind of rules are these! We did nothing wrong! Screw you and screw your gang!" the man shouted as he charged toward Innu.

Park was ready to get up and stop him, but Innu charged forward and kneed the man in the stomach, and his attacker fell to the floor.

"Please, don't make me kick all of your asses, because you know I can," Innu declared. "The rest of you, get out of here, and remember to follow the rules; I know you were all just following procedure, so there's no need to worry about that."

The gang members stood up and started to walk out of the room; however, Park waited until all of them had left and it was just him and Innu.

"I wanted to ask, sir, about that boy; who was he? Should I be aware of his presence as part of the gang, and why was he so . . . skilled?"

Innu smiled at the question.

"I can't really say anything, but I will tell you this. It would be good in the future if you ever did see him to do whatever you can to get on his good side, and to just do whatever he asks."

CHAPTER 78

BROTHER AND SISTER

Eventually Gary reached Cipen. The district was filled with paved walkways, nice restaurants, and all types of shops selling everything from general appliances and fancy clothes to the latest generation of electronic gimmicks. On top of that were some of the top hotels and apartments in the area.

Following the directions on his phone, the teenager finally reached what looked like the outside of a hotel lobby.

This place looks like a castle compared to our old place. At the start of the year I would have never thought I'd live in a place like this, much less own it. Well, I guess it's not completely right to say 'we' are living in a place like this since, seeing as I haven't actually been inside yet, Gary thought.

A man opened the door for him and bowed, welcoming him inside.

"Welcome . . . sir." The man hesitated slightly for some reason. Unsure whether he had the right place, Gary proceeded across the pale marble flooring until he reached the reception desk. The employees behind the counter exchanged looks before they spoke to the new arrival.

"Is there anything we can help you with, sir?" asked a man in a suit whose name tag said *Stin*.

"Um, yes, I'm actually looking for apartment 2306. It's supposed to be located in this hotel," Gary said. Personally, he found it a bit strange that there were apartments in hotels, but Kai had told him that it was quite common with large buildings.

"Ah, yes, we do have that apartment number here, but are you sure you are at the right place? There are plenty of other places that perhaps have the same room number. If you need any help, we could direct you," the man offered with a smile.

Gary looked at his phone, with the texted address from Kai. It said the Biltop Hotel, and judging by the giant sign behind the receptionist, this was without a doubt the Biltop Hotel.

"No, I'm pretty sure that this is the right hotel. Could you tell me how I can get to that apartment?" Gary asked again, politely.

"Sir, is there any reason for you to go to the apartment? Could you share your reason for visiting today? We haven't been informed about any visits, and our rules state that we do have to contact the owner in question in these kinds of situations, to make sure that we don't send someone up by mistake," the man explained.

Gary was starting to find the whole conversation frustrating, but he felt like this level of security for the apartments was quite nice. If it took this much for someone to see his sister, then they were at least doing their job.

"I mean you can do that, but . . . that would be a little weird." Gary scratched his cheek. "I'm actually the owner of that apartment. It's just my first time coming here, so I really don't know the way."

The man appeared stunned, and he looked to his colleague once more. In fact he even chuckled a bit.

"I see now. I hope you have enjoyed your little joke. Now, if you don't mind, we adults have to work. If you wish to exit the building, the doors are that way." The man gestured.

Now Gary was the one raising an eyebrow. *Why is everyone treating me so weirdly?*

"Did I stutter? Can you just tell me how to get to apartment 2306?" Gary asked again, allowing himself to sound annoyed.

"Sir, if you do not leave, we will have to call security."

"Call them!" Gary shouted back. "Maybe they can freaking show me where room 2306 is!"

Now that Gary was causing a scene, people began looking his way. The security staff looked like they were ready to take action.

"Gary!" a voice called out.

He turned around to see a pale-skinned woman approaching, and it could be only one person.

"White?" Gary replied. "It's a good thing you're here. Maybe you can help me get to the room."

The man behind the desk looked nervous as he and White exchanged glances.

Miss White . . . she seems to actually know the boy, the man realized in shock. His manager had warned them to treat Miss White and Miss Amy with the utmost respect, fulfilling their every wish. Apparently, one of the two was related to their latest investor, who now owned 10 percent of their entire hotel.

"I'm sorry!" The receptionist immediately apologized. "We had no clue this boy was a guest of yours. We promise if we see him again we will treat him with the same respect as you! I apologize for my negligence, sir!"

White said nothing, just waved the man off as she escorted Gary to the express elevator that went directly to the twenty-third floor.

As they got on the elevator and the doors closed, White finally let out a sigh. "Have you figured out why they treated you like that? No? It's because you look like a homeless person off the street," White said, as Gary gave her a confused look. "Since you were coming to visit your sister, couldn't you have at least worn something nice for her?"

Gary looked down at himself. Admittedly, his current outfit was a far cry from fancy, but calling him a homeless person seemed like a stretch. He was wearing his comfy clothes, a collared shirt and jeans, though they were scrunched up, a button had been ripped off, and there was even a bit of blood on his shirt.

All of this because of the fight that Gary had gotten in a little while ago.

"At a place as fancy as this, of course they are going to try to stop you if you come in dressed like that. Although they are undoubtedly snobs, I think they had a reason to act like that," White said.

All Gary could do was smile awkwardly; next time he would have to dress up a bit, but if he had fought in an expensive suit, it would cause other problems.

Either way, he could ignore everything that happened, because he was ready to see his sister's smile.

When White opened the door to the apartment, Gary was greeted with a sight he could only imagine in his dreams. A glass window overlooked the entire town.

The living area boasted top-of-the-line wooden flooring and a nice sofa set facing a jumbo TV. The apartment had four bathrooms and a nice kitchen with an island and all the cooking equipment you could need.

However, Gary didn't care about any of that; instead he immediately ran over to the person sitting on the sofa and gave her a big hug from behind.

"Hey, what are you doing holding me so tightly, White?" Amy grumbled, startled by this sudden attack, only to realize that the forearms were far too muscular to be those of a woman.

"I used to look forward to having a room of my own, but honestly I never thought I would miss you so much," Gary said.

Immediately, Amy recognized who it was and stood up. Tears flowed from her eyes and rolled down her cheeks uncontrollably.

"You . . . you big green idiot! Why didn't you tell me you were coming?" Amy complained as she threw her arms around Gary, who held her close.

"Family," White mumbled as she watched the reunion with a smile. "It's . . . a good thing to have."

"When did you get back? What are you doing here? How long will you stay? How was the academy?" Amy had a number of questions for her brother, since the two of them had a lot to catch up on.

"Don't worry, I'll stay here long enough to answer your questions, but I want to ask you some of my own, like how are you doing in the new school? Did you manage to make some friends already? Why don't we talk while we head to the hospital? I thought we could visit Mom together and see how she's doing."

The smile dropped from Amy's face. Gary didn't understand why; he thought it would be good to have the family back together.

Sure, seeing their mother was always upsetting, but it had been a while now since she had been hospitalized, and at least her condition had not worsened. They had visited her together a few times before Gary had left.

"Sorry, I didn't mean to act all weird," Amy said. "I think catching up and going to visit her is a great idea. It's just . . . I think there is something else I need to show you, before we head to see Mom."

Amy rushed off into her room, and a few moments later she returned with a letter.

"Shortly after I moved here, this showed up on the doorstep. I haven't looked inside yet, but the sender is . . . Dad."

CHAPTER 79

LETTER FROM A FATHER

The smell of chemicals, disinfectant, cleaning supplies, and more was entering Gary's nose, and on top of that, there was one that his Werewolf self had come to know quite well: blood.

Despite this being a nicer hospital compared to the others, they all had the same smell in the end, and ever since the day when he and Amy were standing outside waiting for the result of what had happened to his mother, Gary hated coming to the hospital no matter what reason it was for.

"She looks so peaceful since you moved her here," Amy said as she rubbed her mother's hand on the bed.

Surprisingly, or not at this rate, Gary had his mother in a private room. In one of the best hospitals in Slough. Despite all of that, seeing his mother lying there, hooked up to a bunch of needles, bags, and machinery all around her, none of it made him feel good, and he knew Amy's words were just to make him feel better.

Sitting down in a chair by the bed, Gary reached out to hold her hand along with Amy. He looked at her, just breathing in and out.

"Looks like you're still sleeping, Mom. I guess you're tired after looking after us two for so long, but you deserve all the rest you need. You always looked after us," Gary said, his voice choking up. He had to look down at the floor for a few seconds and could feel Amy rubbing his back.

"I'm sorry, Mom, after all this time, I still haven't found the one who did this to you. But I haven't stopped looking, it's just on pause for now, but I promise I will make them pay, but let's talk about some good things.

"The family is doing well. Amy is able to focus on her grades, and she's enjoying the new apartment I got her. I wish you could see it, I think you would love it as well. It has this big kitchen that I asked for. Honestly when I was thinking about it, I was thinking of you and how you loved to cook for us. I really . . . I really miss your meals. I really do." Gary started to sob, his shoulders moving up and down as he couldn't take it anymore.

Leader of the largest gang in Slough, part of the AFA, and an Altered on top of all that, well kind of an Altered. There were many who would dream to be in the position Gary was in right now, do anything to get what he had, but he just wanted his mother back, for her to wake up at this point in time.

After a few minutes Gary had recovered and was just enjoying the time with his sister by his mother. They were sharing funny stories as if their mother were able to hear them, speaking out loud and laughing away, until a serious point came up.

There were no more smiles from Gary as he pulled out the letter that Amy had given him; it was still sealed, and the contents of the letter were unknown.

"I know he abandoned our family, he never came to visit while we were struggling, but you told us never to resent him despite all of that. You told us to trust him if he ever did come back.

"I still honestly really can't, and both me and Amy feel the same way. Which is why I thought it would be best if we open this letter here together as a family."

Gary's heart was beating quite a bit. He didn't even know what his father looked like, and he couldn't remember his voice or even his smell. Which was why Gary found it hard to say he had a connection with such a person.

Yet, for some reason, he was nervous about the contents of the letter. The only reason why Amy knew it was from their father was the writing on the envelope: *To my family.*

On top of that, their father used to write to them long ago; their mother had shown them those old letters, and the handwriting matched.

Gary began reading out loud.

It's been a long time since I last wrote to you all, and for that, I would like to apologize.

I wonder how you are all doing. I wonder how much Amy and Gary have grown up. I hope that they aren't having any problems, and I wish that the life you and they are currently living is a far more peaceful one than mine.

There is a reason why I haven't written to you regularly, and I wish to explain that in person, not on a piece of paper where words can mean nothing. I always believed that actions speak truer than words, and in your eyes I know that my actions have been worthless.

As for writing to you now, the burden of not seeing you all has gotten to be a little bit too much these days. Which is why I plan to end my journey as quickly as I can, so I can see you all soon.

The letter ended there, not really saying much of anything, except for the last part.

"Does this mean Dad will be coming back to Slough?" Amy asked.

Gary scrunched up the piece of paper there and then.

"I don't know, but he wasn't here when Mom was struggling, and he probably doesn't even know about her being in the hospital. He hasn't been in our lives so far, so I wouldn't count on him being in our lives anytime soon."

Amy didn't know what to say about that, but as Gary left the room, he threw the letter in the trash can. She couldn't help herself and picked it back out. Her feelings weren't as strong as Gary's toward her father because in the end, her mother was the one who chose him, and there had to be a reason for that.

After visiting the hospital, Gary took Amy back to the apartment and prepared to say his goodbyes to her and White before he went to the Wolf's Pool Club, but before he left, White asked Gary to step into the hallway just outside the apartment.

"Gary, it was a good thing to do, surprising your little sister like that. She was really happy that you were coming," White said. "But next time, why don't you tell her you're coming? Sure, she's happy today, but if she had known you were coming, she could have been happy the whole week knowing that you were coming. She really misses you."

Gary waved goodbye, and was thankful that he had met White, someone who could be by Amy's side when he wasn't there, because if she weren't, it would have been too painful to leave Amy on her own.

They'd spent the whole day together; the night sky was out, and the Wolf's Pool Club, along with several bars and establishments nearby, was livelier than before. Gary remembered the days when the pool club was on the border between two territories and was constantly involved in fights. No one wanted to establish a business here.

Yet there had been a significant change to the place, thanks to the Howlers gang, and it was nice to see the Howlers having a positive effect after witnessing what had occurred at the bakery.

Gary walked into the club, which was busy with customers, and Miss Degrace was busy working as always. There was no need for her to work at the bar anymore, but she seemed happy with her place at the club and the work she did.

None of the others that Gary was looking for were inside, at least not on the public floor.

"They're downstairs; they've been waiting for you for a while," Miss Degrace said.

As Gary made his way downstairs to Kai's office, Miss Degrace gave him a few passing words.

"Welcome back; we have missed you, leader." She whispered the last word, but Gary could still hear it.

The one thing he still couldn't get used to being called was leader, and his face lit up bright red every time he heard those words.

When he reached the bottom of the stairs, everyone was sitting there, split between two sofas, and Kai sat in his office chair, waiting.

"Gary! You finally made it!" Kai shouted.

Everyone said Gary's name and gave him a big welcome. They stood up and gave him a punch here or there, or even a hug, especially Marie, who squeezed him tight. She wasn't sure if she was imagining things, but it felt like Gary had gotten slightly bigger than before.

"Okay, calm down, everyone, because I need to talk to Gary about something. Have you seen this?" Kai asked as he lifted up his phone, and there was a video: a video of Gary.

CHAPTER 80

BUSINESS TYCOON

Everyone in the room had already watched the video that Kai was currently playing. Since they lived in Slough, they were updated with the latest, and on top of that, Kai always hammered into them that it was important to stay on top of current news.

"What . . . someone was filming all of that?" Gary said as he grabbed the phone out of Kai's hand.

It showed him from behind, a green-haired teenager, quickly dealing with the Howlers members, then giving direct orders to Innu behind the mask.

"This is partly my fault," Innu admitted as he sulked and sat back down on the sofa. "I should have checked to see if anyone had filmed anything, but I was just so focused on punishing those guys, and so surprised to see you return."

The video had been filmed by one of the shop owners. Based on the comments, many of them knew that the black-and-gold clothing belonged to the Howlers gang, which led to many questions in the comments underneath the video.

I'm worried for that kid, the Howlers gang now might send some big guns after him. I mean they took over Slough, how could someone like that stand up to them?

Didn't you watch the video properly? He was ordering them around, and his fighting skills were amazing. He's probably the son of the leader or something and the other members just didn't know who they were messing with.

Who is the green-haired boy, does anyone recognize him?

That green-haired boy, I think it's Gary. He used to go to my school, he's just a normal person.

No way, you must be mistaking him for some other green-haired person.

The comments went on and on and Gary was surprised at how much information was being dug up.

"Is it really that bad? And what should we do about it?" Gary asked.

"Thankfully the video hasn't gone viral. It's only spread around Slough since the Howlers are really only the talk of Slough, but your face is familiar within the AFA now as well. So if it does become widespread, maybe they will find out you were a student of the AFA.

"We were planning to publicly sponsor and support you, but not until you entered the AFC. Right now, while the Howlers are still new and in their expanding stage, I don't want to draw too much attention just yet."

Kai put his finger on his chin, a habit when he was thinking quite hard, and eventually sat down.

"I do have an idea, something that I have been thinking about for a while now, that will help us and you. The number one thing we need to do is make sure that other gangs don't know that Gary Dem is the leader of the Howlers.

"Now, we have already incorporated the masks for the higher-ups of the Howlers gang, so most don't know your face, but once Gary Dem of the AFA gets well known, and your ability is out there for the world to see, some people might be able to put two and two together.

"Which is why my plan is to make you"—Kai pointed—"the Gary Dem right here, another person of greatness!"

Gary raised an eyebrow, and so did many others in the room, because they really didn't know where Kai was going with this.

"People know that the Howlers are a gang in Slough, and there are some businesses and places that are scared of us. It makes them unwilling to take our investment money or to work with us at times.

"Although sometimes companies can see the benefit of working with a gang, that is mainly the larger corporations, and this is where you would come in. I would like Gary Dem to create his own company of sorts.

"The Dem Foundation would invest in small businesses, helping them thrive. Gary Dem would be a business genius who turns around companies and makes a fortune. Of course, most of the funds would be moving between the Howlers' corporation and yours, but the public won't know this.

"All they need to see is the public image that we project of you. In the end, people will think the Howlers listened to you, as you are a wealthy person. At the same time, your mother won't be so suspicious about where the money has come from either. You will have an answer for her.

"We can also approach businesses from both sides; if they have investment opportunities from the family man Gary Dem and the Howlers, they think they have a choice but in reality the offers are both coming from the same person. This is perfect!"

Kai was rambling on, and there was such a large smile on his face that Gary was finding it hard to interrupt.

When do I tell him I have no clue what he's talking about? Kai is a lot smarter than me; maybe I should just trust him with all of this, and I really do need a way to tell Mom how I made all the money.

At first, the Wolf's Pool Club would have been a good answer for how I'm paying all the bills, but it wouldn't explain the apartment and a luxury car, among other things, Gary thought.

Kai was still smirking to himself, mumbling under his breath, and writing on a piece of paper as if he was piecing out his plan.

"By day, you can be Gary Dem, the young business tycoon, and by night, the Howlers' gang leader, the bloodsucking werewolf!"

"What do you want us to do, then?" Innu asked, raising his hand. "There have already been a few people asking who Gary is."

"That's perfect," Kai replied. "We can start spreading the rumor within the Howlers first; if people hear it from the Howlers gang, it'll be more credible."

Kai wrote on a piece of paper, then handed it to the others to pass around. It told them what to say when other members asked about their leader. Everything was moving a bit too fast for Gary, especially since he had just gotten here, but as usual he would just need to ride the wave.

"Is there anything that you need me to do?" he asked.

"For now, just focus on the AFA and other things; we will take care of spreading your name," Kai replied. "Besides, we have bigger things to worry about at the moment. Why don't we all catch up a bit on what has happened?"

The group started to talk about the events that had occurred: everything the members of the Howlers had gone through while Gary was away. He was amazed about what happened to Blake, and wondered if he should pay him a visit.

However, he was even more surprised that Austin had become an Altered. After learning of this, he immediately asked Austin to transform for him, which he did.

Austin also asked Gary if the two of them could have a little sparring match. Gary couldn't lie; he was definitely interested, especially after fighting all the Altered at the AFA.

More than likely, though, after the strength Gary had gained at the AFA, maybe he was another step ahead of everyone here as well.

After that, it was Gary's turn to tell them about everything that had happened in the AFA, and that it looked like there was no easy ride for him there. He explained why he was unable to contact them, along with everything else.

The only thing that Gary left out was the special lessons. He had been instructed to keep them a secret, and although he trusted everyone here to never tell a soul, he didn't want them to get in trouble.

NIRV was a much larger corporation, with its hands in the pockets of the biggest gangs; a gang like the Howlers, although growing, should not upset them, so it was better for him to just keep his lips sealed.

"I'm happy to know that you have not just been doing well but have been doing really well. This will increase our publicity even more when you have your debut match." Kai smirked. "But before all that, I guess we should start.

"Tomorrow will be a big day for you and the Howlers; it could be the starting point of progressing the Howlers from a Tier 3 town into something more, so let me ask . . . are you ready?"

Gary didn't nod right away. He was usually up for fighting, trying his best at physical things, but in situations where he had to use words, that was more up to Kai, but he knew this was a big turning point for the gang.

"I have to be. No . . . I am ready," Gary answered.

CHAPTER 81

THE FAME OF THE HOWLERS

Gary was scratching his head so hard, he feared that he might go bald, but he knew from the system messages that as long as he had Energy the system would revert him back to his original form.

That was one of the reasons why he was unable to change his green hair. This made him wonder: if he had kids, would their hair color be strange as well? Maybe his normal genes would pass on, and his kids would wonder if he was really their dad, because of the strange hair color he had and they didn't.

"Gary, will you pay attention and stop daydreaming? This is important!" Kai shouted as he tapped a large whiteboard several times.

After meeting up with the others at the Wolf's Pool Club, Gary and Kai had left, as they needed to make special preparations for tomorrow. What Gary didn't realize was it was almost a trip back to school for him.

There was a desk, a notepad, and a pencil. Sitting at the desk, directly opposite him, was Kai, in front of a whiteboard. They were in a room at one of the businesses they owned, and Kai had booked a slot for the two of them.

"I'm sorry, but we have already been at this for three hours. I think my brain is going to explode!" Gary said, as he continued to scratch his head, and eventually just placed his forehead on the table.

"Do I have to explain the importance of this meeting to you again?" Kai sighed as he tapped the whiteboard, where the name of a single company was written and circled in the middle: *Cardenez Electronics*.

"This is one of the biggest up-and-coming electronics companies. They are so large that they have more influence in their Tier 3 town than the gangs there, since they supply electronic parts to the Tier 2 cities as well.

"Because of their massive growth, they are now looking to expand, and our town is one of the places that they are considering. Think about it: this is a company that has bargaining power with Tier 2 cities, so much so that they have even been talking about opening up factories and new headquarters in said Tier 2 cities, and they will probably continue to grow there as well.

"Which is why, if we get them to set up a base in Slough, prove to them what we can do, maybe they will move their whole operation to Slough. Gangs might target us because of this, but if we can protect them and continue to show that Slough was the right choice, we can grow together and make this city better."

Gary knew a little bit about the effect of businesses and how they worked to grow in certain places; he had seen the effect on the Underdogs' and other gangs' income when businesses came to the city, but that money had hit a limit to what it could do for Slough.

Lifting his head off the table, Gary looked at the whiteboard again.

"I understand all of that; what I'm struggling with is all these other terms that you are throwing at me. Dilution, gross, net profit. Yearly turnover, buy-back schemes, and more! It's too much to learn in one day, and I never was good at school in the first place."

Kai put the pen down and dropped his head slightly.

"I know this is a lot, Gary. Honestly I don't know why *he* insisted on seeing you. Otherwise I would have taken over all of this for you, but these are just the basics, and if he talks to you directly, I want you to understand a bit of what was going on. I know it's a lot of pressure and not what you're used to."

As usual, Kai was just looking out for Gary, and his passion was coming across in the lesson.

"Come on, let's go over these terms again and see if I can get any of them right."

"All right!" Kai pumped his fist. "This will be good practice for you in the future anyway, for when you become a business tycoon."

Gary shook his head, just wondering what the future held.

The next day had arrived, and for some reason Gary had chosen to sleep at the old apartment instead of the new one. He had told his sister that he was heading straight back to the AFA, even though that was a lie.

This was because he had other business to do, business to do with the Howlers, and he didn't want her to think that he had something else that was more important than her. If he could have, Gary would have happily spent a whole week with Amy before heading back to the AFA, but a break that long would make him fall behind, and he didn't want to miss out on any special lessons.

So a few days back in Slough was the most Gary was willing to give up for now. His eyes felt a bit heavy, as he hadn't had much sleep. The terms he'd learned were repeating in his head every time he tried to get some shut-eye.

Gary dragged himself out of bed and went to the closet, where there was a special outfit that Kai said he had prepared. He was expecting his gang uniform, but instead there was a suit.

"Man . . ."

After putting it on and looking at himself in the mirror, Gary felt like he was almost unrecognizable. He looked like a full-fledged adult, and the suit fit him perfectly in all of the right areas.

It even made him look slightly taller because of how the pants were cut.

Is this a tailored suit? When did Kai even get my measurements? I guess I won't be fighting in this thing anytime soon. I imagine this cost a pretty penny, and I wouldn't want to ruin something so nice.

Two beeps sounded from a car outside. It was the signal that Tyler was there. Gary's heart was thumping. Seeing how serious Kai was about this whole thing just showed the importance of this meeting, which only made Gary even more nervous.

Somehow this feels worse than having to fight someone! he thought.

He left the apartment and walked over to the waiting limo. Tyler stood outside it by the door, but he wasn't the only one. All of the others were present.

Innu, Marie, Austin, and Kai, of course, and even Olivia was with them.

"You're looking sharp, boss!" Tyler was the first to say.

"Yeah, man, how come your suit fits you perfectly. Mine's a bit baggy." Innu showed how his sleeves were a bit too long.

"It suits him right, this look." Kai smiled, glancing at Marie.

"Yeah, it looks good on him," she replied with her face slightly red and her eyes off to the side, but she kept taking another look at Gary.

"You know, all of us in suits and going to a big meeting together like this, it finally feels like we are in a real gang," Austin said.

This was true for all of them, including Gary. Before, everything had felt like they were just going with the flow, while this was a step in the right direction.

"You only feel like that now?" Olivia slapped her forehead. "How did we get taken out by these guys?"

After they all got in the car, Kai explained what was going to happen. Only Gary and Kai would be sitting on the sofa opposite the CEO; the rest were to stand by the side as guards.

This was allowed because the CEO would have the same protection, most likely members of another gang. What gang, though, Kai didn't know. The meeting was to take place in one of the top hotels in Cipen, where the lobby was already booked.

Finally the car reached its destination. The limo had caught the eyes of the guests who were coming in and out of the hotel.

When the door opened, though, they were surprised to see a group of people wearing black-and-gold masks.

Who are they? many of the guests wondered; the group had a certain presence, and it was clear that they were somebody important.

"Wait, those masks, I know them. The Howlers wear those. That must mean something big is going on here," someone said.

As they walked through the hotel entrance, many people brought out their phones to take photos and videos.

"Get used to this, guys, because we might be experiencing it a lot more often in the future," Kai whispered to the others with a smile underneath his fox mask.

CHAPTER 82

THE BIG BOSS

As they entered the hotel, some bolder people followed behind in an attempt to take more photos. However, hotel security quickly intervened and asked them people to move out. A young bellboy quickly approached the Howlers and asked if he needed to take care of any luggage. Following behind him was a middle-aged man in a white shirt with a name tag identifying him as the manager.

"Thank you for choosing to have your event at our establishment, um . . ." The manager looked at all of the masks, trying to discern who exactly he should be addressing. Realizing the issue, Kai pressed his hands on Gary's shoulders and lightly pushed him forward.

"This is our leader," Kai clarified.

"Thank you so much for choosing us, sir," the manager repeated as he bowed down respectfully. "If there is anything that we can do to make your visit here more enjoyable, please let me know. I will make sure that any and all of your requests will be fulfilled at a moment's notice. Please don't hesitate to ask."

This time, the slightly balding man addressed Gary directly, and there was a creepy smile on his face every single time he finished a sentence.

This difference in treatment is truly crazy. Is it just because of my change of clothes? Or because of the level of respect the Howlers have earned here? Gary wondered, but he just nodded toward the man.

"Actually, now that you mention it, we would have preferred to have a separate area to walk through to avoid this kind of attention.

I assume it won't pose a problem to make the necessary arrangements for our exit and for any future meetings," Kai requested.

The manager looked nervous. For hotels, aside from offering rooms for guests to stay in, a good portion of their revenue came from hosting big events for companies, and for an area like Slough this was a first. The hotel knew what a big deal this would be, based on the guest list that would be arriving.

The group was directed downstairs into an area that was much larger than they had expected. It was much bigger than the reception area, and there were several rooms that had primarily been designed for business meetings and more. Eventually the manager led them into the room where they would be meeting.

"As instructed, my staff and I will keep out of the room and remain at the exit, in case . . . anything were to happen that would result in a need to alert the authorities." The manager bowed his head one more time and remained at his place.

"Gary," Kai whispered as he put his hand around his friend's shoulder. "As our leader, it will make the best impression if you are the first to enter. Just take a deep breath and remain confident. This is a formal meeting between us and a company, so there should be nothing to worry about. In the future, if we meet another gang, though, it might be best if you let one of us enter, just in case someone would dare to try and assassinate you."

Gary gulped down hard after hearing this. Kai's words were just making him more nervous than before. Even if there was an assassination attempt on him, he would prefer to walk in first anyway; that way he could stop any of the others getting hurt. If his friends were to die because someone had targeted his life, he wouldn't be able to live with it.

After taking a few deep breaths, Gary pushed the double doors open. The room was large and grand with high ceilings and a chandelier. In the center of the room was a low table with coffee service prepared and several seats. Sitting at one end of the table was the person who had requested to meet with the true leader of the Howlers.

"Please take a seat," Mr. Cardenez said after taking a good look at the gang members.

So that's him, the owner of the up-and-coming electronics company. According to Kai, their company is so big that even the gangs in the big cities are willing to work with them. I have to admit, he has a certain air about him, Gary thought as he took the seat opposite the man.

Mr. Cardenez was wearing a gray suit. It went well with his black hair, which must have been dyed given his age, though it was not obvious at first glance. He was very different from what Gary had pictured when he had been told that he would meet an old man. His aura alone made Gary hesitate about how he should address him.

Kai sat down next to Gary, while the others leaned against the wall on their side of the room, mimicking the group of people behind Mr. Cardenez.

The clothing of his bodyguards was a strange choice, overly large and bright, making them resemble a troupe of clowns. Without a doubt they weren't from the corporation but had to be from a gang, though none of the Howlers knew which one it was.

He seems quite confident in his protection, seeing as none of his men are sitting next to him. Gary or I could just leap from here and take him out in one hit. Unfortunately there is no point in doing that. Companies work differently than gangs, his second-in-command would just take over, and we would have made an unnecessary enemy, Kai mused, before deciding to officially greet their potential partner.

"I'm happy to see you again, Mr. Cardenez. You might have already heard that the problems you've mentioned during our last meeting have already been successfully taken care of. The Howlers have the final say as to what happens in Slough.

"Now, if there are no more reservations from your side, the Howlers would be more than happy to work with the Cardenez group. We have prepared some plans that should make things easy for you. Of course, these are all just suggestions, so everything is subject to change."

Kai handed over a big file of papers. Mr. Cardenez picked them up and flicked through them but didn't look at any individual document for a long time before putting the file down. The blond teenager had to admit that this meeting was nerve-racking even for him. Despite literally wearing a mask himself, he was unable to read the person in front of him.

Was he happy? Angry? What did he want?

Placing both of his hands together in front of his face, the old man leaned forward.

"I have to say that I am quite disappointed," Mr. Cardenez said. "When I first met you, fox mask, I was quite curious about your group. I've done my due diligence and have studied up on the Howlers and Slough. On top of that, you yourself were quite impressive, to the point that I was intrigued about what kind of leader someone as capable as you would follow. And yet . . . what about this great leader? How is this meeting any different from our last one?"

Gary's ears perked up when he heard this.

"You talk about wanting to strike a deal, to work as equal partners, yet all of you sit in front of me, all wearing masks to hide your identity, including this leader of yours. Speaking of which, I have yet to hear him say a single word.

"It appears that I have wasted my time coming here again. One piece of advice: next time you plan on meeting someone, learn some manners beforehand."

Kai had been prepared for this meeting to end badly, but he had also been prepared to offer solutions for any concerns the other party might have. He had considered showing up without a mask, perhaps using his werewolf powers to change his face. Unfortunately, there would be many problems if Gary revealed his true face, and not just because he still looked like a teenager.

Even with makeup it would be very hard to make him look much more mature than a university student. These older folks liked experienced people in the field, and one look at Gary would most likely have been enough to steer him away. In that case, they would have given away valuable information about their identity without gaining anything in return.

"It's truly a shame; I had hoped that the Howlers gang were something impressive, but it appears that you are nothing but a bunch of wild dogs with no idea of where to go or what to do next, no different from all the others who wish to piggyback on our company."

There were a few things about this speech that Gary extremely disliked, and one of them was being called dogs; with a tensed fist, he stood up from his seat.

"Well, Mr. Leader, if violence is your first reaction after seeing that you won't get your way, then there is truly nothing that makes me regret my decision. Our group won't be working with the Howlers. I'll just focus on the Tier 2 city instead."

The old man stood up to leave. Gary stood there, not saying a word. All of the hard work that Kai had put into teaching him was all for nothing.

And Gary couldn't help but feel that it was all because he had appeared.

Maybe we should have used a stand-in, or Olivia should have pretended to be the leader instead, Gary thought, until he felt a hand on his shoulder.

Kai spoke quietly. "Gary, you did nothing wrong. This was a learning experience for all of us, and I know what you're thinking. You're our leader, and we all chose to follow you for a reason, so if he can't see that, well that's his lost cause."

As the old man started to walk out of the room, his group of bodyguards following behind, Kai had a few choice words for him.

"Mr. Cardenez, we thank you for your words of advice, and we would like to offer you something in return. If at any point you find yourself confronted with a problem that neither your money nor your power is able to solve, please remember us. Even if you can't see it now, we Howlers are more than meets the eye, and all we need to convince you will be that one chance."

CHAPTER 83

NOTSBURG

On the car ride back, everyone was quiet. No one asked about what had occurred in the meeting, and it was all because of the energy that Gary was giving off. He still had his hands clenched, annoyed at what had occurred, still blaming himself for what happened.

In the end, he finally spoke.

"I'm sorry, guys. As Mr. Cardenez said, I guess I'm not really fit to be that type of leader. I don't know many things when it comes to business and such, and I know I make ridiculous requests that might make it harder for the gang to operate.

"But I can only really be me in the end, and if someone doesn't like it, I guess that's just it. So what I'm trying to say is, I'm sorry that you guys have to put up with a leader like me."

Immediately, everyone started arguing against what Gary had said, about to say he was a great leader, but because they were all talking at once, Gary couldn't follow what any of them were saying. Kai turned around to Tyler.

"Let's stop on Burnham Street and get something to eat," he suggested.

A short while later, everyone was sitting down at a fancy hotpot restaurant on Burnham Street, and because Olivia was with them, they got top service. They weren't concerned about any onlookers, even without their masks. Since they were wearing normal suits, the other patrons thought the group was just a company out for an evening meal, which it really was.

Everyone was trying to cheer Gary up as they gobbled their food; Olivia, Gary, and Kai were eating the most by far, but nearly everything they ate and ordered was meat. After the meal was done, though, Kai raised a glass of plum juice, because he had a few words to say.

"This meeting was only a small hiccup in the many opportunities to come, but it was also a good chance for all of us to come together once more. Let's enjoy tonight as we say goodbye and good luck to our friend Gary!" The rest raised their glasses as well, with Olivia only the one actually drinking alcohol since the others weren't of age yet.

Gary would be returning to the AFA tomorrow, just in time for his next special lesson. Before leaving, of course, Gary promised that if he was needed again, he would be happy to return at any time. The others were sad to see him go so soon, but that was just the way it needed to be for them to move forward.

For some reason, though, Kai didn't think it would be the end of their involvement with the Cardenez group.

Meanwhile, Mr. Cardenez wasn't the type of person who would wait around doing nothing after such a meeting. His business would have never survived if that were the case, which was why he had set up a meeting on the same day with Notsburg, a Tier 2 city.

Notsburg prided itself on its history. Although it wasn't strong enough to classify itself as a Tier 1, it had cemented its position as a Tier 2.

It had been one of the longest-standing Tier 2 cities, and not once had it been taken over, or the head gang in charge been changed. Of course, the city's leaders would listen to the Kings if instructed to do so, in order to not cause any trouble, but the fact that none of the Kings ever tried to directly own the city showed its strength.

Mr. Cardenez knew this about Notsburg, which was why he was sure it was a confident pick. The city had also shown an interest in his company as well.

Before heading to the Tier 2 city, though, Mr. Cardenez wished to head home, because he was looking forward to picking someone up.

His house was a wide, one-story dwelling, with a large fish pond. As soon as he entered through the imposing gate, his waiting employees bowed their heads and shouted, "Welcome back, sir!"

He walked through the grand entrance and went to his office, a large room with shelves filled with countless books and a window that looked out over the pond, but here was the person he had been waiting to see. He greeted him with the biggest smile on his face.

"Aren't you going to give your father a hug?" Mr. Cardenez asked. "Come on, Numba, there's no need to be shy."

Numba tilted his face to the side, then walked over and gave his father a hug. Mr. Cardenez sat down in his office chair and picked up a framed photograph of himself, Numba, and Numba's mother.

In the photo Numba was only a few years younger than he was now, and there were no photos in the room of Numba as a child; Numba had been adopted by the Cardenez family.

"I got your message and came back as soon as possible. Is something wrong?" Numba asked.

"Nothing is wrong," Mr. Cardenez replied. "In fact, things have been great, especially after learning of all the things that you have done in the AFA. I knew you were a special person, which is why we put so much hope in you, but I'm proud to say that you have exceeded our expectations."

Numba knew exactly what he meant; people usually spent a lot longer in the preliminary stages before entering the real academy, but he had gotten through quickly, and as the number one ranking student no less.

Anyone would be thrilled about this, but Numba knew it wasn't only due to his own efforts, and seeing his father react this way, he couldn't tell his father the truth: that a lot of it was due to his friend Gary's help.

"I know it must be hard for you there, especially with our position. I have heard a lot of things about the AFA and how the students use their backgrounds to bully the others around them, but you have powered through it, and soon you won't have to shy away so much. That is why I called you."

Mr. Cardenez let his smile fade as he moved on to what he believed was a more serious matter.

"I wish for you to attend a meeting today with me. As you are my only heir, eventually you will also take over the family business. I know it will be hard for you to focus on the AFA, the AFC, and the business at the same time, but this is to improve our relations in the future.

"You will become a name that will not be messed with."

This was pretty much the thinking of nearly everyone who sent their kids to the AFA. So Numba was expecting this.

"I see now. I will try my best to learn as much as possible during this meeting," Numba replied.

"Good. Your willingness to learn has always been great. So I will give you a few details beforehand about the whole meeting. This is a chance for our company to make good connections with a Tier 2 city."

Now, Numba knew what his father meant by not allowing himself to be bullied. If they had connections with a Tier 2 city it would put him on par with many of the others.

"The Tier 2 city we will be going to is Notsburg."

The color drained immediately from Numba's face. The name was quite familiar to him, because he had been doing some research of his own on the Tier 2 city.

This city, it's the one that Sty is from.

CHAPTER 84

A TIER 2 BOSS

As someone who had battled against real beasts, Numba would dare to claim that the journey toward Notsburg was far more nerve-racking to him than the AFA's special lesson. One could argue that this was because he was on his own now, but given that his teammates had been Apollo, with whom Numba hadn't had any sort of prior relationship, and Sty, who would be the last person the Goat Altered would ever trust, things weren't that different in the limo that he shared with his adoptive father and two bodyguards.

Ever since that first special lesson, Numba had spent a lot of his free time training. He didn't know if their teams would stay the way they were, but Mr. Corvus had hinted that they might eventually go up against beasts on their own—if they wished to do so, of course.

Having to take care of a business, on the other hand, was an entirely different type of fighting. No matter how excellent the tutors Harry Cardenez had hired to teach Numba everything he needed to know, there was a vast difference between theory and reality, an important lesson that the Howlers had been taught today. There was also a fear at the back of Numba's mind that if he messed up, his father might abandon him, and his life would return to what it was . . .

"Don't look so nervous," Harry Cardenez chided his son. "This is a prime opportunity for you to witness how business is properly conducted between two groups. Just focus on learning as much as you can from this experience. With the Freaks by our side, there's no need to worry about your well-being, either, though I suppose at this point, you're more than capable of protecting yourself. If things get dangerous, make sure to save your old man."

The last comment finally put a smile on Numba's face.

Meanwhile, the two men who sat opposite them, one large and one thin, remained silent. They wore white makeup and bright lipstick, which suited their clown clothing. Others like them were riding in the cars that preceded and followed the limousine along the expressway.

The Freaks didn't start out as a single gang. Just like Slough used to have the Underdogs, the Gray Elephants, the Rising Dragons, the Lock gang, and others, Numba's hometown also used to have multiple gangs fighting for control. However, Harry Cardenez had managed to bring an end to all of this.

The Freaks had been created by combining all the leaders of the gangs, creating a supergroup. The way Mr. Cardenez had done this was simple: through the use of money. It was a fair deal for all parties. The Freaks protected the city and mainly the workings of the Cardenez group, and in turn they got paid and everyone in the town was able to prosper.

Because they were a bunch of gang leaders, the Freaks were a strong group, and sitting next to both Cardenezes were the two strongest gang leaders. Numba could see the confidence on his father's face, but after seeing Apollo's strength during the special lesson, if there were more like him in that city, the Freaks would only be able to buy some time.

No, I shouldn't use Apollo or Sty as the standard. Just like there is only one of me, guys like those two aren't a dime a dozen, and unlike me, I don't think their family would call them back for a meeting like this, Numba thought hopefully.

As the limo entered the city, Numba noticed giant billboards every few hundred yards praising this or that casino. Thanks to the colorful lights illuminating them in the dark, they were easy to spot. Casinos existed in a lot of cities, but in Notsburg they seemed to rival the number of grocery stores.

So Numba wasn't the least bit surprised when their car stopped in front of a giant casino. It was a unique establishment located on an island, with a bridge over a large lake connecting it to the mainland.

The casino itself was beyond large; it looked like one could get lost in the place for weeks without proper directions.

As they entered, the entire group was escorted by men in groups; they walked through the main hall, where the sounds of slot machines going off never stopped. Mixed in were the sounds of people cheering, screaming, and even shouting or arguing with the guards.

It was close to midnight, and yet the place was filled to the brim. Numba could only imagine the sums of money exchanging hands every day. Of course, most of it would enrich the house, or more precisely the person who owned it.

Eventually, they arrived in front of the VIP area. Guarding the large velvet-covered door were two large men with long ponytails, who pushed it open to reveal one of the most extravagant rooms Numba had ever seen. The room had a lot of red inside, and a lot of velvet. The walls, the chairs, the sofas—all of it was red velvet. To the side were glass cabinets that were filled with all sorts of different luxuries. Top-of-the-line watches, jewelry, rare items, and more. All of them looked stunning and untouched, but perhaps what gave off the biggest impression in the room were the two people behind the desk at the back.

The man sitting behind the desk appeared to be in his forties. Strangely, he was sporting a grayish beard, yet the lack of wrinkles on his face suggested that this was more of a fashion choice than his natural color. There were one or two rings on each of his fingers, shining so brightly that Numba thought he might have to close his eyes.

As for his clothes, they looked like an extension of this room, being red and velvet. The man wasn't very large, apart from his eyes that bulged out like those of a bug.

Numba thought, *This has to be the head gang of Notsburg. Does that mean this man is related to Sty? His gang was the leader of a Tier 1 city that had ties with Apollo, who worked for a Tier 1. If so, someone in this room may actually belong to a Tier 1 gang. So the man in front of me is likely Sty's father.*

Those in the AFA were mostly sons or daughters of gangs and corporations. Thinking about what he had done to Sty and how this could be his father was making Numba's legs shake. This was a gang that they were meeting with, a gang of the city, one that had proudly set up base in one of the largest casinos in the area.

But this man wasn't the only person in the room who was getting a lot of focus.

Everyone was told to take their positions as they entered the room. Numba wasn't going to act like Harry was his father, in case he was targeted, and he stood to the side along with the other Freaks in the room.

At the same time, two Freaks stood by Harry's side at all times during the meeting. Harry had taken a seat directly opposite the large man as the meeting.

That was when Numba started to focus on not the leader who was sitting down but the man standing by his side, who Numba guessed was his guard.

The man wore a light blue Hawaiian shirt, unbuttoned to reveal the man's abs and muscular pecs. He was not as large as the seated leader, but there was something fierce about his eyes.

Numerous scars were visible all the way up his body, and his spiky wild hair almost made him look like someone who didn't belong in this room.

Still, Numba kept focusing on the man's eyes, because they reminded him of something, something that shook his very core.

"All right, it's time for us to do business; no one will be going home today until we make a deal," the man said with a big smile on his face; the tone of his voice was enough to convince everyone in the room that he wasn't joking.

CHAPTER 85

A TIER 2 DEAL (PART 1)

Numba didn't know what he should be doing in this meeting; his eyes darted between his father, the gang leader, and the bodyguard. Despite the wild attitude of their host, his swinging arms and creepy smile, Harry Cardenez didn't budge an inch, his facial expressions not changing in the slightest. He kept his hands together, clearly unfazed by the gang in front of them.

"The Scatterbugs have ruled Notsburg for generations, a truly impressive feat. As a gang this means one of two things: either you've managed to earn the respect of most Tier 1 gangs to the point where they don't dare mess with you, or you're under the protection of one of the Kings.

"Now, from what I managed to find out, you have no affiliation with any of the Kings, meaning your gang has solidified its position on its own. I hope that putting my business here won't change that," Harry began.

On the table in front of him, the man pulled out a nameplate that had been hidden behind a few items and placed it directly in front of him for all to read: *Slith*.

"This nameplate indicates who's in charge of the city, and who's in charge of the Scatterbugs. They go hand in hand. As someone from the outside, I can see why you might be worried about others trying to prevent you from expanding.

"Well, let me tell you, all the gangs in Notsburg work for the Scatterbugs. I'm sure you have seen that the city has more than one casino.

We've assigned each gang to protect a casino in their area that has been set up and funded by us.

"As long as they do their job properly, they're paid a percentage of the casino's earnings as a bonus, and believe me when I tell you that they enjoy that treatment. They all know that it would be child's play for us to take that responsibility away from them and hand it over to another group. Thanks to this type of symbiotic relationship, our position is more than just secure.

"In fact, just for a bigger slice of the pie, the small-time gangs are more than happy to check, report, or even fight against any gang that thinks too highly of themselves and dares to try some type of uprising. As for your business, we can offer to work with you directly, meaning you will enjoy the privilege of being protected by the Scatterbugs personally," Slith said, sitting back in his seat with both hands behind his head.

To be honest, as a prim and proper businessman, Harry found the way Slith conducted himself quite rude, yet he knew that it was impossible to expect proper etiquette from gang members. Nevertheless, it irked him that even those Howlers had shown more decorum.

"I see; you've talked about percentages before. In order for us to use your services and set up base here, what conditions can you offer us?" Harry asked.

This was the most important question, but it showed that he was serious. The Scatterbugs had given him confidence that they could protect the business, at least.

"Usually we share ten percent of the profits with the businesses around the area, but since you're a new partner coming from the outside and my advisors tell me that your numbers look more than promising, I've decided to be generous and let you keep a total twenty percent of the profits!" Slith answered in a grand tone.

Mr. Cardenez placed his hands on his armrests. "I've heard you were criminals, but I thought your group would like to do real business. Taking eighty percent of our profits for all our hard work is madness."

Several members of the Scatterbugs stared directly at Harry. It was clear that they didn't like the tone he was using.

"Let me make this clear, you are the one who came into my city. You know perfectly well that without my say-so it will be impossible to operate in Notsburg. Look at it from a different perspective; after all, twenty percent of something is still a lot more than one hundred percent of nothing.

"If you don't like it, you're free to leave. Go ahead, continue doing small-time business in your Tier 3 town. However, if you were satisfied with that alone, would you truly have contacted us and come here?" Slith replied, the smile on his face getting bigger and bigger as he continued.

Harry was silent for a bit as he tapped his finger on the side of his chair, something he did when he was thinking about what to do.

"I believe the two of us are just too far apart. I was looking for a group that wished to treat us like proper partners. In the face of your strength, the rank of your city, and everything you have built up, the most I'm willing to part with will be fifty percent."

Now it was Slith's turn to consider the counteroffer. The thing was, unlike the Tier 3 cities, the Tier 2 cities had a good life. They had businesses that were already flourishing, so they didn't need to attract new ones. There were plenty of people like Harry who were attempting to do so.

However, money was money, and Slith's advisors, who were more informed about that side of the business, had all agreed that it would be a good thing to partner up. By putting his own man at the helm, they would make a lot of money.

"You know what, I like your spunk. I'll agree to your fifty-fifty deal, but on the condition that you move the entire operation of Cardenez Electronics into Notsburg. Furthermore, all deals going forward will be as partners, including us having a say regarding future expansions into other cities," Slith suggested.

Harry's eyes widened. Slith wasn't just asking for a fifty-fifty split in this specific deal but essentially in the whole company. He wanted to be exclusive and own fifty percent of all of Harry's hard work.

The company that he had built up from nothing. From the smile on Slith's face, it was clear he knew exactly what he was doing, and in a high-pressure situation like this one, Harry was sure that multiple gangs might have taken whatever offer had come their way, but they weren't him.

Standing up, Harry straightened his suit.

"It is time I take my leave. I can see that this whole thing was a waste of time." Harry looked toward Numba and the Freaks and started to walk out the door.

The others followed him, but rather than being shocked, Slith began to laugh.

"If you do change your mind, I'll be right here," Slith called after him as the doors closed. A few seconds later, after it was clear they had left the room, Slith's smile left his face.

"That man was awfully rude, don't you think?" Slith asked the room.

"Yes, sir!" several people answered, apart from the man in the Hawaiian shirt.

"Yes, I would have to agree, I think they should receive a nice surprise for being so rude. A gift before they head home." Slith smiled.

CHAPTER 86

A TIER 2 DEAL (PART 2)

Numba didn't say a word on the way back to the limo. His father, although he was a strict and serious person, hardly ever showed his temper. Nevertheless, he had seen his father lose it a few times, and it had always been related to his business.

Right now, if anyone said the wrong word, he would blow his top. The thing was, Numba knew what had set him off: the fact that a gang thought they could just swoop in and take fifty percent of everything he did. They were trying to rob him, and right in front of his nose as well.

They all entered the limo in silence. There was no need to say anything. It was only Numba and the Freaks in the car, and Harry Cardenez, who was the sole director of the company. There were no other partners; he had built the company from scratch and would continue to make it successful, with or without the help of others.

"I'm sorry that you had to see that. Based on their reputation, I believed that things would go a lot smoother than that," his father eventually said. Then he let out a deep sigh, trying to calm himself down. "A true shame, but there are plenty of other Tier 2 cities that we can work with. We will just have to go back to the drawing board and see which ones aren't so influenced by the Kings."

Numba smiled at his father. In truth, he was happy that the deal fell through. If Slith was indeed Sty's father, then things would have been bound to turn bad at some point. Judging by how the meeting went, it was safe to assume that both of them were somehow related, both of them being Grade A assholes, Numba smirked to himself thinking about this.

The car came to a sudden halt as the driver slammed on the brakes. It was so sudden that Numba's seat belt locked up. The next second they heard screeching tires as the car skidded across the ground.

Mr. Cardenez had brought three cars with him, and all three of them had come to a stop.

"What is going on?" Harry demanded to know.

"Sir, it seems like we have trouble up ahead," the driver answered.

Looking through the window, they saw four cars surrounding theirs, and standing outside were a bunch of thugs holding weapons: bats, knives, and more.

They were still on the bridge from the casino to the mainland so it was clear that this wasn't a coincidence but a targeted attack.

Harry's two bodyguards helped him out of the car, while the other Freaks had also left their cars, ready for the inevitable fight. Mr. Cardenez slammed the door so hard that it almost shattered.

"Father, I can help!" Numba shouted as he got out.

"Don't worry, Numba, I know you can, but I can't let you get such filthy blood on your hands," Harry said. "They think that just because I run a business, I don't know how to deal with a few ruffians. Well, Freaks, it's time for you to do your job."

There were ten members of the Freaks going up against fourteen thugs. One of the Freaks had pulled out what looked like a scythe. Another had a pair of nunchucks. The contrast between the gangs' weapons was noticeable.

All of the Freaks' weapons were top quality; some even looked like they had been made from real-life animals. That was because they were; some were Anti-Altered weapons.

"Haha, what the fuck are a bunch of clowns going to do? Get rid of them!" the thugs shouted as they ran across the bridge, the first to act.

None of the Freaks were fazed by this. When the first person got close, the man with the scythe swung it right toward the attacker's legs without an ounce of hesitation. It was so fast that the man immediately fell to the ground, his right leg no longer attached to his body.

The man screamed as his companions continued their attack. The man with the nunchucks swung them, breaking one man's arm and hitting another in the chest, sending him flying back. It was clear that the Freaks greatly outmatched these thugs, and soon only the ten Freaks were left standing.

"I can't believe it. I bet these were the type of people that he would have assigned to protect our business. It looks like there was a silver lining to this whole thing after all," Harry said as he and the others got back in the car and continued on their way home.

Numba, witnessing the Freaks' power, had to admit that he had greatly underestimated them, and wondered how he would fare in a direct confrontation.

Inside the casino, Slith received the news that his attempt at stopping the Cardenez group had failed.

"I knew I had a good feeling about them." Slith chuckled.

"What would you like to do now, sir? Should we send the main group after them?" one of the men asked.

"There is no need." Slith started to sort through a bunch of files labeled *Tier 3*. "It would be embarrassing for a group like us to deal with them personally. It would just give one of the other gangs a reason to sort them out.

"Let's see, how about this?"

Slith pulled out one of the files and pushed it forward.

"A new gang that was rose up recently beat the top gang in their area and took over the town. They must have some strength to do that. Let's see if they can handle this."

On top of the report, the first letter of the gang's name peeked out: the letter *H*.

CHAPTER 87

SOLVING THE PROBLEM

The next day had arrived for the Howlers gang and once again they were without Gary, but it was okay; it wasn't as if the Howlers were planning to go up against anyone anytime soon, and the gangs that had caused disturbances in the past had quieted down, allowing them to take control and work on their day-to-day business a lot more easily.

Kai and Olivia were in Kai's office, and as usual Kai was working on his laptop: doing his morning research, gathering news on what the other gangs were doing, and seeing if there was any way for the Howlers to expand their business.

"You know, you should really get someone else to do this for you," Olivia commented, looking at her newly painted nails. "Whenever I come over you're late by nearly an hour, and yet you insist that I get here on time."

Kai let out a big sigh, rubbing his eyes after looking at the screen a bit too long. Olivia was in the office for their daily training session. Since both of them were werewolves, Kai thought it would benefit them to train with each other.

Although there was no enemy, who knew what they would come across in the future. However, even though they were training, other than learning how to use their bodies and to fight in certain forms, they didn't feel an increase in strength or power like they had before.

"Hmm, Hiring somebody would cost money, and that is something that we don't have plenty of right now, especially after the auction," Kai mused. "I can't even proceed with the plan of making Gary a well-known tycoon at this rate. I was really hoping for the deal with the electronics company to go through, but I guess I will have to look elsewhere."

As Kai continued his research, Olivia received a phone call.

"Okay, we'll be there in a moment." Olivia hung up the phone.

"We'll be there?" Kai repeated.

"I assume you will be coming. It's Burnham Street; they say someone from Notsburg has paid them a little visit and are asking to see the Howlers. A few of our clients used to be from Notsburg, so I know how much of a problem this might be, and with you being the research guru I'm sure you know as well."

Of course Kai knew; he knew every single city in the country, and Notsburg was a Tier 2 city.

"What do they want with us? Is it the gang the Underdogs were working for? If that's the case, we're not ready to deal with a Tier 2 gang yet."

Canceling their training session for the morning, Olivia and Kai headed to Burnham Street. He didn't inform any of the others. At the end of the day, the gang had come to Slough, and had done so unannounced.

If they were planning to attack, they wouldn't have asked for a meeting, and because it was in their own home territory it was most likely to be a safe meeting. At the same time, if it came to it, Olivia and Kai certainly had the skills to escape most situations.

As they stood outside with their masks on, Kai looked up at the sign above.

"Of all the places for them to choose from. Brings back memories, huh."

"Shut up." Olivia cursed as she pushed open the double doors to the seafood restaurant, a place that used to be the old base of the Pincers.

Bursting through the door, Olivia made quite the entrance. All of the workers in the shop bowed down as they knew who it was; even with the mask there was only one person with that figure in the entire city.

The restaurant had been cleared of customers, so no one else was inside, apart from one man wearing a suit and glasses. He looked fairly young, like someone who had just graduated from university.

Just looking at him, most people wouldn't think he was a gang member, but as Olivia approached the four-seat table, she noticed that one of the workers had a mark on their face, a particular tattoo.

Of course, the workers in the restaurant weren't regular employees; they were all members of the Pincer gang who had fighting experience.

He's on his own, and he still decided to start a fight in here, and obviously he made a big enough presence to stop the others from jumping in, Kai thought.

In this situation, Kai knew he had to be the calm one, so picking up his pace, he walked in front of Olivia and sat down opposite the man before she did, for his safety rather than hers.

This person has to be just a messenger; this can't be what I think it's regarding.

"I've heard a lot about you Howlers; to think that you really do wear masks to hide your faces," the man commented, pushing his glasses up with his index finger. "I would assume that none of you are the leader of the Howlers."

"We are high-ranking members," Kai replied. "With enough say in the gang to make decisions. Since this was unannounced, our leader won't be able to visit. Unfortunately he is away. I'm sure you understand, since it appears to be the same with your leader."

Kai gave a smile, which could be seen because his mask only covered the upper half of his face.

"That's good enough for me," the man said as he lifted a suitcase from the seat next to him. "I have a proposal that I think you will be very, very interested in."

He opened the suitcase to reveal that it was full of the one thing the gang needed at the moment . . . money.

CHAPTER 88

BACK AT THE AFA

It wasn't every day that someone from a Tier 2 city came to a Tier 3 town, especially in a place like Slough, to offer money, so it was safe to say that Kai was intrigued.

"That's no small amount," Kai noted calmly.

"Ten million, to be exact, which I'm sure would be able to do a lot for a gang like yours." The man smiled as he closed the suitcase. He could see that he had already caught Kai's attention.

These Tier 3 places are all the same, the man thought.

This certainly would solve their problems, but only for a short while. It wasn't a permanent solution. Maybe for other gangs, who weren't looking to grow out of their own boots, it was life-changing money, and especially for those who would spend the money on themselves.

Which was why the man could see other gangs snapping at the opportunity.

"For that amount of money, I'm sure the task is not a small one," Olivia added.

"No, no, please, it should be fairly simple for you guys, at least based on my research. The Howlers from Slough rose up from nowhere and dominated the Underdogs with sheer strength. Usually a takeover of a place, even a Tier 3 town, would be slow, which just goes to show the wit and strength you guys have.

"And that is why we have come to you. Because we want to use your strength to take care of a problem."

Kai was starting to understand the gist of what was being proposed. They wanted the Howlers to be the muscle. It was quite common for higher-level gangs to do this when they didn't want to use their own people, or when it was just easier to act behind the scenes.

In truth, Kai was just thankful that this didn't seem to have anything to do with the Underdogs; when that time came, he would have to kick everything into high gear.

"I find it hard to believe that there is something we can do that your gang isn't capable of. What's the catch?" Olivia asked.

Kai was glad that of all people, he had Olivia by his side, because she was asking the same questions that he would have, although at times Kai wasn't blunt enough, whereas Olivia was.

"Money isn't important to us, but we know it means a lot to others," the man answered. "I'll cut to the chase. The target is a Tier 3 town, close to Slough; it's not a gang but a business instead. All you need to do is disrupt their business a bit.

"Get in the way of some of their shipments, burn a few warehouses down, it's up to you how creative you want to get. Of course, you might be targeted, or you might have to deal with some guards, which is what the payment is for. There's no reward without a bit of risk."

Honestly, Kai thought the offer was quite fair, and since it didn't involve any direct killing requests, it should be something that wouldn't go against Gary's bottom line, but it did make him wonder. What had that company done to annoy a Tier 2 city like Notsburg?

"What is the name of the company and what did they do? I would hate to do the same thing as they did and offend you guys as well," Kai said.

"That's not really your business, and you know that, even if you did phrase it like that," the man replied. "The company is Cardenez Electronics."

Kai was silent for a while before eventually giving an answer.

"I'm sorry, even though I said we could make the decision, for something like this I will have to consult our leader. You see, our own gang is in our growing phase, and there is quite a bit of trouble here and there. I can give you an answer by the end of the day, and if you don't get a call from me, I'm sorry but we can't accept."

A few moments later, the man from Notsburg was on his way out.

"Are you really going to ask Gary about this?" Olivia asked.

"Nah, that was just my excuse to get him out of here, and a way out of this deal. They seem like the type to bear a grudge against those who don't do what they say. For now, I plan to watch this interesting development and see how things go.

"Maybe a big opportunity will come out of this." Kai smiled.

It was once again time for Gary to return to the academy. With the next full moon farther away than before, he could enjoy his time here in peace, and he could always go back when the full moon was due as well.

On top of that, his one and only Xin Clove also went to the academy.

I wonder if I can see her again. I won't be so out of it this time, and maybe we can start again from where we left off.

Gary still had the picture of Xin kissing him before leaving fresh in his head as he rode the bus toward the academy; he was one of only a few passengers on the bus.

Once he reached the city, he arrived at his stop to change buses and got on the one going directly to the academy.

All Gary needed to do was show his ID to the bus driver. He was expecting the bus to be empty, but there was one person sitting at the back staring out the window.

"No way, what are you doing here?" Gary asked.

"Gary . . . I didn't expect to see anyone get on, much less someone I know. I guess you're heading back to the academy as well," Numba replied.

"Yeah, I didn't know you left; what did you leave for?" Gary asked.

"I . . . just had some family stuff to deal with."

CHAPTER 89

TWO LIVES

Both teenage boys had been prepared to just tune out on their way back to the academy, but ending up together on the ride was a welcome surprise. There wasn't much to catch up on, as the two of them hadn't really missed much. Gary had left the day before yesterday, whereas Numba had left yesterday.

The werewolf had mixed feelings about returning. Part of him was looking forward to it, because the AFA was a dream of his. However, another part of him regretted leaving so soon. After visiting his friends, he couldn't stop worrying about them, his gang, and also Slough as a whole. As a gang leader, even one mostly in name only, he had a lot on his plate.

Since they were alone on the bus, and the bus driver wasn't paying attention, Gary and Numba started discussing their special lessons, though just to be sure they kept it vague. Time passed as they discussed strategies and planned what they would do until the next lesson.

By the time they arrived, the lessons were already over so the two students headed straight for their dormitory. On the floor they could already hear noises coming from a particular room.

"You're the same as always! You invite yourself over and decide to watch whatever you want! This is my room, so at least let me pick the film!" a male voice complained loudly.

"It's not my fault that your taste is garbage! Besides, shouldn't you be studying?" a female voice shouted back.

Since they were both passing by anyway, Gary and Numba decided to tell their friends they were back. The room went silent before they heard someone coming to the door. A messy-looking Ian opened it.

"Hey, Izzy, get over here! They're back!" Ian shouted into the room.

A door slammed, which Ian thought was strange, but he shrugged and let his friends in.

"She probably just went for a shit or something," Ian murmured.

"No, I didn't! I'm just freshening up," Izzy shouted from behind the bathroom door.

As the two of them entered, they saw that Ian's room was a complete mess. Numba shook his head and started tidying up. Gary realized that this wasn't the first time he had seen the Goat Altered clean up behind the two, and from his practiced technique, Numba might have grown used to doing it.

While Ian's guest was making the room more presentable, Izzy came out as well, her face a little flustered. She brushed some crumbs off the seat she had been in earlier and sat down. Unlike before, his childhood friend's hair was no longer a mess; instead it was nicely braided. She was clearly making an effort for someone.

Once Numba was happy about the state of the room, the group spent some time catching up. The two who had been left behind naturally wanted to learn more about Gary and Numba's adventures, yet both just brushed it off as nothing but a boring trip, with mostly some family things.

Neither Izzy nor Ian could contribute much, apart from the fact that they had attended all of their lessons and continued to train with each other, hoping to get stronger and catch up with their friends. Naturally, three days was too short a time to do that.

"I'm happy that you're both still training so hard, but we only got into the main academy. Don't you want to rest a little?" Gary asked. At least that was what he planned to do until their next special lesson. Of course, the werewolf could get stronger from eating the beasts, so training the old-fashioned way wasn't much help to him.

"We need to excel, especially in our physical lessons." Izzy shook her head. "You know they have quarterly assessments for all the students here, right? The AFA isn't like other academies where you study for a year and then move up a grade. This is *the* place to train the next generation of Altered, so they don't care about making us book smart.

"Do you remember those students we fought with when we first entered?"

To be honest Gary didn't remember much of what any of them looked like, apart from Xin. Then again, his mind had been muddled to say the least, but not wanting to explain any of this, he just nodded.

"Well, that should be our goal. As long as you can prove that you're ready for a debut match in the AFC, the teachers will personally take you in and assign you to a coach. After that, you fight your debut match, and then you're pretty much on your own.

"At that point, you technically no longer need to attend the academy, since you pretty much just graduated from the AFA to the AFC. If you want, you can still attend lessons and the academy might ask you to come back once in a while and help them with things, but you're no longer technically a part of the student body.

"That is why you have to show promise in the assessments! No one is expecting you to pass on your first go, but if we perform well the teachers will keep an eye on us, especially if we're showing spectacular growth!"

Thinking about this, Gary realized that Xin was one of those students. Her debut match in the AFC could be any day now. Did that mean that soon she would no longer be in the academy and there would be no way for him to see her again?

Is there even much of a reason for me to stay in the AFA other than the special lessons? Gary thought. *Right now I should be able to enter the AFC and have a debut match. If I show off at the assessment, then I can get out of the AFA as quickly as possible.*

In that case, I could use my new status as an AFC fighter, and then we could turn Kai's plans of turning me into some tycoon into reality. As long as I show up to my matches, I can just live in Slough with my sister and help the Howlers without having to worry.

Gary knew that he should put some more thought into it, but he was pretty sure he had just made his decision. After everyone had run out of things to say to each other, they decided it was best to have an early night.

The two childhood friends assumed that Gary and Numba would be tired from traveling and would like to have some time to themselves before tomorrow's lesson. Waving goodbye to Numba, Gary entered his room, but he stopped when he noticed that he had stepped on something.

What's this? Gary wondered, as he picked up an envelope from the floor, clearly a letter.

Meet me in the octagon room level 4 at midnight tonight. I want to talk about what happened last time.

Gary thought, *A letter left behind in my room . . . could this be from Xin?*

CHAPTER 90

A CONFESSION LETTER

Unfortunately, the mysterious letter wasn't signed, meaning that anyone could have written it. He had never really seen Xin write, so looking at the handwriting wasn't helping him in the least. Luckily, his new senses gave him one way to try to identify the writer.

Taking a sniff, Gary tried to catch a whiff of a particular scent. Back when his crush had been kidnapped, he had managed to find her. Since that day, Gary had had her scent locked away in his mind, yet there was no trace of it on the letter.

It could still be her, right? Gary thought, his heart starting to beat a little slower. *Our rooms get cleaned daily, and the letter had to have been dropped off not too long ago. What should I do?*

On one hand it could be Xin calling out Gary after being unable to talk with him during their last meeting. Still, it was highly unlikely that she would do it this way. If she wanted to contact him, why not meet him in person or at least ask for his number, if not directly, indirectly through his friends?

Then there was the location, the octagon. Whoever wanted to meet him might have chosen the place for a fight. The question was how many people in the academy wanted to fight Gary? He had only encountered a handful of people.

Ah, man, I know I should just leave it . . . but we're in the academy, so it should be safe, right? Even if it's not her and someone challenges me, nothing is stopping me from walking away . . . Besides, if it's not her, whoever wants to talk to me will probably keep pestering me, Gary thought.

There was still quite a bit of time for him to change his mind. Eventually, curiosity got the better of him, so instead of waiting around, he decided to go to the meeting place beforehand. It felt impossible for him to just ignore it now.

It was evening, around nine p.m., and to his surprise quite a few students were training by themselves. Some were hitting away at the special heavy bags; others were doing drills. There were even a couple of students in the sparring ring, though they weren't really sparring, just imitating moves in slow motion and letting the other person react to them.

It reminded Gary that he was more safe than he realized. He had completely forgotten that in the main academy they were only allowed to fight with the teacher's permission. Sitting down on one of the side benches, he watched everyone hard at work, pouring sweat as they did their best to improve their bodies to the next level.

One person in particular caught his attention, as well as that of the people around him. The student was hitting the heaviest bag in the room, with a large amount of force. With each hit, the bag swung out, but he would hit it again as it swung back. The impressive thing wasn't just the force but also the student's stamina. Gary watched him for a couple of minutes, and he was hitting it with the same amount of force, speed, and power without looking tired.

That guy's name was Wu if I remember correctly. I didn't realize it during the special lessons, but that guy can really hit.

Gary continued to watch him, and more and more students were stopping their own training to watch him as well; he kept hitting the bag, not caring that his whole body was dripping with sweat. There was a dark mark around him from all the sweat his body had made.

I thought I had a crazy amount of stamina as a werewolf, but I pale in comparison to him. I'm not even sure how to feel about that.

Eventually it was time for Gary to have his meeting with the mystery person, but when he looked around the only two people left were him and Wu.

It can't be . . . was Wu the one to send that letter? Gary scratched his head. *But what reason would Wu have to send it? Hang on . . .* "I want to *talk about what happened last time." Does he want to ask me about what happened during the special lesson?*

Gary continued to wonder what he would be asked and what he should say, but Wu simply continued training until the clock struck midnight. At that point, he stopped midpunch and grabbed the sports bottle that was at his side. After quenching his thirst, Wu finally seemed to notice Gary and raised an eyebrow.

"What are you doing here? Don't tell me you were watching me the whole time; I feel . . . so exposed," Wu exclaimed as he covered his chest, though for some reason only his nipples.

"Oh, shut up!" Gary shouted, red-faced, not having expected this level of shamelessness. Seeing as Wu had been hanging out with Apollo, Gary had unconsciously believed him and his friends to be the serious type, yet now it seemed that at least one of them might be a bit of a goofball. "I was just waiting for someone, that's all. You just happened to be training in here."

It was quite clear that Wu hadn't written the letter. Gary was left still wondering who it was. He intended to wait a few minutes before giving up, but soon enough the doors opened on the other side of the room.

A dark-skinned man with several bracelets on both arms walked in. Gary racked his brain but was unable to remember where exactly he had seen the other person.

"Oh, so your date is with one of the debut students. Interesting, you do you, man, I don't judge," Wu noted from the side. That's when it hit the werewolf. This was one of the students who had fought against his group when they first came to the real academy, although Gary didn't remember much about his fight.

"It's nice to meet you again, Gary. You don't seem to remember me, but that's okay. My name is Shingi. I'm happy to see that you could make it today." As Shingi spoke, his voice was shaking slightly and so was his body; he grabbed one arm with his other hand to stop himself.

"I know you might find it weird as to why I called you, but ever since I saw you train in here, since I saw you rip a hole through that bag, I haven't been able to sleep properly. I was worried about what would happen in the fight, fearing for my friend's life. To be honest,

I thought that you might kill him, accidentally or not, but in the end, he lived.

"However, that whole fight that day was strange. For someone with your capabilities, that fight should have been a walk in the park, especially since my friend didn't believe me when I warned him about you. That's why I wanted to ask you, why didn't you use your full strength in that fight?" Shingi asked with a serious look, and suddenly there was a larger figure behind him; he wasn't alone.

"Coincidentally, I'm also curious about the answer to that question," Eddy asked, his arms folded.

CHAPTER 91

A DEBUT (PART 1)

Gary had to admit, of all the things that he thought he would be asked, this wasn't one of them. The thing was, they were right; Gary had been having an off day for more reasons than one during the fight.

On top of that, if Gary were to truly show his absolute full strength in a fight against a supervisor, he would have to use his full transformation skill.

Wu, who was still in the room, found the conversation quite interesting, especially since for some reason a teacher was involved. So he decided to take a step to the side, with a towel placed over his head, as he listened to the conversation.

If Shingi had just asked the question, I could have played it off, but why is Eddy the teacher, asking as well? Gary thought.

"What do you mean?" Gary replied with a smile. "I barely won that fight, and I felt really sick that day, which is why I acted like that. Honestly, I think I was barely conscious because I felt so sick." Gary chuckled.

"If what you say is true, then you wouldn't mind having a match with me," Shingi said, tensing his fist. "I have to fight you to get over this fear. Are you special, one of a kind? Maybe I'll find out once I fight you, and I'll be able to progress myself."

Wu looked up again.

"Did Gary say he won his fight? I noticed him, so I'm guessing both my group and his group fought against the same guys, but we all lost our fights. Unless they fought against someone else; that wouldn't be possible."

"I'm sorry," Gary replied. "After what happened last time, I really don't have an interest in fighting others. Not when there's no reason to. I still have a lot to learn at the academy, including how to control my powers properly."

Shingi looked disappointed; he had sought out Eddy, telling him his worries and what he was hung up over. Since Eddy had received a few hits from Gary himself, he was interested in this student as well, and agreed to help Shingi out.

"A reason to fight." Eddy stroked his chin. "Maybe I can give you one. You and Xin, you both know each other, right? I have a feeling that you like that girl, correct?"

Gary's face made it impossible to hide the fact as he turned away. He was quite honest, based on his facial expressions, and a terrible liar.

"You know, I am directly in charge of Xin's lessons before her debut match. There is a reason why you haven't seen her as much, but if you take part in this match, maybe I can make some favorable situations for you."

"Can you even do that?" Shingi whispered, questioning the morality of a teacher using one of his students like that.

A little kick from Eddy quieted Shingi, though, since this was all for him in the first place.

Maybe such a simple thing wouldn't have convinced the others, but Xin was half the reason why Gary had come to the AFA in the first place.

I can show my strength a little, right? I already passed their checks, so anything I do now won't be so suspicious, Gary thought. *And the better I show that I am, the closer I can get to Xin.*

He imagined the two of them rising through the ranks, and then maybe in the future they would be set up to have a match together. Before the match was started, though, Gary would bow down and forfeit the match, saying, "I'm sorry, I can't hit the one I love."

The crowd would cheer and whistle as Xin showed her cute shy side and confessed her feelings there and then. It would be a moment for the history books.

As Gary was thinking about all of this, all the others could see was his shoulders moving up and down and the weird expressions on his face as he went into a daze.

This guy . . . this guy beat one of the top students in the entire AFA . . . no way. I know he did quite well in the special lesson, but I still can't see too much of what Apollo sees in him, Shinji thought.

"All right, fine!" Gary said. "I'll win this fight, and teacher, you better keep your promise."

The octagon was set up, and this time Eddy would be in the cage. He was unsure if anything strange would happen like last time, but Gary certainly did seem like a different person compared to the last time.

Gary was a little concerned because after consuming the beast, he was stronger than before. He didn't have the boost of the moon on his side, but he was a completely different person, one who wasn't fighting with himself, which would allow him to show the full extent of his skills.

"I have a favor to ask," Gary said, just before the match was about to start. "I know it might sound cocky of me saying this, but if you feel like there is a large difference between the two of us, then give up straightaway. For my sake as well as yours."

Although Gary hadn't fought much since coming into the academy, he did realize something after turning into his werewolf self. With each fight he was growing with excitement, and sometimes he got carried away, making it harder and harder for him to stop.

"Fine, let's do this!" Shingi declared.

CHAPTER 92

A DEBUT (PART 2)

Shingi believed that both students had a fair advantage, because he had displayed some of his Altered form last time, even though they weren't supposed to, and he had seen Gary's wolflike form.

The truth was, though, that Gary couldn't even remember what this person could do, and he was just going to go with the flow and react. If he showed his absolute strength, he was sure that these guys wouldn't bother him again.

"Since you were so nice to give me a tip, let me give you one as well," Shingi said. "When the fight starts, use your Altered form straight away. Otherwise you won't be able to survive the first attack."

Gary smiled at this comment as he looked at his stats.

Grade: Bishop
Class: Warrior
Level 22
Health 250
Energy 300
Exp 8788/11564
Strength 36
Dexterity 26
Endurance 32

The system didn't give me a quest. I'm sorry, I know you might be skilled, but according to my system you're not enough to warrant giving me Exp, Gary thought.

"If the fighting gets too dangerous, I will have to step in like last time," Eddy declared.

Wu stood up and moved closer to the cage. Everything he was hearing about the teacher having to get involved just made him imagine a crazy situation that had to have occurred the last time Gary fought.

The thing was, whatever Wu was thinking, it was not crazy enough compared to what had actually occurred.

"Match start!" Eddy shouted.

Gary felt like he could win the fight without transforming, but he didn't want to give everything away, so to make it look like he was trying his best, he transformed his arms, and brown fur started to grow on his legs and part of his face as well.

Right now, essentially his whole body had been transformed, but not quite to the point where he was a full werewolf, just around 60 to 70 percent.

As for Shingi, he immediately threw both of his arms forward, and they stretched to the other side of the arena. He was extremely fast, but his arms ended up hitting nothing but the cage.

Where did he go? Shingi thought.

"Brace yourself," said a voice from underneath him, as Gary threw a fist right into his stomach, lifting Shingi's body up into the air. Quite a bit of liquid came out of Shingi's mouth, but in truth he wanted to throw up.

Eddy, who was standing on the side, had seen the whole thing.

I knew Gary was skillful when he kept dodging all of Ryan's attacks, but he moved the instant Shingi started his attack, and that speed and strength is crazy. Maybe I should stop the fight here, Shingi is clearly outmatched, Eddy thought.

While in the air, Shingi gritted his teeth. There was a reason why he was one of the top students about to debut. He retracted his arms and stretched them out again, grabbing both of Gary's shoulders.

Honestly Gary thought this would end the fight, and he was interested to see what Shingi would try to pull next.

The top of Shingi's head had turned a strange silver, as if his skin had hardened into a type of metal; then, as he pulled forward and leaning his head back, it stretched out slightly. He was going for a headbutt.

Seeing this, Gary smiled.

I know you wanted me to go all out, but I can't do that. I have deadly skills, and if I turned into a full werewolf you might find out that I'm not really an Altered, but there is something I can show you: that my endurance is top notch!

Shingi and Gary swung their heads at the same time and bashed into each other. Gary's head held steady instead of being flung back, and he grabbed both of Shingi's hands in his own. "You're better than I thought . . . but you should rest now."

Shingi's whole body weakened, and he collapsed to the ground, passing out there and then.

Gary's forehead was a little sore. It was safe to say that Wu was left a little confused as to why Shingi was on the floor, when Gary had attacked only once, unless one counted the headbutt.

Eddy walked over to Shingi on the ground and smiled at him.

"You did well. You were already out of the fight after that first hit, but you decided to stay in there a little longer and show him everything you had instead, didn't you?"

Gary had also noticed the look in Shingi's eyes halfway through the headbutt; he was already gone, like a person who had passed out. Gary was surprised he had held on after the first punch; he was aiming to finish the fight quickly so he didn't have to show more, and he had done it.

A few moments later Shingi came to, and when he saw Gary, he immediately went to the canvas and touched his forehead to the floor.

"Thank you so much for having a match with me. It's as I thought. You're really something special, but there is one thing I'm happy about."

Shingi thought back to the punch he'd received and the damage to the bag he had seen. He was happy that he was able to take Gary's punch and survive.

"Hey, please, we are all students here, learning. I . . . just have gone through a lot in my life," Gary said as he gave a hand to Shingi and lifted him off the floor, both smiling at each other.

"Well, now that this is out of the way, I have a big question that I need to ask." Eddy grinned. "I think you're more than ready to join the AFC. Why don't you join the debut students and practice with them?"

CHAPTER 93

BECOMING A DEBUT STUDENT?

Although Wu had to admit that Gary had been impressive in the match just now, he couldn't believe what he was hearing. The teacher had just asked Gary to bypass all of the procedures and prepare for his debut match.

This was the goal of every student in the AFA, and it was being handed to him right there and then.

For Eddy, though, it was a simple matter. Gary had beaten Ryan, the number two of the debut students. Some might have thought it was down to luck or his out-of-control powers, yet he had beaten another student with ease.

It wouldn't make sense not to put him at the same level as them, and staying in the academy for whatever reason would just be a waste of his time. It was clear that he had managed to hide under the scouts' radar.

Gary started to think about the benefits. He had already been thinking about trying his best at the next quarter assessment. That way he could quit the academy and go back to the gang, but he hadn't expected to have that option arrive so soon.

If I accept, it means I'll be under a private coach like Eddy, and then in the academy until my official first match. After that I'll no longer be here, Gary thought.

"If I say yes," Gary replied, "does that mean I'll be taken out of my dormitory and all of my current lessons, including the special lessons?"

Eddy didn't reply right away, because he knew the special lessons were good for growth, but in his opinion the special lessons were below Gary. In fact, after completing the special lessons, students normally came out of them at the stage where Gary was now.

On top of that, there was something else Eddy didn't like about the special lessons. It was the fact that students had died before. Students just as promising as Gary had lost their life and in doing so never got to see the stage.

Eddy didn't know much about what occurred in the special lessons—he wasn't allowed to—but it still gave him a bad feeling.

"When you become a debut student, you will be given a set date for your first match. You will then follow the coach's schedule and only the coach's schedule. You will also be sent to a different part of the facility, one that can move you away from distraction, but of course you can come back to visit if need be," Eddy answered.

Hearing that, Gary made his decision, or at least he thought he had. But as he opened his mouth to reply, he closed it again as images flashed through his head. An injured Numba in the preliminaries, a shy Izzy, and an energetic Ian cracking jokes.

He was enjoying his time at the academy, and so far they had passed everything together. Taking a shortcut like this . . . it just didn't feel right.

"How long until the next assessment?" Gary asked.

"Four weeks; if you get a fight it will take eight weeks of preparation time as well," Eddy answered.

"I'm sorry, but I'm going to have to decline," Gary replied. "But I promise that as long as I prove myself at the assessment, you will see me then."

Eddy smiled at this answer; after all, there was no doubt in his head that Gary would pass, so waiting an extra four weeks wasn't too much to ask. As for Gary, this also meant four more weeks of special lessons.

After that, it would be the end of his time at the AFA, and he would return to the gang to see where his path would lead him. With the conversation over, Shingi thanked Gary once more before leaving.

Giving out a big yawn, Gary walked down the hallway as he thought about what a tiring day it had been, but he couldn't wait for the morning breakfast; being a werewolf was certainly a tiring job for being only once a month.

Wu watched Gary as he walked down the hallway.

"Honestly, I thought he would have jumped at the chance. I know I would have," Wu said to himself. "Crazy, though, how Apollo said the same thing when he was offered it as well."

The next day after waking up, Gary attended his lessons as usual, learning about Altered fighting techniques and more. It was still somewhat a dream for him, and unlike in high school, Gary paid close attention to everything.

On top of that, whenever anyone asked questions while they were analyzing videos and such, he was able to answer most of them.

Is that how Gary is able to grow at a fast speed? Izzy thought. *He seems like a bit of an airhead, but when it comes to things like fighting, he's quite the genius.*

Whatever the reason, Izzy would have to work harder, especially since she was the least physically capable out of the entire group; she didn't want to be left behind.

As they were leaving class, several students looked to the left of the door, as if they saw someone strange, and when Gary and Numba made it into the hallway they understood why.

"AH COO COO!" Crowley said. "I was looking for you two. I thought that you might have both gone to the loo."

Izzy and Ian looked at each other with raised eyebrows.

"Who is this . . . weird adult?" Ian couldn't help but ask.

"He's our special lesson teacher," Gary answered.

Suddenly Izzy and Ian didn't feel so bad missing out on the special lessons, if that was the teacher.

"Enough!" Crowley said, lifting his hands along with his black feathered cape. "There has been a change of plans, as we have a special guest today. COO! You must attend an extra special lesson today."

CHAPTER 94

A SPECIAL GUEST

The special guest hadn't announced his arrival, but when he arrived, even the professors felt the need to pamper him and treat him with respect.

In fact, it was an honor that he had even decided to come to the AFA; although they had expected he would come someday because of a particular person.

Currently, the special guest was ensconced in one of the many meeting rooms, and the only others in the room were the three professors who practically ran the AFA: Hai, Wood, and Humfree. He had made a request that even they didn't expect.

"You would like to see the results of the last special lesson?" Humfree replied as he stroked his beard. "That certainly is possible, but I'm surprised you're interested. You didn't ask about the other sessions, just the most recent one."

The man smiled. "I had just heard that someone interesting had arrived, that was all. I just wondered how they might have done."

The professors looked at each other. The person who had made the request already knew of the content of the special lessons, so they saw no trouble on their end, and they thought it might be good to get his opinion on the students as well.

As the video was being set up, six reports were handed across the table so the special guest could check them out.

Finally the video of the lesson started to play. It showed both groups fighting what should be the first beast of their life. However, for some students in the video, it certainly didn't look that way.

"I see," the man remarked. "These certainly are some special students. You have had quite a few good prospects in the last couple of years. As they say, the new crop of Altered just keeps getting better and better."

After sorting through the files he had just received, he handed two of them back to the professors.

"If you were to ask me, these two are the ones that you need to look out for. They certainly will become something big."

The professors looked at the two chosen files, and all of them nodded, because they had the same inkling. The files belonged to Apollo and Gary.

"You have done a lot for me already," the man said. "But if you don't mind, I have one more request that could be beneficial to you."

Numba, Sty, and Gary were all following Crowley once again. They had already passed through the large steel doors, and in the small waiting room they met up with the other trio: Wu, Snow, and Apollo.

Gary noticed that Apollo was looking at him and smiling. The relationship between Apollo and Gary wasn't significant by any means; they had only had one or two interactions here and there, but not enough for Gary to judge his character.

"Man, I really didn't expect them to have another special lesson so soon. I'm really not sure if I'm ready for this, Gary," Numba whispered.

"Honestly, I'm quite happy about there being a surprise lesson," Gary replied, smiling back. The extra stats, the Exp, all of it could only be found here.

"Man, Gary, I wish you were just a little bit weird; sometimes I feel like I'm the crazy one for worrying too much," Numba said, as he saw Apollo smiling as well.

"Don't worry too much," Wu said. "I'm a bit nervous too."

Wu couldn't deny it after what had occurred, and since they would be fighting with students they didn't know well, they didn't have their normal friends to back them up.

After they had followed Crowley to the red and blue rooms and put on their clothing, he cleared his throat.

"COO!" Crowley shouted, catching their attention. "In today's lesson, both teams will be taking part together."

Immediately, the students realized that the beast they would be facing today must be a tough one. They had been warned about this beforehand, but then why did it have to be a surprise lesson? Why couldn't it have been scheduled at the normal time?

"Although you will be working together, your colors still signify your team, and the assessor will be judging each team on their performance. The ones who do the best will be allowed a special request." Crowley smiled.

"Wait, didn't you say that when the task forces the two teams to work together, we should do anything we can to survive?" Numba asked with a raised hand.

"Yes, I did, and that is still true apart from this special special lesson," Crowley answered. "You will understand when you proceed."

"The special request?" Snow raised his hand. "Is it like last time, something we ask for from NIRV?"

"This one is a little different," Crowley replied. "It will be limited to whatever the academy can do, within their power."

With no other questions, Gary looked across to Apollo, who did the same. This was a contest between the two teams, and they would be in the same room. Finally they would be able to see what the other had.

Both doors opened, and they entered a separate chamber as the doors closed behind them, and then when the doors opened again, both teams entered a bright white room, just like before, and a single person stood on the other side.

"I'm guessing you are all slightly confused," said the man standing there.

The others all froze for a moment, as they couldn't believe who they were looking at; meanwhile Gary covered his face with both hands, closing his eyes.

"Today, your special lesson will be fighting me. I will be testing all six of you. Come at me at once, and show me your full strength, especially you, streaker boy," the man said.

CHAPTER 95

THE END GOAL

The academy didn't have many students compared to those that focused on academic studies, or those that accepted anyone as long as they were an Altered, but for some reason the AFA was incredibly large.

This was due to a number of reasons, one of them being their multiple training facilities. Others thought that the academy did more than just train students, using facilities such as labs and for other companies.

A little ways away from the main area, past the main field, stood a large square building that would look more like the outside of a swimming facility if it was anywhere else, but there was no swimming going on inside. Instead all anyone could hear was loud grunts.

"Harder! Each punch needs to be as strong as your first!" Eddy shouted, clapping his hands.

Several loud thuds echoed throughout the room, as Eddy looked at his students and gave them a nod. Right now he was training the debut students. They were in a special facility designed just for them.

Currently all were present: Xin, Ryan, Shingi, and the others, on green artificial turf, punching a large punching bag. It wasn't a regular bag; in fact it was even tougher and heavier than the ones at the academy.

On top of that, the bags were part of a special system. Each time a student punched a bag, it moved away on a pulley system. When it stopped, a red mark was left where the bag reached, and it would then come back.

Each time the bag came back, the students were to hit it again as hard as they could, either reaching the same distance as before or surpassing it. This was how Eddy could see if each punch was stronger than the one that preceded it.

All of them were drenched in sweat, and as Xin's bag came back her way, she mustered up her strength again and threw a punch, sending it three-quarters of the length of the room.

Ryan, looking to his right, saw that Xin's bag went the farthest.

How can she still hit it that hard, even after going at it for twenty minutes?

Ryan's Altered form was somewhat similar to a gorilla, and he had extreme power even when he wasn't transformed. At first, his bag had gone farther than Xin's. It wasn't by much, but it was a win in Ryan's eyes.

However, after ten minutes he realized that he could no longer hit the bag as hard as he could before, not reaching his red marker, yet Xin was still reaching hers.

It doesn't look like she's pulling her punches either. I guess that's just Xin; she's on another level compared to us.

As Ryan saw the bag come back to him, he really wanted to hit the red mark he had made before, and as he threw his punch he started to summon his power; his forearm grew slightly and his knuckles became slightly hairier as he hit the bag and sent it flying past his original red mark.

"*Ryan!*" Eddy shouted as he pressed a button and reset the mark. "I told you already that you are not to use your Altered form. You have to build a strong foundation without your form.

"Improving your natural body is the first step to allowing you to bring out everything you can in your Altered form. When transformed, you rely on that state, so it's hard to train your Altered state, but when you build your everyday state, your Altered state will improve with it!" Eddy nodded, proud of his lecture.

The lesson went on for a while, until everyone collapsed on the floor, out of breath and worn out, apart from Xin. She was breathing deeply but slowly.

She had taken in a breath as the bag came toward her, then exhaled at the right time as she punched it, once again hitting the red mark.

"I . . . just don't understand her," Ryan said, taking deep breaths between his words.

"All right!" Eddy clapped. "That is enough. You all did well. Let's rest up for now, and then we will get to the next training session."

Xin walked over to the others and then just like them, she sat on the floor and started guzzling water; it was clear that she was actually tired, but while the training session was going on, she had a fierce look in her eyes that she was able to switch on and off.

"Come on, you've got to tell me what juice you're on," Ryan said, throwing her a snack bar to eat.

Catching it, Xin quickly dropped it to the floor.

"I'm not on anything, it's just . . . in each of these training sessions, I give it my all no matter what, no matter how exhausted I feel."

Everyone wanted to hear what Xin had to say, but they too felt like they were giving it their all; it was just that their bodies weren't letting them succeed. It wasn't the answer they were looking for.

"Okay, then let me ask you this instead: what pushes you to work so hard?" Ryan asked. "And don't flake out like you usually do. Whenever I ask this question you just give me a fake answer and duck out, but it's clear you wanted to be part of the AFC for a reason."

For Xin there was more than one reason, but how to explain that her father was an overprotective person because of his position, and he thought his daughter was weak?

On top of that, she would always be compared to her brother, whom she cared for dearly, but she wished to be on the same level as him, or at least surpass his achievements, which was a big ask for anybody.

"I want to be free," Xin answered. "I want to live a life where I can walk the streets, go to whatever city I like, and do as I wish. To do that without having anyone to look out for me or worry for me, I'll have to become the best, right?"

"Wow!" one of the others said. "Well, that's a better answer than mine. I'm just doing it because I want to become famous. I mean, after a few matches in the AFC, then I can go get an acting job or something."

"We can see why you're the first one to collapse, then," Ryan joked.

"I wonder what his reason is for being here," Shingi mumbled. "I wonder how he would have done on the test as well."

"Who are you talking about?" Ryan asked.

Shaking his head, Shingi looked to be on the defensive.

"Oh, no one, just forget about it."

"No, come on, just say who it is you were thinking about. Who's caught your eye?" Ryan asked again.

Looking down, Shingi really didn't want to say the name of said person, because of what had happened, but he also knew that Ryan would keep pressuring him until he got an answer out of him.

"It's Gary," Shingi said.

Everyone went a bit quiet. They all knew it was a taboo subject around Ryan, as it reminded them all of what had happened during that match.

"It's all right, guys, I'm over it, I promise. You don't have to treat his name like he's some bogeyman around me." Ryan laughed, and the others laughed nervously around him.

"Oh, really," Eddy said, having just come out from the side. "That's a good thing, then. I was worried that if he accepted the invitation to join us, you would be affected, but now that I've heard this, it might motivate you to work even harder."

"What? You asked a student who's barely been here a couple of weeks to join us?" one of the others shouted.

"Will you all calm down, he said no anyway." Eddy folded his arms. "That also reminds me: Xin, I might need to speak to you later on . . . about him."

The others were certainly interested to know what this was about. Why would she and Gary be involved? They had stayed away from the subject so far, as to not annoy Ryan, but now he said he was okay with it.

"Enough, we don't need to know about that," Ryan said, red faced, trying to change the subject; what he hated more than talking about Gary was talk about Gary and Xin. "Speaking of which, teacher, do you know why Jayden Tiger is at the academy?"

"Jayden is here!" Xin almost jumped up. It was a secret to everyone that he was her brother, but why didn't he come see his sister? she thought, folding her arms.

"Yeah, I thought he might be coming over to train us for a bit or something?" Ryan asked.

"Oh really? I guess I should look into it," Eddy said with a smile, wondering what was going on.

CHAPTER 96

SIX VS. ONE (PART 1)

"I must be dreaming, but that's Jayden Tiger, right?" Wu asked with glowing eyes. His fellow students were just as baffled to see the Altered celebrity in person, but without a doubt, this was the famous "White Tiger."

Snow frantically started searching his pockets for something to give to his idol, eventually pulling out a carrot while also dropping a few on the floor. It was amazing itself how one could hide so many carrots on one's body.

With the carrot in hand, he ran to Jayden's side.

"Would you mind signing this for me?" Snow asked with some slight embarrassment. "It's the only thing I have on me right now."

In some situations, this might have been embarrassing, but the others were just jealous that they didn't have anything that Jayden could sign right now.

"Just what strings did the AFA pull to get the forty-eighth strongest AFC to teach us a lesson?" Sty wondered out loud. It was normal for students to be starstruck when meeting someone from the AFC, even more so since this wasn't just a regular fighter but someone within the top fifty of the world. Even those who didn't watch AFC fights would recognize him with ease.

"Thanks for all the praise, but I'm actually back to rank 49 after yesterday's fight. In the end, I lost by a few points," Jayden admitted freely. Since he didn't have a pen on him to sign Snow's carrot, he simply transformed his fingernail into a claw and used that to make an indentation of his signature instead. "There you go. It's my rest day today, so I decided to pay a visit."

"Do you think it was the AFA or NIRV who asked him to come here to teach us? I mean, his schedule must be filled to the brim with training, shoots, and more," Numba whispered to Gary. Although they weren't on the same team, since they were friends it was natural for them to stand next to each other, but Gary had moved to the back of the group, still covering his face with his hands, even though nobody seemed to have connected the dots after Jayden had addressed him with that awful nickname.

"What are you getting all shy for, shouldn't you at least say hi?" Jayden prompted, as he looked toward the back of the room, making everyone turn their heads. "When I heard that you not only managed to make it into the real AFA but also joined the special lessons, I just had to pay you a visit. It's been a while since we last fought, so I'm looking forward to see how much you improved."

Gary . . . y-you actually know Jayden personally? Just what kind of relationship do the two of you have for him to not only be interested in you but also make time to teach us a lesson? And what does he mean, since you last fought? Numba's head was filled with questions, but now didn't seem like the right time to ask his friend about those.

He wasn't the only one whose opinion about Gary had changed drastically.

I knew it! Apollo smirked. *Someone that strong couldn't have come from some no-name Tier 3 town. He has to have connections, I just never thought that Jayden Tiger would be one of them. I'll seriously need to ask one of the teachers to allow me to have a match against him, but for now . . . I'm more excited to see how I fare against an actual AFC fighter.*

Apollo punched his fist into the palm of his hand, and Jayden saw this, which made him clear his throat.

"Ahem, let's focus on the contents of this extra special lesson, please. There will be more than enough time for us all to talk afterward, provided you do well enough," Jayden said, not forgetting to offer them some extra motivation. "For the next fifteen minutes, both teams are to attack me as if I were your enemy. There's no need to hold back, so I advise you to turn into your Altered forms.

"I will be the one grading both teams, and the one that does better will win the reward. It's up to you whether you want to work together or get in the way of the other team. From what I saw from your last special lesson, unless the six of you come at me together, you won't stand a chance of actually defeating me."

With the rules explained, it was time to get ready. The red team, Apollo, Sty, and Numba, stayed on the right side, while the blue team, Gary, Wu, and Snow, stayed on the left. Then there was Jayden, who stood on the other side of the fifty-yard fighting room.

"*Begin!*" Jayden shouted, and it sounded almost like a growl as his face started to change. White fur with loose black marks appeared on his face as his nails turned into claws. It was a small partial transformation, but just this slight change made the teenagers feel a slight form of pressure.

The last time we fought, he didn't transform but I did see him use some of his strange skills against the red color gang. We have to be careful, Gary thought, but just when he wanted to warn his team members, he saw that everyone else had decided to recklessly charge in.

Numba had transformed into his goatlike state, the horns on the top of his head pointing at Jayden. Wu had the same antennae as before, with his body covered in sweat. Then there was Snow with his fluffy white fur and large legs, hopping around. Sty was in his buglike state, flying overhead.

All of them seemed confident in their skills as they charged Jayden, and even Apollo was positioned toward the front as well.

"Really, your big plan is to charge at me all at once?" Jayden scratched the back of his head as he let out a low sigh. "I guess you're confident in numbers. If people saw this many Altered coming at them, even if they were Altered themselves, they would be frightened, but you have to remember . . . I'm not your regular Altered."

Jayden placed his leg back slightly as he got in position and swung his hand back; the next moment he threw a fist with massive force. The group had yet to reach him; there was still a good fifteen yards before any one of them would be in striking distance.

A large, powerful gust of wind immediately hit the others like a concrete wall. They were knocked off their feet into the air, their bodies spinning as they crashed to the floor. The wind was too strong for Sty to continue flying, and he fell as well.

"Oh, one of you managed to break through that. Good job." Jayden praised them as he saw something akin to a giant white polar bear rush through his attack. Apollo's Altered form still made him look human, but it was as if he had grown an entire size. His cheeks had transformed a little, making them puffier, but the details of his face were still there. Charging ahead on all fours, he was moving incredibly fast for someone of that size.

"You're good," Jayden said as he glided across the floor, being pushed by the wind. He didn't even move his feet; it looked like he flew over. Apollo had carefully watched his feet, but because of that he was unprepared for Jayden to suddenly appear in front of him, launching a fist right into the Polar Bear Altered's stomach; once again a large rush of wind came out of the strike, lifting Apollo high up in the air, causing him to crash and land on the floor.

Only a few seconds had passed, and Gary had just stayed at the back and watched everything.

One swing knocked down four of them, and a single punch was enough to do Apollo in. Is this what it means to be the best of the best? No, he himself admitted that there are Altered out there even stronger than he is . . . and he isn't even taking this completely seriously!

"They don't call me White Tiger and Master of the Wind for nothing," Jayden boasted proudly, making a fist.

If I want to protect my family and the gang in the future, I need to become stronger than him, Gary thought.

Skill activated: Controlled Transformation
New Quest received
Honorable Fight 3.0!
Among your team, you're the last man standing!
Condition: Survive fifteen minutes or knock your opponent out
Reward: ???
Failure: ???

CHAPTER 97

SIX VS. ONE (PART 2)

If Jayden fully transformed, then Gary could never dream to win this fight without transforming himself. However, since the AFC fighter was obviously holding back, Gary decided to transform to around 80 percent of his Full Transformation. His face was the only thing that remained as it was. Although it was now covered in brown fur, he did not have a large muzzle, nor had he sprouted his large canines.

This looks just like the quest the system issued when I fought against Xin. It's the only one I ever failed so far. Should I thank you, system, for giving me a chance to redeem myself? Gary thought as he ran forward.

He was fast, and all of the others who were still getting up from the first strike watched him go right past them.

That guy's even faster than when he fought against Shingi, Wu thought.

Seeing this, Jayden prepared the same strike he had used against the others, and he swung his arm out, letting out a large gust of wind. Gary waited for his fur to rustle a little bit, and when the wind wall came at him at full force, the werewolf pushed off the ground and swung both his hands as if he were striking the air.

To those watching it looked silly, since the wind was invisible to the eye, but Gary's strong force and use of his sharp nails allowed him to cut right through and continue forward.

"I see, so far the wolf and the polar bear get equal points. Let's see if you can get through the next part." Jayden smiled.

When Gary was close enough, he was ready to swing at Jayden's head, but the Altered swung his arm slightly, and a gust of wind hit the teenager, moving his body off to the side.

Using this opportunity, Jayden continued forward and kicked Gary with his powerful leg. Gary felt the force of the wind send him flying back and crashing across the ground. In the end, Gary had to use his claws to stop himself from bouncing all over the place as he returned back in line with the others.

–10 HP

240/250 HP

The wind is strong, but it looks like he's still holding back to make sure he doesn't hurt us too much. Unlike against those gang members, he isn't using fatal attacks. I can't believe that Jayden is so much stronger to the point that he can pretty much play with us like this, without having to worry, Gary thought, and the realization dampened his mood.

If Jayden had wanted to, he could have easily ended the fight then and there, but since he had come here to teach the teenagers a lesson, he stayed in place and waited for everyone to get up. This time, none of them were quick to charge in again.

"Great, it looks like you've learned your first lesson. It's always smarter to study the skill set of your opponent rather than just rushing in to attack. This is true for fighting humans and Altered, but also beasts. Never make the mistake of thinking you fully know what your opponent is capable of, just because you might have studied him beforehand.

"I bet you all thought that just because you've seen me on TV many times, you already knew my skill set. I hope I don't burst any bubbles, but as you will learn in the future, the AFC prohibits the use of special attributes for Altered like me.

"So this wind power that my Altered form grants me has never been seen on TV. Well, streaker boy over there might have warned you, since he's seen me use it already. This is why I told you that you needed teamwork. If Gary had informed you of that beforehand, then you all would have fared better, right?"

The others turned to look at Gary, including Wu and Snow. Their eyes were questioning him about whether he had withheld that information on purpose, just so he could impress Jayden the most.

Don't blame me, when you guys were the ones who ran off before I could even say anything! Gary thought as he rolled his eyes, frustrated at the lack of trust, and at Jayden obviously scapegoating him.

Now that everyone was a bit more cautious, they had naturally split up around the room in their various forms. Apollo surprisingly had actually moved backward, while Gary moved forward to act as part of the attack force this time.

The idea was simple: with them split up, it should be near impossible for Jayden to use his attack like he had done before. The White Tiger was glancing around him, smiling, and the first to make a move was Sty, as he spat strange green liquid from his mouth.

Jayden moved away to avoid the attack, but the second he did, Numba charged forward, horns first. Unfortunately, Jayden stopped his charge prematurely, horns first.

"You have quite the explosive power there, and the two of you worked well together; a point for the red team!" Jayden announced, just before he slammed Numba's head into the floor, and his transformed state was reverted back to normal. Judging by the cracking sound, it was safe to say that Numba was out of this fight.

Sty continued to spit out the green acidlike substance at Jayden, who avoided it easily, and Snow, getting impatient, jumped in with his rabbitlike legs. It seemed like the perfect time, since Jayden would have to move to dodge the acid, but with a flick of his wrist, the wind splashed it right into Snow's eyes and burned him.

Jayden was ready to finish him off with a kick to the head, but Wu punched him in the leg. It was a powerful punch that matched even Jayden's strength.

"That's impressive power you have there. Extra point for your team, but I'm afraid I have to get a little more serious on you," Jayden said, as cuts that looked like claw marks appeared across both Wu's and Snow's bodies. They had no idea how Jayden had done it.

With two swings of his hand, Jayden bashed their heads together, knocking both out. At that moment, Gary jumped out from the side, launching in with his claw.

The Altered moved back, avoiding it, but midstrike Gary used Controlled Transformation to extend his claws longer and scratch the top of Jayden's chest.

"You aren't the only one with skills."

Claw Drain
+2 HP

"You waited for the right time to strike, but you ended up losing your teammates in the process, so I can't give you any points. You in the back are making the same mistake," Jayden said, criticizing Apollo. "I already told you that you would need to work together; if you continue the special lessons like this, you'll end up in serious trouble in the future."

CHAPTER 98

A WINNER

A lot of what Jayden said went unheard by the students. After all, he'd already knocked out more than half of them. Even Sty had been hit by a wind blast at some point, banging his head into one of the walls.

This left Apollo and Gary as the only students able to listen, but since Apollo was on the other side of the room, it was unlikely he heard anything; as for Gary, he was so focused on Jayden that his brain was drowning out the words coming from his mouth.

I scratched him . . . which means I can hit him as well, which means I can win this fight! Gary thought, as he burst off the floor, swinging his arms at Jayden. Although his attacks were fast, Jayden saw them relatively easily, and he parried the strikes away without touching Gary's hand.

Right now, Jayden couldn't feel Gary's strength because not a single hit was landing.

I only have a few skills—Claw Drain, Last Stand, and Howling Force—but in this situation none of them can help me. Did I make a mistake? Should I have focused on increasing stats and converted some of my Pawn points into Skill points to unlock a skill?

I still have two Pawn points that I can use, but getting a skill I don't know how to use in the middle of the fi—

"You're thinking far too much," Jayden said, as he jumped, flipping over Gary and stabbing his hand right into the wall. Gary didn't even realize that they were this close to the wall because he was so focused on hitting Jayden.

In a ring, Gary's speed and tenacity would certainly put most AFC contestants in trouble. His speed, his strength, and his deadly claws . . . his transformed state is one of the strongest I've ever seen. Under conditions where one isn't allowed to use their special abilities or attributes, he may very well become champion, but outside the ring . . .

It will be hard, Gary; if you continue down this path, you will meet fighters who are far more powerful than me, with far more dangerous skills. You have to learn how to fight them. I'm glad I came here, because you need to learn a lot more than what the AFA can teach you if you're going to survive.

I know you're the one who defeated Kirk, and I know you're involved with the Howlers. I've been watching the news carefully to see what you have been doing, and it looks like Slough has become a better place . . . but there are people who will try to take advantage of that. It was the same for me.

With a double palm thrust, Jayden unleashed a strong wind that pushed Gary into the wall further with his claws, as another fighter was coming toward him.

Apollo had been waiting for the right time, and while Jayden and Gary were busy fighting, he had begun his charge, reverting to his full Altered form, looking more like a polar bear than a human, and was running on all fours.

He was slow at first, but soon he picked up speed and was running as fast as a car as he came straight toward Jayden. When he launched forward, Apollo's form was changing into his half-state, making him appear more human, and Apollo had the biggest grin on his face, because he could tell that this was too fast even for Jayden to react.

I got him.

Apollo grabbed him by both of his arms, holding them tightly.

Now he can't use his wind against me, Apollo thought as he lifted Jayden into the air and threw him against the floor as hard as possible.

The professors and the observers from NIRV who were watching were worried; they had seen Apollo's strength, and even Jayden would be hurt by this.

At the last moment, with his hands facing backward, Jayden unleashed a large amount of wind, using all of his power to stop himself from touching the floor.

"You're good, you're really good. Too bad I'm awesome," Jayden said with a smile, as he used a burst of wind to loosen himself from Apollo's grip.

"You're a big guy, so I think you can take this!" Jayden swung his hand, releasing another wind, but not as strong as before; Apollo felt the special armor across his chest ripping, along with parts of his flesh, drawing blood, but he still stood there strong as Jayden created distance between them.

At the same time, Gary quickly reverted to human form to get his claws out of the wall and then transformed back to his werewolf self.

I can feel it, I'm close; I have to keep trying new things, Gary thought, as he returned to Apollo's side.

These two, Jayden thought. *Both of them are incredibly strong. It makes me wonder, if the two of them were to get in a fight, which one would win? What a talented new generation we have. Xin, you have a lot cut out for you if you want to stay at the top.*

He put his hands down, and the buzzer went off shortly after.

"Fifteen minutes have passed; the special lesson is over," the voice from the speaker said.

Jayden had known exactly how much time had passed; it showed how skilled he was to be able to focus on different things during the fight.

"I guess it's now time for me to declare the winner." Jayden smiled.

CHAPTER 99

A SPECIAL REWARD

Before announcing the results, Jayden waited for the knocked-out teenagers to wake up. This didn't take long, since a specialized medical team was already on standby. Usually they only needed to take care of wounds caused by beasts, so treating the fighters who had been only lightly injured by the AFC fighter was a welcome change.

"No need to make a fuss; if those guys weren't strong Altered they never would have made it into the special lesson classes. Besides, I held back, so most of those are surface wounds." Jayden shrugged as he waited for the medics to do their job.

In a matter of minutes, both teams were lined up, all of them sharing unsatisfied looks on their faces. One of them was Apollo, who cursed himself for not lasting longer. He had wanted to try so many more things, but time had run out. Gary knew exactly how he felt, because it was the same for him as well.

"Man, we suck so much!" Snow complained. "We were one of the first ones to get knocked out."

Wu was also feeling down. When they had faced off against the debut students, it hadn't seemed like there was such a big gap, but fighting against a top ranker made it clear to him that outside the AFA, a whole new world awaited them. Even scarier was the fact that until the end, the White Tiger hadn't taken them seriously.

"Now, now, don't get your knickers in a knot. You guys didn't do that bad, and your bravery is commendable. Still, I hope that one of the lessons you take with you today is that there will be times when being brave could get you killed," Jayden lectured. "You need to be prepared that you might meet another Altered with special abilities, as well as beasts that have special abilities. In fact, you yourself as Altered might have yet to unlock your true talent and powers."

These words were quite encouraging to the six teenagers. For a while some of them had felt that they had hit a plateau in their training. They felt that they weren't improving as quickly or as much as they used to, but hearing this and seeing what was possible inspired them to push themselves even harder.

"Now here comes the hard part for me: as your stand-in teacher, I need to decide which of your teams sucked less—ahem—performed better than the other." Jayden quickly cleared his throat to distract from his verbal blunder and placed his finger on his chin, as he thought back to the events.

"Gary, let's start with my critique toward you. I get that you're more of a lone wolf, but you have been assigned your teammates for a reason. But what did you do? Rather than make use of their strength, you stood back twice waiting for a chance, even going so far as to sacrifice them to get a chance to hit me. The same, though to a lesser degree, applies to you, Apollo. Nevertheless, at the end of the day, I give you equal points for having managed to circumvent my wind wall and get to me, in Gary's case even scratching me.

"Snow, Wu, Sty, Numba, the four of you might have been knocked out, but you still showed at least a semblance of teamwork. If you had focused on it, you might have done far better. Snow, I'm sorry to say but your performance was the worst of the six. While it was a good idea to attack me at the position I would appear at, after seeing how I could use wind, you should have been prepared to be hit by the acid attack.

"Wu, your mentality to attack me when I was going to dispose of Snow isn't that much better than Gary's or Apollo's, yet I noticed a slight hesitation when you attacked me, since you made sure Snow was okay. As passionate as that is, in those situations you should focus on doing your job, and you should have attacked me with all you had, rather than allowing yourself to get distracted.

"Sty, I think you already know that while your wings give you the advantage over many enemies, they're not almighty, and your attack capabilities aren't the best against those who either are tough enough to brace against your acid attack or can dodge or evade it.

"Numba, while your charge attack might certainly pack a punch, you need to work on it, especially on not making it that obvious. Still, good usage of the opportunity that came from me not knowing about Sty's attack. That was the closest thing to teamwork that came out of this lesson today, and for that reason I have to give the win to your team."

Numba cheered and raised his arm to high-five the person next to him, only to realize that it was Sty, who kept his arms folded and turned his head away. Then there was Apollo on the other side, but he didn't look to be in the mood to high-five either.

"You guys will get to ask the academy for a reward. Ask for a day off, some nice food, or something. Anyway, the real reward will be what you take away from today's lesson."

With that said, it was time for Jayden to leave, but as he walked past Gary, he put his hand on his shoulder and whispered in his ear.

"Meet me on the roof of your dormitory; we need to have a little catch-up chat before I go."

Gary gulped, not knowing whether this was a good thing or a bad thing. In the past Gary wasn't bothered about Jayden too much, but now after seeing his display of skills, it made him worry. What would happen if he and Xin got in an argument one day? Would Jayden come knocking on his door?

Why am I worrying about that now when me and Xin aren't even together? Besides, as an Altered, she could probably fight me herself if I ever pissed her off. Jayden never seemed to mind the two of us in the first place, unlike her father . . . Gary thought.

Once again the werewolf found everyone's eyes on him. With the lesson over, Crowley sent them back to the dormitory to rest, but not before he explained that the regular special lesson would still be on Friday, and reminded everyone to take to heart what they had been told, especially since Jayden had been a part of these special lessons.

It was no surprise, otherwise they would have never let him in there, but did this mean NIRV had control of many of the big shots in the AFA? If that was the case, they were a far bigger and powerful organization than the outside world was aware of.

As they walked back to the dormitory, Numba couldn't help but smile.

"I can't believe you know Jayden. So what is the deal between you two?" Numba asked the question that had been plaguing him ever since the White Tiger had shown himself. He wanted to ask before but didn't want the others to find out, even though he knew they must be just as curious.

"I wouldn't really call it knowing him. Not a lot of people know this because they don't really advertise it, but he has folks living in my home-town. In the past, I did something . . . stupid, and he helped me out."

All of what Gary said was technically true, but he wouldn't mention the reason behind his embarrassing name.

"I see. It's still cool that you know someone like that. He seemed to like you, at least." Numba started to rub his hands. "I can't wait, though I don't even know what to ask for as a reward. Maybe I can ask to get a personal coach who can help push me to the next level. After all, I don't want to fall behind in the special lessons . . . Oh sorry, I forgot, you didn't get a special reward."

Numba was just too excited, and since Gary was his only friend in the special lessons, he sometimes forgot that they weren't on the same team. Now he felt a little bad about the bargaining he had just done.

"It's okay, seriously, I'm not that upset about it," Gary replied with a smile. He wasn't lying; after all, he did get something out of it.

Quest completed
You managed to survive against one of the best, though next time he might take you seriously!
Hopefully, you've learned a valuable lesson.
The system wishes to help you by unlocking part of your strength!
Please choose one of the following skills
Lethal Pounce
Berserker Mode
LOCKED (Failed to achieve the optional part)

You really know how to motivate me, system. Still, getting to choose one out of two skills is better than nothing. Now, if you only could at least provide me with a bit of description in the future . . .

There was a skill that Gary perhaps could have used against Jayden, and that was Magnetic Howl. However, it was an ace in the hole that he didn't want to reveal too soon, but one of the skills that kept coming up was one that had interested Gary.

I think this skill could work well with what I have at the moment.

CHAPTER 100

REACH ME

In the past when a tough decision came up, Gary would have confided in Tom for advice. Since he was on his own, he pondered what his best choice would be. Although there was no description, the skill names themselves gave him some information.

Lethal Pounce had to be a movement skill. In the fight with Jayden, it might have allowed him to cover the distance between the two of them quickly. It had been tricky getting through the wind attack, but he had managed to do it without a special skill. Of course, the skill could have some other effects, but there was no way to know that without choosing it.

Then there was Berserker Mode, which promised a lot more synergy with his current stats. From what Gary knew, Berserkers usually focused on their rage, gaining pure power in favor of defense. The more wounds they took, the more power they could exhibit, so in his case, he assumed that less Health would translate to a bigger boost to his Strength.

Fortunately, his Endurance had always been high, and coupled with his Last Stand skill, Berserker Mode might prove to be a deadly combo. Unfortunately, it was once again a skill that seemed like a double-edged sword, and it might be more suited as a last resort.

I don't like the idea of playing around with death. I get that taking this skill might very well mean that I would be at my strongest at that point, but if I miscalculate even slightly, that might be it for me ... Stupid system, why did you have to taunt me by showing me that I missed out on a potential choice? Now I can't help but be curious!

As he rolled from one side of his bed to the other bed, the system suddenly informed him that it was past midnight, one less day until the next full moon.

"System, can't you give me a tip or suggestion? Is it possible to trade those in for a more useful skill? How about something that allows me and others to have a peaceful time during the full moon?"

Unsurprisingly, Gary got no answer. He started listing the pros and cons once again, but in the end the decision was so tough that the exhausted teenager was starting to fall asleep. As he closed his eyes he pushed his finger forward and picked one of the skills.

A brief nap later, he suddenly woke up with a scary realization. Taking a look at his phone, he noticed that he had been asleep for over an hour. *Ah crap, Jayden's going to kill me.*

Taking the quick way to the rooftop, not wanting Jayden to wait any longer, Gary opened the outside window and started climbing. With his strength and grip he was easily able to throw himself a few ledges up with a single hand.

He continued to do this until he reached the roof, and there he saw the one and only waiting in the distance.

"*Finally!* I was just about to walk to your room and drag you here. Do you have any idea how many people would be willing to pay me to get to hang out with me, and yet here you are taking your sweet time." Jayden tapped his foot in anger—the crooked smile on his face showing teeth.

"I'm so sorry." Gary immediately apologized, clasping his hands together. He even went as far to get onto his knees like he was begging. "I promise, the teachers . . ."

"Relax, there is still one more person I need to see before leaving anyway; besides, I like being on rooftops," Jayden said as he turned around and looked at the view from atop the academy.

"Gary, there is a lot I want to speak to you about. The academy, the AFC, the Tier cities, the gangs, my father, Xin. The list is huge, but we don't have too much time, and I'm afraid at the moment, most of that stuff will just unnecessarily put pressure on you."

Jayden then turned around with a very serious expression on his face. It wasn't his usual smiley self; instead it was a worried look. Gary knew what this was like, because it was the same for him when he was in the Underdogs.

"Jayden . . . is everything okay? Do you need help with anything?" Gary asked.

Those words seemed to snap Jayden out of his daze as he shook his head. "Help? From you. I appreciate the gesture, Gary, but if I can't solve my problems, then what do you think you could possibly do?"

It was true, but for some reason at that moment Gary wanted to offer his hand to pull Jayden out of whatever struggle he was in at the moment.

"I'm amazed at the speed of your growth. With what you've shown, I don't doubt that you would fare well in the AFC's lower ranks, but until you reach where I'm standing, my problems should not be yours to worry about. I do sometimes wish there were someone at my side to discuss these things with, and maybe it's stupid of me to say this but I'm going to anyway."

Jayden took in a deep breath as he walked over to Gary and then stopped right in front of him, putting a hand on his shoulder.

"Get stronger, strong enough so you can stand by my side, and when you do, we can have that type of conversation."

For some reason, Gary felt like whatever problems Jayden was having must be relatively serious if, one, he couldn't solve them, and two, he needed someone just as strong as he was. For Jayden, though, who had helped him every step of the way, of course Gary would take his hand.

"Of course," Gary said. "I promise that I will get as strong as you, and when I am, if there is anything you need help with, I will be there."

A spoken deal has been made, would you like to mark "Jayden Clove"?

This was a promise that Gary didn't want to break himself, no matter who he became, so he decided to make the mark anyway. Not that he thought he would need it anytime soon.

"Haha, you surely have balls. Well, should you become strong enough to stand by my side, I might actually have to give you my blessing for Xin. Well, getting her to agree, is still up to you first, of course."

Gary let go and put both hands behind his head as his nostrils grew slightly bigger. "Haha, yeah."

"I'm sorry about this, but my message basically is, reach me where I am," Jayden confirmed.

With that said, Jayden was off. The werewolf didn't know when they would see each other again, but eventually, when Gary felt he was strong enough and had the power to help, he would find Jayden and repay him.

CHAPTER 101

SPECIAL LESSON 2

The normal days at the academy were going quite slowly for Gary. There wasn't much to do, and since he had already been offered a chance to debut, the lessons felt somewhat pointless now. Sure, it was interesting, but none of it was as interesting as what was happening in his life at the moment.

After speaking to Jayden last night, Gary couldn't stop thinking about what the problems could be, and he knew one thing: he needed to get stronger.

Gary Dem
Grade: Bishop
Class: Warrior
Level 23
Health 250
Energy 300
Exp 8788/11564
Strength 36
Dexterity 26
Endurance 34

Which was why he couldn't wait for Friday to come. Still, Gary got to enjoy his time with the others, and Numba had done as he said he would, getting a private instructor to teach him, just like the debut students.

Which meant that Numba was away from the others a lot more than he usually would have been. Friday finally came and Gary was back in the strange room wearing his blue clothing, taking part in the special lesson.

"Before your lesson begins today, I am to take you to the observation deck," Crowley announced. "Coo! I want you to know, you are all to be on your best behavior, for there are many people up there from NIRV."

"Sir, what exactly will they be doing?" Snow asked.

"That is not for me to know, but I think there may be a weekly assessment for you all. Before you take part, perhaps they are monitoring your growth," Crowley said.

The two groups went into the large fighting area as usual, but at the side of one of the walls was an open door. As they walked in, they realized that it was actually an elevator.

Gary had noticed that the NIRV research team that had taken the crystal out of the beast had gone into these rooms before.

Man, I hope I don't meet that creepy guy again. I have a feeling he already had an idea what was going on, Gary thought.

As the elevator dinged and the door opened, the students were surprised by what they saw. It looked like a large lab. There were several machines, recording equipment, and men in white shirts and suits.

To the right was a long glass wall that would allow them to look down at the fights taking place. Now they knew why it was called the observation deck. However, one of the first people that Gary saw was the NIRV employee he had been thinking about.

"Ah, it's very nice to meet the new Retrievers in person!" James said, as he walked forward with his thick, black-framed glasses and his annoying pen in his hand. Every so often he clicked the top of the pen for no reason and, with Gary's sensitive hearing, he noticed it more than the others.

James looked at all of them, smiling, but when his eyes met Gary's, the smile grew even bigger.

"Please, none of you have to be nervous, we are just checking your Altered information. After all, we want to give you the best chance of survival, as you will be fighting stronger beasts from now on. Once we know your skills and the type of Altered you are, it will allow us to match you up with more appropriate beasts."

Crowley stood between James and the students with his arms folded; if there was one thing Gary was happy about, it was the fact that Crowley also seemed to dislike these guys.

"But if there is a danger, then you will do everything in your power to stop it, correct?" Crowley said.

"Of course!" James smiled. "Please just follow along; this will only take fifteen minutes or so, and after that you should be ready for your next assessment."

As Gary walked along with the others, he realized something. What if these tests figured out he wasn't an Altered? What would happen then? There was still the fact that the Underdogs were supposed to deliver the package that had made Gary into a werewolf to someone. From all the things he was finding out about NIRV, it seemed like they would be a good suspect.

My only bet is to plead to Crowley that I don't want to take these tests, he should understand, right . . . right?

"Please, my employees will take great care of you," James said as he walked off and brushed past Gary. His heart was beating fast, but as he turned his head, he smiled.

"You shouldn't worry too much. It's just a questionnaire and a health checkup. We can't take that much information from you guys. Rules of your academy and whatnot," said a soft voice that Gary hadn't heard in a while.

He nearly shouted out when he saw him, but the person winked at him as he held the clipboard.

"Ah, don't worry, I was just trying to be friendly," the other person said nervously. "Anyway, let's get going to the test."

As Gary followed the others, it was hard for him to stop smiling.

Who would have thought, of all places, I would meet you here. Well, it's nice to meet you again, Tom.

CHAPTER 102

A SPECIAL ITEM (PART 1)

Tom had been working for NIRV for just as long as Gary had been at the AFA. When the two of them had split up that day and left school, Tom had resumed his prior work as a special case. His grades were more than good enough, and although he was younger than usual, as the son of two of their prominent researchers, NIRV had agreed to make an exception and sign him up for their program aimed at students who had just graduated, offering him a nice career.

Of course, as soon as Tom had heard that some NIRV employees worked at the AFA, he did his best to be a part of it. He couldn't imagine the look on Gary's face when he appeared in a white lab robe, and he was quite pleased with the result today. In a way, their meeting showed that although they were taking different paths, they could still be involved in each other's lives; they just needed to get out of their current rut.

It's nice to see you again too, and from what I've learned about these special lessons, it seems that you have been doing well at the academy, and you don't have to worry about a thing now that I'm here; I will make sure your secret stays a secret, Tom thought as he conducted the tests on each of the students.

Honestly, at the moment there was nothing in the test that would out Gary, as the students were just going through some small checkups.

They were connected via cables to a machine that checked their heartbeat, respiration rate, and a few other vitals.

After that, each student received a questionnaire about their current Altered forms and their powers. Many of the questions asked them to rate themselves on a scale from one to ten, such as how strong they felt compared to other Altered. The questions were quite subjective depending on their experience.

When Tom handed out the clipboards, Gary's form, which was on the very bottom, was already filled out. When the werewolf looked up, Tom just mouthed *pretend*, so the green-haired teenager quickly picked up the pen and "used" it.

This is the safest way to do it. Gary could always answer something that would raise their suspicions, so it's best that I do it for him. I'm a really good friend, aren't I? Tom smiled to himself.

Gary would have to agree that Tom was going above and beyond. If NIRV caught him doing such things, he might be lucky if all they did was kick him out. It just showed how much Tom treasured their friendship.

With all the tests over, the students were free to go, but before they left, James had come back because he had something to say.

"Today's test will be the same as last time. You will be split into two teams, but for your own safety, we'll be doing one group after the other," James explained. "The red group will start, so the blue group is free to relax, or even watch and come up with a strategy."

"Isn't that a bit unfair?" Sty asked. "If they see what the beast is capable of, then they will have a better chance of beating it easier and quicker."

"This is not a contest," Crowley quickly interrupted.

"Your teacher is right. Although today you will be fighting the same beast again, it's unlikely to happen often in the future. The primary goal of these special lessons is to strengthen you, so that you can work as full-fledged Retrievers. Knowing your enemy beforehand is a luxury, not a guarantee.

"Of course, depending on the estimated degree of danger, it's likely that we will put both groups together to face the beast, but regardless, most Retrievers do their job going in blind, so you'd best get used to it.

Also, and you should take clear note of this, if at any point we decide that you're not Retriever material, we'll no longer allow you to take part in these special lessons."

This was the first time the students heard that if they didn't demonstrate good enough skills, or couldn't prove they were strong enough to survive, they would be kicked out of the lesson. Gary guessed that this was more the academy's doing than NIRV's. The corporation couldn't possibly care whose life was lost and whose wasn't.

Apollo, Numba, and Sty headed back down to the training room, while the blue team was allowed to stay on the observation deck and watch from above. Just before the test was about to begin, Tom coughed loudly and informed his supervisor that he needed to go to the restroom. The older NIRV employee seemed annoyed, and chided the intern that he was old enough to just go on his own.

Seeing this, Gary assumed that Tom was sending him a signal, so he turned to Crowley. "Actually, I might go quickly as well, before the test begins."

As Gary entered the restroom, Tom was waiting by the sink. "I'm so happy that you understood what I wanted. I was worried that I might have to be in here for ten minutes before you got the message."

Gary chuckled because there had been a few moments when he was second-guessing himself, but he thought it would be a nice time for the two of them to talk anyway.

"Anyway, we can't stay in here for long, otherwise they will be suspicious, but I wanted to give you something. During my research I found something that I think you might like."

Tom placed what felt like a large medallion in Gary's hand. It bore a shield and the face of a wolf; that wasn't the only interesting thing about it, though, because the system recognized it as well.

[An ancient item has been received]

CHAPTER 103

A SPECIAL ITEM (PART 2)

"Tom, where did you get something like this? Are you sure it's all right to give this to me?" Gary had to ask, because he still couldn't believe that the system had had such a reaction to this object.

"It's pretty cool, right?" Tom smirked. "You better accept it, because it wasn't easy getting it out. I pretty much swiped it from work. Don't worry, I wasn't stupid enough to do it in one go, and it's also nothing too precious, at least by NIRV's standards. In fact, they won't even miss it. They found it when digging for fossils, but after a few rounds of experiments they found no link to any ancient beasts.

"It has a wolf on it, so according to the notes, the researcher assumed that it was just a piece of art depicting what could have been a beast. Since it was gathering dust in the archives, I thought it might be better off with you rather than getting auctioned off to some museum. Anyway, I thought it would be a nice gift for you, to remember me, you know, in case you forget."

"Tom . . ." Gary replied, wanting to make a joke that they weren't a couple like that. There was no need for him to get Tom a gift, but there was so much on Gary's mind because he doubted that Tom even knew what he had just given him.

An ancient item has been received

A werewolf artifact of old
The artifact cannot be activated with your current power

It doesn't just have a normal wolf on it; this picture on the medallion is a werewolf. Does this mean that werewolves also existed back then, when the strong beasts used to roam the earth?

An image appeared in Gary's head of werewolves fighting against the large beasts. It seemed to make sense, but the other thing was the fact that this item could be activated but the system said he didn't have enough power.

What does it mean by power? Does it mean that my level is too low, or something else? If it belongs to werewolves of the past, then werewolves should be able to open this thing. The next time I see them, I should have Kai or Olivia hold it and see if there's any reaction.

Gary wasn't going to refuse something like this, and he put it in his trouser pocket. In the suit he was wearing, the pocket wasn't really the best place.

"Are you sure that thing . . . is going to be comfy there?" Tom asked.

"It's the only place I can put it for now," Gary replied, wondering how to make sure it wouldn't suffer in the middle of the fight.

"All right." Tom couldn't help but stare at Gary's junk area, trying to see the outline of the object. "There is something else I wanted to warn you about. NIRV seems to be quite worried about a black liquid.

"It's a substance that is just like Altered DNA, and it can be used the same way; the only thing is, only a small amount of it is needed. Because of that, many groups have been researching it, not just NIRV, but there is quite a nasty side effect; it makes people turn into Crazed Altered."

Immediately Gary's mind went to the orphans in Slough as well as a couple of redheaded twins he had come across.

"Of course they're trying to get rid of the side effects, because this could be a huge breakthrough in the Alterification process. People would no longer have to pay a fortune to become Altered! But that's only if they can do it. Anyway, my point is, the black liquid's origin is from the beasts.

"There have been some cases, when creating a beast from the crystal, that a beast shows signs of being infected. Purple skin, dark eyes, and sometimes a strange shadow floating from their skin. There are two things: these beasts that are infected are stronger than your average beasts, and some Altered who have been seriously injured by these infected beasts have turned crazed as well.

"So, while taking these lessons, if you ever come across a beast that looks like this, I advise you to run."

All of this information was interesting to Gary. Meeting Tom had taught him a lot. Now Gary was starting to see the advantages of having people in different areas of expertise. Gary could gather information in the academy, from Tom at NIRV, and from Kai in the gang world as well.

"Come on, let's get out of here, before they think the two of us are up to something," Tom said as he exited the restroom first, and then a few moments later Gary followed him.

How did the Gray Elephants get their hands on the black liquid? Did they work with an organization like NIRV? No, I doubt that they would want something like this to get out. Does that mean that someone is selling this defective liquid to the gangs for some extra money? I'll have to update Kai about this and make sure none of it reaches Slough. Once was more than enough . . .

As they returned to the observation deck, Gary heard James the NIRV scientist and others talking.

"Wow, impressive. This beast was harder than the last, we can see that, but in the end they managed to defeat it quite quickly," James said.

Gary rushed to the glass, where he saw a beast that was unrecognizable, as most of its body was torn apart. Apollo still appeared to be in a transformed state, as he was covered in blood, while Sty and Numba looked somewhat injured, clearly still alive.

Judging by their wounds, this beast had not been as easy to defeat as the last one, and once again Apollo had done most of the grunt work.

"It looks like that surprise lesson from Jayden helped him reach another level," Crowley said, and it was clear he was talking about Apollo.

"All right, blue team, it's time for you to get ready." Crowley smiled.

Gary was excited. *A stronger beast than last time? Perfect, that just means I'll be even stronger afterward!*

CHAPTER 104

SPECIAL LESSON 3

There was a fine line between nervous and excited, and, as Gary stood there in the white room, he didn't know how he felt. A way to grow stronger! But what type of beast would come out this time?

But he also knew how dangerous this was; these creatures were trying to outright kill them, and there was also the warning from Tom. Before the assessment was to start, Gary looked up toward the glass screen. Now he knew what kind of people were keeping an eye on him.

"Hey, Gary," Wu said, already punching the air to warm up. "You know we have to impress these people to stay in the lessons; you heard them, right? So give me and Snow a chance."

"Give us a chance, what are you talking about?" Snow angrily complained.

Wu had never acted like this before, even after the last assessment. Yes, he knew Gary was good, but the way they were talking to him made it sound like he was on another level.

Of course, this was Wu's evaluation after seeing him take on the debut students and fight with Jayden.

A buzzer sounded, and they had no time to argue or fight each other, because in front of them was the beast that they were facing. The door opened wide, and unlike the last time, they saw nothing.

There were no heavy, intimidating footsteps, which made them wonder if there had been a mistake. That was until they saw the beast crawling along the wall. Its body was the size of half a car, but it was almost as long as a small train, and it had hundreds of legs that they could hear scurrying as it walked on the side of the wall.

It had a hard outer shell, which made the beast look like a centipede, and the two large claws in front of its mouth didn't make it look any less like one.

"Is it going to stay on the side of the wall?" Wu asked, as his two antennae were already sticking out of his head. Now that he was seeing what looked like another bug, his instincts were kicking in.

Bug-type Altereds were dangerous for a few reasons; one of their main strengths was that they were far superior to humans in strength and speed. As insects, they were already fast; when they increased in size, they became even more deadly.

Now, seeing a bug-type beast, Wu felt that this was going to be a tough challenge. The beast started to climb the wall, out of reach, and was going from the side wall to the back wall at an incredibly fast pace.

"Is this the beast we have on file?" Tom asked on the observation deck. "I thought we were still giving both teams the same type of beast to evaluate the students' limits."

Something was worrying Tom; perhaps it was the fact that he had never seen this beast on file. Meaning he didn't know how to categorize it. Through research, they were starting to learn that the crystals the beasts left behind after death—depending on what type of crystals— said a lot about their strength.

So from the plenty of fossils they had, they were able to tell if it was a basic beast, intermediate, advanced, and so on. Yet if it was a beast that wasn't on file, they had no idea what level it was either.

The other students also realized that this wasn't the same beast they had fought, and the first thing that Apollo noticed was that it was a lot faster and a lot more agile.

"You're right, I switched it," James answered. "However, you have nothing to worry about. From our research we are beginning to understand the levels of beasts before they are created. Don't worry, I wouldn't let something so dangerous out with a bunch of amateur Retrievers. What type of person do you think I am?"

That was the thing; Tom had no clue what type of person James was. He was always smiling and friendly to everyone, but at times he would do wild things with the experiments or the teams he ran as well.

James continued, "Based on their last assessment, I just thought they could do with more of a challenge."

"James!" Crowley shouted. "Remember what I said. If these students are seriously hurt because of something you did, I don't care what organization you have behind you. I will do everything in my power to hurt the person responsible."

James just looked at the teacher, nodded, and continued to watch the match as if it were no big deal.

Snow, seeing the beast so high up on the wall, was getting frustrated, and he couldn't take it anymore. He transformed his body, and his bottom half once again became that of a rabbit, while both of his small ears became large and floppy.

That bug thing is pretty high up. I know that Snow has strong jumping power, but how is he going to reach up there? Gary thought.

The only thing he could think of was using his claws to climb up the wall. The problem was, then he would be in a vulnerable state. Which was why Gary thought it was best to wait for the beast to attack them first.

Squatting directly up against the wall, Snow jumped up high, reaching halfway up the wall of the large room, but by then the centipede was nearly to the ceiling.

When it looked like Snow was slowing down and about to fall, he pushed off again in midair. There was nothing for the rabbit-like Altered to push against, but somehow he was on the floor again, and a burst of energy sent him upward.

Snow threw a fist toward the centipede. When he got close, though, the beast used its body like a whip, swinging its body outward, with most of its weight in its large head, and hitting Snow out of the air and right into the wall, where he slowly slid to the floor.

I'm quite happy that I didn't decide to go through with my plan now, Gary thought, as he imagined that he would have ended up in the same situation. The beast was incredibly fast, and thanks to its segmented body, it was able to create a powerful strike just like a whip.

There was a dent in the wall where Snow had struck it, but Snow was the number two student, so something like this wouldn't kill him; at least that was what Gary hoped anyway.

However, the centipede was on the move again, and it was going right for where Snow would land, aiming to finish off its injured prey.

When Snow touched the floor, the centipede opened up its two large pincers, ready to cut him in half. Snow was slightly dazed, but he was coming to and had only just seen the beast.

"Don't worry, I got you!" Wu said, as his forearms grew larger and his skin tone changed to a dark brown, black. Stretching out his arms, Wu stopped the pincers' strike. His arms were shaking but he was unable to stop the momentum of its body.

The centipede carried on, pushing Wu into the air. He held his hands out at full width, stopping the pincers from crushing him. Although Wu hated the thought, the only one he could rely on now was Gary, who had already transformed.

As Gary swung his arm, the centipede's body suddenly twisted the other way, and Gary's claw hit nothing but air.

Was my timing off? Gary thought, as he ran after the bug beast again and swung his claw at a different part, but the same thing happened again, with the beast curling its body and avoiding the strike.

But its head is focused on Wu, and it isn't looking this way. It must have some type of sixth sense . . . At first Gary was worried, but then he smiled. *I guess this is an opportunity to try my new skill.*

CHAPTER 105

NEW SKILL ACTIVATED

The large centipede-like beast continued to move, and unlike with the last beast, Wu wasn't pulling any of his punches. He was using the full strength of his current Altered form as he stopped all of the power in the pincers from crushing him.

The struggle continued for a while, but eventually they reached the end of the wall, and the centipede, with no fear of hurting its own body, crashed into the wall, pushing Wu right up against it.

The body weight, speed, and strength of the beast made it a powerful blow, but Wu was proud of one thing, other than his strength, it was his body. Having not passed out, Wu was still fighting against the pincers crushing in on him, and his hands were starting to bleed as well.

One snap of these pincers and I'll be dead, not just me but any Altered. Isn't this too much of a step up from the last beast that we fought? Wu thought.

Just then he saw someone coming through the air from a distance.

"Don't worry, this is teamwork!" Snow shouted as he landed on the beast's head, feet first, then pushed off with all his strength, and the centipede's head crashed into the floor.

Though Snow was falling, he wasn't done yet. As he prepared to kick the top of the centipede's head, it moved out of the way and the rest of the body scurried off, leaving Snow's foot to kick at the empty floor.

Snow's attack had damaged the floor, but the centipede had retreated back up the wall.

"Damn it, that might have been our best chance, while it was close to the floor! What are you doing, Gary!" Snow shouted.

"Sorry, I was just checking something." Gary smiled awkwardly, as he stood in the center of the room scratching the back of his head. But now he was sure of his options.

The skill he had selected while half-asleep was perfect to use on an opponent like this; he just needed the right opportunity.

"What are we going to do now?" Snow asked as he approached Gary and Wu, whose back was raw and red.

To be honest, Snow wasn't in great shape either.

"It looks like that thing is just going to stay up there, but if we try to attack it, we know what happened last time," Wu said.

This was the problem: the beast was too far away and all of them were physical fighters. Even Gary didn't know what to do, and with the other two stumped, he had to come up with a solution.

"I will try to get it to come out of the corner. Maybe it will do the same as last time, if it grabs me in its claws again, but it also might go after you two . . . the thing is so fast."

"Don't worry about us," Snow said, interrupting Gary. "We're top students, and we're in this lesson for a reason. If you get that centipede out of the corner, we can handle ourselves."

Heading to the other end of the room, Gary looked up at the centipede in the corner. It wasn't the best situation, and he didn't know if it ever would be, so he would just have to go with the flow.

Using his claws, Gary climbed the wall quickly, digging his nails in. As he got closer, and saw it crawling over its own body, he started to slow down.

I saw what that thing did to Snow . . . do I really have to? Gary thought.

In the end, he had no choice; he climbed right up to the centipede, which was moving and lifting its head, just as before, right before it hit Snow like a whip.

Gary was worried that he might get crushed, so the only thing he could do was match power with power. Placing his legs up against the side of the wall, Gary pushed off as hard as he could with his claws in the air.

Swinging part of its upper body, while its slower body parts remained clinging to the wall, the beast whipped around, hitting Gary just like it hit Snow. There seemed to be no difference, despite Gary using his claws and his power, as he was sent crashing into the wall.

–66 HP
184/250 HP

That's a big hit, a couple more of those and I'll no longer be standing.
Quickly recovering and not allowing himself to slide down the wall, Gary prepared to fight the beast again, but it was no longer in front of him.
Where did it go?
He looked down and saw that it was now on the floor, heading straight for Snow and Wu.
This is what I was afraid would happen! Gary jumped down and ran off after the beast.
At the other end of the room, Snow asked Wu, "Do you have any ideas?"
"I was going to hit it until it stopped moving," Wu replied.
"I thought as much." Snow smiled as he hopped away toward the beast.
When he got close, Snow jumped into the air, and the centipede used its pincers to try to grab him. Once again, Snow kicked the air, doing a double jump to avoid the hit altogether.
With this jump, Snow had leapt over the body and reached the end of the tail with both legs tucked in toward his chest.
At the last second, he pushed off with his legs as hard as he could, hitting the very last segment. The attack broke through the hard shell, revealing bare flesh, and pinned it to the floor, but it didn't stop the beast.
As the centipede used its legs to continue forward, the last segment detached from the body and headed toward Wu.
Once again, Wu was unable to do anything other than use his hands to stop the pincers from closing down on him.
"I need to help Wu somehow," Snow said.
"Leave it to me," Gary replied, catching up to the beast halfway along its long body; Wu had used a lot of energy defending himself, and soon his muscles would give out.

"I have to do something now!" Gary jumped to the side with his claws out, and saw the beast use its sixth sense to twist its body away. "Now!"

Lethal Pounce activated

The second Gary's feet touched the floor, a burst of energy exploded from him, and to the others watching it was like a blur as Gary launched forward and stabbed his claws right into the beast's body.

However, his power was so great that he ripped off a segment of the beast's body, detaching it from the head.

"This isn't enough, I have to finish it!" Gary said, running toward Wu. "Throw its head toward me."

Wu wasn't sure that was a good idea, but the beast did seem slightly weaker. He threw the centipede's head toward Gary, and it opened its pincers again, ready to attack.

They looked like they were about to touch Gary, but before they could:

Lethal Pounce activated

The same rush of energy flooded Gary again, enabling him to jump with enough force and speed, with his claws in front of him, to pierce the beast's head.

The beast had successfully been killed and the special lesson had come to an end.

Skill Lethal Pounce
This skill can only be used within a certain range of the enemy. The skill will light up when it can be used on an enemy. The user pounces on their enemy, giving them a 50 percent speed boost. The skill can be used in succession, and there is no cooldown.
Energy cost: −50

CHAPTER 106

A CRYSTAL

The newly acquired Lethal Pounce was quite strong, for a few reasons. The skill boosted his speed, and it seemed to scale with his actual Dexterity. As long as that stat continued to increase, so would the skill, since it gave him a 50 percent boost.

The only sad part was that the boost was limited to the execution of the skill itself. Nonetheless, it was impressive. A speed increase coupled with strength, resulted in a devastating attack, as the others had just witnessed.

So far, the werewolf had been focusing on his Endurance, Energy, and Health, working to become more and more of an unkillable monster. However, his fight against Jayden had taught him an important lesson: stats alone wouldn't help him against certain kinds of opponents. Skills were needed to make up the difference, and Lethal Pounce was a great start.

One downside to the skill was its relatively large Energy consumption. Gary had thought that his days of worrying about that were over, but using the skill twice had cost him a third of his reserve. Controlled Transformation and the fighting itself also took their toll, leaving the green-haired teenager with slightly less than 100 Energy.

Luckily, he had had only one opponent, but in the future, if he had to fight multiple opponents, or a beast that was even more formidable than this one, he would have to conserve the skill and use it as an ace in the hole.

Just like last time, after the beast was defeated, cleanup crew entered the facility to look after the students and retrieve the crystal. Gary's eyes were fixed on the men as he made mental notes as to where the crystal was pulled from the beast's body. In the future, he hoped to be able to locate it on his own.

I was sure it would be in the head, but when I broke through I couldn't find it . . . maybe next time, Gary thought.

An Advanced tier has been defeated
A first-time bonus for defeating the beast will now be awarded
15,000 Exp received
You are now level 24!
You have gained a stat point

This is it, Gary thought. *I'm only one level away from reaching Level 25. Then something is supposed to happen to my Warrior Class at that stage. Fighting these beasts or high-level Altereds is the only thing that gives me Exp these days. I hope after the next lesson, I reach Level 25, and if not, I still have one more lesson after that.*

Then I'll have used my time at the AFA and in the special lessons to my best advantage.

Gary had been given his reward for completing the task; the body parts of the beast had been placed in a private room. But before he went in this time, Crowley had decided to go in first. Gary wasn't sure what his strange teacher intended to do, but he believed that it was in his best interest. Afterward, Gary looked left and right to see if James would pop out of nowhere; he did not, so Gary went in straightaway, looking at the strange beast parts in front of him.

If my theory is correct, I need to eat this thing as quickly as possible in order to maximize how many stat points I can gain. Without the energy of the crystal, these bodies have expiration dates. With this in mind, Gary did his best to ignore the fact that he was going to eat a giant insect carcass.

As usual, even though the beast parts were several times bigger than his own body, he managed to devour them eventually.

That was when he saw the message appear, and he couldn't be more pleased.

The beast that you have defeated has been consumed
You have received the following stats
+2 Dexterity
Dexterity 28

Hmmm, since the system called it an Advanced tier, I had hoped for more. Still, it's not as much as I get when consuming an Altered. I shouldn't complain too much; after all, this is double what I got from the last one. Most likely because the beast was quite strong, and since this one was fast it also makes sense for me to get something speed-based.

Would it have been more if I had eaten it earlier? Too bad they dry out once the crystal is taken out . . . I wonder what would happen if I were to eat one of those?

Since he gained strength from the beast mainly because of the crystal, it seemed reasonable to assume that eating the crystal directly might provide an ever bigger boost. Part of him had hoped to be able to find it, but he had failed . . . at least this time. If he ever got lucky, he would have to be sneaky about it; NIRV did not care about losing the worthless body, but a crystal . . .

Maybe I can do that on my last test or something; then even if I'm caught and they kick me out, it shouldn't matter, Gary decided.

All he had to do now was wait for the rest of the body to disappear. It was a shame that Gary wouldn't be able to speak to Tom again before he left, but he assumed that they would be able to see each other again some other time.

Like last time, once the lesson was over, their phones and other personal belongings were returned to them, and finally Gary could pull the medallion out of his special place and into his pocket as he changed back into his suit.

While Gary and Numba were walking back to their dormitory and discussing the assessment, Numba's phone started to ring.

"Sorry, Gary, it's my dad. He never calls, so it's probably urgent. I'll be with you in a moment." Numba excused himself as he walked off in the opposite direction.

Gary continued ahead, but as usual his sensitive ears picked up the conversation.

"Son . . . I just wanted to be the one to tell you. Right now . . . right now it might be for the best if you stayed in the academy. However, do be careful there as well, and make sure nothing bad happens to you."

"What do you mean, Dad? This isn't like you. Is everything okay?" Numba said, but that was the end of what Gary was able to hear, because the phone call ended.

CHAPTER 107

A LESSON LEARNED

A few days had passed since Harry Cardenez had visited Notsburg in the hopes of striking a deal. Just like he had said in the meeting, there was more than one Tier 2 city that they could do business with, and so he had spent these last few days in an attempt to set up another meeting. Just as he was sifting through the reports of the Tier 2 gangs in those areas to avoid another such situation, frenetic knocks came from behind his doors.

Bursting into his office was one of Harry's newest assistants, a promising young man whose clothes were drenched. "Sir, we've just been informed that one of our factories is under attack! It looks like it's coming from one of the gangs."

Harry didn't even look up; rather, he huffed out a loud sigh as if this news was bothersome.

"This happens once in a while. The gangs in the city forget who exactly took over this place just because we don't shove our name everywhere. Just notify the Freaks to deal with them, and tell them to leave behind some men to protect it for the next few days."

After giving his order Harry went on with his business, but his assistant still stood there. "Sir . . . are you sure that this will be sufficient? According to the reports, the gang that is currently attacking us isn't one of the local ones. It's too early to say who they are, but they're definitely from an outside city."

This finally got Harry's attention; he placed his pen down and closed his laptop. He'd known that this would happen some day, another city attempting to take over theirs. They were doing well so far, which was one of the reasons he wanted to collaborate with a higher-tier city: to avoid becoming the target of an attack.

"Send out a full force. We need to send out a message so other groups won't do the same thing."

"Yes, sir!" The man bowed down.

The Freaks were sent to the factory location, and with their strength and power it didn't take them long to deal with the outside gang. After some interrogation, they discovered that the attackers came from a nearby Tier 3 town, though this was more of a scouting party.

The Freaks didn't hesitate, deciding that slicing off their heads and sending them back to the town would send a clear message, in case the gang leader would want to come for them as well. Harry wasn't sure that that wouldn't provoke them, but he trusted in the Freaks' judgment.

The next day, the same thing happened again, only this time another factory was targeted. Once more, the Freaks were able to deal with the mess, yet they found out that it wasn't the same gang that had attacked them the day before.

One attack could be called a coincidence, but two in such a short time frame . . .

"Two attacks, one after another and both at the factories. Although they didn't manage to destroy much, this is cause for concern." Harry mumbled to himself. "Fixing the damage will take some time, though fortunately we've been ahead of the schedule so far. Still, if this continues to happen, our workers might start to quit."

The third day, things got even worse; both factories were attacked at the same time by two different groups. The Freaks were strong, but there weren't many of them. In this situation they would have to deal with one attack and then the other.

As they cleared both places, they found that many of the workers were injured, and equipment had been destroyed in the second factory. As Harry had thought, many workers quit because they were too afraid to go back in.

He slammed his fist on the desk.

How do I solve this situation? Two groups have decided to go after us. Both of them are local towns. If I send the Freaks to deal with one of them, then we will be defenseless.

At that moment Harry's phone started ringing with several calls. He answered them, dealing with them one by one. The men stationed outside the room heard him shouting and cursing.

After that, things settled down, but the calls didn't stop. Harry was lost as he put down his phone.

Those clients just canceled their orders all of a sudden. It should be impossible for them to have already heard about the factory attacks . . . or maybe they were targeted as well. As this thought came to Harry's mind, so did the image of a man in a red suit: Slith, the man he had recently met.

Harry's phone rang once more; this time it was an unknown number. Usually he wouldn't pick these up, but this time he answered the call.

"Hello, dear friend." A deep voice entered his ears.

"You're behind everything, aren't you? Is this your way of trying to force my hand?" Harry asked, but all he heard on the other end was the sound of soft chuckles.

"I don't have the slightest idea what you might be talking about; neither I nor anyone in my city has even lifted a finger," Slith replied.

Harry knew that the business he had built up with his own sweat and blood was falling apart. Which was why he decided to swallow his pride to salvage what he could.

"Please stop . . . I will sign the deal with you under your conditions, and we can work together. That's what you want, right?" Harry asked.

Slith laughed again. "Sorry, but I thought I made it clear that that offer was only valid during your stay with us. You were given a chance, and you rejected it. You wanted to sit at the big table, but there's a reason why people like you can't reach it. Now, have fun dealing with the consequences of your own actions, and enjoy watching your whole company burn down."

The phone call ended, and Harry was left staring at the desk in front of him. At this point the only thing he could do was talk to his son.

CHAPTER 108

A LITTLE TASK

The next day had arrived and it was now morning. However, Numba didn't get much sleep; his father sent him multiple messages updating him on the situation, and after that Numba had received one more call in the morning.

For the first time since he had been adopted by the family, he had heard his strong and unmovable father break down and cry over the phone. It broke Numba's heart.

Why hadn't he been born a few years earlier? Maybe then he would be part of the business already, helping them sort out this mess. In fact, Numba even offered to come back. He was a lot stronger than before, and being part of the AFA already meant that he was a lot better than other Altereds out there.

"No!" Harry shouted back. "I . . . haven't given up yet, but you being here will make no difference. In fact, I'm more worried that you might get involved in all of this because I was the one who brought you in. You have always been a great son, and it's only right that you got into the academy for never backing down, going above and beyond to further your powers.

"If anything ever happens to the company or me, then I want you to continue doing well in the AFA, and live a good life."

His father had hung up the phone, and immediately afterward, Numba hit the redial button, attempting to call him.

"We're sorry, the number you are trying to call is currently not—"

"No, please! Please! Why are you doing this?" Numba said, his eyes swollen, too tired to even produce tears, his throat was all swollen up. After trying to call for the third time, Numba threw the phone onto the bed. It bounced and almost hit the ceiling.

"Don't you understand?" Numba moaned. "Everything I was doing in the AFA was as a thanks to you . . . a thanks for getting me out of my shit life!" He continued to sob.

Meanwhile, Gary and the others were waiting in the hall. He, Izzy, Ian, and Numba usually left the dormitory at the same time, so they could all walk to class together. Numba was usually the first one out of his room, but there was no Numba in sight.

The three of them approached his door.

"Maybe we should knock; he might have forgotten to set his alarm," Izzy suggested.

Just as she was about to knock, Gary grabbed her by the wrist, stopping her.

"We should just let him rest and leave him be. I'm sure he'll join us later," Gary said.

They agreed and headed to class. But Gary was a little worried, because he had heard the sound of crying through the door, and it sounded like Numba was in incredible pain.

Back at the Wolf's Pool Club, Kai had also been following the situation quite closely. He had asked Olivia and her gang to gather reports.

"As I expected, they didn't just come to us, but to all of the gangs in the areas surrounding Cardenez Electronics," Kai said aloud and smiled. "From the looks of it, three other gangs in the area had accepted the deal.

"The group protecting the Cardenez company is strong, to deal with attacks from all three sides. If we had accepted as well, they would have been done by now, and to top things off, they would have only had to hire us. Still, it was a good excuse to tell them that Gary was away, because the Scatterbugs seem to be quite the petty gang.

"The only thing I don't understand is why Harry hasn't accepted their offer yet. I was sure if they were pushed to this situation, he would have accepted, unless . . ." Kai had to remind himself what Daimon was like, and how many people like him existed in this world. If that was the case, he knew exactly what had happened between the two.

"Interesting . . . Now how can I take advantage of this situation?"

Back at the academy, Numba had missed the entire first lesson. Because it was the weekend, they only had a half day compared to a full day. The second half allowed them free time, where students were allowed to study, practice, or just rest. Rest was important, but being Altered, the students required less rest than regular people. However, during the second lesson of the day, Numba finally entered the classroom.

They all quickly realized that he wasn't himself, though; he was dragging his feet and avoided eye contact with everyone, but when he reached where the others were sitting he looked up and forced himself to smile.

"Your face, it's so—"

Before Ian could finish his sentence, Izzy gave him a quick jab in the ribs with her elbow.

As Numba sat down, Izzy tried to make the atmosphere as comfortable and normal as possible, but it was quite hard, and the group was unable to talk the same way as before.

I wonder . . . should I ask what's going on? I heard some of the conversation that he had with his father, but if it's personal business, then it might not be my place to get involved, Gary thought.

Regardless, Gary couldn't stay silent; it just wasn't his style. So right as the lesson ended and everyone was leaving, he called out to his friend.

"Numba! Remember that we made that alliance. It goes both ways, right? So whatever you need help with, if there's anything bothering you, you can always talk to and count on us."

Izzy thought this was the right thing to say. It wasn't prying into Numba's life or asking what happened, but just letting him know that they were there for him.

"Thanks, Gary," Numba said. "You are a good friend."

And with that, Numba just walked away, as the rest of the day would be a free period.

Thank you for the offer, Gary, but this matter is practically a gang war, and I doubt even you could do anything to help, he thought as he walked off.

Meanwhile, a loud voice called out, "Gary, there you are!"

Gary turned his head and saw Eddy, the debut teacher, waiting for him by the entrance.

"I checked your schedule and you should be free right now, so come over with me for a second. I think I have a nice surprise that you might like." Eddy smiled.

With nothing else to do, and since he was the only one being invited, Gary waved the others off, while Izzy assured him that she would look after Numba while he was away.

During the free period, some students had decided to return to their rooms rather than train, as Numba had done. He wanted to get his anger out and hit something. One of those people was Sty; he had received a message to call someone as soon as he could.

"Great, you got the message then." A cheery voice answered his call. "I'll get straight to the point. I believe there is a student named Numba Cardenez in your school."

Sty recognized the voice; in the pre-assessments this person had been doing everything he could to make his life hell.

"Yeah, there is," Sty replied.

"Great, well, I have a task for you. It should be relatively easy, but I want you to make his life hell, and make sure you get evidence of it as well. Can you do that?"

Sty's heart started to beat faster, and Gary's gaze entered his mind once again. If he were to touch Numba, then . . . and on top of that, the last time he and Numba fought it had ended in a draw.

"Hey, this is important!" the voice shouted. "A son of mine should easily be able to take out a no-name from a Tier 3 city. Are you really saying the task is too difficult?"

"No!" Sty replied back. "I can take care of it. I definitely can. I won't let you down, Father."

CHAPTER 109

FOR HOURS

Following Eddy, Gary had no clue what this was about, and it didn't look like Eddy was going to explain. He was leading Gary through areas of the academy the teenager had never seen before, while whistling with a giant grin on his face.

Eventually, after they had passed some fields, they headed for a large rectangular building. Once they were inside, Gary started to have an idea of what this place was. There was high-tech training equipment inside, similar to what they used in the academy, but the latest models.

In addition to this, the person who was in the room pretty much gave it away.

"Shingi, how many times have we been over this?" Eddy asked in an annoyed tone. "Resting is an equally important part of your training period!"

The teacher could only let out a frustrated sigh, because Shingi had been like this even before he had come to the real academy. He was the type of student who would train at the slightest opportunity, no matter where he was or what state he was in, even ignoring the advice of his trainers.

Right now, Shingi was training with the automatic punching bag. The person would hit it as fast as they could, and then the bag would come back on a pulley system for them to hit it again. It was one of Shingi's favorite pieces of training equipment because he could easily tell when he was doing better.

For one, he could measure whether his punches were stronger than before by how far the bag went. After that, he could see how long he could keep the punches strong before he hit the bag less than his original punch.

"Shingi, stop that now!" Eddy shouted to get his student's attention. "Somewhere in that thick head of yours, you should know that this training is pointless with how tired you were after the earlier training session!"

But it did look like Shinji was able to hit the bag just as hard as before. It made the teacher wonder what had lit a fire in his belly, even more so than usual.

"Ahem!" Gary cleared his throat, unwilling to just stand there. "Could you please tell me what we're doing here? I already told you that I didn't want to become a debut student until I took the assessment."

"Don't worry, I haven't forgotten, and that's not why we're here. We're a bit early, but you will see in a moment," Eddy replied without looking away from Shinji, who continued hitting the bag. Only this time, he noticed that it fell a bit short compared to his last hit, making him stop.

Shingi had managed to last about sixteen minutes, throwing punches with equal power. As he wiped the sweat away, he turned around only to notice that Gary was here as well. He was so focused that he had barely registered Eddy's voice, much less that of someone he hadn't recognized immediately.

"Oh, this is great." Shingi smiled. "Gary, did you see what I was doing with the bag training? This is something we debut students do quite a lot."

Shingi went on to explain the rules, stating that you weren't allowed to transform and what all the equipment meant.

"So what do you think, do you want to give it a try? It's quite fun," Shingi suggested.

Ever since doing this type of training, Shingi had wanted to witness Gary on the machine, because he wanted to get an idea of how far along he was compared to the others.

Gary looked at the bag for a few seconds as he wondered whether he should take Shingi up on it. After his lunch meal, his energy was full at 300.

"I mean, this doesn't really help too much. Because my energy goes down when I transform, or when I get hurt, to heal my body, as well as using my skills . . . but I do want to try it."

Soon Gary was set up and so was the punching bag.

"We're short on time, so just hit the bag a few times to get a feel for what it will be like. If you like it, we can talk about you coming here later," Eddy advised.

As the bag came toward Gary, he readied his right hand and threw an overhead right straight. It was the same punch he had seen Shingi throw, so he thought he should do the same. The impact was strong and his speed was fast, and he propelled the bag 85 percent along the length of the room.

That's a good hit, especially for someone who's doing this for the first time. Usually it takes a few hits to familiarize yourself with it, but Gary beat my score and his strength is higher than Xin's, though not as high as Ryan's, Shingi thought.

Although Gary was strong, he wasn't at his peak strength, which he would only reach in his transformed state. However, since this was just a type of training, he saw no need to use Controlled Transformation, especially since Shinji hadn't transformed either.

As the bag came back, Gary was ready to hit it again. It took thirty seconds for the bag to be hit, stop, and come back before one could hit it again. This was regardless of how far one hit it, so they could measure their time more easily.

Gary punched once again, making great contact with the bag. It was satisfying to say the least, and the werewolf could picture himself coming here on bad days to get his Energy out.

The bag went back as much as it had on the first hit, showing that Gary knew how to control himself well. After that Gary hit the bag three more times before finally stopping. He didn't seem out of breath or tired at all.

Most people would be exhausted just doing five punches at full strength, but Gary hit it to the same distance every time, Eddy thought.

"So . . . what do you think, how long do you think you could last on the machine?" Shingi asked in excitement.

There was a reason why Gary had stopped after five hits, though it had nothing to do with him being exhausted. No, he had stopped because a sudden revelation had shocked him: after the last punch his Energy had dropped to 299. So far, as long as he didn't transform and fought in his normal state, without using any skills, he could literally go for hours.

"I'm sorry, give me a second, I need to do some quick math," Gary replied.

Shingi and Eddy looked at each other in confusion. Why would Gary have to do math? He should know his own body well enough to just give a general answer.

"I'm not sure but if it's just doing this, then it should be . . . around ten hours, give or take? Although I would probably get tired just standing around during the day and would need to eat something if I did that," Gary replied after crunching the numbers in his head.

"*Ten hours?*" Eddy couldn't help but repeat this and laugh. "Gary, I know you feel fine now, but trust me, the strain and tiredness builds up after a while. You would be lucky to even last one hour."

Hearing the adult's opinion made Gary feel embarrassed. After all, maybe his math was wrong. Ten hours sounded ridiculously long to him as well. However, Shingi didn't feel quite the same way. He felt like Gary hadn't said it to be funny.

Just then they heard the doors opening, and all of them turned to look.

"All right, Eddy, why did you call me this time? It's our rest period and you're the one who keeps repeating how important it is for us to not skip out on that." The female voice slowly drifted off as the person's eyes fell on Gary.

Xin! Gary screamed in his head, and his heart started to thump louder. Then the thought of what had occurred the last time echoed in both of their heads. She had attacked Gary because it had been the only thing she could do to calm him down, while he felt extremely embarrassed as he remembered how he must have acted like a crazy person in front of her.

"Well, look at you two, all shy like that." Eddy smiled. "Anyway, you should have dressed up rather than coming in your academy uniform, but this will have to do. I'm sorry, Xin, but I promised our green-haired friend here that as long as he agreed to a request of mine, I would give him a date with our local star."

"A date?" Xin shouted back. "How could you do that without even asking me?"

"Calm down, call it whatever you will, it's just spending time together, and you two obviously have some shared history. It's not like you can go off academy grounds anyway. So it will just be like spending time with another student; whether it will be a traditional date or not, I'll leave that up to you."

Xin looked at Gary, then shook her head. "No . . . it's fine. I'll go on this date. I want to go on this date," Xin answered. "But, Eddy, you owe me for not asking or warning me beforehand!"

Gary's heart felt like it was going to come out of his chest, but Xin had always been this type of person: straightforward and honest with her feelings.

"I-I do as well," Gary stammered.

CHAPTER 110

THE DATE (PART 1)

Shingi and Eddy waved Xin and Gary off, giving the two "lovebirds" the rest of the afternoon to do whatever they wanted. The only problem was that neither one of them really knew what they were supposed to do, because of the lack of their dating experience and neither one having been told about this date beforehand. It didn't help that the AFA students had to apply for leave in advance, so they were unable to do anything exciting outside the academy.

As they thought about what they should do together, they walked in silence toward the large field. It was more or less a track field that had multiple pieces of equipment for the debut students to train outside. It wasn't used a lot because most of the students in the AFA were aiming for the AFC, making them prefer practicing indoors, specifically in the cages where real fights would occur.

"I'm sorry." Xin eventually broke the silence, which was starting to get awkward. "About zapping you before, I mean. However, in my defense, you did seem like you were out of it."

Gary tried to laugh it off, trying to come up with a good excuse, but he couldn't think of any. "No, no, you were totally right to do that. I just got a bit too hungry that day, I guess."

"That was all from you being hungry?" Xin asked with a raised eyebrow. "In that case, I should probably be happy that you must have eaten before you came over to meet my parents."

Hearing Xin tease him like this, Gary felt that the awkwardness of the whole situation had lessened. His crush always seemed up for anything and was quite forward, and not hard to read either, making her all the more charming in his eyes.

"Yeah, we should avoid dates at restaurants in the future . . . assuming you want to have another one, of course . . . oh God, I'm messing up already, aren't I?" Gary cursed his own tongue for being faster than his brain. However, to his surprise, Xin just chuckled at his antics. "Relax, let's just enjoy the time together and play it by ear."

Eventually, they approached what looked like an archery field with a large round board at the back. Strangely, there were no bows or arrows in the vicinity, but a row of heavy metallic-looking balls to one side. They were dense weights, and picking one up, they figured out that one was meant to throw them at the target from around fifty yards away.

"How about we start our date with this?" Xin suggested. "It's easy, each of us gets five balls, and the one to score the most points wins. Hmmm, let's make it a bit more fun. Usually we play this with some ante, so why don't we do the same? Is there anything that you want if you win?"

Looking at her from head to toe, the teenage boy blurted out the first thing that came to mind. "A kid!"

Xin dropped the heavy ball to the ground. "Don't you think you're moving a little too fast, Casanova?"

Gary's face turned bright red. "*Kiss!* I meant to say *kiss*, I swear!"

"Oh, yeah, that seems reasonable. All right, but if I win, I'm gonna ask something from you, but I have to warn you, I'm pretty good at this," Xin replied as she threw the ball. It went flying through the air and hit the target right in the center, scoring her the maximum amount of 100 points.

I guess since this is next to the other training place, she has done this a few times, but it doesn't look too hard, Gary thought as he picked up the weight. It was heavier than he had expected, and he imagined that a few people would be unable to throw the ball without transforming, but since Xin didn't transform, he wasn't going to either.

Gary hurled the ball as hard and as fast as he could. It went through the air faster than Xin's had, hitting the inner middle ring and scoring him 75 points.

That's pretty good for his first try . . . it's hard to imagine Gary is really the same person as that lunatic I had to knock out, Xin thought.

"I guess we didn't really get to talk since then, huh?" Xin suddenly realized. "I'm sorry I didn't even look for you. Say, when did you even become an Altered? It had to be after I left, right? What made you join the AFA?"

While she asked her questions, the teenage girl was still concentrating on their game, focusing her aim. Gary watched everything she did so he could imitate her form.

"It was pretty much after you left. A company called the Howlers decided to invest a lot of money into Slough and they had a trial run, looking for candidates to join them, going around schools and scouting. In the end, I was lucky enough to get selected, so I'm now a representative of their company. Since I was very compatible with my Altered, they let me try out with the AFA, and here I am," Gary answered confidently.

It was a lie that Kai had prepared for him in case anyone ever asked. Xin believed it since she had seen how talented he had been, though she was mistaken in that she had seen him before his turning. The only hard part to believe was the story about a new corporation investing in Slough of all places, especially seemingly out of nowhere. Then again, Slough was neither the first nor the last town that a company might choose to invest in, in case they saw some potential.

Honestly, Gary was quite nervous; after all, Xin's father, the mayor, might have told her about the Howlers, although it might just have been a comment in passing.

"Although, if I'm honest, I also asked for a chance to come here . . . Jayden was the one who recommended that I do so."

Xin was just about to throw the ball, but this sudden piece of news made her flinch, resulting in her throw being off by a bit. Nevertheless, her second throw ended up giving her 75 points.

"Jayden? As in my brother? He told you to come here?"

CHAPTER 111

THE DATE (PART 2)

Turning away, Gary answered, a bit embarrassed. "He told me that if I wanted to be with you, I should come here."

Not many things startled Xin, but this was certainly one of them. If she was hearing Gary right, he had come here because of her. Although that was sweet to hear . . . it saddened Xin.

It must be nice for someone to be so free that they can join the AFA just for a reason like that, while here I am trying to gain my freedom, Xin thought, her mood souring a bit.

Gary threw the ball again, and although he believed he had copied Xin down to the last part before her flinching, his ball hit the 75-point mark again.

"Have you visited Slough lately, or talked to your father about anything?" Gary peeked from the corner of his eye when he asked this question.

Xin then threw the ball perfectly, hitting the same spot dead in the center, scoring 100 points.

"No, I've put all my attention into the AFA. For now, that's all I want to think about until I've achieved my goal of reaching the top fifty in the AFC."

It was the first time Gary had heard Xin's goal so clearly. Top fifty was a tall task; it meant she needed to at least get as strong as her brother, which coincidentally was a goal that Gary had set for himself as well.

When Gary threw the ball a third time, his aim was even more off than before, though it was enough to score him 50 points.

"Stop trying to throw it as fast and hard as you can," Xin advised. "This isn't a contest of strength. Not everything is about how strong or fast you are. Treat this like a fight; you aren't just running to your opponent to clobber them. You need to have the right technique; use your head and some self-control."

Gary nearly jested that as a werewolf, self-control was the last thing he had, but he quickly swallowed it down. Besides, this was something that he needed to learn. Xin's fourth ball hit the center again, scoring her another 100 points. Gary could foresee that there was no realistic way for him to beat Xin at this game, but he wanted to hit the center at least once, and he had two more throws to do it.

Control myself, and aim for the center, Gary thought as he breathed in and out slowly. His heart rate started to slow down. He threw the ball, and it went straight . . . falling to the ground midway, not even reaching the target.

"Hahaha!" Xin burst out in laughter, making the green-haired teenager turn red again. His crush tried but couldn't stop laughing as tears came out of her eyes. "Gary, you can't just completely focus on one thing, but that was good. It shows that you are willing to listen. You're a bit like a sponge, soaking up the knowledge that everyone tells you. It's a good trait as long as you can tell the bad advice from the good."

The game continued and in the end, Gary managed to hit 75 again. He had come close to the center but never hit it, while Xin had ended with a score of 475. With that, he had lost their little bet.

"Xin, with you being so busy, do you think the two of us will ever have a proper date? Just live our own lives?" Gary asked, thinking about his own circumstances with the gang. Xin turned to Gary and smiled.

"Of course," she replied with confidence. "That's why I'm fighting so hard. Anyway, it looks like someone lost the bet, so now you need to do something for me."

Sulking about missing his chance to earn the kiss he wanted, he was now a bit worried what she might ask of him. To never bother her again, perhaps? To wash all her clothes and be her servant for a while? Frankly, Gary wouldn't mind the latter too much; after all, it meant he would be able to see her more.

"Close your eyes," Xin said after some slight deliberation.

Gary did so, wondering what would happen, when he suddenly felt something soft on his lips, and a small pressure soon after. Opening his eyes, Gary saw Xin with her eyes closed and her lips pressed against his.

Your heart rate is rising at an incredibly fast rate
Suggestion: see a doctor or a vet!

Fuck off, you stupid system, let me just enjoy this, Gary thought, closing his eyes again. For a short, sweet moment, all his worries were forgotten, but the next he focused on slowing down his heart to avoid transforming. Eventually, the moment that he dreaded the most came, when Xin ended the kiss and took a step back.

"I never got to tell you what my reward was for winning . . . but it's because we both wanted the same thing." Xin smiled cheekily. "Keep chasing after me, Gary. One day, we should be able to go on a proper date without having to worry about stuff. Until then, although I know it makes me selfish, I like that I have one person who cares about me in their own way. It makes me feel not alone."

At that moment, Gary felt like he would follow her anywhere she went. It was impossible for him to put it into words, so he just stood there and nodded.

"Come on, we still have a few hours together," Xin said as she grabbed Gary's hand, and they continued to walk. The werewolf's brain had seemingly short-circuited, still trying to process his second kiss with her. It was undoubtedly better than the first one, and longer. For the moment he was more than content to walk with Xin holding hands.

The trees, the sky, even the garbage bins stationed around the school seemed prettier in his eyes now.

Is this what they call love? How does everything look so nice to me now? Gary wondered.

They continued to walk around the academy and eventually arrived behind one of the buildings, and Gary picked up the sound of someone arguing.

"Did you really think you could take on ten of us? You really are an arrogant piece of shit!" one of the voices screamed.

"Come on, why don't we head in another direction?" Gary suggested to avoid getting involved.

"Why . . ." He heard another voice. "Why are you doing this to me? Why are you doing this to my family?"

Gary stopped in his tracks there and then, and Xin felt him gripping her hand. She looked over and saw that his eyes were glowing slightly red.

"Why can't they just leave him alone? And why did they have to do this today, of all days?"

CHAPTER 112

WHY ME?

During their free period in the afternoon, Numba decided to go off on his own toward the dormitory. Having found out what his father was going through, he couldn't get it off his mind. A part of him was afraid that if he stayed around his friends, there was a good chance that he would just blurt something out by accident.

Before Numba had met the others, he hadn't really been one to filter his speech, a trait that hadn't exactly gotten him a lot of friends in his life. For that reason, the last thing he wanted to do was get his new friends involved in his family's mess. When he got to his room, a student wearing a beanie stood in the hallway, leaning up against his door.

"Hey, you're Numba, right?" the student asked while chewing a piece of gum. "My name's Mike. Miss Patel sent me to fetch you."

The Goat Altered didn't recognize this student immediately. There were only so many students in a class, yet there were multiple classes because the number of students fluctuated depending on how fast someone was able to graduate. Numba had only focused on the students who had come in just before their batch. That way he could compare his progression to theirs.

"What does she need me for?" Numba replied.

Mike shrugged. "Beats me, I'm just the messenger boy. My guess is that it might have something to do with your absence this morning. If you wanna know, just ask her." With that, he walked away.

Numba didn't think much of it, because that theory was quite sound. After all, he hadn't informed Miss Patel about his absence, nor had he requested time off. He followed behind Mike, who seemed to be showing him the way. However, when they ended up in an outside area, only then did Numba start to suspect that something else was going on.

Wait a second, I'm pretty sure the teacher's office should be in the same building, so where is he taking me? Numba wondered. Of course, there was the chance that Miss Patel might be somewhere else, but in that case, what would be important enough that it couldn't wait for when she was back at her office? Besides, was there really a need for a student sent to pass on the message to guide him, rather than just tell him where to go?

"Hey, I don't want you wasting this free period. How about you just tell me where she is. I can head there on my own," Numba suggested carefully.

Mike stopped dead in his tracks; they were about ten yards away from the main academy building.

"I thought that this would be a simple, easy job." Mike turned around, still chewing his gum. "Look, all you need to do is follow me, okay? And before you think of running away, let me tell you that there is a particular girl with curly hair who is waiting with my friends for you to show up. Surely you don't want her to get hurt just because you didn't show up, right?"

Numba's heart thumped louder for a second. Whoever this person was, or this group, they had to know a bit about him, because they knew that Numba and Izzy were friends.

How . . . did this happen? Izzy and Ian are nearly always together. How did they manage to split them apart? Numba wondered as he proceeded to follow Mike.

Sure, there were plenty of strong students in the academy, but in a lot of cases, Numba would classify Ian as a better fighter than he was. The two of them would also have been in school, so Ian would have been able to do something for them to get away.

"Ah!" Ian let out a sigh as he pushed the bathroom door open. "I really needed that, I don't know what it was that I ate yesterday . . . Izzy?" Ian turned his head left and right. *I swear she said she would wait for me. Maybe yesterday's food didn't agree with her either. Anyway, they say it's best to stay put when separated, so I guess I'll just stay here for now.*

Eventually Numba was led to a deserted part of the school. It was between the main academy and where the debut students gathered.

When they turned the corner, Numba saw ten students waiting, a mix of some he had seen and others he might have only noticed in passing. The group was all male; the only odd one out was Izzy, who was up against the wall. There was a bloodstain on the wall, and her face was beaten and bruised, with dried blood around her nose. Her eyelids were swollen and it looked like she had passed out.

"You bastards!" Numba screamed. "You wanted me, right? Why would you hurt her?"

The rage was too much, and Numba had already started to transform. Long white fur was growing on his arms, and horns appeared on his head.

In an explosive takeoff, Numba blasted his way to Mike, throwing a fist that hit him square in the face, sending him flying through the air and onto the ground. Blood dripped out of his mouth, and he did not get back up.

"Hahaha!" One of the other students laughed. It was the one who was closest to Izzy. He was tall and skinny, with bags under his eyes. He also had bruised knuckles.

He must be the one that hurt Izzy! Numba thought.

The Goat Altered ran toward her, but his explosive power only took him so far. It was more like an explosive kick from the ground, and then he would need to kick off again.

As Numba slowed down, all the others had transformed. This wasn't just a gang of ten ordinary teenagers, or a group of thugs loitering around the school. This was the AFA, an Academy for Altered where the best came to train, and that was when Numba realized the situation he was in. A strange, long, wet-looking limb whacked him right in the stomach.

At the same time, something he couldn't even see had hit him in the top of the head. Before he could recover, he was been lifted by another pair of arms and slammed into the concrete, and then he was getting hit and kicked from multiple sides.

Why is this happening? Why are these people attacking me? Numba remembered the words of his father, that he had to be careful in the academy. It was too much of a coincidence to just ignore. He had been going through his academy days fine until this point.

That man, the one I saw at Notsburg! His eyes, I knew they weren't normal. This gang must be related to Sty . . . is he behind this? Even if he isn't, he will surely know something about it, but first I need to survive!

The group of nine didn't stop, and Numba's vision was getting hazy from blood loss. *Because of me . . . they hurt Izzy . . . I'm the worst type of friend.*

"Stop!" a man shouted from next to Izzy, and the attack stopped. Numba was in no condition to fight or get up. It was unclear just how many bones they had broken, but it was obvious he would need weeks to heal.

"It was a great idea to bring her here, don't you think? Seeing your girlfriend like this was a sure-fire way to get you to attack us first," the man said, gloating. "One of the first things you learn about this part of the academy is that no fighting between students is allowed without a teacher's permission.

"However, there is one addendum to that rule. Students are allowed to act in self-defense. You were the first to strike, so you have nobody to blame but yourself."

Numba, unable to move, could only move his mouth slightly. "Why are you doing this to me? Why are you doing this to my family?"

"Oh, so it looks like you figured out why this is happening to you." The man laughed again. "Either way, it looks like you might no longer be in the AFA after this."

The group started to laugh again, until they heard a grunting voice. "What are you guys doing?"

They turned to see a green-haired teenager standing next to a gray-haired girl.

"Oh, are you a friend of his? Well, too bad you can't get revenge, otherwise you'll get kicked out of the academy as well." The man laughed.

Gary's eyes were beaming red as he shouted at them, his body starting to transform.

"You think I give a fuck about following the academy's rules when scum like you attack my friends? I'll kill you all!"

CHAPTER 113

A SPARK OF POWER

Numba had been so badly hurt that he was fading in and out of consciousness, but a deep rumbling voice that shook even his core caused him to look through his blurry eyes.

That can't be . . . is that Gary? . . . How is he here? Why is he here? Numba's brain was too muddled to make sense out of the situation. He hadn't had a chance to tell anyone where he was going, and they weren't in an area that a student would just stumble across.

"Please . . . don't get kicked out of the academy for my sake," Numba quietly muttered with his limited strength.

Under normal circumstances, Gary might have listened to him, but the werewolf was only seeing red. The scent of blood from both Izzy and Numba had wafted into his nose, so his instincts told him to punish those responsible for hurting his friends.

"Look at this guy!" A student in the back ridiculed Gary's tough-guy approach. "Something is seriously wrong with your whole batch. Your friend down there also thought himself a hero, and look what it did for him. Take a look around. Do you seriously think you're capable of taking *all* of us on?"

Although the student next to Izzy seemed confident enough to taunt the green-haired teenager, the rest of his friends had yet to act. If they could, they would have attempted to attack Gary, but those closer to the werewolf could feel some invisible pressure radiating from him. Their brains told them that it should be impossible for one student to fight off nearly a dozen, but with how crazy he looked, nobody wanted to sacrifice themselves for the others.

As Gary approached the first student, he clenched his fist tightly. When he got within attacking range, the student reacted instinctively. Mid swing, his arm turned into a limb that resembled a tentacle, indicating that his Altered was based on a creature from the sea.

As the tentacle came toward Gary, he dodged under it and kicked off the ground, aiming for the Altered's face. His fist was inches away, yet before he could connect, his opponent suddenly fell to the side, making his attack hit nothing but air.

For some reason, he remained on the ground, though his body randomly shook as if someone were electrocuting him. It reminded Gary of when he had been in a similar situation. Turning his head in the other direction, he saw Xin preparing to attack.

"You're too angry. You may seriously end up hurting someone and regretting it for the rest of your life, so let me deal with it!" Xin shouted as she ran toward the next student who was close to her.

She jumped into the air, spinning her body and landing a kick to the head. When her foot made contact, sparks appeared. Even though the kick wasn't very hard, he ended up zapped and suddenly sent flying away.

"What are you doing? Don't attack her just one at a time! Get her all at once!" the student from the back shouted.

The rest of the students headed toward Xin as they all began to transform; Gary was ready to rush in and help, but lifted her foot above her head; yellow sparks started to surround her leg and she slammed it into the ground.

The sparks went in every direction, striking the other students and sending a current of electricity up their bodies. It wasn't painful like some of them imagined, they soon found out that it was a lot worse.

They all fell down, completely creeped out, feeling like someone else was in control of their bodies. But Xin's attack had simply messed up the signals from their brains.

Before they could recover, Xin punched one in the stomach, lifting him into the air, and moved right to the next one, kicking him into a third. Each one was dealt with in a single hit, and there was no need for her to do more.

What is this? Nobody told us that someone like her would interfere! The older student next to Izzy thought. Not many students could take on ten Altereds at a time. When she was finally done and was walking toward him, he saw her face clearly, and everything started to make sense.

"You . . . you're Xin! Why is a debut student like you getting involved? You should know the rules! Do you even know this person?"

It was clear he was startled, and he had good reason to be. Never in his wildest dreams did he think he could take on the best student in the whole academy, and as a way to get out of it, he reached toward Izzy.

"You idiot!" Xin shouted as she threw her fist; there was still about five yards between them, but a single electric current came out of her fist like a lightning strike, throwing the student against the wall and causing him to pass out immediately.

Gary was mesmerized. Xin didn't even have to transform to fight against the others, yet she was able to use a strange power. A skill or, more accurately, an attribute just like her brother Jayden.

She's so powerful without even transforming. Just what type of Altered is she? I have no clue, but it has to be really powerful given her current status and the electric powers it lets her use. Damn, how is it fair that others get all the cool powers?

For a second Gary was actually feeling jealous, wondering if he hadn't been turned into a werewolf, what type of Altered he could have been. However, when he thought about it some more, he realized that while his Werewolf System might not have granted any flashy of skills, something like Last Stand was too good to give up.

Getting a one-minute extension of life was an extremely extraordinary skill.

Snapping out of it, Gary quickly went to Numba's side, checking the true extent of the damage. It was clear that his friend had more than a couple of broken bones. He gently lifted the Goat Altered's head, as he could see that Numba was still alive and conscious.

"Gary . . . I'm sorry! I'm sorry for getting you involved and you having to help me again," Numba blurted out.

"I think you might have hit your head a bit too hard," Gary replied. "For one, I'm not the one you should be thanking. I didn't even get to do anything. Second, how is it your fault that those scumbags attacked you? You don't have to explain yourself; let's just get you to the medical office as soon as possible."

Gary lifted Numba by his shoulder alone, so he could put as little pressure on his one working foot as possible. Xin came over and picked Izzy up off the ground, helping to place her on Gary's other shoulder.

"Look after them, Gary. I'm sorry that our date had to be cut short by this, but I will stay here and handle the aftermath. Don't worry, as the top-ranking debut student, they won't kick me out, and I'm also close with the teachers. I'll do my best so that something like this won't happen to any of your friends in the future."

Gary nodded, appreciating how reliable Xin was. Although a tiny part of him wanted to suggest continuing their date after dropping off his friends, he understood that he needed to be there for them now. Using Controlled Transformation, he lightened his load and left to get to the nurse's office as quickly and gently as possible.

Once the three were out of sight, Xin knelt down to the man she had shocked earlier. Grabbing his head, she let out another few sparks, forcing him awake. The older student groaned in pain as he opened his eyes, directly staring into Xin's.

"Me and you are going to have a talk, and you're going to tell me everything about this little stunt of yours."

The nurse's office looked more like a hospital, and there were many trained staff going from room to room. It only took a few minutes for someone to come over and bring the two injured students into rooms of their own. Because they were Altered, Gary was certain that they would heal in due time, but the pain they had gone through was still the same as anyone else would have suffered.

Half an hour later, Gary was allowed to visit Numba, as he had woken up. From what the receptionist had told him, Izzy was still asleep. Gary entered the room and went to his friend's side; for a second Numba looked away, gripping the bedsheet tightly.

"Izzy . . . she was hurt because of me," Numba admitted as tears fell down the sheets one by one.

"True, but were you the one who hit her? Or were you the guy who bravely tried to attack those who did that to her?" Gary asked. Numba cried even more.

"No, but . . . Gary, I don't know what to do . . . I don't know what to do." His friend sobbed, wiping his tears away. "Please . . . help me. Help . . . my family."

CHAPTER 114

A CRY FOR HELP (PART 1)

Kai sat in his office at the Wolf's Pool Club, twiddling his fingers on his desk, but once again, he wasn't on his own. He was with Olivia, and both of them had their masks next to them.

"What a very interesting development," Olivia couldn't help but note with a devious smile. "Tell me, did you know this was going to happen?"

Shaking his head, Kai smiled back. "Do you really think I somehow have the ability to see into the future? The only thing I can say is, people are more predictable than you think. There are only so many scenarios that I can account for; I just do what I can to prepare for all of them equally. Even now, I'm unsure what will happen."

Looking toward the staircase, Olivia folded her arms. "Sometimes I forget that you're just a seventeen-year-old brat. If only you were a few years older."

"Sorry, but even though you look this young, I'm not really the type to date someone who is—"

Before Kai could finish his sentence, Olivia had pulled out her whip, her eyes shining blue as she dared him to finish the sentence. The teenager knew better than to piss her off.

For the day, the Wolf's Pool Club had been closed, and upstairs the rest of the core members were present. Innu, Marie, Austin, and the others . . . Unlike those below, they were already wearing their masks. They stood in place waiting for the double doors to open.

Eventually, they heard the sound of cars from outside. Two black cars with tinted windows had arrived, and coming out of one of them was none other than Harry Cardenez, followed by his close aide, Will. The young man was his newest personal assistant and had a tendency to be on point, having a tablet in his hand, glasses with thick black frames, and a perfectly tidy suit.

"I can't believe it," Will grumbled, shaking his head. "They have asked you to meet in a place like this, in this area? This is nothing like the last time! Was that all for show?"

Harry had called up Kai asking for another meeting after their last, and to be honest Harry himself was surprised about the location change. He had never seen a gang operate from such a small place.

"Will, remember why we are here!" Harry lectured the young man as he continued to walk forward.

As before, several members of the Freaks accompanied them, one from the car they were riding in and two from the other. Most had to be left back in the city, in case of more attacks.

Walking side by side, Harry and Will pushed the doors open, and as soon as they saw the others standing there with the masks on their faces, they knew they were in the right place.

"The person you are waiting for is ready to meet you downstairs," Marie said. As a girl with a small frame, she seemed like the perfect choice to guide their guests without putting them on alert. What didn't go unnoticed were the Anti-Altered weapons that Marie had strapped to her body, a spear and a crossbow.

"Sir, I don't like the feeling of this place; this could very well be a trap," Will whispered while covering his mouth.

"We have no other option," Harry replied as he walked forward, following the masked girl.

She went down the stairs first while the others remained upstairs in case anything strange happened. When they finally reached the bottom, they saw Kai sitting at his desk and Olivia standing by the side, both with their masks on.

Harry started to look around the room, to see if there was anyone else.

"If you are looking for our leader, he isn't here. He is a busy person, you see, and since we don't know the outcome of this meeting, I hadn't asked him to come along," Kai explained.

Will was burning up inside. Even for a gang, the whole thing was disrespectful. Kai hadn't come to greet the owner, and now the leader of the gang wasn't even here. Still, unlike last time, Harry seemed to ignore all of that as he waved a hand to tell the others to stay where they were while he stepped in front of Kai's desk.

"I have one question first before I tell you my request," Harry said, while Kai remained silent. "Did the Scatterbugs ask you to attack Notsburg?"

Bringing both of his hands up toward his mouth, Kai hid his smile from the others; only Olivia could see it.

"Yes," Kai answered after a heavy pause. "They even offered up a very nice incentive."

Harry's response shocked everyone in the room. He fell to his knees and placed his hands and head on the floor.

"Our two groups were once close to reaching a deal, but in the end I decided to look for other opportunities, which is why right now the only thing I can do is plead, no, beg for your help.

"I don't know why you didn't agree to help the Scatterbug group, but I'm sure you are aware of the situation. We, the Cardenez group, are asking for your help! If it is within your power, I want you to save our company, and in return we will become a part of the Howlers."

"Sir, how could you?" Will shouted. "You put your blood, sweat, and tears into building this company from the ground up. How could you give that to a gang, a Tier 3 gang that we don't even know if they can help or not?!"

"*Silence!*" Harry shouted at the young man by his side. "What's the use of all my former achievements in our current situation? If we do nothing now, then there will be no company left!"

It was more than that; Harry knew that the Howlers were unlikely to accept such a proposal, because getting involved could mean the end of them as well. It was a crazy idea for two Tier 3 groups to team up to take on the other Tier 3 gangs as well as the Scatterbugs, but this was his last hope.

Before Kai could give him an answer, his phone rang.

"I'm sorry, but this is a very important call."

Once again, this angered Will, but he bit his tongue; since Harry was down on his knees, it was the least he could do.

"How are you doing, Green Fang?" Kai asked.

CHAPTER 115

A CRY FOR HELP (PART 2)

Inside the medical bay in the academy, Gary had stayed by Numba's side; his friend hadn't said much after asking for help. Eventually one of the nurses informed them that Izzy was back to her normal self. Not long afterward, she entered the room, with Ian at her side.

Numba would still take some time to heal. While Gary stayed by Numba's side, Ian had done the same for Izzy. Immediately after finding out what had happened, Ian burst into the room asking who they were and wanting to take them all down.

But as they left, multiple students were being brought in: the ones who had done this to Izzy. It looked like someone had already gotten to them, before Ian could.

They both decided to go visit Numba, and since he wasn't allowed to leave, they were worried that he was much worse. Thankfully Numba was okay, and now Gary, Ian, and Izzy all sat around their friend as he lay in his hospital bed.

"So . . . are you going to tell us? Why did they attack you?" Ian asked. "Izzy said they captured her to get to you, but she knew something was up, and then this happened."

Izzy once again kicked Ian's shin. She knew that it would hurt Numba to think it was his fault, but Ian seemed unaware of this.

"Can you stop kicking me? That shit hurts! I know it might be hard for him, but we need to either teach those guys a lesson so they don't do it again or find out why they did it," Ian explained with a tear in his eye.

"I agree with Ian," Gary added. "Numba, you asked for my help, but since then you haven't said a word. Just tell us what's going on, so we can find a way to help you."

Numba took a deep breath as he prepared to answer. He was well aware that without an explanation, they would constantly nag him either way. The Goat Altered repeated what his father had told him and his own findings.

Every day he had been checking the news from his city, and it was getting worse. The constant attacks, people closing businesses, withdrawing from deals, and how his father had warned him to be careful.

"That's why I didn't want to tell you guys. There is nothing that we can really do." Numba clenched his fists. "This is business between cities . . . I heard that all the other towns in the area close by have started sending gangs as well . . . and I . . . I . . ." Numba started to break down in tears again. "Can't do anything about it."

It hurt the others to see Numba like this, but Izzy and Ian didn't know what to do. They were heirs to restaurants and other businesses. They could ask their families to send financial support to the Cardenez group; however, they knew that their families would most likely decline, based on what was happening. If anyone got involved, they ran the risk of being targeted as well.

"Numba . . . I don't like seeing you like this. Earlier you asked me for help. I saw the desperate situation you were in, and it's worse than I thought. For them to use students to attack you as well . . . for them to get you involved in all of this. I can't forgive them. So I'm going to help you." Gary stood up and walked toward the door.

"Gary, what do you mean?" Numba shouted. "You can't be thinking of fighting them yourself. Don't do anything crazy. This is a Tier 2 gang we are talking about. I could never ask you to get your whole gang involved in this."

Turning around, Gary asked, "Do you not remember what I said to all of you? We are an alliance now, and one of our members needs help. It's only right that I act, and don't you remember? I owe you one from that assessment. With this we can call it even."

"What are you thinking?" Ian said. "Are you really going to try to fight the gang . . . I mean, even you aren't *that* crazy, right? Are you going to ask your gang to help?"

This was what Numba was worried about: more people getting involved because of him.

"Numba, I wouldn't worry too much. If anything happens to you and your family, we will look after you. As for Gary, I know you're worried about him, but I'll be honest, it's unlikely his gang will get involved.

"Gary is just someone the gang sponsored. Sure, he might have some say, but to use a whole group to go up against a Tier 2 gang won't be possible. No gang would start a gang war just because of the request of a member."

The second Gary left the room, the smile disappeared from his face, and he grabbed his phone, pressing speed dial. It rang only a couple of times before he got an answer.

"How are you doing, Green Fang?" Kai asked.

"Kai . . . I need you to prepare the whole gang," Gary said. "I'm asking you all for a favor, as the leader of the Howlers."

ABOUT THE AUTHOR

JKSManga is the pen name of UK-based, *New York Times*–bestselling LitRPG author Kawin Jack Sherwin, whose series include My Vampire System, My Dragon System, and My Werewolf System. His works have sold fifteen million copies worldwide, and several have been adapted into comic books.

RESPAWN YOUR CURIOSITY

follow us on our socials

 podiumentertainment.com

 @podiumentertainment

 /podiumentertainment

 @podium_ent

 @podiumentertainment